CRITICAL ACCLAIM FOR

Scoundrel

Debra Dier

"This great romance has a cast of lively characters and fast-paced action that brings you right into the story. A thoroughly enjoyable book!"

—*Rendezvous*

In *Scoundrel,* "delightful Debra Dier provides her myriad of fans an exciting and very enjoyable…romance."

—*Affaire de Coeur*

"Another great read for Ms. Dier, *Scoundrel* sizzles with romance, intrigue, and memorable characters."

—*Paperback Forum*

RAVE REVIEWS FOR DEBRA DIER'S OTHER ROMANCES!

"*The Sorcerer's Lady* is a warm and touching love story!"

—*Romantic Times*

The Sorcerer's Lady is "a marvelous tale with a grand maze of twists and turns that will mesmerize you and spark your imagination....A keeper!"

—*Rendezvous*

"*Deceptions and Dreams* is tightly plotted with plenty of well-developed characters....Ms. Dier's writing is skillful and sure, painting with words a story filled with passion, adventure, and emotion."

—*Rendezvous*

"*Shadow Of The Storm* is a powerhouse of intense emotions, a brilliantly crafted, cleverly plotted novel that lures the reader and holds your attention from beginning to end."

—*Romantic Times*

"*Surrender The Dream* has sparkling dialogue, suspense-filled intrigue, and sizzling love scenes!"

—*Affaire de Coeur*

CLOSE ENCOUNTER

"Tell me something." Simon held Emily with his look, his black eyes probing hers. "Just why did you invent a husband?"

"It's none of your concern."

"Couldn't you find any man willing to put up with the temper that went along with your beauty?"

Emily's back stiffened with indignation. "There were plenty of men who wanted to marry me."

"And yet you didn't choose one." He brushed his fingers over the ivory silk counterpane that lay folded at the foot of her bed.

"Why?"

Emily followed the slow trail of his fingers, her body growing taut deep inside. "I don't intend to explain my actions to you."

"I see." He lifted away from the bedpost. "Then you leave me to my own conclusions."

She stepped back as he stalked her. "Just what do you think you're about?"

He smiled. "I'm about to test a theory."

She backed away as he drew near. "Keep your distance."

He shook his head, his dark eyes glinting with mischief. "I don't think I can test this particular theory from a distance."

Other *Leisure* and *Love Spell* Books by
Debra Dier:
THE SORCERER'S LADY
DECEPTIONS & DREAMS
A QUEST OF DREAMS
SHADOW OF THE STORM
SURRENDER THE DREAM

Scoundrel

Debra Dier

LEISURE BOOKS NEW YORK CITY

A LEISURE BOOK®

January 1996

Published by

Dorchester Publishing Co., Inc.
276 Fifth Avenue
New York, NY 10001

Printed in the United States of America.

For Beth, Jan, and Joyce. You've listened to my manic-depressive chatter and helped keep me sane. Thanks for always being there to share your advice and your friendship.

Scoundrel

Chapter One

England, 1812

This was much more difficult than she had imagined. Emily Maitland stepped back into a corner of the ballroom in her parents' home near Bristol, staring at the swarm of guests gathered beneath the glitter of crystal chandeliers to celebrate her recent marriage. If she weren't certain that one of her family would question her absence, she would escape the crowd, retreat to her room, and hide like a coward.

Deception did not suit her. In the past she had always prided herself on her honesty. In the past, she had never told a lie of any proportion. Yet, the lie she had created six weeks ago in London was more than just a small prevarication. No, her first foray into the fabrication of fact was about the size of Gibraltar. And she could feel that lie pressing against her heart like a solid chunk of granite.

Emily stiffened when she noticed her grandmother step from a crowd of people near one of the refreshment tables. Dear heaven, she was headed in Emily's direction. One look at Lady Harriet Whitcomb's face and Emily knew her grandmother was not pleased with her performance this night.

Lady Harriet paused close to Emily, close enough to be heard above the combined noise of music and conversation. "Emily dear, you look as though you are waiting to be marched to the gallows. We don't want your guests wondering what is wrong with you, do we?"

"Look at all of these people, Grandmama," Emily said, her voice nearly drowned by the bright notes of a cotillion flowing from the orchestra perched high in the minstrels gallery. "They all believe this monstrous lie."

Harriet rested her gloved hand on Emily's arm. The warmth of her palm radiated through the buff kid leather, like a brand against Emily's cool skin. "May I suggest the rather obvious fact that we want them to believe this monstrous lie."

"I know. I simply didn't realize it would be so difficult. I'm afraid deception doesn't suit me."

Harriet pursed her lips. "You have little choice but to grow accustomed to it."

"I keep thinking of how disappointed Mother and Father would be if they knew the truth of what I've done."

"Precisely why I suggest we never allow them to discover the truth. I doubt they would have much sympathy for either one of us."

Emily watched her parents as they glided through the steps of a cotillion. Small, with dark hair and brown eyes, Audrey Maitland looked like a young girl dancing with her first love. The way she gazed up at her tall, fair-haired husband mirrored the adoration in Hugh Maitland's green eyes as he smiled down at his beautiful wife.

Emily had never seen a couple more in love than her parents. Growing up with that love as a standard for what she expected from her future marriage was part of the reason Emily found herself in this awkward situation tonight. "I didn't realize how difficult it would be to face everyone and maintain this illusion we've created. I feel as though I'm betraying everyone."

Harriet tightened her grip on her granddaughter's arm, her fingers pinching the skin beneath Emily's short sleeve. "Emily, look at me."

Emily tore her gaze from her trusting parents to look into her grandmother's taut features. The silver threads that liberally streaked her dark red hair, the lines that crinkled at the corners of her amber eyes, could not steal Harriet's beauty, even though she was past sixty. Just how far past sixty she had progressed, no one knew. Lady Harriet Whitcomb, the dowager Countess of Castlereagh, believed every woman should keep a degree of mystery about her.

"I expect you to play your role well. You aren't a green girl."

Emily cringed at the reminder of her age. In two months she would attain the advanced age of five and twenty, far too old to be subjected to another London Season. Indeed, her parents should have allowed her to remain on the shelf, where she belonged. Her sister Annabella should have been the one to plunge into society. Yet, no one in her family had been inclined to allow Emily the peace of spinsterhood. Instead, her adoring but misguided parents had forced her to endure another Season in town.

Another round of boring parties and balls.

Another chance for the endless rank of fortune hunters to snag a rich heiress.

Another bout of guilt when she found no one with whom she wished to spend the rest of her life.

Guilt because Hugh and Audrey Maitland insisted that Emily have the opportunity to marry before any of her four younger sisters were allowed to enter into society. In this her parents were every bit as stubborn as she was.

"You aren't going to do anything foolish, are you my girl?" Harriet's golden eyes were filled with an uneasy mixture of dread and determination. "You shall remember you convinced me this was your only course of action. And of course, you will bear in mind that both of our reputations are now at stake. Your parents trusted me to launch you safely into society.''

The responsibility of her deception rested across Emily's shoulders like an iron yoke. If the truth were ever discovered, the scandal would not only ruin Emily and her grandmother, but her entire family. No, she was far too tangled in her own web of lies to hope of escaping. She looked into her grandmother's worried eyes and managed a smile. ''I would do nothing to jeopardize my parents' trust in you. I won't fail you.''

''Of course you won't, my girl.'' Harriet dropped her hand, frowning at the red marks her fingers had left on Emily's arm, below the emerald silk of her short sleeve. ''You are, after all, my granddaughter. The only one of your sisters who had the excellent sense to inherit my looks.''

Emily rubbed the tingling flesh of her upper arm. ''Mother has always said my temperament is related to my red hair.''

''Yes, well, you've also inherited my unfortunate propensity for being just a bit headstrong.'' Harriet flicked open her fan, the gilt-trimmed edge glittering in the candlelight. ''Still, all in all, I'm quite satisfied with how you've turned out, even if you are a trifle stubborn, and far too reckless at times. You are quite an original. Indeed, you remind me remarkably of myself at your age.''

Emily smiled as she thought of how her penchant for rich colors and medieval decoration had set her apart in the eyes of the ton. ''Thank you, Grandmama.''

''Emily!''

Emily turned as her sister Annabella glided toward her, her pale hair glowing in the golden candlelight cascading from the chandeliers.

''Isn't it a wonderful party?'' Annabella waved her fan in an elegant sweep of the ballroom. ''I can't wait until my first London ball.''

Harriet smiled. "You shall be the rage of the Season, my dear."

"Do you think so?" Annabella clutched her fan to her chest. "They won't think me too countrified?"

Harriet smoothed her fingers over Annabella's flawless cheek. "My dear, they will think you a diamond of the first water."

A blush rose to brush a pink stain across Annabella's cheeks. "Oh, I do hope so."

"We shall make certain of it." Harriet snapped her fan closed. "Now, my sweetings. I see Lady Chadwick has arrived, and I really must speak to her."

Emily watched her grandmother wend her way through the crowd surrounding the dance floor, making her way to where Lady Chadwick stood near the base of the three curving stairs leading from the entrance of the room into the swirling mass of people below. People stood aside to allow Lady Harriet passage as she sailed like a queen across the crowded room in her gown of pale blue sarsenet. Her grandmother always had such wonderful confidence. Confidence was one thing Emily lacked at the moment.

They had only done what was necessary, Emily assured herself. They had . . .

A military man dressed in full regimentals walked through the entrance of the ballroom. He stood for a moment on the top stair, framed by the white arched entrance, looking across the room like a hunter seeking prey. Emily watched as he descended the stairs, a tingling sensation rippling through her. It was like watching a hawk descend into a covey of doves. Even from a distance, she could sense an aura of danger about this man. She could imagine him astride a huge black stallion, like a knight of legend, leading his troops into battle. Looking at this commanding figure, she had little doubt he had only recently left the battlefields of the Peninsula.

Candlelight slipped golden fingers into his black hair, the glossy mane curling in luxuriant waves over his collar. The fringe of his golden epaulets dangled like gilt in the candlelight, emphasizing the incredible width of his shoulders. White braid marched down the front of his short coat, the blue wool hugging the planes of his wide chest. A gold dress sword brushed the side of his thigh, buff-colored breeches molding the muscular curves of his long legs before plunging into shiny black Hessians. One look and Emily forgot to breathe.

"Emily, there is something I've been meaning to ask you," Annabella said.

"What?" Emily asked, her gaze never wavering from the tall, dark-haired man who was making his way across the room. He moved with the easy elegance that came when strength blended with agility. Power was evident in his every stride. This was a man men would follow into hell. And women would wait breathlessly for his return.

"I've been worried."

"Worried?" Emily noticed heads turn as the officer made his way through the crowd. Women cast admiring glances his way. Men gazed with a touch of envy at this tall, commanding figure.

Who was he? Emily was quite certain she had never met him. Oh no, she would never have forgotten this man. Even if she had merely glimpsed him before.

"About your marriage." Annabella kept her voice so low that Emily had to incline her head to hear her sister. Although Emily was not excessively tall for a woman, her sister was several inches shorter than she was, small and delicate, a perfect flower of the ton. "Emily, you didn't abandon your dream, did you?"

Emily tore her gaze from the military officer, glancing down at her sister. "What do you mean?"

"You didn't marry simply to allow me to enter into society, did you?" Annabella twisted her fan, crinkling the ivory lace trim. "Oh, Emily, I couldn't stand it if you married someone you didn't love for any reason."

The concern in her sister's huge blue eyes tugged on

Emily's heart. They had always been close, sharing their hopes and dreams. In fact, this was the first time she had ever kept a secret from her sister. She resisted the urge to confess everything, knowing she had no choice but to keep her secret. Annabella would never approve of her deception. "You mustn't fret about me."

"But, Emily, it all happened so quickly. I still can't believe you were married by special license. An elopement! Emily, you do love your Major Blake, don't you?"

"Of course I do." Emily glanced down at the embroidered ivory lace edging one short sleeve of her sister's pink muslin gown. As she progressed in her career as a liar, she was discovering it was most difficult to look into someone's eyes when she twisted the truth. "You and I made a pact, remember. Neither of us would ever marry unless we were as deeply in love as Mama and Papa are."

"I know. But, Emily, I also know how hard you fought to have Mama and Papa send me to London this Season, even though I wanted you to go. I couldn't live with myself if I thought you had married someone simply because of me."

"Then it is time you stopped torturing yourself. I'm quite content with my handsome major."

"Then it is true?" Annabella's eyes pleaded for the confirmation of her hopes. "He swept you off your feet?"

Emily took Annabella's clenched hands in hers. All the lies made sense when she looked into her sister's sweet face. The chance to see Annabella happy was worth the price of her own integrity, she assured herself. "One look at Major Sheridan Blake and I knew he was the only man for me."

"I know how careful you've been ever since . . ." Annabella caught her lower lip between her teeth. "Ever since that unfortunate incident that happened during your first Season."

Emily stiffened at the memory of her near escape from a disastrous marriage. "It was an excellent lesson. One I have not forgotten. One you should never forget.''

Annabella nodded. ''But you married Major Blake so quickly. How can you be certain he is not the same type of horrible creature that awful Lord Avesbury was?''

''I am no longer the same wet goose I was that first year in London.'' Emily squeezed Annabella's hands before releasing her. ''You can be certain Sheridan Blake is not a fortune hunter.''

Annabella sighed, the strain leaving her pretty face. ''And do you tremble when he touches you?''

''Like a leaf in a strong breeze.'' Emily glanced past Annabella's shoulder to where the officer was greeting her parents near one of the two refreshment tables in the room. In some strange way this man had stepped straight out of her fantasy. This is how she imagined Major Sheridan Blake would look, if he truly existed. He didn't, of course. That was the problem. Emily had invented him. Sheridan Blake was no more than a figment of her imagination.

''You always said that for each of us there is one person destiny has meant us to meet,'' Annabella said.

''Only one.'' Emily drew in a breath that trembled in her lungs as she stared at the officer. There was something about him, an aura of command, a solid strength that she could feel all the way across the room.

''And now I know it's possible. I can find that one special man destiny has meant for me.''

''Of course you can. We must never settle for anything less than to marry for affection, Anna. And we must be very careful not to be tricked by clever frauds.''

Annabella touched her arm, and when Emily glanced down at her sister she saw admiration shimmering in her eyes. ''I only hope I can be as strong as you are, Emmie. I know how much Mother and Father want to see each of us settled.''

''When you think of the lifetime you will spend with your husband, you will know you can't live with an imitation of love.'' Emily would never abandon her dream of finding her one and only love. Not if she had to wait until she was eighty before she met that very special man. For now, he lived only in her imagination.

Six weeks ago, out of a sense of duty and sheer desperation, Emily had given this fantasy a name she had borrowed from a popular playwright and one of her favorite poets. Sheridan Blake became an army officer who had been in London for a few days before heading back to the Peninsula, just long enough to elope with Emily. At least that was the fairy tale she and her grandmother had concocted.

It had all seemed so simple at the time. The perfect solution to her dilemma. She could stop the fruitless search for a husband among the fortune hunters and bores of London, and Annabella could enter society.

Of course, she didn't plan to stay married to her fictitious husband forever. She fully intended to become a widow after a few months. As a widow, she could take her time to find the one man she was meant to marry. He was out there. She was certain of it.

Emily stared across the room to where the army officer was talking with her parents. She could tell even from a distance that this was the type of man she had always dreamed of meeting. Honest. Brave. Loyal. The type of man a woman could trust with her dreams. Who was he?

"You always were the impetuous one, Emmie."

Impetuous. And a hopeful romantic, Emily thought. She would never give up hope. She had a peculiar notion that her special gentleman might be close. She watched the army officer press his lips to her mother's hand. Yes, he might be very close indeed.

"An elopement, imagine. How utterly romantic."

"Yes." Odd, her mother and father were greeting this man as though he were a long-lost son. Father couldn't seem to stop shaking his hand. Mother was staring up at this dark-haired officer with something close to awe in her light brown eyes. If her parents knew him so well, why hadn't they ever introduced her to this intriguing man?

"I do hope Grandmama is right," Annabella said. "I hope I'm accepted by London society."

"London society consists of arrogant aristocrats, foppish bores, and ever so charming fortune hunters. They will find you delightful. With your inheritance, you will be the target of every fortune hunter in London. You must be careful, Anna. You must remember my folly and avoid their tricks."

"I will try to do my best."

They were coming this way! Mother was leading the officer her way, while Father was headed for the spiral staircase leading to the minstrels' gallery at the back of the room. Emily's heart crept upward in her chest until each beat throbbed at the base of her throat. She couldn't breathe.

"Emily, my goodness." Annabella touched Emily's arm "Will you look at the officer coming this direction with Mama?"

Emily wasn't merely looking at the man, she was staring. She couldn't help herself.

"He is really quite dashing, isn't he?" Annabella whispered. "In a dark, formidable way. Still, he's much too fierce looking to be called handsome."

He wasn't handsome, Emily thought. No, not when male perfection was measured by the soft, petulant, pretty looks of Lord Byron. There was nothing soft in the sculpted lines and curves of this man's face. Nothing petulant in the sensual curve of his finely molded mouth. Nothing pretty in the overall effect of towering strength and bold masculinity.

He was compelling. Mesmerizing. Overwhelming.

Emily had never seen a more blatantly attractive man in her life. Here was a warrior who could easily have stood before her in polished armor awaiting a token from his lady to take with him into battle.

"Emily, look who is here!" Audrey said, rushing toward her daughter, clutching the army officer's arm as though she were afraid he might get away from her. "Isn't it a marvelous surprise?"

Emily glanced at her mother, dazed by the presence of this bold warrior.

"Emily, darling." Audrey hugged Emily, then stepped back, pressing her hand to the base of her neck. "I can see you are overwhelmed."

The tears in her mother's eyes startled Emily's already confused senses. "Mother, I don't understand . . ."

Emily's words dissolved in a gasp as the officer gripped her shoulders in his big hands and drew her near. She caught a glimpse of his smile, a glimmer of the amusement in his dark eyes as he lowered his head and kissed her.

Emily had been kissed before. A few bold suitors had presumed overly much in the past, grazing her lips before she could protest. Yet never in her life had she been kissed this way. And never in her life had she been kissed by a man such as this.

He slid his firm lips across hers, slowly, deliberately, as though he had every right to kiss her, as though he had every right to do more. Shock and confusion solidified into a shimmering excitement within her. This was a kiss straight from her wildest fantasy. This was a bold knight claiming his lady. Not with cold steel and brute strength. But with the intoxicating elixir of a single kiss.

He wore no cologne. Yet a beguiling aroma of leather and wool mingled with a scent that was entirely masculine. A scent that teased her. A scent that made her want to press her face against his neck, fill her senses with his essence.

The music and voices in the room dissolved into the distant roar of her own pulse pounding in her ears. Although he did not hold her pressed against his chest, she could feel the heat of him, the strong radiant warmth of his body stroking hers through the emerald silk of her gown. And for some inconceivable reason, her body sought that warmth.

She felt a shifting within her, a yielding of muscles that

made her sway until she could feel the press of his chest against her breasts. Sensation shimmered in the tips of her breasts, spiraling in all directions, like sparks escaping a flaming pinwheel. He tightened his grip on her arms, holding her close. For an instant. Only an instant. And then he was pulling away, leaving her breathless and hungry for more.

She stared up into his dark eyes, seeing a flicker of what could have been confusion melding with the heat of a desire she could recognize even in her innocence.

"I've missed you, Em," he said, his lips curving into a smile that sliced a single dimple into his tanned right cheek.

Emily blinked, stunned by her overwhelming response to this man. For one extraordinary moment she wondered if he had indeed stepped straight from her fantasy. "Missed me?"

His eyes sparkled with a bedeviling light. "More than words can say."

The bright notes of the orchestra faded only to erupt in a stunning crescendo. A moment later her father addressed the room. "Ladies and gentlemen, please give me your attention for a moment."

Her father's voice sliced through the fog clouding Emily's mind. Reality swept through her with a vengeance. Dear heaven! The rogue had kissed her. What was worse, she had kissed him back, as though she had known him a thousand years. What would people think of her kissing a stranger in this manner? Especially now, when she was a *married* woman.

She glared at the man. "What the devil do you mean by . . ." Her words dissolved in a startled exhale of breath as the tall stranger pressed his fingertip to her lips.

"Hush, sweetheart, your father has an announcement to make."

Emily frowned as she glanced to her mother, looking for support in her indignation, finding none. The world suddenly seemed to be spinning in the wrong direction. A man had kissed her. Here in the middle of her parents' ballroom. And her mother was all smiles. She glanced around her. Four hundred people stood in the huge room, staring up at the minstrels' gallery, where her father stood at the black wrought-iron balustrade, commanding the attention of everyone present.

"As you all know, we are here tonight to celebrate the marriage of my daughter Emily to Major Sheridan Blake, who is in service to His Majesty, King George the Third." Hugh paused a moment, staring down at his guests, his lips curved into a smile. "We thought the major was unable to attend tonight, due to a prior engagement in the Peninsula."

Thought the major was unable to attend. Emily stared up at her father, an uneasy shiver skittering up her spine, a sense of impending disaster settling over her like a heavy cloak.

"Through a twist of good fortune"—Hugh's smile grew as he looked to where Emily stood near the back of the room and raised his arm in her direction—"he was able to join us tonight. It is my great pleasure to introduce all of you to my new son, Major Sheridan Blake."

Chapter Two

Emily dropped her fan. The ivory sticks hit the tip of her emerald satin slipper and plunked against the polished oak planks of the floor. She stared up at the rogue who had slipped his arm around her shoulders. "What the devil do you . . ."

"Oh, Emily, this is wonderful!" Anna said.

"Emily, he is everything you said, and more," Audrey said, squeezing Emily's hand. "I'm so happy."

"But you don't understand. This man is . . ." Emily could manage no more as the guests began descending upon her and the impostor by her side. Smiling faces of friends and family swirled in her dazed vision. Voices buzzed in her ears.

"Congratulations, my dear."

"Oh, what a charming couple."

"Always knew it would take a strong man to win Emily's hand."

"How fortunate you could return, Major."

Emily's thoughts whirled. She received the good wishes

of her guests as though she moved through a dream. Stunned. Speechless. This could not be happening. She felt as though she had been yanked from the ground by a whirlwind. Her head reeled. Her heart pounded against the wall of her chest. She had to stop this!

Her father stepped from the chattering crowd that had gathered around Emily and the impostor. "You've made me very happy, daughter," he said, touching her cheek.

"Father, this man . . ."

"Counts himself among the most fortunate men of the world," the impostor said, holding Emily close to his side. "To have the honor of your daughter's hand in marriage."

Emily glanced up into eyes as dark as a moonless night. There was amusement in those endless depths, and a subtle warning that stole the words of protest she had meant to speak. He trapped her with that look, and suddenly she felt like a dove held in the talons of a hawk.

"I've sanctioned another waltz, Emily," Hugh said. "One for my daughter and her new husband."

Emily was vaguely aware of the violins as they sang the first few phrases of a waltz. The man holding her shifted his grip, sliding his arm around her back as he led her toward the dance floor. Guests parted and formed an aisle of smiling faces, like peasants seeking a glimpse of their lord and lady.

"Just what do you think you're doing?" Emily whispered as the rogue took her in his arms.

"Dancing with my bride." He grinned, that solitary dimple peeking at her. "Smile, sweetheart. We don't want people to think you don't like me."

"Like you?" Emily stumbled as he swept her into the graceful swirling motions of the dance.

He caught her, easing her through the first turn. "I didn't realize you were so inexperienced in the waltz. Just relax and follow my lead."

"Inexperienced! I'll have you know I'm an excellent dancer."

He lifted one black brow, his midnight eyes sparkling with mischief. "So you say, my lady."

Emily glared up at the scoundrel, aware of an odd tingling in her limbs. Through the white kid of his glove, the heat of his hand seared her through the emerald silk of her gown, his warmth seeping into her blood. "Don't try to distract me," she said, painfully aware that his very presence distracted her.

"But I think it will be quite enjoyable distracting you." His smile turned positively wicked. "I'm looking forward to an entire night of marvelous distractions."

There was a note of sensuality in his deep, velvety voice, a dark promise that whispered to a need lurking deep within her. A tremor rippled through her. She missed a step, her slippered foot coming down on his toes. He flexed his hand at her waist, gripped her hand, imposing balance until she regained the proper rhythm.

He cocked one dark brow, his eyes sparkling with an understanding any decent gentleman would disavow. She was certain the man was aware of every wayward tingle he could conjure inside her. And he wanted her to know how very easily he could read her thoughts. Oh, she wanted to strangle the man. "Just what are you about, coming in here pretending to be my husband?"

"Pretending?" He gave her a look filled with cultivated innocence, a look completely at odds with the roguish glint in his eyes. "Why, Emily, I assure you that even though we were married in haste, everything is quite legal."

"*We* were never married." She kept her voice low, acutely aware of the couples who had joined them on the dance floor, even though they were nothing but a blur of color in her vision as he swept her in bold, flowing turns around the floor.

"I know I've been away for several weeks, but I'm shattered to think you could have forgotten that one glorious night we shared."

"Oh, will you kindly stop talking such nonsense!"

"Emily, how you wound me," he replied, his grin spoiling the melancholy in his voice.

Oh, she wanted to slap that mocking smile right off his handsome face. "Not yet. But I will, you know. I'm quite capable of using a pistol."

He laughed, the deep tones rippling with the bright sounds of the violins. "I find I'm trembling in my boots."

"Oh you . . . villain! How dare you come in here and play this loathsome game?"

"Game? Emily, darling, I'm afraid you have me at a loss."

Emily halted in the middle of the dance floor, ashamed to find her legs were trembling. It was from anger, she assured herself. She certainly was not trembling at this rogue's touch. "I've had all I intend to take of your insolence. I believe it is time to announce you as a fraud."

"That wouldn't be wise."

"Oh, and why, pray tell?"

He smiled, a lazy curve of his lips that reminded her keenly of how those sensual lips had felt moving against hers. "Because your family and guests would be quite distressed to discover you had deceived them into believing you were married."

A cold hand squeezed her heart. She stared up into his eyes, seeing the reality of her situation mirrored in the dark depths.

"Yes, sweetheart, I know everything."

A small sound escaped her lips, the startled sound of a rabbit trapped by a lion. Dear heaven, how had he discovered the truth? What did he want? If he whispered the truth to anyone, her entire family would suffer.

He lifted her hand and glanced down at her clenched fist, his expression growing solemn. "I believe it's time you and I had a little talk," he said, slowly sliding his thumb over her knuckles in a gesture meant to soothe.

His gentleness was lost in the storm of Emily's emotions. Still, she didn't resist as he took her arm and led her from the dance floor. She glanced around the room, spotting her parents sitting together on an ivory Grecian chaise longue that stood against one of the pale green walls. Her parents had always done what they thought was best for her. They loved her. Trusted her without question. What would they think if they knew she had deceived them? Her stomach clenched as she realized how much pain she would cause them. And her entire future lay in a scoundrel's hands.

Lady Harriet met them as they left the dance floor. She stepped before them, like a palace guard in pale blue, her head high, her golden eyes glowing with fury. "Just where do you think you are going with my granddaughter, *Major Blake*?"

Even though her grandmother kept her voice low, Emily flinched at the venom in her tone. She glanced up at her tormentor. The rogue didn't look the least bit intimidated by a woman who had a reputation for freezing an opponent with a single glance.

"There is much we need to discuss, Lady Harriet," he said, his dark voice low and filled with command. "I believe you have a stake in all of this. Please join us."

Harriet looked at Emily, sudden doubts clouding her topaz eyes. "Emily?"

Emily moistened her dry lips. "He knows."

Harriet closed her eyes, her lips moving in a silent oath. When she opened her eyes, there was a hard glitter in the golden depths. "Very well. Follow me."

Emily's mind churned as she followed her grandmother out of the ballroom and down a hallway where candles flickered behind glass, casting wavering shadows against the mahogany-paneled walls. She had weaved every inch of this terrible tangle. Now it threatened to strangle her grandmother as well as her entire family. Not for the first time in her life, she cursed her own reckless nature.

Emily set her jaw as she entered the library behind her grandmother. She stared at the man who strode into the room beside her. Heaven help her, somehow she would find a way to wipe that maddening grin off his beguiling lips.

"I suppose I should be glad you aren't carrying a pistol at the moment." He touched the tip of her nose with his fingertip. "You look angry enough to shoot me."

Emily slapped aside his hand. "An excellent idea. Shall we meet at dawn?"

He tilted his head, smiling at her in a way that sent a tingle along her spine. "Lovely lady, I would meet you any time. Of course, pistols would not be the sport I had in mind."

Emily turned away from him, aware of how his bold words brought warm color in her face. Oh, she wanted to hang the man! She marched to one of the open windows, welcoming the cool evening breeze against her warm cheeks.

Harriet closed the library door, squeezing the music that flowed from the ballroom into a trickle of silvery notes. She stood for a space of a dozen heartbeats, glaring at the scoundrel with her most glacial stare. Yet the rogue only smiled in return. "Now then, young man. Just what is it you believe you know?"

He strolled to the fireplace and rested his arm along the smooth white marble mantel as though he were master of the house. On either side of the mantelpiece, carvings of Apollo and Venus stood with heads turned toward the rogue, staring as though fascinated by this mortal in their midst. "I know you and Emily invented Major Sheridan Blake six weeks ago."

"What nonsense is this?" Harriet demanded.

"We're beyond the point of denial, Lady Harriet." He smoothed the tips of his long fingers over the marble beneath his hand. "I know you had your solicitor obtain a special license for marriage between Major Blake and your granddaughter. He also paid a magistrate to forge marriage papers. I, by the way, have a copy of those papers locked away for safekeeping."

He truly did know everything. The blood drained from

her limbs as Emily realized she was well and truly trapped. "How did you discover all of this?"

"It doesn't matter." He glanced up at the elaborate marble chimneypiece above him where Jupiter tossed Vulcan from Mount Olympus, father and son locked forever in conflict. "All that matters is I do know your secret. And we both know that if the truth were ever told, you and your family would never again be able to show your faces in society."

Emily stared at the dark-haired rogue, wondering how she had ever believed he had stepped out of her fantasy. The man had come straight out of a nightmare. "I won't let you do this."

He looked at Emily, holding her in a dark, penetrating gaze. "Although you might be reckless enough to jeopardize your own reputation, I doubt you would sacrifice Lady Harriet, Annabella, or your other three sisters. Not to mention what the truth would do to your parents."

Emily clenched her hands into fists at her sides. Impotent rage surged through her. How could he do this? She wanted to scream. She wanted to snatch a pillow from one of the Sheraton sofas and toss it at him. How could she have been so wrong about this man? How could she have imagined he possessed all the qualities she had ever wanted in a man? Honesty. Bravery. Loyalty. Dear heaven, this man was nothing but a scoundrel. "Villain!"

He smiled, a surprisingly gentle curve of his lips that softened the fierce look in his eyes. "I don't want to hurt you or your family."

"Liar." She glanced away from him. She stared at the fire screen standing on a rosewood frame beside the hearth, where the delicate needlepoint stitches revealed a knight on his knee to his lady. She had been thinking of her own true love when she had fashioned that screen. A man she had been so certain she would recognize with one glance. She had mistaken him once. And now she had managed once again to commit the same folly. Dear heaven, would she ever learn?

"Tell me, just what is it you do want?" Harriet asked.

He rested his foot on a brass andiron and stared into the lifeless hearth, the muscles of his leg flexing beneath the close-fitting wool of his breeches. "I'm a soldier who has returned from the battlefields only to find he has no way of making a living."

So, he truly was a soldier. Somehow Emily had known it. He wore the uniform and the look of a predator far too well. And there was more. There was a darkness she sensed inside him, as though he had crawled his way out of hell but could not escape the memories. And somehow that darkness beckoned her. "Who are you?"

"It doesn't matter." He inclined his head, glancing up from the blackened streaks of fires long dead to give her a smile. "You can call me Sheridan."

Sheridan, the man of her dreams. Emily crossed her arms below the high waist of her emerald gown. "I would prefer not to call you anything, except gone."

He chuckled under his breath.

Emily clenched her teeth. How dare the villain laugh at her!

Harriet lifted her quizzing glass, studying him for a moment before dropping the glass, the lens swinging on a blue satin ribbon pinned beneath the high waist of her gown. "How much do you want?"

"Although you have a substantial income, I believe I can do much better as Miss Maitland's husband."

The full import of his statement hit Emily square in the chest, like a blow from a prizefighter. "If you think for one moment I will sanction your fortune-hunting scheme, you are very much mistaken."

He looked at her, his dark eyes reflecting the light of the candles burning in the wall sconce above his head. "You need a husband, I need a position."

"This is preposterous." Emily paced the length of the

library. She turned when she reached the glass-fronted mahogany bookcases across from the smiling rogue, her body trembling with fury. "I have no intention of allowing you to waltz in here and step into the role of my husband."

He studied her a moment, a smile playing at one corner of his lips. "I believe you have little choice in the matter."

"I have spent the last few years of my life avoiding fortune hunters like you. If you believe for one moment—"

"Emily," Harriet said, her voice cutting like lightning through Emily's tirade.

Emily glanced at her grandmother. "What?"

Harriet tapped her fan against her open palm. "He has us at dagger's point, my dear."

"But I . . ." Emily hesitated, the reality of her grandmother's words seeping through the fury fogging her mind. The man had her trapped. She stared at the rogue, anger congealing inside her along with a terrible fear. Dear heaven, she had invented a husband to avoid marriage to a fortune hunter, only to find herself trapped by her own scheme. "Never in my life have I met a more contemptuous—"

"Calm yourself, my dear," Harriet said. "There are a few matters we need to clarify with the gentleman."

"Gentleman. Hah!"

Harriet ignored Emily's outburst. "Now, I would like to clarify the terms under which we shall operate, Major. I understand you expect to live in this house as my granddaughter's husband."

"I would rather live with swine." Emily crinkled her nose at the rogue. He grinned in reply.

"Emily, please control your temper." Harriet tapped her fan across her palm. "This is a matter to be discussed with a cool head. I don't believe I have to remind you who is responsible for this situation."

Emily's throat tightened. "No."

"Now behave, while we negotiate a few points."

"Grandmother, you can't expect me to live in this house as that scoundrel's wife."

"Relax, Miss Maitland. I have never in my life seduced an innocent woman. I'm after a position. Not your virtue."

He might have slapped her across the cheek. He felt nothing for her. Nothing at all. While she had imagined him the life and blood of her fantasy. Oh, it was all far too humiliating to discover how very wrong she had been.

A scoundrel.

A fortune hunter.

Dear heaven, it was entirely too much to absorb. Emily sank to the edge of a couch near the windows and listened as her grandmother made a bargain with the devil.

Harriet stared at the tall man standing near the lifeless hearth. "I will expect you to behave as a gentleman toward my granddaughter."

"An intelligent man knows better than to get too close to an angry tigress." He smiled at Emily. "Especially a tigress who likes pistols."

"Yes, well, my Emily does possess a temper. I'm afraid it's something she inherited from me." Harriet lifted one finely arched brow. "You would do well to realize that if you harm her in any way, I will find a way to make sure you are punished. Quite severely, *Major*."

The scoundrel didn't flinch as he held Harriet's intense gaze. "As I said before, I don't have a taste for seducing virgins."

Harriet nodded. "I assume, since you will not find comfort with my granddaughter, you will seek companionship with some Cyprian or another. In doing so, I must insist you be discreet."

"Grandmother!" Emily stared at Harriet, appalled at her grandmother's meaning. "I cannot believe you are giving this man leave to carry on some tawdry affair while he is masquerading as my husband."

"Well, dear, he is a man. If you don't plan to satisfy his needs, then I think we must be realistic in acknowledging that he shall have them satisfied elsewhere.''

''I will not have my husband consorting with some bit of muslin.''

''Emily dear.'' Harriet addressed her as though she were speaking to a bewildered child. ''He isn't really your husband.''

''That isn't at all the point.'' Emily clasped her hands in her lap, trying to keep them from trembling. ''What would people think if they discovered that the man claiming to be my husband was seeking his pleasure in a brothel?''

''Precisely why I'm insisting he be discreet.''

''I won't have it.'' Emily felt a shivering deep inside her, where memories of past humiliations slithered from shallow graves. ''My husband will not maintain a ladybird.''

Harriet pursed her lips as she stared at Emily. ''I doubt you shall have any say in the matter.''

Emily looked at the rogue who had invaded her life. He was watching her, a smile barely lifting one corner of his lips. He looked like a lion who was lazily contemplating whether he would eat her for dinner or amuse himself with her for a while first.

''Are we agreed, Major?'' Harriet asked. ''You shall be most discreet in these matters?''

''I will do nothing to cause the lady any embarrassment.'' His lips curved into a devilish grin, mischief lighting his eyes. ''It wouldn't do to have people believe Miss Maitland is unable to satisfy her husband.''

Emily shot to her feet. ''My husband will find no need to seek comfort in the arms of another woman.''

He shrugged, broad shoulders lifting beneath blue wool, golden epaulets glittering, a mockery of every ideal she had attributed to that uniform. ''I can only wait to see if what you say is true.''

Emily curled her hands into fists at her sides. ''You shall wait until the sun freezes over.''

He laughed, a dark rumble that came from deep in his

chest. "You display such passion, I must say I am quite overwhelmed."

"Oh, you—"

"Emily!" Harriet drew a breath in exasperation. "Please control your temper."

Emily opened her mouth to protest, but the stern look on her grandmother's face quelled her. She nodded, silently calculating ways she would repay the man for his insolence.

Harriet looked at the rogue. "It seems there is little more to say. If you don't mind, I would like a few moments alone with my granddaughter."

"I'm certain the young lady will need some reminding of the advantages of playing along with this little drama." He looked at Emily, his dark eyes probing hers, as though he could pierce her defenses and read her mind. "Think of it this way, Miss Maitland, you need a husband as much as I need a fresh start. It is to our mutual benefit to co-operate with one another."

Emily lifted her chin. "I would never have taken a scoundrel like you as a husband."

"No? And here I thought we were rather well suited."

"In your wildest dreams."

He smiled, a wistful look entering his midnight eyes. "Perhaps you're right."

A disturbing sense of despair settled over her as she watched him stride from the room. She couldn't stop that hopeful, terribly romantic girl within her from wishing things were different. If he were only the heroic figure he appeared, she could quite easily fall in love with him. As it was, he was her enemy. And she must find a way to best him.

Harriet spread her fan and stared down at the painted silk. "Quite an intriguing man."

"I find nothing intriguing about the scoundrel."

"No?" Harriet eyed Emily with a look that told her she knew otherwise. "I thought you might have found him quite exceptional."

"Perhaps, when I first saw him." Emily toyed with the gold satin ribbon at her waist. "I might have thought him attractive. In a fashion."

"Yes, he is certainly that. And such a quality of command about him."

"Grandmama, you can't possibly find anything of quality about such a cad."

"I believe you are mistaken, Emily." Harriet tilted her head, pale blue ostrich feathers bobbing in her hair as she stared at the space where the stranger had stood in front of the mantel. "I would wager he comes of excellent stock. You can see the aristocratic cast to his features, those high cheekbones, the sharp line of his nose. And his address—learned from the cradle. I wouldn't at all be surprised to find he is a second or third son of an English peer. Yes, I definitely can see the blood of nobility in him."

"Nobility!" Emily paced the floor like a tigress testing the limits of her cage, crossing squares of gold edged in black, her satin slippers silent against the wool carpet. "That man is an out-and-out villain."

"I understand it can be very difficult for a man who wishes to leave the army these days."

Emily paused beside a globe on a walnut stand in a corner of the room. "Grandmama, you aren't suggesting you are in accord with the blackguard? He is blackmailing me into accepting him as my husband."

"Yes, well, there is that." Harriet tapped her fan against her chin. "Pity, he is such a splendid-looking man."

"His looks conceal a black soul." With a flick of her wrist Emily set the globe spinning. Her own lack of judgment infuriated her as much as the fact that the man had failed to live up to her expectations. She was a fool. How could she ever have looked at the man and imagined him the embodiment of her dreams? "How do you suppose he discovered the truth? Do you suppose Beamish let it slip?"

"Never." Harriet was quick to defend her coachman.

"But Beamish took us to the magistrate. He is the only

one who knew what we were about that night.''

''Beamish has been with me for eleven years. I took him in when the world was through with him. When he could no longer amuse gentlemen with his performances in the boxing arena. When he had no place else to go. He would defend me and my secrets with his life.''

Emily nodded, thinking of the big man with the flattened features who served her grandmother like a devoted mastiff. ''Then how did the scoundrel discover the truth?''

''Emily, it doesn't really matter. The damage has been done.''

Emily groaned her frustration. ''I cannot believe you agreed to his demands without a fight.''

''Tell me, my dear, what did you expect me to do?''

''We can't let him get away with this.''

''And what do you propose we do to prevent him from carrying on with his plan?''

''I don't know.'' Emily paced the length of the room, slapping the drapes as she passed the windows, setting heavy gold velvet swaying. Oh, she wanted to scream. She wanted to march into that ballroom and announce to the world he was a fraud. Of course, she could do nothing. At least not at the moment. She might be in check, but the scoundrel would find it difficult to put her in checkmate. She paused at the fireplace, tapping her foot on the spot where he had stood. ''I shall not allow that man to ruin my life.''

''Emily, you aren't going to do anything foolish.''

''Of course not.'' Emily lifted her chin, smiling as she imagined the day she would see her ''husband'' pay for his sins. ''But you can trust I shall think of a plan.''

Harriet rolled her eyes to heaven. ''I was rather afraid you were going to say that.''

Chapter Three

Deception suited him. At least, Simon St. James had come to believe it suited him. In the past few years he had volunteered for one dangerous mission after another. All requiring an altered identity. All for crown and country. He hadn't really explored his reasons for taking such risks. Perhaps because he didn't want the answers. He didn't like to think he was still trying to impress a father who had tossed him away a long time ago.

Still, as he stood near one corner of a refreshment table, watching Emily Maitland enter the ballroom beside her grandmother, he admitted to a few qualms about playing the role of Major Sheridan Blake. He was attracted to Emily Maitland in a way he had never been attracted to other women. That kind of attraction could prove fatal if he weren't careful.

Simon watched her, following Emily's every move as she drifted through the crowded room, the intricate ivy design embroidered in gold at the hem of her gown rippling around her ankles with every step. It was a medieval design.

A design that might have graced the gown of a lady in the days of knights and chivalry. And there was something about her that made him imagine himself carrying her token into battle.

With her emerald gown and red hair Emily glided like an exotic tropical bird across a lake crowded by pale swans. She was not beautiful. Not by the standards of society.

She was not a pale, ethereal creature like the beauties so cherished by the ton these days. No, she was filled with the fire that burned in her beautiful golden eyes. A fire that could consume him if he weren't careful. Yet, looking at her, he realized he craved the warmth of her fire.

He thought of that one moment he had held her in his arms, recalling the soft flutter of her lips beneath his. The warmth of her sigh against his cheek. The brush of her breasts against his chest. His body reacted immediately, as it had at the first touch of her lips against his, a sudden surge of blood pounding low in his belly, a spark of desire setting fire to his blood. Damnation! He was growing hard just thinking of her.

He sipped his champagne and realized he had been too many nights without a woman. As soon as the thought formed, his innate honesty forced him to dismiss that assumption. He suspected Emily Maitland would have that disconcerting control over his body even if he had just spent a month indulging himself in a harem.

"We have some lovely canapes this evening, sir. Chef's been fussing about them all day."

Simon smiled at the sound of the rusty male voice. He glanced over his shoulder, where a short man in dark blue Maitland livery was replenishing a platter of canapes. The white wig he wore hid his thinning sandy brown hair, but couldn't disguise the thick jaw and alert brown eyes of Sergeant-Major Horace Digby.

Simon moved to the table and examined the platter of canapes. "So I see you've finally found a suitable station in life,'' he said, his voice kept low enough for Digby's ears alone.

''It ain't all bad, sir.'' Digby grinned, deep creases lining his sun-darkened face. ''A sight more comfortable than crawling through every smuggling hole in England. And the company is a damn sight better than your pack of smugglers, if I do say so myself. Learned to sleep with one eye open I did on that last mission.''

''That pack of smugglers is providing a valuable service to the crown, Digby.'' Simon selected a thin wafer topped by a slice of lobster and red sauce. ''The gentlemen now form a rather fine network of communication, providing a wealth of information for our commanders. If it hadn't been for them, we might never have discovered the smuggling being done through Maitland Enterprises.''

''Aye, sir. Not many men would have seen the worth of using smugglers as spies.'' Digby cocked a brow as he looked up at Simon. ''Most men might think they should be hanged.''

''Although there are many true scoundrels among those engaged in illegal trade, I've found a surprising number of smugglers to be men loyal to their country. Men who feel they do a service by providing goods most people would not be able to obtain without their assistance.''

''Aye. There is that side to it. There's a fair number of people here at home who like to sample a bit of smuggled goods.''

''It's difficult to find someone in this country not buying contraband.'' Simon glanced around the room, his gaze lingering on Emily Maitland. He watched her move through the steps of a cotillion with her father, the emerald silk of her gown swirling around her long legs. ''Half the women in this room are wearing silk. And I would wager most of it came from France, even though they would swear it came from the East Indies.''

''Aye, sir. I noticed even the lordships in the ministry carry silk handkerchiefs. And no one can deny your pack of smugglers provide a fair amount of information on Bonaparte and his army.'' Digby frowned as he transferred an oyster canape from the tray he held to the silver platter on the table. ''Wish I had some information to report, sir.''

''You haven't been able to learn anything?''

''No more than what already came through the network, sir.'' Digby placed another canape on the platter with the care of a man building a castle of cards. ''We know someone in Maitland's company must be involved in the smuggling being done, but I haven't caught a whisper that might lead to the blackguard.''

Someone in Maitland's organization was smuggling more than sugar and wool to the French. Someone was smuggling black powder and weapons in Maitland's ships. Weapons that were sending young Englishmen to early graves. Simon's chest tightened, memories stirring inside him, ghosts that refused to remain buried. He was going to catch the traitor and personally escort him to the gallows.

''We know the cargo is initially destined to be shipped to a customer in Tangier. That customer is an agent for the French. We have to find out who he is,'' Simon whispered. ''The weapons are stored in barrels of sugar. I suspect the crew of the merchant vessels have no idea what they are carrying. The traitor has to be someone who can control the shipments. Someone in a position of authority.''

Digby nodded. ''I think you're right about suspecting someone high up in the organization.''

Simon watched Emily and her father, seeing the easy affection between the man and his daughter. An odd sense of dread seeped into his blood. The traitor could very well be Hugh Maitland. And for some reason, the idea of hanging that beautiful redhead's father didn't set well with him.

''Looks like you managed to make your way past the castle guards, sir.'' Digby shook his head in wonder. ''I'll be telling you, I wasn't of a mind that the young lady would go along with your play acting.''

''I didn't give her a choice in the matter.''

Simon had spent most of his life in the army, hardly a profession that allowed a man sufficient opportunity to learn all the intricacies of a woman's nature. If any man could ever learn all those intricacies. Still, instinct told him to watch his back with the red-haired hellion.

"She's a beauty, if you don't mind me saying so, sir."

"You can say anything you like about the woman, Digby." Simon watched her, fascinated by the way the candlelight ignited the fire in her hair. "Aside from allowing me access to her father, the little hellcat means nothing to me."

"Aye." Digby placed a canape on the mound he was building. "But I'm thinking her looks will make the work go easier, being that you're supposed to be her husband and all."

"This is business." Simon frowned as he realized he needed reminding of that fact when it came to Miss Emily Maitland. "The last thing I intend to do is get involved with the woman."

"Wise of you, sir." Digby eased the last canape onto the mound and stepped back to admire his creation. "You know, I've been thinking how strange it is that she came up with this make-believe husband. I'm wondering why."

"What man can fathom the workings of a woman's mind?" Simon had his own theories as to the reason Emily hadn't chosen a real husband. If she were seen to be a married woman, the beauty could carry on romantic liaisons without fear of the consequences, or the burden of a husband who might object. Infidelity was common among married men and women of the ton. Far too common.

He recalled the passionate look in her beautiful golden eyes as she had gazed up at him, her lips parted from his kiss. He knew enough about women to recognize desire when he saw it, and Emily Maitland's eyes had burned with it. The woman glowed with inner fire. The army had taught him to find an enemy's weakness and use it to best advantage. Had he already found the crack in Miss Maitland's defenses?

"Strange, isn't it? The lady coming up with an army officer as a husband. A tall one with dark hair. A major even. And you being just that rank. Almost as if there was something more going on here than what meets the eye."

Simon glanced down, meeting Digby's smile with a frown. "You haven't been talking to Gypsies again, have you?"

"No, sir, I haven't. But, I'm thinking it's a bit of destiny, the way Miss Maitland described you to everyone, as though she knew you."

Simon glanced at Emily Maitland, trying to shake the odd feeling of familiarity that had nagged him since the first moment he had looked at her. For some strange reason, he felt as though he had met her somewhere before. He was certain he hadn't. He never would have forgotten her. "I'm not in the mood to hear any talk of kindred spirits and superstitions."

"Aye, sir. I know you don't believe in nothing you can't see." Digby chuckled to himself. "Still, it's a strange thing, it is."

Simon frowned. "Coincidence. Nothing more."

Digby nodded, humor glinting in his brown eyes.

"I want you to visit the various pubs along the waterfront. We know a few of the smugglers have loose tongues when their gullets are full of rum. Otherwise, we might never have discovered this operation in the first place. See what you can find out."

"Aye, sir. Now if you don't mind, sir, I best get back to the kitchen or I'll have some explaining to do."

"Fine, Digby." Simon watched Digby walk away, the little man strutting like a rooster, his bowed legs encased in white stockings and dark blue velvet breeches. Digby was a good man, even if he was a superstitious fool. Nothing had brought Simon into Emily Maitland's life except a mission. A mission that could very well send her father to the gallows.

Emily stared into the mirror of her vanity, frowning at her own reflection as her maid worked a brush through her thick red curls. The man had managed to charm them all. Her mother. Her father. Annabella. Everyone. Everyone who had met the scoundrel had walked away admiring him. Could no one see the man for what he was? Were they all as blind as she had been? How could she ever have looked at him and imagined him a chivalrous knight?

Foolish woman. It was insanity to imagine for a moment that he could be the man she had waited for all of her life, her knight straight out of the pages of a legend.

She closed her eyes, recalling each detail of his face. The way his midnight eyes had sparkled with mischief as he had taken her in his arms. And his kiss. A tremor rippled through her at the memory. Dear heaven, his kiss had left her breathless.

"Did I hurt you, miss?"

"No, Nellie," Emily said, realizing she had sworn under her breath. "I was just thinking of something, that's all."

Nellie nodded and returned to her task of brushing out Emily's curls. "You have such thick hair, miss, I always fear I'll hurt you with the brushing."

"She has beautiful hair. Just like my mother's."

Emily glanced over her shoulder, finding her mother standing in the doorway to the hall.

"That will be all, Nellie." Audrey crossed the room. "I'll finish taming my daughter's wayward curls."

"Aye, milady." Nellie handed Audrey the brush and left mother and daughter alone in the room.

The love and pride glowing in her mother's eyes as she looked down at her shamed Emily for her deception. She turned back toward the mirror, staring down at the intricate embroidery of roses and leaves along the border of the Irish linen runner stretching the length of her vanity.

"I haven't done this in a long time." Audrey lifted a handful of the red curls that tumbled to Emily's waist. "Since you were a little girl."

Emily traced the curve of a rose leaf she had embroidered in the white linen, as her mother stroked the brush through her hair. As a little girl she had always enjoyed her mother's soft touch as she brushed her hair. Now, all she felt was guilt for the lies that lay between them.

"I can tell you, now that you're married, how very concerned I have always been about you. More than I have been about the other girls."

Emily looked up, meeting her mother's warm brown eyes in the mirror. "Concerned? In what way?"

"You were always so terribly romantic." Audrey smiled as she drew the brush through Emily's hair, candlelight from the wall sconce shimmering like dark fire in the auburn strands. "I remember the first time we took you and Annabella to the ruins of Ravenwood Castle—I believe you were eight and Annabella six. Annabella saw a dark, frightening place. You saw King Arthur's castle."

"It's a magical place." Emily smiled as she thought of the Norman castle that stood at the eastern edge of her father's property. "When I'm there, I can almost see Lord Ravenwood and his lady strolling about the place."

"Yes. I know you can. You have a lush imagination, a firm belief in the truth of legends and myths. That is the main reason I feared that you of all the girls were destined to be disappointed with life."

"I'm not certain of your meaning."

"Annabella is a sweet, biddable girl. Many a nice young man might fill her ideal of a charming husband. But you—" Audrey shook her head. "I always knew it would take someone very special to win your heart."

Emily glanced at a small book lying near one corner of the vanity, a black leather blot against the white linen. The book of Shakespeare's sonnets had been a gift, given on the day she had agreed to marry a man she had imagined as her Galahad. She kept the book as a remembrance of the naive young woman she had been. A talisman against future mistakes. "Do you believe I want too much from marriage, Mother?"

"Of course not." Audrey rested her hand on Emily's shoulder. "As you may recall, your father and I married against my father's wishes."

"But it's rare, isn't it? The kind of love you share with Father comes only once in a lifetime."

"Yes, I believe it is rare." Audrey worked the brush through Emily's hair. "I was always concerned you would allow your one mistake in judgment to turn you away from men. And I'm so very glad you didn't. After meeting your handsome young army officer, I can see that you and Major Blake were meant for one another."

Emily stared at the book of poems. "Can you?"

"Oh my, yes. Even though I haven't your gift for the romantic, I can imagine him as a legendary knight of old."

A dragon was more like it, Emily thought. A dragon who had seared her with a single kiss.

"I'm so thankful your father and I didn't surrender to your wishes and allow you to don the cap of a spinster." Audrey drew the brush across Emily's head, the soft bristles stroking her scalp. "You have so much love inside you, my beautiful child, so much spirit, so much to offer the right man. I couldn't bear it if you had given up your chance to find him. I can't tell you how happy I am to see you settled so well."

Emily closed her eyes, a tight band of guilt closing like steel around her chest. Her mother would be devastated if she ever learned this was all a terrible lie.

"I'm afraid we would have bowed to your wishes next year. We couldn't force Anna to wither away."

Emily looked at her mother's reflection. "You intended to allow Anna to have her first Season this coming spring?"

Audrey smiled. "You look shocked, my darling."

"I thought you were going to keep sending me until my hair turned gray."

Audrey laughed softly. "We couldn't very well tell you this was your last Season. You might never have decided to marry."

Emily stared at her mother, realization seeping into her blood like ice. She had invented Sheridan Blake for nothing. Dear heaven, she had allowed that scoundrel to invade her life for no reason at all. She flinched as someone knocked on the door.

"Ah, that should be your handsome husband," Audrey said, heading for the door.

Emily stood up so quickly her chair wobbled. She snatched the back of the chair, her fingers clutching the lyre-shaped rosewood. "What does he want?"

Audrey glanced over her shoulder, her lips curved into a gentle smile. "I suspect he wants to retire for the evening, dear."

"In here?"

Audrey's soft laughter rippled through the quiet room. "There is no need for modesty, Emily."

"But . . ." Emily searched for a reason for her mother not to open the door. "Mother, I . . . he . . ."

"Relax, my darling." Audrey paused with her hand on the brass door handle, smiling at Emily. "I realize you and Major Blake didn't have much time together before he had to leave, and you're still a little shy. But all of that will change now. You'll have a lifetime to get to know each other."

Emily stood beside the vanity, feeling trapped as her mother opened the door. Her heart tripped at the sight of him, this tall, broad-shouldered warrior who strode into her room, his long strides filled with a powerful elegance, reminding her of a lion on the prowl.

He smiled as he noticed her standing beside the vanity, a lazy curve on his lips, his eyes sparkling with the devil's own amusement. Oh, she wanted to hang the man.

"Have a pleasant night, darling," Audrey said, before leaving the room.

Emily flinched at the soft click of the door.

He arched one black brow as he looked at her, mischief sparkling in the dark depths of his eyes. "You seem a little tense, sweetheart."

"It comes from having a scoundrel turned loose in my bedroom."

Simon rested his shoulder against a carved mahogany post at the foot of her bed. "Now, is that any way to talk about your husband?"

"You aren't my husband." Emily gripped the lapels of her dressing gown together, her fingers sinking into the sapphire-blue satin. "And if you think for one moment I will submit to . . ."

He held up his hand, halting her words. "Relax. I've never taken an unwilling woman to my bed, and I don't plan to start with you. I give you my word, I won't try to force you to perform the repellent duties of the marriage bed."

Did he find her so unattractive that he wouldn't even try to seduce her? A stab of wounded pride jabbed her. "I feel so much more secure now, having the word of a man of such sterling character."

He touched his hand to his heart. "You're safe, Miss Maitland."

For some unfathomable reason, she believed him. The man had a way of dredging trust from a person, even when she knew he was a complete charlatan.

She should be frightened of him. He was far too fierce to be standing in her bedroom amid the scent of lavender potpourri and the perfume of roses that drifted in from the gardens on the cool evening breeze. He looked far too masculine surrounded by the ivory silk and thick embroidered lace that fell in swags from her canopy and dripped from her bed. This was a soldier who belonged atop a black stallion, leading his men into war.

Yet, there was something in his eyes as he looked around her room, a wistful look that lent a vulnerable cast to his chiseled features. Did he long for comfort and always find it out of reach? And then she realized she *was* frightened.

It wasn't the strength so obvious in this man that frightened her. It wasn't the threat of ravishment. For she truly believed this man had never found the need to force a woman into anything. No, she had the feeling this man could charm a woman as easily as he could bring down an enemy. With one look he could make a woman understand what it truly meant to feel feminine. With one kiss he could bend her will. And that power frightened her.

"Tell me something." He held her with his look, his black eyes probing hers. "Just why did you invent a husband?"

"It's none of your concern."

"Couldn't you find any man willing to put up with the temper that went along with your beauty?"

Emily's back stiffened with indignation. "There were plenty of men who wanted to marry me."

"And yet you didn't choose one." He brushed his fingers over the ivory silk counterpane that lay folded at the foot of her bed. "Why?"

Emily followed the slow trail of his fingers, her body growing taut deep inside. How odd. How very intimate to watch those long, elegant fingers trail across her bedclothes. "I don't intend to explain my actions to you."

"I see." He moved away from the bedpost. "Then you leave me to my own conclusions."

She stepped back as he stalked her. "Just what do you think you're about?"

He smiled. "I'm about to test a theory."

She backed away as he drew near. "Keep your distance."

He shook his head, his dark eyes glinting with mischief. "I don't think I can test this particular theory from a distance."

Emily stepped back, hitting the low sill of the open window beside the vanity. She felt her balance shift with her backward progress. She gasped. She snatched for something solid as her body continued through the dark cavity of the open window.

''Careful!'' Simon shouted, grabbing her arms as she threw them up before her.

Her breath escaped in a whoosh as he hauled her against the solid wall of his chest. Without a thought she clung to him, her arms tight around his waist, her cheek pressed against the white braid slashing across the blue wool covering his chest. Her entire body trembled in his embrace.

''Good God, Em,'' he whispered, tightening his arms around her. ''That was close.''

Too close. She dragged air into her lungs, each quick gasp filling her senses with the intriguing aroma of wool and leather and man.

''I haven't a fancy to become a widower before I've even had a chance to sample the bliss of married life.''

She pulled back in his arms, staring up into the endless depths of his eyes. ''I shouldn't need to remind you that we are not truly married.''

''No, there is no need to remind me.'' He smiled, that intriguing dimple slashing his right cheek.

She was painfully aware of the powerful arms that still held her, his long fingers curved at her waist. Yet, she couldn't find the strength to pull free.

''If we were truly wed, we wouldn't be standing here like this,'' he said.

It seemed right, standing with his arms around her, the cool June breeze swirling the perfume of roses around them. ''We wouldn't?''

''No.'' He slid his hands upward along her back, slipping beneath her unbound hair, spreading a warmth that soaked through the satin of her dressing gown, the chaste white linen of her nightgown. ''If we were truly wed, I would be lying beside you in that big, soft bed of yours.''

''Oh.'' Emily stared up into his eyes, captured by the flames flickering in the dark depths.

''If we were truly wed''—he brushed his lips against the sensitive skin beneath her ear—''I would learn every lush curve, every elegant line . . .'' He nipped her earlobe. ''Every secret little hollow of you.''

Emily trembled beneath his touch, tingles shimmering along her every nerve. *If we were truly wed*—the thought rippled across the pool of longing hidden deep within her. Her body responded to him in a way she had never imagined, even in her dreams. She felt a shifting within her, a slow melt of muscles that flowed toward him, until her breasts nestled against the solid wall of his chest, and her breath escaped on a heated sigh. His muscles tensed against her.

''You're so very beautiful,'' he whispered, his lips brushing her cheek.

Emily felt her will unraveling. Dear heaven, she had to put a stop to this. ''You're trying to seduce me,'' she said, pulling back as far as his strong arms would allow.

''You have a way about you, Miss Maitland.'' He lifted his head, a smile curving his lips as he looked down at her. ''It's the fire in your hair, the flicker of flames deep in your big amber eyes. It makes a man want to discover if there are truly fires burning deep within you.''

''You're being most impertinent.'' She pushed against his granite-hard chest, appalled at the quiver that stole the strength from her protest.

''Am I?''

''You certainly are.'' Emily stared up into his eyes, wondering what chance she would have if he truly decided to claim her. Yet it wasn't his physical power she feared. No, it was a power that couldn't be measured. A power to make her wish for dreams to come true. ''Kindly take your hands off me.''

He slid his hands downward, caressing the curve of her back. ''If that is what you truly desire, my lady.''

Emily swallowed hard. "Of course it is."

He released her.

She stumbled back toward the window.

"Careful," he said, grabbing her arm, steering her clear of danger.

She jerked her arm free of his grasp. "I can manage quite well without your help, thank you."

He shrugged. "I'm simply trying to make certain your family isn't plunged into mourning."

"They would be if they realized what a terrible mistake I've made." She lowered the window, shutting out all but a breath of the cool evening breeze.

"In your choice of husbands?"

"Precisely."

"What would they think if they knew we weren't really married?"

Emily shivered when she thought of what would happen if anyone knew she was in her bedroom alone with a man who was not her husband.

"Precisely," he said as though he had read her mind. He lifted the book of poems from the vanity. He flipped through the pages as though he hadn't a care in the world.

"Give me that," she said, snatching the book from his hand.

"You're very tense. You should try to relax, Miss Maitland."

"How do you expect me to relax when I'm being blackmailed by a scoundrel?"

"I'm not about to reveal your little secret."

"It would ruin your own budding career as a fortune hunter, I believe." She hugged the book to her chest, staring at the rogue, appalled at how he could read her thoughts. "My father would no doubt see you thrown into prison."

"It seems we both have much to lose if our secret is discovered."

"It might be worth the scandal just to watch you rot."

He laughed, a deeply masculine sound that made her smile, despite her anger. ''You really are a bloodthirsty little chit.''

''Keep that in mind the next time you try to seduce me.''

''Tell me something, Em. Would you be more offended if I tried to seduce you''—he smiled, a lazy curve of finely molded lips that sparked memories of his kiss—''or if I didn't.''

''Don't be ridiculous.'' She turned away from him, hiding the blush she could feel rising in her cheeks.

She stared out at the gardens and lawns that rolled away from the back of her father's house. Grass sprinkled with moonlight stretched to the edge of a deep gorge where the river flowed like a shimmering silver serpent in a legend. A night like this was straight out of a fairy tale, an evening for gallant knights to rescue fair ladies. Except her knight had turned out to be a dragon in disguise. ''I can assure you, I certainly do not enjoy being mauled by a scoundrel.''

''Is that a fact?''

''It certainly is. Your actions are quite . . . bothersome.'' The heat of his body brushed against her back as he drew near. She resisted the urge to run, determined to show this man she was not afraid of him.

''That's going to make our time together rather difficult.''

''An ordeal.''

''Tell me something, my lady,'' he whispered, his lips brushing her ear.

Emily closed her eyes, the velvet whisper sending tingles skimming across her shoulder. ''What?''

''Do you want the right or the left side of the bed?''

Chapter Four

Emily spun around to face him, her glorious dark red curls spilling around her shoulders. "What nonsense is this?"

Simon slipped off his dress sword and propped it against the vanity. "It looks as though there is only one bed."

"You can't seriously expect to . . ." Emily stared up at him, realization dawning in her eyes. "Under no circumstances shall I share a bed with you."

"Suit yourself." He began flicking open the brass buttons lining the front of his blue coat. "But that couch doesn't look very comfortable."

She smiled, a smug little twist of her lips. "Since you have insisted on staying here, it would seem you are destined to sleep on that couch."

Simon looked at the Grecian chaise longue standing near the white marble hearth. It was an elegant little affair, sleek and narrow, covered in mint-green damask silk. Definitely not accommodations for a man who stood several inches over six feet. "I'm afraid you misunderstood me, Miss Maitland."

"In what manner?"

He peeled off his coat and dropped it over the lyre-shaped back of an upholstered armchair near the bed. "I have every intention of enjoying a good night's sleep in the comfort of this bed. If you don't want to share, then that is your concern. Not mine."

Emily stared at him, her eyes wide with astonishment. "You can't mean to say you would force me out of my own bed?"

"Never." Simon sank to the edge of the bed, sighing as the soft mattress cushioned his weight. After years of sleeping on hard pallets, he wondered if he would ever take a decent bed for granted. He pulled off one shiny black Hessian and let it fall. It hit the swirls of green and ivory in the carpet with a soft plunk. Emily flinched. "You are welcome to join me at any time."

"Why, you . . ." She watched as he pulled off the other boot and dropped it to the floor, a wary look entering her golden eyes. "What are you doing?"

He started unfastening his white linen shirt. "Preparing for bed."

Her lips parted, then closed, then parted once more. "You can't do that."

"No?" He tugged the white linen from his breeches and slipped the shirt up over his head.

"Dear heaven," she whispered.

Simon ran his hands through his hair, smoothing back the shaggy dark waves, watching Emily as she followed his every move, her eyes so wide the whites showed all around the amber irises. She was staring at him as though she had never before seen a half-naked man. And she looked fascinated.

The heat of her golden gaze skimmed his shoulders, the look of fascination fading into a frown as she caught sight of the ragged scar below his left shoulder. He expected her to turn away, shocked and disgusted by the ruined flesh. Instead she lowered her gaze, absorbing every detail of his chest, as though he were an infinitely intriguing tapestry of dark curls and sleek muscle. Her heated look stole the breath from his lungs. He felt the heat rise in his blood, the pulse pump low in his belly.

Damnation! The woman had a way of ambushing the control he had long ago learned to exert over his more primitive needs. A man could get killed if he allowed what was in his breeches to rule his head. He stood, determined to take control. "Miss Maitland, unless you want your delicate sensibilities injured, I suggest you turn around."

She glanced up, looking at him with wide, startled eyes. "Pardon me?"

He flicked open the top button of his breeches. "I'm about to remove my breeches."

"Oh!" She spun around, lifting her hands to her face.

He drew a deep breath, trying to ease the tension in his chest, before he peeled off his breeches, revealing the full extent of Miss Emily Maitland's unrelenting influence over him.

She marched to the vanity and restored the volume of verse to its place. "You really are a complete barbarian," she said to the top of the vanity.

"Nonsense, Miss Maitland." Simon slipped between the soft white sheets and breathed in the scent of freshly washed linen dried in the sunshine. "If I were a complete barbarian, you would be on your back in this soft bed, with me between your smooth white thighs."

Emily gasped. She spun around to face him, her cheeks brushed high with color. "How dare you!"

"Perhaps you're the one who should dare."

"And just what do you mean?"

Simon sank his elbow into one plump pillow and rested his cheek on his open palm. He smiled at her, knowing he was teasing her unmercifully, unable to resist. He liked to see the blush rise in her cheeks. "The world thinks we're married. Why not enjoy each other?"

She lifted her chin, meeting his smile with icy defiance.

"I can assure you, I would not enjoy your bestial rutting."

"Certain of that, are you?"

She folded her arms and stared at him. "Quite certain."

"And you're basing this theory on your vast experience with other men."

Emily's mouth dropped open. "How dare you imply that I would stoop to such depravity?"

"A fake marriage seems an excellent opportunity for a woman who would like to taste forbidden fruit and still live within the strictures of society."

"Ooooh, you are a perfect beast!"

Laughter welled up inside him as he watched her snatch the counterpane from the foot of the bed. He couldn't help laughing. She looked so indignant. So incredibly innocent. So painfully seductive.

He allowed himself the pleasure of imagining what it would be like to have her lie beside him in this big comfortable bed—the warmth of her skin radiating against him, the sleek length of her legs rubbing against his, the soft brush of her breasts nestling against his chest. He wanted to spread all that fiery hair of hers across his pillow, bury his face against her neck, breathe in the sweet scent of lavender. It had been a long time since he had held a woman who smelled of lavender. A lifetime.

Ah, to make love to a woman who didn't reek with the stench of the last man who had slaked his lust upon her body. To hold a woman through the night. To feel something more than emptiness after his lust was spent. To live for tomorrow and the day after, instead of the moment. These were things other men took for granted. Yet, the life he led did not allow for these simple gifts.

He looked into Emily Maitland's eyes and wondered what it might be like to have this woman look at him with something more than the incipient desire he had glimpsed in those golden depths when he had held her.

She stood at the foot of the bed, clutching the counterpane to her breasts, staring at him as though he had crawled out from under a rock. "I shall have you understand, there is only one man who will ever know my love."

Simon's chest tightened when he learned that the little beauty had already given her heart to some man. He thought of the inscription penned in her book of sonnets, and wondered why he had a sudden urge to strangle a man he didn't even know. "And who is the lucky fellow? Is he the Henry who gave you the book of sonnets?"

She stiffened. "He is none of your concern."

Simon ran his fingertip over the delicate lace stitched across the edge of the sheet on the bed beside him. "I assume Henry is already married. Otherwise there would be no need for this deception. With a fake marriage you and your lover can carry on a liaison without fear of consequences."

"You are filled with base notions, aren't you?"

He looked at her, fighting the urge to grab her slender shoulders and shake her. The woman had no business wasting herself on some man who couldn't even give her his name. Still, if the lady wanted to toss away her life, it was her business. "I suppose it really isn't any of my concern."

"No. It isn't." She pivoted and marched toward the couch, the ivory silk of the counterpane dragging on the floor behind her, her dark red head held high, like a tigress who has fought her first fight and come up short.

"Emily."

She flung the counterpane across the narrow couch. "What?"

When she turned to face him, he tossed one of the plump pillows at her. It smacked her chest, white lace fluttering as the pillow tumbled to the floor.

He smiled in the face of her furious glare. "I thought you might like a pillow."

"How very thoughtful of you." She growled deep in her throat as she retrieved the pillow and tossed it on the couch.

"Good night, sweetheart," he said, staring at her stiff little back.

She huffed in response.

He bit back a chuckle. "Are you going to put out the lamps, or do you want me to do it?"

She glanced over her shoulder. "You stay right where you are."

"My pleasure."

She stalked to the sconces along the walls and with quick, efficient motions extinguished the candles, then marched to the oil lamp perched on a small mahogany table beside the bed. As the flame died, the moonlight took command, silvery columns spilling into the room through the windows.

She stood for an instant beside the bed, looking down at him, as though the sight of a man in her bed was something she couldn't quite absorb. Moonlight captured her in a silvery frame. Her face was as pale and smooth as fresh cream. Her hair tumbled over her shoulders in a cascade of dark fire. The sight of her stole his breath.

There were times in his life, when he had allowed himself to wander into a realm of fantasy, when he had imagined what it might be like to have a home, a family, one woman to share the rest of his days. So far fate had denied him such luxuries, but he had his dreams. And as he looked up at Emily, he could easily imagine she had stepped from those dreams.

On impulse he grabbed her wrist, holding her when she tried to break free. "Don't waste all your fire on a man who will never truly be your own, Em."

She ceased her struggle, pausing like a deer entranced by the sight of a lion, not knowing if he intended to destroy her or let her live. "If you must know, I have never in my life had a lover."

The tension eased in his chest. Women could lie as easily as they could breathe. Yet he believed her. Because in that moment, as he looked up into her face, he wanted to believe no man had ever felt the heavenly burn of her fire.

"I certainly would never be so foolish as to become involved with a man who is married to another woman."

He stroked the smooth skin of her wrist with the pad of his thumb. "It has been known to happen."

She slid the tip of her tongue over her lips. "I can assure you I would find nothing appealing in a dishonorable blackguard who would betray his wife."

"Love does not always obey the rules of propriety."

"I would not expect you to understand the concept of honor."

She was trembling beneath his touch, like a wild bird captured in the palm of his hand. She was so fragile. He sensed her weakness, and knew it was also her strength. A firm belief in her own dreams glowed inside her, as bright as sunlight. And inside him, where shadows crept into every corner, he craved that light. "Tell me, why did you invent Sheridan Blake?"

She stared at his hand as though she were intrigued by the sight of his fingers curled around her narrow wrist. "My parents insisted I marry before Anna could have a Season."

He rubbed his thumb over the heel of her palm. "And since you couldn't find the man of your dreams, you invented him."

She nodded. "It seemed to be a good plan at the time."

"Interesting. You created a military man. I would think you would aim for something higher."

"I am not so green as you might think." She pulled her wrist from his light grasp and hugged her arms to her chest. "My father is a wealthy man, but to the *haut ton*, he is in 'trade.' That makes his daughters somewhat beneath their touch."

"You're also the late Earl of Castlereagh's granddaughter."

"Oh, yes." Emily smiled, a grim curve of her lips that left her eyes glittering like gold in the moonlight. "My grandmother made certain I received all the prope invitations, every opportunity to fully display my wares on the marriage mart."

Simon frowned, sensing the bitterness inside her. "I have to believe that more than one gentleman wanted to make you his bride."

"You're quite right. Father's fortune was much more powerful than my lack of proper pedigree."

"I see. You think every man who has ever been interested in you has been after your fortune."

Emily arched one brow as she stared at him. "So it would seem."

Simon leaned on his forearm, studying her a moment. "I suspect your attitude is what has kept you unmarried, Em."

She frowned. "My attitude?"

"You see phantoms where they don't exist."

She lifted her chin, her lower lip puffing in indignation. "You are hardly the one to lecture me on the noble spirit of the aristocracy."

He wondered what she would say if she discovered he was a member of that class. No doubt he would drop in the lady's estimation. If, in fact, he could fall any lower. "It seems obvious you never met a member of the aristocracy who could sway your opinion."

"I have no taste for an arrogant aristocrat who seeks only a plump purse. I do not wish for a man who expects to maintain his ladybird after he has spoken vows of faithfulness to me. The man I marry shall be honest and true. He shall know the meaning of loyalty and integrity. And he shall love me as deeply as I love him."

"Like a knight of legend." He smiled as he recalled the legends of knights and castles he had devoured as a boy. "A warrior who will pledge his heart and sword to his lady."

"I realize this is all very amusing to you."

"Is it?" He looked up into her eyes, seeing the light that burned like sunlight in the golden depths. "You're a woman determined to marry only for love. A woman reckless enough and intelligent enough to invent a husband and fool the world."

"And you think I'm—"

"Extraordinary."

"Oh!" She stepped back, bumping into the mahogany table near the bed. The glass chimney of the lamp clattered. She snatched it, her hand hitting a carved rosewood frame housing a small watercolor of a Norman castle. The painting tumbled to the floor.

He smiled as he watched her retrieve the painting, her hands trembling as she placed the frame back on the embroidered lace doily. For some unholy reason, this woman had a knack for making him smile. If they had met in another time and place, they might have become friends. Perhaps lovers. Perhaps more. They might have had a chance at forever. Mentally he shook himself. He had learned long ago not to dwell on the twisted threads of fate.

"So tell me, who was he?"

She backed away from him, smoothing her hand over her wayward curls in an effort to repair her dignity. "Who do you mean?"

"The man who made you bitter enough to suspect that every man who paid an interest in you was only after your fortune."

She bumped into the elegantly curved arm of the couch. "If there were such a man, he would be none of your concern."

"I'm your husband. That makes it my concern."

"We are *not* married," she said, enunciating each word as though she were talking to a backward child. "And I shall find a way to be rid of you."

Simon propped his chin in his hand and grinned at her. "It was Henry, wasn't it?"

"Oh, you are . . ." She sank to the couch and tugged the counterpane over her knees as though she were trying to hide from him.

"What did Henry do to hurt you?"

She drummed her fingers on the ivory silk covering her knees. "Why are you so interested?"

A question he might have asked himself, if he truly wanted to examine the answer. He didn't. "We're going to spend a great deal of time together. If we're going to convince people we're married, we should know more about each other."

She released her breath in an irritated sigh. For a moment she sat staring at him, drumming her fingers on her knee, a silent debate reflected in her eyes.

"Come on, Em. Who is Henry?"

She stared at him, her lips pursed, a single line digging between her brows.

"Someone else will tell me if you don't."

"I shall not appreciate it if you go about asking questions concerning me."

"All right. So tell me, who is Henry?"

She released her breath in a sigh. "Lord Henry Coverdale, Viscount Avesbury."

Simon frowned, trying to place the name among the aristocrats he had met during his few dips into the pool of London society. He couldn't place the man. "What did he do to make you distrust men?"

She smiled, yet the bitter twist of her lips left her eyes as cold as gold in the dead of winter. "He asked me to marry him."

Simon's inner tension grew as he chipped away at the walls she had built around her past. "Did you love him?"

He hadn't intended to ask the question. He knew it really wasn't any of his concern. Yet, for some unfathomable reason, his next breath seemed to wait on her answer.

"I thought I did. But I was wrong."

He breathed again.

She glanced down at her hands, drawing her fingers against her palms, shaping her hands into small fists. "I was young, barely twenty, in my first Season. So full of dreams. And he was so handsome, tall, and fair, and quite the darling of the ton. I was so flattered when he took an interest in me."

He could imagine Emily in London, a breath of spring in the frigid drawing rooms and ballrooms of aristocrats who had long ago turned into ice sculptures, existing without the spark of life. Like his father.

"I met Avesbury my first night at Almack's. I remember standing beside my grandmother terrified of how I would disappoint her if no one asked me to dance. She had taken such pains to make sure I received a voucher." Emily smoothed her hand over the ivory silk covering her knees, as if to soothe the terrified girl she saw in her memories. "I was convinced I was too tall, my hair was much too red, my address too countrified. I would have given anything at that moment to be small and fair like Anna."

Simon caught himself wishing he had been there on that night. He would have taken great pleasure in leading the beautiful young redhead onto the floor.

"It seemed I stood there a lifetime, waiting for someone to save me from complete disaster." She pressed her palms to her knees, stretching her long fingers like a cat unsheathing her claws. "And then Henry came to my rescue. After he danced with me, the other gentlemen in the room took notice of the Green Girl from Bristol. I danced the rest of the night, but Henry was the one man in the room who had become my hero."

Simon frowned at the bitterness in her voice, the self-loathing that remained after all these years. Avesbury had plunged his dagger deep inside her soul. And it startled Simon to realize how much he would like to be the one to help heal the wound.

"I knew him less than a fortnight when he asked me to marry him. And I remember feeling so honored." She laughed, a bitter sound that made Simon want to find Henry Coverdale and throttle the man.

"It was grandmother who first heard the gossip about him. Henry had left for Bristol intending to ask my father for my hand. But the rumors of our impending engagement had already spread through London. So naturally, grandmother's friends felt impelled to tell her the latest *on dit* concerning my future husband."

Simon had a feeling this was one time he owed a debt of gratitude to the waspish old ladies who ruled town society. "What did you learn about him?"

"Aside from the fact that he kept a fair-haired mistress in a lovely townhouse on Park Lane, it seems Henry had lost a fortune at the gaming tables. In truth, he was deep in dun territory. After I accepted his proposal, he went about issuing notice of his impending marriage to the Maitland fortune as a guarantee to cover his vowels. The strange thing is, even after hearing the truth, I didn't believe it."

"I take it you finally did come to believe all the rumors."

Emily plucked at the ivory silk above her knee. "Not until he confessed everything to me. It seems he thought I would be anxious to trade my inheritance for his title. And it also seems he thought it quite natural for a gentleman to keep his mistress even after he was married."

No wonder the lady had reacted so passionately to the discussion of possible arrangements for his own bit of muslin. "Why do you keep the book he gave you?"

She kept her eyes lowered, but he could see the tight curve of her smile. "As a reminder of my foolishness."

"Avesbury was the fool."

Emily glanced up at him, her eyes reflecting the moonlight, revealing the hard glitter in the golden depths. "He was only trying to improve his position in life."

Simon clenched his teeth, uncomfortable with the position in which he found himself—viewed as an equal with a man Emily justifiably detested.

"Since questions seem to be the order of the day, perhaps you will tell me how you managed to get that scar."

Simon managed a grin. "Which one?"

"You have more than one?"

"A few minor ones."

Emily pursed her lips. "I would hardly call that scar on your shoulder minor."

He rubbed his fingers across the puckered flesh below his collarbone. When the weather turned wet and cold the old wound still pained him, but not as much as the memories. "It's a little reminder I brought back with me from the Peninsula."

"So you really were in the army."

"Surprised?"

She shrugged. "I didn't realize they allowed scoundrels to enter the army."

"A few of us slip by."

"It must have been quite terrible."

"War is never pleasant."

"No." She glanced up at him. "And this is war between us, you realize."

He sighed, acknowledging the fact that he would like something more than animosity between them. "I would prefer that you didn't see me as your enemy."

"I'm afraid you leave me no choice." She turned, pulling her legs onto the narrow couch. "This is war, and I don't intend to lose."

War. The lady had no idea what the word meant. He hoped she never did. "Sleep well, my lady."

"I am *not* your lady."

"You are." He glanced at her, meeting the angry glare she cast him with a smile. "At least until you find a way to be rid of me."

"Smile your smug smiles while you can, *Lord Scoundrel*, for I intend to wipe the smile from your face."

"I have a feeling you will prove a worthy opponent, milady."

She lifted one finely arched brow. "You have no idea, *milord*."

Simon flopped on his back and stared up into the shadows of the canopy, frowning. She was right. They were enemies. He had to keep his mind on the business at hand. Not on a beautiful redhead who could set his blood on fire with a single glance. Women could be treacherous, he reminded himself. Involvement with this particular woman could be deadly.

He rolled his head on the pillow, looking at Emily who now lay curled beneath ivory silk, recalling the feel of her in his arms, the warmth of her lush body pressed close to flesh that even now hardened with the memory.

Simon released his breath in a frustrated sigh. Her father could very well be a traitor. Simon could very well be the man who would send Hugh Maitland to the gallows. Any thought of a future with Emily was nothing more than foolishness. And foolishness in this business could get a man killed.

Chapter Five

Morning sunlight teased Emily. Warm rays brushed her face. Golden light glowed against her closed eyes, coaxing her from slumber. She opened her eyes and blinked against the light, her body making the slow transition from slumber, her mind grappling with wisps of dreams and scraps of reality. A man stood near the window across from her. A tall man dressed in nothing more than buff-colored breeches and sunlight. A portrait of potent masculinity framed by elegant ivory silk brocade. For a moment she was certain this was a dream. Where else but in a dream would she find this man?

Sunlight poured through the open window, slipping pale yellow fingers into the thick black hair that tumbled in wayward waves against the back of his neck. Sunlight slid shimmering fingers of gold along his wide bare shoulders. Sunlight taunted her, touching him the way she longed to touch him.

She stared at his back, skimming the intriguing valley of his spine, sunlight and shadow sketching the thick, smooth muscles tapering to his narrow waist. She imagined touching him, pressing her face against the sleek muscles, slipping her arms around his lean waist. She imagined all of this and more—*if we were truly wed.*

He turned his head, gazing at her over his bare shoulder, a pagan god spotting a mortal woman who had been spying on him in his lair. Amusement sparkled in the dark depths of his eyes. His lips tipped into a grin that left little doubt the man knew exactly how fascinating she found him. "Good morning, Em."

Emily flinched as though he had tossed a glass of water in her face, reality hitting her squarely between the eyes. She sat up, sucking in her breath as the tortured muscles in her neck and shoulders stretched painfully. "Must you parade about my room dressed like that?"

His look was pure innocence etched on the face of a fallen angel. "Like what?"

She pursed her lips as she rubbed her stiff neck. "Like a half-naked barbarian."

He laughed softly. "Emily, love, you're married now. Time to set aside maidenly sensibilities."

"We are *not* married."

He pressed his fingertip to his lips, warning her to lower her voice. "Careful, Miss Maitland. We don't want to brew any scandal broth. What would people think if they knew we had spent the night together without benefit of marriage?"

"How dare you remind me of the situation you have put me in?"

He moved toward her, his smile tipping into a devilish grin. "It's a situation that could be worse, if you don't control that rather fiery temper of yours."

"Insufferable, odious blackguard. I wish you would just go away."

He lifted one black brow, his amusement mocking her anger. "Is that any way to talk to the man who has given you his name?"

''It's exactly the way I speak to a scoundrel.'' She rubbed her stiff neck, trying not to look at the man who stood before her in nothing but buff-colored wool that hugged his narrow hips and long, muscular legs.

''I had a feeling you might be a little stiff this morning.''

She glared at him. ''You needn't look so smug about it.''

He shrugged those wide, bare shoulders. ''You can't say I didn't give you the opportunity to share the bed.''

''Your generosity overwhelms me.''

''You know, Em, that's a big bed. Chances are we wouldn't even collide during the night.''

Emily stared up at him, trying to appear nonchalant, as if the sight of his bare chest hadn't added a beat to her heart. ''There isn't a bed large enough to give me ample distance from you.''

He lifted a lock of hair from her shoulder, sliding the dark red strands between his fingers, enjoying the feel. ''Frightened of me?''

She snatched her hair from his hand. ''I believe a measure of caution is in order when dealing with a black-hearted rogue.''

''Your virtue is safe with me.'' He looked straight into her eyes, and for the life of her she didn't understand how the man could manage to look so utterly sincere. ''I told you before. I have never in my life forced a woman to endure my villainous advances. Please believe me, I don't want to hurt you in any way.''

Emily felt a shudder of longing that came from dreams that refused to see reality even when it was standing right in front of her. She kept her gaze pinned on his face, fighting to ignore the smooth expanse of his shoulders, and those intriguing black curls that started just below the hollow of his neck. ''You will pardon me if I fail to believe a word you utter.''

He touched the tip of her nose with his fingertip. ''I suppose I can understand your having some small measure of distrust under the circumstances."

Emily swatted away his hand. "You are my enemy, *Lord Scoundrel.* There is nothing you can do to make me change my mind."

He grinned, a mischievous light entering his eyes. "Are you brave enough to let me try?"

She stared up at him, her eyes narrowed with suspicion. "What do you have in mind?"

"Nothing as sinister as you obviously believe," he said, walking toward the corner of the chaise longue.

Emily turned her head, keeping her eye on him as he walked around behind her. "What are you about?"

"Don't be frightened. I won't bite."

"I'm not frightened of you." She flinched when he rested his hands on her shoulders. "Just what do you . . ."

"Relax." He lifted her hair, dropping the heavy mass over her shoulder.

The heat of his body whispered against her back, stealing the breath from her lungs. She was overcome by a feeling of weakness that threatened her resistance and every good intention she had ever possessed.

He gripped her shoulders when she tried to bolt. "I thought you were made of stronger stuff, Em. Don't tell me you're really a coward?"

Emily clenched her teeth. "I am not a coward."

"Then you have no excuse for running off like a scared little rabbit."

"A scared little rabbit!"

"That's right." He settled his hands against her shoulders, close to the base of her neck. "I'm not going to hurt you."

"I'm not frightened." She only hoped he couldn't feel the way her body was trembling beneath his touch. "I simply do not care . . ." She hesitated as he began massaging her stiff muscles. The heat of his hands seeped through the satin of her robe, the soft white linen of her gown. "Ah, I don't care to be . . . mauled."

"I promise not to maul you." He pushed his thumbs into her tight shoulders, kneading her muscles with his long fingers, gently easing away the knots.

A sigh rose inside her, escaping her lips before she could prevent it. She clasped her fingers over her lips, hoping he hadn't heard. If he had, he chose to ignore the wayward sound of pleasure.

"How long do you intend to sleep on this thing, Em?"

She closed her eyes, the heat of his hands penetrating into her blood. "Until I find a way to be rid of you."

"Should I fear for my life?"

"Murder is tempting." She lowered her chin, her will dissolving beneath the heat and strength of his touch. He worked his hands back and forth across her shoulders, and her stiffness melted.

"I'm serious about sharing the bed. You have nothing to fear from me."

She nearly laughed. "I cannot believe you would actually imagine I would sleep in the same bed with you."

"You should realize people are going to assume we are sleeping in the same bed, even if we don't."

"I have no intention of consorting with a scoundrel, no matter what people may believe."

He rubbed his thumbs upward along the back of her neck. "I had hoped we might strike a truce, but I suppose there isn't much chance of our becoming friends."

"None." Emily released her breath in a long sigh. "You are my enemy."

"Pity. Your father told me there is a pool chamber connected to the house, with a bath fed by one of the hot springs in the area. I'm looking forward to a nice hot soak." He brushed his lips across the top of her ear. "I had hoped you might join me."

The soft touch sent an army of shivers skittering across her shoulder. Startled by her own reaction, she sprang to her feet, bumping her shoulder against his chin. "How dare you imagine I would bathe with you?"

He rubbed his chin, his lips curving into a smile as he held her furious glare. "I'll scrub your back."

"Why, you . . . you . . ." Emily clenched her hands into fists at her sides. "You are the most arrogant, black-hearted man I have ever had the misfortune to meet. To imagine . . ."

He laughed, a dark sound that rumbled from deep in his chest and shredded her self-control. She suddenly realized the man was only teasing her.

"Oh!" She snatched her pillow from the sofa and swung it at him, smacking him across the shoulder.

"I'm unarmed," he mumbled through his laughter.

"Scoundrel!" She swung the pillow with both hands.

He threw up his arm, blocking the blow she aimed at his head. The plump pillow plopped against his forearm. His deep laughter stoked the angry fires blazing inside her.

"Ooooh!" She swung the pillow and missed as he dashed around the corner of the elegant chaise longue and headed for the bed. She chased him, the pillow slung over her shoulder. He paused at the bed, snatching a pillow. She wielded her linen-clad weapon, whacking him across the back. "Blackguard!"

"Termagant!" He pivoted, smacking her across the hip with the plump pillow.

"Villain!" She hit his chest.

"Vixen!" He returned the blow, hitting her shoulder, laughing as she squealed her outrage.

She recognized that he was restraining the power of his blows, yet it didn't stop her from hitting him with all her might. She had been tense for months, apprehensive about the future, and each blow drained some of that anxiety.

A low groan escaped his throat as she smacked the pillow across the side of his head. He stepped back, hitting the edge of the bed. Emily planted the pillow against his chest and pushed, catching him off balance. He toppled backward, sinking into the soft feather mattress.

She pressed her advantage. She swung the pillow up and

slammed it against his chest with enough force to pop the stitches beneath the linen cover. Plumes of white goose down sprayed in all directions, shooting upward like a geyser.

Emily gasped. She stared at her enemy through a shower of white feathers, her weapon dangling limp in her hands. Simon coughed, waving feathers away from his face. Feathers rained upon him, frosting his black hair, coating his wide bare shoulders, tangling in the black curls on his chest.

She stared down at him, feathers drifting all around them like snow in a paperweight. He sneezed, scattering feathers everywhere. Without warning, a giggle flickered deep inside her, rising from a place where her laughter had taken refuge months ago. The laughter bubbled upward, streaming from her like water from a fountain that had been dry for an eternity.

"Look . . . at . . . you," she sputtered between giggles. "Lord Scoundrel . . . all dressed up in white feathers. Pity I haven't any tar."

"Smug little hellcat." He surged upward, feathers flying in all directions. Before she realized what he was about, he had his hands on her waist. In one fluid movement he yanked her off the floor and tossed her to the bed beside him, feathers flying all around them. He pounced, pinning her to the bed with the weight of his body.

"Scoundrel." Her giggles spoiled the severity of the epithet.

"Temptress," he said, smiling down at her.

Feathers drifted over them, dusting his tousled waves, kissing her brow, her cheeks, her neck, like soft white rose petals. She stared up into his dark eyes, suddenly aware of each place his body touched hers, the heat of him soaking through satin and linen, drenching her skin.

Each breath she took brushed her breasts against his broad, bare chest. Each touch sent sensation shimmering along her every nerve. The fires she saw awakening in the midnight depths of his eyes mirrored the flames igniting inside herself. And as the flames flickered to life, her resistance began to melt.

She remembered the way his lips had felt against hers. The taste of him, more potent than wine. And, as shocking as she found it, she could not deny she wanted to once again experience that illicit pleasure.

She arched her fingers against his chest, testing the strength of sleek muscles. He was an intriguing collection of textures—warm skin, firm and smooth, black curls silky against her fingertips. He drew in his breath, his chest expanding into her hands, his heart pulsing against her palm in time to the beat of her own heart.

A part of her screamed in protest—this man was her enemy. She shouldn't be within reach of this scoundrel. Yet, she could form no words that might slay the dragon who lay against her, his breath falling warm and soft upon her face. It was as if he had entranced her, as if he had cast some ancient spell that had stolen her will.

His thick, black lashes lowered as he gazed at her lips. She held her breath, watching as he lowered his head, his lips parting, his moist breath spilling across her cheek before his lips touched hers.

Before this moment, she had wondered if the thrilling excitement she had felt when he had kissed her the night before had been an aberration. Before this moment, she had harbored a measure of hope that circumstances had embellished that kiss. Yet now, with the slow slide of his firm lips against hers, and the pleasure seeping into her every pore, that slender hope evaporated.

She curled her fingers against his chest, wanting to slip her arms around his neck and hold him. This was what she had craved all of her life, this man and the way he made her feel. He was the one man destiny had claimed for her. He was the one man who could fill her heart with a heavenly song.

Only it was nothing but illusion.

Dear heaven, the man who could make her heart sing

could destroy her with that power. She turned her head, breaking the kiss, her breath coming in ragged gasps.

He lifted himself above her, searching her eyes for answers to his confusion. ''What is it, Em?''

''Get off of me!''

He did not move but stayed close against her, his heart hammering against her palm, his dark eyes probing hers.

She turned her head, afraid of what he might see in her eyes. ''I seem to recall you saying you had never forced a woman into enduring your villainous advances.''

He touched her cheek, a soft brush of warm fingers across her skin. ''Is that what I was doing?''

Emily clenched her teeth, wishing she had the strength to throttle the man. ''If you think for one moment I am enjoying being crushed by a brute, think again.''

He released his breath in a long sigh. And then he was lifting away from her, releasing her from the intoxicating influence of his powerful body.

She scrambled from the bed in a flurry of blue satin and white feathers. Her knees threatened to buckle as she marched to the windows, putting the length of the room between them.

She took a deep breath, gathering the shreds of her defenses before she turned to face him. He was lounging on the bed in a pool of white feathers, his elbow planted in the soft mattress, his cheek cradled in his open palm, watching her like a lion amused with his prey.

She clasped her trembling hands at her waist. ''If we are to carry on this farce, I must insist you refrain from your more bestial behavior.''

His lips tipped into a devilish grin. ''Sweetheart, you have never even glimpsed my bestial side.''

She stiffened. ''And I prefer never to glimpse it.''

He lowered his eyes, sweeping her figure with a lazy look that made her feel as though he were peeling away her clothes and touching her with the heat of his hands. She shivered, but not from revulsion.

When he lifted his head and looked straight into her eyes, she had the uncomfortable feeling he could read her every thought. "Don't worry, Em. I promise never to push you into anything you don't want."

Emily squeezed her hands together, glaring at the man. "I can assure you, I do not want anything you have to offer."

He stood, feathers swirling around him. He studied her a moment, a smile curving his lips before he spoke. "If you don't want what I have to offer, then you have nothing to fear."

Yet, if she did want him, she had everything to fear. She watched as he crossed the room and withdrew an emerald silk robe from the dressing room where his clothes had been stored the night before. When he drew the robe over his bare shoulders, she noticed the dragon embroidered in gold and scarlet threads along one side of the emerald silk, its fiery tongue curving near his left shoulder—an appropriate crest for *Lord Scoundrel*, she thought.

He gathered fresh garments, tossing each over his arm. She stared at him, knowing she should look away, finding it impossible. Each movement he made was somehow fascinating.

He turned at the door leading to the hall, a devilish grin curving his lips as he caught her staring at him. Again. "Are you certain you don't want to join me?"

Emily clenched her hands into fists at her sides. "Quite certain."

He shrugged his broad shoulders and left her alone.

Emily moaned in frustration. Oh, that man! She had no business finding him attractive. None at all. She paced the length of her room, feathers fluttering from her hair and clothes. She had to find a way to get rid of him. She had no choice. None at all. She had to get rid of him before she committed the supreme act of foolishness. Oh yes, she had to get rid of him before she managed to lose her heart to the scoundrel.

The door opened. Emily pivoted at her vanity, her heart surging with the expectation of seeing him once again. Lady Harriet stepped into the room, closing the door behind her, like a spy afraid of being detected by the enemy.

"I saw him leave."

Emily released the breath she hadn't realized she had been holding. "Headed for the pools."

Harriet leaned back against the door, her eyes wide as she stared at the feathers strewn across the bed. "What happened here?"

"I made the mistake of hitting him with my pillow. Next time I shall try something more substantial." Emily smiled as she imagined her next battle, in which she would be the victor. "Perhaps a chair."

Harriet frowned. "Did he try to force his attentions on you?"

"No. The man claims never to have forced his 'villainous advances' with any woman."

"I would suspect that young man has never had a problem finding intimate companionship."

Heat flickered across her breasts when Emily thought of the way his body had pressed against hers. "I pity the foolish women."

"I rather suspected that young man would keep his word." Harriet stared at the bed, a thoughtful expression on her face. "The man has quality. In spite of everything, I believe he is essentially honest."

"How can you say that? The man has stormed into my life and upset all of my plans." Emily plucked a feather from her tangled curls. "The scoundrel even stole my bed."

Harriet tilted her head and smiled. "I wondered which one of you would end up on that chaise longue. I had a feeling it wouldn't be your scoundrel."

"I would prefer if you didn't refer to him as *my* scoundrel." Emily snatched her brush from the vanity and slashed at her curls. "Can you imagine, the scoundrel actually implied I had invented a husband so I might carry on illicit affairs.''

Harriet tapped her fingertip against her chin, considering the statement a moment before she spoke. ''I suppose that would be a logical conclusion.''

Emily stared at her grandmother, stunned that Harriet would take his side. ''Only a scoundrel would see such base notions in the most innocent of actions.''

''I would wager that young man has seen the darker side of life, Emily. You cannot blame him for relating your actions to what he has come to expect from other people.''

''That doesn't signify. He should know I wouldn't do anything so . . . so . . . vile.''

Harriet studied her a moment, a smile hovering about her lips. ''How would he know you are a woman of principle? He doesn't know you. At least, not yet.''

''But . . .'' She hesitated, realizing that what she was about to say made little sense. It was impossible to explain the way she felt, as though she had known the man all of her life. ''We know each other as well as we are going to know each other.''

''Emily, I'm afraid you are saddled with the man for the rest of your life. You must learn to adjust to the situation.''

''No.'' Emily turned and stared out the window where Ravenwood Castle rose like a gray phantom from the rolling green hills. ''Ever since I was a child, I always knew I would never settle for anything less than a marriage built on love.''

''Emily, we can't always make our dreams come true.''

''This is too important to abandon.'' Somehow, she had to find a way to get rid of the scoundrel who threatened her very existence. ''I refuse to allow that man to destroy me.''

Chapter Six

Simon stood near the open French doors in Hugh Maitland's study. A gravel path led from the stone terrace outside the study to the rose garden. Beyond the roses, Emily, her mother, the two sisters closest to Emily in age, and Lady Harriet were engaged in an archery contest on the lawn, shooting at paper targets attached to bales of straw.

Simon watched one of Emily's arrows pierce the target a foot wide of the mark. She lowered her bow, shaking her head as though she were disgusted with herself, the golden ribbons on her bonnet rippling in the breeze. Judging by the wildness of Emily's shots, he suspected the lady was distracted. And he had a fairly good idea of what was distracting her.

"How does it feel to be out of uniform?" Hugh asked.

Simon turned to face his host. Hugh Maitland was sitting on the edge of his large mahogany claw-footed desk, his long legs stretched out before him in a relaxed pose that still managed to convey the man's quiet sense of command. Tall and lean, with a mane of golden hair and a clear, direct gaze, Maitland certainly didn't look like a man who would betray his country, but Simon had learned a long time ago that a man would stay alive longer if he never judged anyone or anything by appearances alone.

"I'm already accustomed to the new attire." Simon flicked the lapels of his dark gray coat, part of the wardrobe he had acquired in London while investigating Miss Emily Maitland. He had intended to pay court to the woman, looking for a way into Hugh Maitland's kingdom, when the lady had dropped the drawbridge for him.

"I hope you don't mind me pulling you away from your bride for a while. But I thought we should get to know each other better."

"I agree." Simon already knew a great deal about Hugh Maitland. Still, he needed to know more. He needed to know if the man should be sent to the gallows. "I realize our marriage was quite sudden."

"To tell you the truth, I had almost given up hope that Emily would ever marry." Hugh twisted a crystal paperweight in the shape of a square rigger on his desk. Sunlight pouring through the open windows behind the desk glittered on the facets carved into the crystal, casting rainbows of light across the bookshelves built into the mahogany-paneled walls. "A few years ago she was hurt very deeply by a man calling himself a gentleman." He looked up at Simon. "I assume Emily has told you about Avesbury."

Simon's muscles tensed at the mention of the man's name. "She has."

"I suspected she would." Hugh glanced down at the crystal ship. "The first time I met the man I knew he wasn't right for Emily. There was a weakness about his mouth, a soft, petulant look. He looked like a bloody poet."

"Apparently she had an affection for poetry." Simon turned his face into the warm breeze drifting through the open door. He watched Emily fit an arrow to her bow, aware of a strange emotion curling like a viper inside him.

"Her first London Season was delayed because of the

death of Audrey's father. Even so, at twenty, Emily was terribly naive. She has always been filled with romantic notions, and I'm afraid her mother and I have always encouraged her dreamy side.''

Simon stared at Emily, watching as she drew back her bow. He had known the woman barely a day, and here he was contemplating strangling a man he had never met for hurting her. Foolish notion. He might amuse himself with the lady for the time he was here, he reminded himself, but he couldn't entertain thoughts of any lasting connection.

Emily released the bowstring. Her arrow sliced through the air, piercing the heart of her target.

''I can't tell you how many times I have given thanks that Emily discovered the truth before it was too late. It never would have worked. Emily would have grown tired of Avesbury within a year. She has always been strong-willed. She needs a strong man. And I'm glad she found one.''

Guilt nipped at Simon as he held Hugh Maitland's gaze. He pushed the feeling aside. Guilt was just one of the emotions he couldn't afford. Not on this mission. ''Still, you weren't upset by our hasty marriage?''

''Emily has always been impulsive. Stubborn, in fact, if you don't already know.'' Hugh chuckled beneath his breath. ''How could I be opposed to her elopement, when Audrey and I eloped? Against her father's wishes, I might add. He didn't care much for the idea of his daughter marrying a man in 'trade.' On top of that, Whitcomb sold Ravenwood Castle and the surrounding land to my father to cover a gambling debt. Even though my father had nothing to do with Whitcomb's going into debt, the earl resented him for buying Ravenwood. It had been in Whitcomb's family since the first Baron of Ravenwood. I'm afraid it took several years before he forgave Audrey for eloping with me.''

''And what do you think of your daughter marrying a military man?''

Hugh lifted his cup of coffee. "The way you ask the question makes me think you've heard a few things about my opinions on the war."

Simon rested his shoulder against the door casement, intending to appear casual as he baited his quarry. "I have heard you're against the war with Napoleon."

"I am." Hugh sipped his coffee, studying Simon over the rim of the ivory porcelain. "I'm not at all certain our government has done a fair job of trying to make peace."

Simon held Hugh's steady gaze, looking for something that might betray the man. "I understand there are those who believe England would be better off under Napoleon's rule."

"Including a few of the peers." Hugh settled his cup in the saucer on his desk, staring down into the dark liquid a moment before he spoke. "Although I feel our government could do with substantial reforms, I am not overly fond of the Monster. But this war must end. This war is draining all of the life from our country. I say let Napoleon have his empire. Bring our men back home."

"And what would prevent Napoleon from invading England?"

"If he did indeed invade England, would England not survive? We survived the Normans and became stronger in the bargain. Think of what might be if England were joined with the continent, with no barriers to trade."

"A man with a shipping company could make a fortune."

"True." Hugh smiled, his green eyes remaining cool, like a general assessing his troops for the first time. "But all of this must sound like treason to a man who has just come back from fighting against Napoleon's army."

Simon smiled. "Not all soldiers love war."

Hugh studied him a moment, as though trying to penetrate his mind. "Have you given any thought to what you might like to do now? Emily told us you are the last of your family. I assume that leaves you with few connections.''

''I know Emily could have done much better in her choice of husbands.''

''I have never judged a man by the coin in his pockets.''

''I'm afraid there is very little coin in my pockets.'' Simon held Hugh's cool green gaze. ''I have been in the military most of my life. I believe I have gained a few skills that would be beneficial in a business. I would like very much to earn a position in your company.''

''As you probably know, I have substantial business interests, and no son to carry on after I have departed.'' Hugh studied Simon a moment, the cool, appraising look in his eyes warming with his smile. ''I have a feeling you might be an answer to a prayer.''

Simon drew in his breath, filling his tight lungs with the scent of roses drifting from the garden. If this man was involved in the slaughter of English soldiers, Maitland would need more than prayers.

Simon turned to look at Emily, watching as she yanked an arrow from the target. Sunlight slipped into the curls caught by a golden ribbon at her nape, spinning the dark red strands into shimmering fire. An image from this morning flickered in his mind—Emily lying beneath him, those dark red curls spilling across a white linen sheet, her lips parted as she stared up at him. A pulse throbbed low in his belly as he recalled the feel of Emily snug against his body.

He might have spent most of his life in the military. He might have had only a few liaisons with women who weren't purchased by the hour. Still, he could recognize desire when he saw it in a woman's eyes. And Miss Emily Maitland burned with it. What she needed was a man to make love to her until she shimmered with that fire, until she felt the flames lick across her skin, until she succumbed to the blaze. It was a damn shame he couldn't be the one to give her that taste of forbidden fruit.

''What the devil?'' Hugh muttered, coming to his feet.

Simon frowned as he watched one of the Maitland ten-year-old twins dash across the yard toward the ladies. Her blond curls bounced on her shoulders. Her white gown fluttered behind her. Her shrill young voice sliced the air with cries for her mother. He didn't know if the child was Jayne or Olivia, since they looked alike, but he did know she was terrified.

Audrey bent to meet her young daughter, the curiosity on her lovely face dissolving into a look of sheer terror. A moment later she was running toward the far corner of the house, with Emily and the other women on her heels.

"I wonder what that is all about." Hugh started for the open doors.

Simon was already out the doors and running toward the far end of the house. When he rounded the corner, he found the ladies gathered beneath a huge oak tree, all except Emily. His beautiful lady was perched on a wrought-iron bench at the base of the tree, her hands pressed against a limb below her waist.

As he ran toward the tree, Emily climbed upward, disappearing into a tangle of green leaves and gray limbs. Why the devil would Emily be climbing a tree?

"Major Blake!" Audrey said, grabbing his arm. "Thank goodness you're here."

Simon stared up through the leaves, his heart squeezing in his chest when he saw Emily ascending toward the little girl perched on a narrow limb high above him.

"What the devil is going on?" Hugh demanded as he reached the small group of worried spectators.

"It's Olivia," Audrey said. "The girls were playing with Misty when the silly cat darted up the tree. Now Livie and the cat are both stuck, and Emily has taken an insane notion to get them down."

Hugh frowned as he looked down at his young daughter. "Where is Miss Wentworth? Why the devil isn't she looking after the two of you?"

"She went for a footman," Jayne said, staring up at her

father, her big green eyes wide. ''But Livie wouldn't wait.''

''Apparently neither would my wife.'' Simon's palms grew damp as he watched Emily work her way toward her sister. Bloody hell! He hated heights.

When she reached the limb where Livie was perched, Emily sat astride on the slender branch, her golden gown riding high on her thighs, exposing white silk stockings and a fair amount of pale skin. Simon stared up at her, torn between admiration for her courage and fury for her recklessness.

''Emmie, I can't get down.'' Olivia straddled a narrow branch, hugging her cat close against her. Misty meowed deep in her throat, a rusty sound of protest for the tight hug, or perhaps for the pink muslin gown and matching bonnet the girls had forced her to wear.

''Don't worry, Livie, I'm here.'' Emily glanced down, looking through the leaves and branches to her family, who were staring up at her from the ground. She swallowed past the fear that had formed a knot in her throat. As a child she had often climbed this very tree. But somehow it had never seemed this high.

She could do this, she assured herself, easing her way along the upward slope of the branch. With her hands she lifted herself, scooting a short distance, her legs dangling over the sides of the narrow branch. She gripped a slender limb above her, seeking balance as she reached for her sister. ''Put the cat down and give me your hand.''

Livie shook her head. ''Misty can't get down without help.''

''Livie, you have to put down the cat or I won't be able to help you.''

Olivia's lower lip trembled. ''But I can't leave her.''

Emily scooted closer to her sister, oak leaves ripping from the limb she still grasped, sending a sharp tang into the air. ''Let's get you down first, and then Misty.''

Olivia hugged her cat. ''Promise you won't leave her here?''

Emily forced her lips into a smile. "I promise."

Livie lowered the cat to the bough. The animal promptly dashed past the girl, out toward the end of the limb. "Misty!" Livie shouted, turning to chase the cat.

"No!" Emily leaned forward, grabbing Livie's arm. "You get down, and I'll get the cat."

Olivia hesitated a moment, staring at her cat, who sat near the end of the limb. Misty's green eyes were narrowed beneath her lace-trimmed bonnet, her fluffy orange and white tail switching beneath the pink muslin gown.

Emily tugged gently on her sister's arm. "Livie, I promise I'll get Misty for you. But you must climb down. Mama and Papa are very worried."

Livie cast one more glance back at Misty. "All right." She allowed Emily to help her back to the massive trunk of the tree. When she had her feet planted on a thick lower branch that jutted out perpendicular from the one on which Emily sat, Livie gazed up at her sister with trusting green eyes. "Now you have to get Misty," she said, leaning against the massive trunk. When Emily hesitated, she added. "You promised."

Emily drew in her breath and turned back toward the cat. "Come here, Misty."

The cat meowed but didn't budge.

Emily gripped the limb, scooting toward the end of the branch, the soft muslin of her gown snagging on the rough bark. "I'll give you a nice bowl of cream if you just come to me."

Misty sat hunched on the limb, her tail swishing back and forth, batting thick green leaves.

Emily tugged on the delicate golden muslin of her gown, trying to maintain some measure of modesty, and at the same time preserve her backside from the rough scrape of tree bark. "Come here, Misty. Come on, I'm not going to hurt you."

Misty meowed deep in her throat as she crept toward Emily.

"That's it," Emily murmured, holding out her hand. "Come on."

Misty nuzzled her outstretched hand, rubbing her face and the muslin bonnet against Emily.

"That's it." Emily grabbed the pink muslin gown and hauled the cat into her arms. Misty growled, her body growing rigid with protest.

"It's all right." Emily hugged the cat to her chest, squeezing the limb with her legs to keep her balance. She stroked the cat through the soft muslin, crooning softly, soothing the cat until the animal settled in her embrace. "You're safe, you silly cat."

As if in response to her words, the bough groaned beneath her. The sound sent fear slicing through her. The cat growled as Emily's arm jerked against her.

"Damnation, woman! What are you trying to do, get that beautiful neck broken?"

Emily released her breath in a sharp sigh at the sound of that deep male voice. She glanced over her shoulder to where her scoundrel stood against the trunk, his feet planted on the thick branch where Olivia had stood a few moments before. "Where is Livie?"

"On the ground." He took a deep breath, keeping his gaze fixed on her. "Where you and I should be."

"For once I can honestly say I'm glad to see you."

"Although the sentiment appeals to me, I would much prefer to hear it under different circumstances."

Emily frowned. "You look a little pale."

Simon drew his lips into a tight line. "I suppose you didn't notice just how high this limb happens to be."

She stared at him a moment. "Don't tell me you're frightened of heights?"

He started to say something, then clamped his mouth shut. He stared at her, the arrogant scoundrel gone and in his place a man who looked more than a little uncomfortable.

She giggled. She couldn't help it. Not when fear already

had her nerves stretched to the breaking point. "Why in the world would you climb a tree if you are frightened of heights?"

He lifted his chin, his eyes filled with wounded pride. "If you are through discussing my fear of heights, I suggest we get down."

"I agree." Emily moistened her dry lips, staring at the juncture of the limb and the trunk, where yellow wood showed through a crack in the dark gray bark. "Any suggestions?"

He nodded. "Put down the cat and get the hell over her."

"I can't. I promised Livie I would get Misty down."

He swore under his breath. "All right." With one arm hooked around the trunk, he leaned out over the limb until he was stretched like a bowstring. The breeze rippled the wide white sleeve of his shirt, tossed a thick lock of ebony over his brow. "Hand the bloody nuisance to me. And be careful."

Gripping the limb with one hand, she held out the cat with the other, holding her by the scruff of the neck just above the lace-trimmed collar of the gown. Misty dangled from her hand, hissing, clawing at the air.

Simon grabbed the animal, swearing as Misty batted him across the chest, her claws sinking into his white linen shirt and the skin beneath. "Bloody hell!"

Emily cringed. "Sorry."

"If you aren't nice, I'll give you a chance to see how well you can fly." Yet in spite of his words, his voice was soft and soothing as he stroked the terrified animal and cradled it against his chest. "Emily, ease your way over here."

Emily stared at the crack at the base of the limb. She couldn't move. She sat on the branch, her fingers digging into the tough bark, terrified that any movement might snap the branch.

"Emily, you have to come here." He unfastened the first

few buttons of his waistcoat as he spoke. "The branch won't hold my weight."

Emily watched as he slipped the cat into his waistcoat, wishing she were the one snuggled against his broad chest. Sunlight penetrated the canopy of leaves overhead, dripping golden drops of light across his broad shoulders. In spite of the small fact that he hated heights, he managed to look so strong, so powerful, so very capable. A man who could conquer his own fear to charge to her rescue.

"Come to me, Em," he said, holding out his hand.

She couldn't move. She wanted to, but she just couldn't move. "I can't."

He closed his eyes, a sigh escaping his lips. When he looked at her, determination sparkled like polished ebony in his eyes. "I'll come out and get you."

"No!" Emily gripped the limb as he started to mount the broken branch, planting his hand near the crack. "It will never hold your weight."

"It's not going to hold *your* weight much longer." He reached for her, stretching as far as he could manage. "You have to move toward me."

Emily stared at the man who held his hand out to her. The breeze ruffled his thick hair, tossing a dark wave over his brow, but it didn't soften the hard lines of his face, or the determined glitter in his midnight eyes. He looked like a man who could defy the devil and win.

She drew a deep breath and scooted toward him. The limb groaned, and she was certain she could feel it giving way, tilting toward the ground.

"Come to me, Em." He stretched toward her, his long fingers reaching for her. "I'll keep you safe."

She eased back along the limb, praying it would hold her. The limb groaned, tipping her forward. Emily clawed at the bark, squeezing hard with her legs.

"Come on, Em." She felt his fingers graze her arm. "Move toward me."

Emily bit her lower lip, fighting the pitiful whimper lodged in her throat.

"You have to move. Now!" He grazed her arm, and she realized he was struggling to reach her. He was behind her. Just a few more inches and she would be safe. She closed her eyes and scooted back, landing hard on the weak limb.

The limb snapped.

Chapter Seven

The falling limb smashed against smaller branches like a bear crashing through the woods. Leaves ripped from their moorings. Twigs snapped. Emily screamed as she pitched forward toward the ground.

Simon grabbed her. "I've got you."

Emily pressed her back against the bark, gripping the drooping limb with her legs. Golden sunlight and blue sky peeked through the leaves above her. Below her, the ground waited for her fall.

Simon tugged on her arm, trying to haul her toward him. "Let go of the limb."

"I can't." Emily squeezed the limb, the rough bark digging into her thighs. "I'll fall."

"I won't let you fall." Simon flexed his fingers against her upper arm. "Trust me."

"Trust you?" Emily tilted her head back, staring up at the man who had turned her entire world upside down. If she weren't dangling in the air, she might have laughed. "You won't even tell me your real name, and you expect me to trust you."

"It doesn't matter what my name is. All that matters is I won't let you fall." Simon squeezed her arm, holding her in a tight grasp. "Let go of the limb."

She stared at him, seeing the determination in his black eyes. She could imagine this man with sword in hand, riding to his lady's rescue. There was something about him, an aura of command, a quality that inspired trust in spite of everything. And she realized he was all that kept her from a killing fall. She released her hold on the limb, pinpoints of pain flaring in her thighs.

"That's it." He hauled her toward him, her gown snagging on the rough bark, shredding as he dragged her to the relative safety of the thick branch beneath his feet. Her knees shimmied beneath her when he helped her to her feet.

"It's all right," Simon whispered, slipping one arm around her. He held her against his chest, cradling her back against the sturdy tree trunk, providing a safe harbor in the middle of a storm. "You're safe."

Emily gulped the air like a drowning woman, taking the intriguing scent of his skin deep into her lungs. The heat of his body radiated through the layers of their clothes, warming her, easing the fear that streamed through her veins like an icy river.

"You're safe, Em."

She looked up into his midnight eyes, seeing the tenderness there, the strength of a man who might have led knights into battle. Misty meowed from deep in his waistcoat. Emily felt the cat squirm against her side, heard Simon's sharp intake of breath, and realized Misty had sunk her claws into more than white linen.

"Bloody hell," he whispered.

"It would seem Misty doesn't appreciate your efforts to rescue her."

He shifted his waistcoat. "So it would seem."

"But I think you did fairly well," she said, smiling up at him. "For a man who is frightened of heights."

"Never show a woman the chink in your armor. She

won't let you forget it." He growled deep in his throat, flinching as though Misty had used her claws once more. "I think Misty is ready to end this little adventure. Are you ready to go the rest of the way?"

"I'm ready."

"That's my lady." He kissed the tip of her nose.

Heat flared deep inside her at the gesture that seemed all the more intimate for its simplicity.

"Follow me," he said, squeezing her arm. "I'll be with you every inch of the way."

She obeyed, following him as he made a slow descent from limb to limb, accepting the strength he offered as he helped her each step of the way. When her feet touched the ground, he slipped his arms around her, holding her close. She didn't protest. It felt too good, having his powerful arms around her. She pressed her face against the comforting strength of his chest, and breathed in the scent of his skin.

For one glorious moment, he held her as though he never intended to let her go, as though they were bound by more than deception and lies. She realized in that moment this was exactly where she had always longed to be, and in a very real sense that fact was more terrifying than being trapped on a breaking limb.

She stepped away from him, leaving the warmth of his arms, bumping into the bench at the base of the tree, as her family gathered around them, and she sought to find her balance.

"Emily, you frightened the life out of me," Audrey said, throwing her arms around her daughter.

"I'm sorry, Mother."

Simon smiled, his midnight gaze on Emily as he pulled Misty from his waistcoat. He handed the squirming bundle of pink muslin and white and orange fur to Livie, who promptly threw one arm around his waist and hugged him. He glanced down at the child quizzically, as though she had slipped beneath his defenses and taken him by surprise.

A smile curved his lips as he patted her small shoulder, a wistful look entering his eyes.

Emily glanced away from the rogue, finding the sight of him oddly disquieting. He fit into her life far too well.

"You could have been killed." Audrey pulled back to look up at her daughter. "I don't know what you were thinking."

Emily managed a smile. "I saw Livie, and reacted."

Harriet shook her head. "You always were impetuous."

"Thank you for saving my girls." Hugh squeezed Simon's shoulder. "I'm glad you're here, son."

Emily inwardly cringed at the deception her father so thoroughly believed.

Simon glanced away from her father as though he couldn't hold his look. "I only did what needed to be done."

"I'm terribly sorry about all of this," Miss Wentworth said. The little gray-haired woman had been governess to all of the girls. She stood between Phoebe and the new footman, clasping her hands at her waist. "I'm so glad nothing happened to either of you."

"It's all right," Emily said, patting Miss Wentworth's shoulder. "I realize Livie is as difficult to manage as I was."

Miss Wentworth smiled up at her, lines flaring from her gentle gray eyes. "You were a bit of a handful, miss."

"She still is." Simon retrieved his coat from the bench and slipped it around Emily's shoulders.

The scent of his skin lingered on the superfine wool, ambushing her senses, tempting her to press her face into the soft gray wool. She shivered, but not from cold. She stripped off his coat and handed it to him. "I'm not at all chilly."

Simon frowned. "Emily, you . . ."

"Thank goodness you were here." Anna stared up at Simon as if he were wearing the shiniest armor. "You saved Emily's life."

Emily cringed at the thought, unwilling to accept the fact the man had saved her life.

"You were wonderful," Phoebe whispered, adoration shining in her brown eyes.

Simon shrugged. "I'm glad I was here to help."

No doubt the rogue believed she owed him something now, Emily thought. She could only imagine what he might expect as a reward. Still, he didn't look like a man determined to collect a reward. The man actually appeared uncomfortable with the praise. Nearly as uncomfortable as he had looked perched on that limb.

"Emily, I think you should wear this." Once again, Simon slipped his coat over her shoulders.

Emily glared up at him. Did the man think she was an invalid who needed a coat on a summer day? She snatched the coat off her shoulders and tossed it at him. He caught it before it hit his chest. "I told you I'm quite fine."

"I still think you should wear the coat." He smiled, a devilish little curve of his lips as he offered her the coat. "At least until you reach your room."

"Thank you. But I don't need your coat."

Hugh cleared his throat. "Blake is right. I think you should slip on his coat and go change your gown."

"My gown?" Emily glanced down at her gown, seeing the snags in the golden muslin, feeling the breeze whisper against her back, cool against her scraped bottom.

"Oh my." Audrey clapped her hand over her mouth. "Emily, your gown is a bit tattered."

Emily turned, glancing over her shoulder, trying to get a look at the back of her gown.

"Begging your pardon, Miss," Digby said, turning away from her.

"Oh my goodness." Anna stared at her sister with wide eyes. "Emily, your gown is in shreds."

The twins giggled. Phoebe gasped. Lady Harriet rolled her eyes toward heaven.

Emily brushed her hand over her backside, feeling the

tattered remains of her gown and petticoat, and the smooth curve of her bare bottom. She gasped, clutching at the shreds of her gown. "Why didn't you tell me?" she demanded, glaring at Simon. "You must have noticed my gown was torn when I was climbing down that tree!"

"I certainly did." Simon's eyes sparkled with mischief as he offered her the coat.

Emily's blush burned her cheeks when she realized how much of her person the rogue had seen. A gentleman would have averted his gaze. She snatched the coat from his hand and threw it over her shoulders. "Please excuse me," she said, lifting her chin. "I think I shall change."

Simon watched Emily march toward the house, her pride as tattered as her dress. Yet she managed to hold her head high. The little hellcat had courage. More than her fair share. When he thought of how close she had come to breaking her beautiful neck . . . he drew in his breath.

"That was a near thing," Harriet said as she approached him.

Simon turned to face her, meeting the curious look in her golden eyes. "Too near."

Harriet rested her hand on his arm, staying him as the others headed for the house. "I find it is truly a lovely day, much too fine to go in just yet. Will you stay and talk with me a while?"

Simon smiled, even as he was mentally reaching for his sword, preparing to do battle with this shrewd woman. "I would be honored to keep you company, Lady Harriet."

"Such a dear young man," she said, the corners of her eyes crinkling with her smile. She glanced over her shoulder, watching as the last of her family disappeared around the corner of the house. "Did it occur to you that you might have been killed in your heroic attempt to rescue my granddaughters?"

That was only one of the things that had rushed through

his mind as he had stood on that branch. ''I climbed a tree, hardly a heroic act.''

''Modesty. That's something I wouldn't have expected from you. You are an intriguing young man.'' Harriet stared up at him, her eyes narrowed as though she were trying to piece together a puzzle. ''There is something very familiar about you.''

Simon stared down into Lady Harriet's eyes, knowing there was little chance she would guess who he was. ''I'm certain we have never met before.''

''No. I would definitely remember you.'' She smiled, her eyes lighting with humor. ''I would hazard most women would remember you.''

''Are you flirting with me, Lady Harriet?''

''If I were forty years younger, I would be flirting with you. As it is, I'm only making an observation.'' Harriet snapped open her fan and smiled at him over the gilt-trimmed edge. ''I have a rather infamous habit of knowing everyone there is to know in society. I suspect I know your parents.''

Simon suspected the lady was on a fishing expedition.

''Your father is a peer, isn't he?''

''What makes you say that?'' he asked, keeping the surprise from his expression as well as his voice.

''It shows.'' Harriet flicked her fan back and forth beneath her chin. ''Who are you?''

He held her steady gaze, a smile tipping one corner of his lips. ''Sheridan Blake.''

''I see.'' Harriet turned away from him, her pale yellow gown rippling in the breeze as she took a seat on the bench beneath the oak tree. When she looked at him, he had the distinct impression he was facing a tribunal. ''You are very secretive about yourself. I trust you aren't a murderer seeking an escape from justice.''

He shook his head. ''There is no hangman waiting for me.''

"Then tell me, why does it matter if I know who you really are?"

"Who I am no longer matters."

"Poppycock!" Harriet snapped her fan closed. "You are married, in a fashion, to my granddaughter. You have altered her life. And I want to know more about you."

He couldn't risk this woman discovering his true identity. Still, he sensed she would persist in one way or another until she had her curiosity satisfied with a few scraps of information. "What would you like to know?"

She smiled slowly as she opened her fan, one slat at a time. "How long have you been in the military?"

Simon stared at the roses that spread out from the corner of the house like a colorful carriage wheel, bright blossoms bobbing in the warm breeze. "Seventeen years."

"Seventeen years?" She stared at him, her lips parted, her eyes betraying her surprise. "You must have been a child when you took your commission?"

"Twelve."

"A child of twelve sent off to war." She pursed her lips. She flicked her fan under her chin, fluttering the red and gray curls framing her face. "Your father must have been quite a tyrant. What could have possessed him to send you off to war at such a tender age?"

Simon clenched his jaw. "I wasn't the first twelve-year-old to be sent off to war."

Harriet lifted one brow as she studied him a moment. "Still sensitive about him, I see."

Simon drew in his breath, taking the scent of roses deep into his lungs. "Remind me never to play casino with you, Lady Harriet."

She smiled a smug little grin as she patted the bench beside her. "I have a feeling you could hold your own, Major Blake."

He sat on the bench beside her and stared at the house. His eyes followed the twisting ivy that rose along the stone walls to the windows which stood open in Emily's room.

The breeze fluttered against the ivory brocade drapes framing the windows. He imagined Emily standing somewhere beyond his sight, slipping out of her tattered gown. "Emily is in no danger with me."

"Poppycock!"

He glanced at her, seeing amusement where he expected to see anger.

"Don't try to look innocent. It doesn't suit you." She rested her fan on her knees, spreading the slats, revealing the watercolor roses painted on the ivory silk. "I've seen the way you look at her. You're a virile young buck and there is nothing more you would like to do than to make love to her."

"I can't imagine a man with blood in his veins who would not want to make love to Emily." Simon smiled when he thought of what Miss Emily would think if she knew what he and her grandmother were discussing. "But she is safe enough. I won't force her into anything."

"Few people can force Emily into anything." Harriet tapped her open fan against her knees. "Of course, there are different means of persuasion. And I suspect you are very good at them."

Simon held her piercing gaze. He thought of the few stolen moments when he had held Emily close against his body, his blood warming with the memory. A fire ignited when they touched. A fire that could consume both of them. He had little doubt he could coax the beauty into his bed. He could ease the ache in his loins, and allow Emily the opportunity to bed the man who might send her father to the gallows. It would prove to be a betrayal that would haunt both of them the rest of their lives. "I have no intention of seducing her."

Harriet lifted one brow as she stared at him. "You seem quite firm in your resolve. Since you have already confessed your attraction to Emily, I wonder why you aren't planning your conquest."

Simon shrugged. ''Perhaps I simply don't think seducing virgins is much sport.''

''Perhaps. Then perhaps it has something to do with who you really are.''

Simon lowered his eyes, retreating from Lady Harriet's penetrating stare. He stared at her fan. Golden drops of sunlight dripped through the leaves, splashing on the painted silk.

''Have you ever been married?''

Simon watched a red and black ladybug land on the green leaf of one of the pink roses painted on her fan. ''No.''

''What do you think of marriage?''

He thought of his parents' marriage: two strangers, sharing the same house. Hostile tigers forced to share the same cage. Until his willful, passionate mother had ended the farce. He would never settle for a marriage based on money or position, a convenient union empty of warmth. ''I think it's difficult to find a marriage based on mutual affection.''

''And that's important to you?''

He stared at the ladybug, watching as it spread its bright spotted wings and took flight from the imitation flower. ''Yes.''

''But you have essentially cut off your chances for that type of marriage by entering into this bargain with Emily.''

Although Harriet's assumption was not quite on the mark, Simon well knew that this mission had severed any chance he and Emily might have had for a future together. He drew in his breath, aware of a tightening near his heart as he stared at the painted roses. ''We can't always obtain everything we desire.''

Harriet was quiet a moment. In the periphery of his vision he could see her studying him, trying to dissect him, taking him apart piece by piece, examining every flaw.

''What qualities would you look for in a wife?''

An image stole into his mind, of a woman with golden eyes that burned with inner fires. ''Intelligence to challenge me. Honesty.'' He glanced at Lady Harriet, a smile beginning to form. ''A woman capable of deep passion, and all of it directed toward me.''

''I see.'' She lifted her fan, flicking the painted silk beneath her chin. ''I rather suspected you were a man who would appreciate a woman with spirit.''

Simon frowned as he studied her, seeing the speculative look on her face. ''Lady Harriet, why do I have a feeling that a scheme is brewing in your beautiful head?''

''I have no idea what you mean.'' She pressed her open fan against her chin, smiling at him over the gilt trim. ''Now I suggest you run along and change, young man. It looks as though that silly cat drew blood.''

Simon glanced down at the red smudges staining his white shirt where Misty had sunk her claws into him. He had the uncomfortable feeling that if he weren't careful, another little hellcat would leave her mark on him.

Chapter Eight

Emily paced the length of her bedroom, turning as she reached the door. She marched back to the windows. Her grandmother was still sitting there under the oak tree, fanning herself and smiling as though she had a secret she intended to keep.

What on earth could her grandmother have found to discuss with that blackguard? And she had actually seemed to be enjoying herself. A few times, as she had watched them from a hidden corner of her window, Emily was certain her grandmother had actually been flirting with the rogue. She crossed her arms at her waist, tapping her toe against the smooth oak planks at the edge of the carpet. Dear heaven, did the man have that same unsettling effect on all women?

Her skin tingled. The breath settled in her lungs. There was no noise. No sign of his presence. Yet, she sensed it the moment he entered the room. Although she scarcely knew him, she was becoming familiar with his ways. He could move as silently as a shadow at midnight, like a jungle cat who survived on its cunning.

She turned and found him standing near the closed door. His hair was tousled into thick black waves around his face, his lips curved into a grin that made her wonder what he was thinking.

Emily pressed her hand against her neck, trying to ease the pulse that fluttered there, the blood sprinting through her veins at the sight of him, this dark-haired angel who had fallen from grace. "Do you ever knock?"

He grinned, that infuriating dimple slashing his right cheek. "Not on the door of my own room."

"This is *not* your room."

"I'm surprised at you, Em." Simon's smile grew crooked as he held her furious look. "Didn't anyone ever teach you to share?"

She released her breath in a hiss between her teeth. "I don't care to share what is mine with a scoundrel trying to steal everything I own."

"You have me all wrong, sweetheart." He pulled open the door to the dressing room and slipped his coat onto a hanger. "I'm not out to steal anything."

"Oh, pardon me." She watched as he stripped off his waistcoat and laid the blue silk in one of the drawers built into one wall of the dressing room. "I must have you confused with some other scoundrel. The one who is parading around my life, pretending to be my husband."

Simon rested his shoulder against the door frame, smiling at her as he unfastened the cuffs of his shirt. "I intend to work for my living."

"Oh?" She stared as he pulled his shirt from his tight-fitting pearl gray trousers, revealing white linen tails creased by the heat of his body. "Did you manage to convince my father you could be of some benefit to his company?"

"As a matter of fact, your father was thrilled to have me." He tugged the shirt over his head and stared down at the smudges of blood staining the front.

She tried to moisten her lips, but her mouth had turned

to parchment. Sunlight streamed through the open windows, sliding golden light across the smooth skin of his shoulders. ''My father doesn't realize this is all a terrible farce.''

He tossed the shirt into a wicker hamper. ''Your father had almost given up hope of you ever finding a man brave enough to marry you.''

''Brave enough?'' Emily stared as he poured water into the basin on the washstand, fascinated by the play of taut muscles beneath golden skin. It felt strange to be this close to a man in the middle of his toilet, especially a man such as this one: beautiful, untamed, like a magnificent wild animal bathing in the heart of a wilderness. ''I wasn't aware that bravery was required for marriage.''

''It isn't required if a man plans to marry a sweet, biddable girl.'' He bent over the basin and splashed water on his face and chest. ''A girl like Annabella.''

''Oh?'' His words pricked her pride. Did he really find Anna so much more attractive? ''I suppose you think most men would prefer to marry Anna?''

''I doubt that Anna would ever climb a tree to rescue a cat.'' He slid his wet hand over his chest, wiping away the dried blood.

His action drew her eyes to the black curls that spread like arched raven wings across his chest. She curled her fingers into her palms, remembering the silky feel of those masculine curls against her fingers. ''I climbed that tree to rescue Livie.''

''True.'' He lifted a white linen towel from the rack beneath the basin, his lips in a lopsided grin as he looked at her. ''Still, I doubt that Anna would ever engage in a pillow fight.''

''You're fortunate I didn't hit you with a chair.''

Simon shook his head. ''Anna would never even imagine hitting a man with a chair.''

''No. She wouldn't.'' Emily stared down at the vanity, her gaze resting on the book of sonnets.

In her heart she knew most men would prefer Anna. There was no reason to feel crushed because this scoundrel thought she couldn't compare to her beautiful little sister. It would take someone very special to love a stubborn woman. A woman with far too fiery a temper. A woman past her prime. He simply wasn't that man. Still, she felt as though he had kicked her hard in the ribs.

In the corner of her eye she saw him move toward her in long, loose-limbed strides. He paused in front of her. So close she could feel the warmth of his skin reaching out to her. She lifted her eyes, staring into the mirror, seeing his reflection beside hers.

Her breath tangled in her throat as she stared at their reflections. An odd sense of familiarity swept over her, as though she had stood this way before, beside this man, in a different time and place. Sunlight streamed around them like shimmering liquid amber, capturing them for all eternity in the silvered glass—a bold warrior and his lady.

He touched her face, his long fingers stroking her cheek with warmth, slipping beneath her chin, urging her to look away from the reflections in the mirror, coaxing her to look into the reality of his eyes. Fires flickered in the midnight depths. Fires that kindled kindred flames deep inside her.

He smiled, a gentle curve of generous lips that made her want to capture that smile beneath her fingertips. "I think Anna would be ill equipped to deal with a scoundrel," he said.

She swallowed hard before she could use her voice. "Anna would never find herself in this tangle."

"No." He stroked his thumb over her bottom lip. "Only a woman of fire would have done anything quite so daring as to invent a husband."

She stared up into his eyes, knowing she should pull away from this beguiling creature. Yet, the heat of his body radiated against her, shriveling her will. Her body leaned toward him, like a delicate rose seeking the warmth of the sun.

He lowered his eyes, staring at her lips. "Only a woman of fire would ever suit me."

Only a man as bold as this would ever suit me, she thought. He was so close. If she rose just a little, lifted her lips, she could taste his kiss once more. She shivered with the temptation of it.

She placed her palm on his chest, intending to push him away. Yet, she lingered, absorbing the feel of him. Silky black curls tantalizing her fingers. Damp heat radiating against her skin. The powerful pulse of his heart throbbing under her palm.

His muscles tensed against her palm. He stared down into her eyes, all the humor she had seen in the dark depths consumed by the flames raging there. He slipped his hand into her hair, his long fingers curving around her nape, cradling her head. "You could tempt a saint, Miss Emily."

She felt as though she stood on the edge of a cliff. One step and she would fall. "You are hardly a saint, Lord Scoundrel."

He flexed his fingers against her nape, as though he wanted to pull her close and push her away all in the same instant. "No, I'm not."

She should pull away. Now. But her body wouldn't listen to reason. "If you think what you did this afternoon changes anything between us, think again."

"Relax, Miss Maitland." His slow smile made her want to capture it beneath her lips before it was gone. "I told you before. If you don't want me, I won't force you."

Emily stared up into his eyes, straining against the invisible cord that tugged on her, threatening to draw her to disaster. "I certainly don't want you."

"So you say, my lady." He slipped his arm around her waist and drew her close. So close she could feel the heat of his body through the delicate muslin of her gown. So close she could feel the press of taut muscles against her belly, her thighs. So close, and yet not close enough.

"I don't want you. I mean it."

"Do you?" He held her with his look, a dark gaze that stripped away pretense and exposed all the secrets she might have tried to hide.

"Yes, of course I do." She had to pull away from him. Now. Yet it felt so right, standing this way, with this man.

She watched as he lowered his head, sensual lips parting, warm breath spilling across her cheek. He slid his lips against hers, igniting a warmth that spiraled down inside her, like a slowly spinning ember, setting fire to all it touched. Logic melted in the heat of his kiss. Nothing mattered but the feel of his body—warm and hard against her.

She slid her hands upward, brushing the silky black curls on his chest, the smooth expanse of his wide bare shoulders, sinking her fingers into the soft black waves at his nape. He growled deep in his chest, a dark husky sound that filled her with an odd sense of power.

He touched the tip of his tongue to the seam of her lips in a gentle prodding she had never before experienced. Instinct guided her, coaxing her to part her lips, to welcome the slow slide of his tongue into her mouth. Even as that small voice of logic in her mind not yet drowned by sensation expressed shock and confusion, her body recognized the rhythm, the slick thrust and withdrawal of his tongue that tripped a pulse low in her belly. A delicious ache pulsed and expanded in that part of her she was only now beginning to understand.

She leaned into him, nestling her breasts against the solid strength of his chest, instinct seeking surcease for the ache throbbing there. Sensation rippled through her. Yet it wasn't enough. Not nearly enough. She snuggled against him. Seeking more. Something she didn't quite understand.

"Feel what you do to me," he whispered against her lips. He slid his hands down her back, his palms warming her, sliding lower, over the curves of her rounded bottom, pulling her up into the wicked heat of him.

She gasped against his lips, feeling the hard thrust of his aroused flesh through the layers of clothing. Shocking. Exciting. She wanted to strip away the barriers. She wanted to touch him. She curled her hands in his hair, pulling him closer.

"Emily. Beautiful, fiery Emily." He kissed her cheek, her jaw, her neck, moving his lips, touching her with his tongue as though he loved the taste of her.

She arched against him, pressing into him as he slid his hands upward along her back, the curves of her shoulders, his fingers slipping inside her gown. The soft summer breeze whispered through the windows, brushing her breasts as he pulled the muslin low, exposing her flesh to his midnight gaze.

"So lovely," he whispered, staring down at her as though she were something rare. Something precious. A gift that left him awed.

He touched her, a soft brush of his fingertips across one rose-colored tip. She gasped with the sensation. He smiled, lowering his lips, kissing first one, then the other nipple, a soft brush of his lips that left her breathless.

She tilted back her head, her hair brushing her bare back like cool strands of silk. She caught a glimpse of them in the mirror, two strangers entwined: a woman standing with her gown pushed low, half naked in the arms of a man, his dark head bent, his mouth closing over her breast. It was a shocking sight. Scandalous. Wicked. Provocative.

Sensation spiraled from her captured nipple, a fiery arrow that shot through her, straight to the heart of her woman's flesh, where feminine tears dripped like warm honey. She moaned with the pleasure as he flicked his tongue over the taut little bud, as he teased her with his teeth, nipping her flesh. He brushed his cheek against her breasts, his body rigid against her.

"Oh, God," he whispered, a man in pain.

He released his breath against her skin, the damp heat searing her skin. And then he was pulling away from her. The breeze rippled across her damp nipples, chilling the flesh he had warmed. She opened her eyes, staring up into the turbulent depths of his black eyes.

"You don't need this," he said, his hands tensing on her upper arms.

She moistened her lips, staring up at him through the fog of desire still hanging thick and sweet over her. His words made no sense. None at all.

"Bloody hell!" He fumbled with her gown, yanking on her sleeves, tugging on her neckline. He was breathing hard, and she noticed his hands trembling as he straightened her clothes, forcing the muslin up over her breasts.

She touched his cheek. "What are you doing?"

"Damnation, woman! What does it look like I'm doing?"

His sharp words ripped the delicate tapestry of sensation he had woven around her. Reality sluiced through her veins like a stream rushing through a broken dam.

She stepped back, bumping into the vanity, knocking over a bottle of lavender water. She snatched the bottle, setting it right with trembling hands.

"Emily," he whispered, touching her arm.

She flinched at the soft brush of his fingers against her skin. "Don't touch me."

"I'm sorry." He swept his hands through his hair, pushing the black waves back from his face. "I didn't mean for this to get so out of control."

Emily stared at him, her face burning with shame. If the scoundrel hadn't stopped, she would have given him everything she had to give. But he had stopped. And she knew it had nothing at all to do with morals or gallantry. Since he possessed neither. "You did this to humiliate me, didn't you?

"Emily, I—"

"No. Don't say a word. Because I won't believe a word you have to say."

She spun on the ball of her foot, a blade of pain twisting in her chest. She marched to the door, trying to ignore the shaking of her legs. Dear heaven, she had been willing to give him everything. And he had rejected her. Tossed her aside like an ugly old shoe.

What was wrong with her? What did he see when he looked at her? What was she lacking? Tears stung her eyes. She clenched her teeth, fighting the humiliating weakness. She needed some distance. She needed to gain her balance. She would not fall to pieces because of this man.

Emily sank into an upholstered armchair next to the mahogany vanity in her grandmother's room. "The man is impossible."

"What do you think?" Harriet turned in her vanity chair, facing Emily. "Do I need a little more rouge?"

"More rouge?" Emily stared at her grandmother. "Have you heard anything I've been saying?"

"Of course." Harriet turned back to the mirror. She stared at her reflection, smoothing her fingertips over the crests of her cheeks as she continued. "Sheridan is a beast. He swaggers about your room, half naked, as though he owned the place."

Emily crossed her arms under her breasts. "You're certainly sanguine about all of this."

Harriet glanced at Emily, a smiling. "If I were you, Emily, I should enjoy the view."

"Grandmother!"

Harriet laughed. "Don't look so scandalized. You're hardly a green girl, Emily. And you have to admit, the man is devilishly attractive."

"The man is a devil."

"He is quite exceptional." Harriet tilted her head, the curls piled at the crown of her head, brushing her shoulder. "In spite of everything, I believe he has a solid core of honesty inside him."

"How can you believe such a thing?"

"There is something about him, a certain quality that commands respect." Harriet rested her fingers on a crystal atomizer bottle that stood among other bottles and jars on the white embroidered lace runner covering her vanity. "I wish I knew more about him."

Emily frowned. "I wish I could think of a way to get rid of him."

Harriet twisted the bottle in her fingers, candlelight from a wall sconce sparking fires in the cut crystal. "Would it really be so terrible if he should stay?"

"Grandmama!" Emily came to her feet. "You spend a few minutes in conversation with the man and you think I should accept that fortune-hunting scoundrel into my life."

"Emily, calm yourself."

"How can you even imagine I would ever entertain the thought of allowing that man to stay? It's unthinkable."

"Is it?" Harriet smiled, her eyes filled with understanding. "I think you're frightened of your own attraction to the man."

"Grandmama, please, don't talk such nonsense. I am not attracted to the rogue."

"No?" Harriet studied her granddaughter a moment. "From the way you look at him, I would say you find him devilishly attractive."

Emily turned away from her grandmother's perceptive gaze, her restlessness bringing her to the windows. Was she really so terribly obvious? Could everyone see how she had fallen under his spell? At least they didn't know how very foolish she truly was. She stared into the distance, where dying rays of the sun streaked scarlet and gold across the clouds above Ravenwood. "I want him out of my life."

Harriet sighed. "Emily, try to put aside how he came into your life. Become acquainted with the man behind the mask of Sheridan Blake. I think you might like him."

"Like him?" Emily turned, staring at her grandmother. "The man is a complete scoundrel."

"I don't think so." Harriet smiled. "A complete scoundrel would have stood by and watched as you fell from that tree."

Emily curled her hands into fists at her sides, resenting

the fact that the man had saved her life. "I didn't ask for his help."

"No. He gave it without being asked."

"It doesn't change anything." Emily batted one of the burgundy drapes, the heavy silk brocade swinging, scraping brass rings against the brass rod. "The man only wants money."

"Emily, perhaps he wants more than money. Perhaps he wants a home."

"Then he should find one of his own."

Harriet was quiet a moment. "Did you know he was sent off to the army when he was twelve?"

"Twelve?" Emily turned to face her grandmother. "Dear heaven, what type of man sends his son to war at twelve?"

"My thoughts exactly." Harriet twisted the perfume bottle in her fingers, shards of light striking Emily's face. "Can you imagine what it must have been like, being sent away at such a young age, tossed into battle. It's a wonder he survived."

A steel band tightened around her heart when Emily thought of what he must have suffered as a boy, ripped from his home, forced to fight for his life.

"I doubt that young man has known much compassion in his entire life."

"He is hardly a boy any longer." Emily forced air into her tight lungs. "Although I think his circumstances were unfortunate, I'm not responsible for his past."

"No, you aren't. But what you do will shape your future as well as his." Harriet lifted the crystal bottle and squeezed the atomizer, spraying perfume on her neck, releasing the scent of gardenias into the air. "I suggest you try to find a way to live with him."

"I can't believe you expect me to allow that man to march into my life and take over without a fight."

Harriet lifted one dark brow as she studied Emily. "I don't think you have a choice."

Emily stiffened. ''I can find a way to be rid of him.''

''Or you can find a way to live with him.''

''Never. I shall never surrender to that scoundrel.''

Harriet shook her head. ''Many things can happen between now and never, my darling girl.''

Emily turned and stared out the window. On a nearby hill, Ravenwood Castle stood like a phantom from the past, tall and pale in the moonlight. She wouldn't let the scoundrel destroy her dreams.

Harriet came up behind her and rested her hands on Emily's shoulders. ''I only want what is best for you.''

''What is best for me is to banish that man from my life.'' Emily kept her eyes focused on Ravenwood. ''And I shall find a way to do it.''

''Yes, I suspect you will.'' Harriet sighed, squeezing Emily's shoulders. ''Come now, darling, it's time for dinner. Try to smile. Pretend nothing is amiss. We don't want the rest of the family to suspect you aren't the happiest of women.''

As Emily withdrew her hand from her bishop, Simon moved one of his pawns, winning a chilling glare from his opponent. He grinned in response.

''You always move so quickly, Major,'' Olivia said, scooting to the edge of her seat to gaze across the chessboard. ''I've never seen anyone play so quickly, have you, Emmie?''

Emily glanced at her sister sitting beside her sham husband, her lips pulled into a tight line. ''No.''

Olivia gazed up at Simon, something close to worship in her big green eyes. ''Even Father has a difficult time winning when he plays with Emmie. You don't even look as though you're trying.''

Simon smiled at his opponent. ''Oh, your sister is a challenge all right.''

Emily pressed her finger on the top of her remaining knight, glaring across the battlefield at Simon.

Jayne tugged on Simon's arm, trying to win his attention. The twins sat on chairs on either side of him, as they had at dinner, flanking him like two little fair-haired bookends. "You could beat Napoleon at chess, couldn't you, Major?"

Emily took her fingers off her knight. "He hasn't won yet."

"No." Jayne gazed up at Simon, as though he had the power to place every star in the sky. "But he will."

"We shall see about that." Emily stared at the battlefield, a line forming between her brows. She planted her elbow on the curved mahogany arm of her chair, propped her chin on her fist, and stared at the chessboard as though the fate of a nation rested on her next move.

She wanted to beat him so intensely that he almost considered allowing her to win. Almost. Somehow he knew she wouldn't appreciate a hollow victory any more than he would. He leaned back in his chair and glanced around the large room.

Candlelight from wall sconces glowed in the carved gold frames of the landscapes and portraits hanging on the ivory walls. Above him, more candlelight flickered through a crystal chandelier, raining a warm light upon the family gathered in the drawing room.

Emily's parents sat at a round mahogany table near the carved white marble fireplace, playing piquet with Anna and Harriet. Phoebe sat in an upholstered armchair nearby, her dark head bowed over the book she was reading. She glanced up as he looked in her direction, giving him a shy smile before returning to her novel.

Simon drew in his breath, filling his lungs with the fragrance of roses that drifted with a cool evening breeze through the open French doors, a sense of peace settling over him like a warm cloak. It had been a long time since he had spent a quiet evening in the comfort of a drawing room. A lifetime. Still, even in those distant memories, there had never been a single moment such as this, when a family gathered simply to share conversation and pass a pleasant evening together.

There was a lure to this place. A lure to these people. He sensed it tugging on him, drawing him toward the warm circle of this family, and toward the woman who could set his blood on fire with a glance from her golden eyes.

He gazed across the chessboard at his opponent. All of Emily's glorious curls were swept back from her face and caught in some intricate weaving near her crown. Yet, a few shimmering coils were allowed to fall free. They tumbled over one pale shoulder, dark red fire against pale ivory. She tugged one long curl as she contemplated ways to banish him from his kingdom.

He watched her, following her slim fingers as she tugged on that abused curl, his chest growing tight as he contemplated things beyond his reach. It would be far too easy to become accustomed to spending every night in Emily's company. Too easy to forget what had brought him to this place and these people. Too dangerous.

A man in his position couldn't afford an attraction to this woman. Whether he liked it or not, he and Emily Maitland were enemies. Ice trickled into his blood when he looked at the reality of this situation, spoiling the warmth he had found in the circle of this family. It was possible he would be the one to rip this family into shreds.

Emily moved her knight, leaving her fingers on the carved wooden piece a moment until she was satisfied it was the move she wanted to make. She sat back in her chair and smiled, a smug little twist of her lips. "Check."

He glanced at the board, then looked at his smiling opponent. "Are you certain you want to make that move?"

She nodded. "Quite certain."

Simon moved his queen, sliding the lady across the board and straight into Emily's king. "Checkmate."

"Oh." Emily leaned forward in her chair, staring at her fallen throne. "I didn't see that."

Simon grinned. "Obviously."

"I knew you would win!" Jayne said, clapping her hands.

"You're the best chess player in the whole world," Olivia said, gazing up at him like an adoring puppy.

A heaviness settled in his chest. The weight of guilt he couldn't afford. His first loyalty was to England. Not to a little girl who gazed at him as though he were a hero. And certainly not to the beautiful woman who could plunder his soul, if he weren't careful. He had to maintain his distance.

Emily glanced up at him, golden eyes narrowed like a tigress about to pounce. "Would you care to play again?"

"It would be a pleasure, my lady." He returned her prisoners, replaced his own soldiers on the battlefield, and prepared to fortify his defenses.

Chapter Nine

Simon leaned his shoulder against the frame of the window in Hugh Maitland's Bristol office. The offices of Maitland Enterprises resided in a three-story wooden building on the quay along the river. Sugar refineries and brass, glass, and soap factories were wedged shoulder to shoulder with shipyards and warehouses, all crowding the harbor, wooden buildings rising two and three stories from the edge of the gray water. Simon stared at the masts of square riggers rising like gray ghosts above the river, trying to concentrate on the conversation going on behind him, and on the three men who were gathered in this office to discuss shipping.

"If we don't get a naval escort, the ships bound for the Indies will be in jeopardy."

Hugh tapped his clenched hands on his desk, emphasizing the importance of his words. Still, Simon had to force his attention so that thoughts of a red-haired lady would not distract him.

Emily talked in her sleep. Not every night, but once or twice in the few days since he had taken up residence in her room, Simon had heard her, a soft murmur of words that made little sense, except in her dreams.

What dreams awakened inside of her when she closed her eyes? Were they as innocent as the lady appeared while she slept? Lord, he would give a year of his life to share her dreams, to escape the ugliness that haunted him at night.

"Turrow Shipping lost two ships last week," Hugh said. "To American privateers."

The scent of smoke from a hundred coal fires drifted on the warm summer breeze, rising in black columns from the buildings along the river. Yet it was the scent of lavender that haunted Simon. He went to bed with the fragrance teasing his senses. He awakened each morning to the fresh scent. Emily's room was like a field of lavender, the fragrance wafting from the dried potpourri in small porcelain bowls placed throughout her room.

Memories stirred in his mind. Memories of Emily trembling softly in his arms. Her eyes drowsy with passion. Her pale breasts rising and falling with each breath. Her nipples growing taut and tingling beneath his tongue. Heat flared deep in his belly.

He had kept his distance from her the past few days. But he couldn't get far enough away from the beautiful hellcat to stop the memories. Memories that had no business lingering inside him.

He went to bed wanting her. He awakened wanting her. In his dreams he had held her in the way he longed to hold her. In his dreams he had made love to her a hundred times. Still there was no surcease in dreams. Dreams only enhanced his longing for Emily.

Simon drew a deep breath, coal smoke streaking an acrid taste across his tongue. He had to stop thinking of the woman. He had no business standing here, staring at the morning sunlight glittering on the river, daydreaming about Emily Maitland as though he were a cub with his first infatuation.

No, he definitely should not linger on the memory of

how Emily looked in the early morning when sunlight rushed through the windows to touch her face, her hair. All of that dark red hair.

Every morning her hair tumbled over the side of that painfully elegant couch, a cascade of dark red curls gathering like a pool of fire on the carpet. Lord, how he wanted to gather that fire in his hands, rub his face in the soft, lavender-scented tresses, feel the dark red silk brush his bare chest. Memory twisted a blade of longing low in his belly. He definitely shouldn't think of Emily.

He had a mission to complete.

Emily's father could be a traitor.

There could be no future with the lady.

Simon reached within himself for the discipline that had sustained him for the last seventeen years. One of the three men seated in this room could very well be selling his country to the enemy. He wasn't about to let his fascination with a beautiful woman jeopardize his chance to put an end to the blackguard's smuggling operation.

"I suppose we should be grateful the Mediterranean runs have been unmolested."

Simon's back stiffened at Hugh Maitland's words. He turned, facing the other three men in the room.

"We don't have the Americans to worry about on the Mediterranean run." Laurence Stanbury tapped his fingers against a wooden arm of his chair. "I don't care if they call themselves privateers. They are nothing but bloody pirates."

"And damn fine mariners," Hugh said.

From what Simon had been able to discover, Maitland had been friends with Stanbury's father. Stanbury had come to work for Maitland three years ago, after Stanbury's father had committed suicide—a result of losing most of his fortune and all of his sugar plantation at the gaming tables. Thirty-two, unmarried, Stanbury stayed at home when he wasn't working. And from what Simon could tell, the man was always working. But how did Stanbury really feel about taking a position working for a man who should rightfully be his equal?

"It isn't bad enough that we can't clear up the war with France." Hugh clasped his hands on the emerald leather desk pad on his mahogany desk. "But I never conceived that our government could be so cork-brained as to provoke a war with the Americans."

"It is inconvenient, I'll grant you. It certainly has some of our captains in a pucker. Thought I'd have to take the *Fair Isle* to Jamaica myself." George Whitcomb flicked open a silver snuffbox. After offering the contents to each of the gentlemen, and finding no one interested, he took a pinch between his forefinger and thumb. With practiced elegance, he extended his little finger as he delicately inhaled the snuff. He sneezed, whipping a monogrammed handkerchief to his nose.

Simon studied Whitcomb, wondering what able-bodied seamen would leave port with this dandy impersonating a captain. The points of Whitcomb's collar reached the crests of his cheeks, swallowing the lower part of his face. His neck was swathed in what must be a yard of white linen, intricately tied in an excruciating slavish attempt at fashion. One lock of his chestnut brown hair fell over his wide brow, as it did every day, no doubt placed there to give him a poetic air.

"Ain't a bad notion by half," George continued, nodding, his chin sinking into the folds of his cravat. "Always had a notion to take command."

One corner of Hugh's mouth twitched as he looked at his young brother-in-law. "Yes, well, I'm certain it won't come to that, Whitcomb."

Laurence Stanbury cleared his throat in what sounded suspiciously like a man trying to hide a chuckle. He smoothed his hand over his thinning light brown hair, smiling as George cast him a curious glance.

Hugh looked to Stanbury. "What about the escort we requested?"

Laurence shook his head. "I'm afraid the only escort the Admiralty is able to give us will put our ships returning from the Indies straight in the middle of hurricane season."

"That puts us between Scylla and Charybdis. We can risk privateers if we run the ships without a naval escort, or hurricanes if we wait for the Admiralty." Hugh released his breath in a long sigh. "Not a happy choice."

"Have you considered defending yourself?" Simon asked.

Hugh glanced up at him, a hint of surprise in his eyes. "Each of our ships is armed, but you must realize our ships are about half the tonnage of an average East Indiaman. Because of their size, the guns we are able to carry are only six or nine pounders. Which makes us a poor match against a well-armed privateer. Even when we run in convoy, the bloody bastards manage to pick off a trailing vessel."

Simon was aware of the other two men in the room, watching him, wondering if this soldier who had married the owner's daughter had anything to contribute to the company. "Is there anything that would prevent you from establishing a few frigate-sized ships in the line?"

George laughed. "You have obviously spent much too much time among your fellow brethren of the blade, Major. It's obvious that solution don't come up to scratch. Far too much blunt for the ready."

"I've already ordered the ships, Blake," Hugh said, ignoring George with the ease of long practice. "Unfortunately, by the time the ships I've commissioned are available to sail, the company could be sunk."

"You've ordered more ships? Hummm." George sat back in his chair, nodding. "Well now, it does sound like a cracking good notion. Build our own frigates. Yes, a cracking good notion."

Hugh gave George an indulgent smile. "I thought it was."

"The Admiralty has supply ships regularly sailing a circuit to and from America," Simon said. "What we need to do is sail on their coattails."

"Blake, my man, we've tried that. Haven't we, Maitland?" George looked up at Simon, his narrow chest pumped with self-importance as he reiterated the earlier conversation as though it were a secret he alone could divulge to the newcomer. "The Admiralty don't intend to provide us with a timely escort."

Although Whitcomb was four years his senior, Simon felt like Methuselah looking into Whitcomb's vacant blue eyes. "The Admiralty has a war to fight. They might not consider your request for a special escort a high priority."

"That's it." George nodded his head. "Now you've got the run of it. Knew you would be up to snuff in no time at all."

Simon continued, keeping his voice as quiet and patient as he would with a green recruit facing his first battle. "They might also not consider a regular run of one of their supply convoys *as* an escort."

"They might not consider a regular run an escort," George said, as though speaking the words might make them conform to a logic he didn't quite grasp. He leaned forward, his brow knitted in concentration. "They may not consider a regular—"

"I see what you're saying," Hugh said. "We asked for an escort. The liaison for the Admiralty put our request under a list of 'special requests.' What we need do is ask if we can tag along with one of their regular convoys."

Simon smiled. Seventeen years of living in the tangled administration of the military had given him a particular insight into how to circumvent that system. "You might find protection more forthcoming."

Laurence frowned as he looked at Simon. "You can't mean to imply the Admiralty has actually neglected to give us an escort because of something so simple?"

Simon held Laurence's skeptical stare. "That's exactly what I'm implying."

Laurence pursed his lips. ''I suppose we have nothing to lose if we try.''

''And a great deal to gain. Stanbury, I would like you to get started with our new approach.'' Hugh smiled as he looked up at Simon. ''And perhaps Blake can tell you a good person to contact.''

''Commander Jonathon Lovelle. He's an aide to Admiral Westgate. He should be able to expedite matters.''

''All right.'' Laurence rose from his chair. ''I'll see what can be done.''

''I'll be out of the office the rest of the day, Stanbury.'' Hugh leaned back in his chair. ''I want to show Blake more of the operation.''

''I hope you don't overwhelm the good major.'' Laurence's lips formed into a stiff smile as he looked at Simon. ''Maitland Enterprises is a long way from the Peninsula.''

Simon sensed the animosity behind the smile, and wondered what was at the root of it.

''I'm certain Blake will handle it,'' Hugh said.

''Of course.'' Laurence clenched his hands into fists at his sides. ''Now, if you will excuse me.''

''By Jove, ain't you a deep one, Major.'' As Laurence left the room, George came to his feet and offered Simon his hand. ''Yes, sir, I knew you'd be a dab at business.''

''Thank you,'' Simon said, pumping the hand George held limp in his grasp.

''Glad to have you on board,'' George said. ''Yes, sir.''

Simon had the urge to run a handkerchief over his palm when he released Whitcomb's hand.

''Glad to see Emily finally settled. We were beginning to wonder if the chit would ever get buckled.'' George winked at Hugh. ''She's a beauty, even if she is a termagant. But I'd say you've got what it takes to tame her.''

Simon had a feeling that any man who tried to tame that red-haired tigress would not walk away unscathed.

''Whitcomb, I've got a few more things I would like to discuss with Blake,'' Hugh said.

"Oh, yes." George sauntered toward his chair. "We must get on with business."

"Whitcomb, I would like to speak with Blake alone."

George hesitated, glancing at Hugh, realization dawning in his eyes. "Oh, of course." He nodded as he walked toward the door. "Got a few things I need to do myself. I'll see you both at the party tonight." He paused with his hand on the brass door handle. "Expect a crush. You know Claudia, she don't think a party is a success unless she has people packed shoulder to shoulder. If you need me, remember I'll be in my office."

"I'll remember that." Hugh released his breath in a long sigh after the door closed, leaving him alone with Simon. "He means well."

Simon sat in an upholstered armchair near the windows, pressing his back against the wooden back, hooking one booted ankle over his thigh. "I'm not quite certain what it is Whitcomb does for the company."

Hugh grinned. "Welcome to the club."

"I see. Lady Harriet and your wife must be pleased to know he has a position."

"And I am pleased to keep both ladies happy."

"Wise man."

"Time has taught me well." Hugh leaned back in his chair, the dark green leather sighing beneath him. "I want to thank you for your contribution today. It could make a substantial difference in the company's profits."

Simon wondered if that were true. Maitland Shipping was only a part of an empire that included sugar refineries, colonial plantations, brass and glass factories, mining interests. No, he seriously doubted that a few privateers could destroy the Maitland empire. And he wondered why a man of such considerable means would turn to smuggling.

"How does it feel?" Hugh rested his fingers on a miniature globe that sat in a mahogany stand on one corner of his desk. "Spending your first day at work?"

"I think I'm going to enjoy it."

"I hope you will." Hugh turned the globe with the tips of his fingers. "I had worried there would be no one capable of taking over the reins, until now. I know I've said it before, but I want you to know, I'm delighted to have you in this family."

Simon stared down into the harbor. He watched the river lap against the hull of a square rigger, searching for the discipline to keep his defenses strong. It sounded too appealing, becoming part of this family. It had been a long time since he had felt as though he had a home. And his own home had never felt this warm, this loving. Each night he spent with Emily and the other members of her family reminded him of everything he had always dreamed of having.

He had to remember that none of this was real. *He* wasn't real. No matter how attractive life as Sheridan Blake might appear, it was nothing more than an illusion. An illusion he found himself wishing might become reality.

Mentally he shook himself. He couldn't afford the luxury of wishes. It could get him killed. Still, he knew he was going to need all of his self-discipline to keep from getting involved with Hugh Maitland's beautiful daughter.

Hugh came to his feet. "Shall we take a look at the rest of Maitland Enterprises?"

"I would like that."

"This is where we store the sugar when it arrives from the islands. And after it leaves our refineries." Hugh closed the door after Simon entered the warehouse, the thud of oak hitting oak echoing against a wall of stacked barrels. "There isn't a shipment due in or out until tomorrow, so it's fairly quiet in here."

"Like a country cemetery." Sweetness hung in the warm air of the warehouse, so thick Simon could taste it on his tongue. He followed Hugh down a narrow aisle. Sunlight streamed through the second-story windows, slanting across the barrels stacked on shelves that rose on either side of the aisle, shaping a dark brown canyon.

"The raw sugar is partially refined in the Indies, then shipped here. We store it on the other side of the building until it can be used at the refineries." Hugh glanced up at the barrels they were passing with pride in his eyes. "These barrels are filled with sugar straight out of our refineries. My father started with one plantation in Jamaica. He moved to Bristol when he decided he wanted to control the entire sugar process, from planting to the day it shows up on a tea tray in London. After I took over the business, he and mother moved back to one of the six plantations we now own in Jamaica."

"You expanded the business considerably after you took over."

Hugh shrugged, as though his accomplishment were insignificant. "It's easy to expand when you have a solid foundation to begin with."

Simon drew a deep breath, the thick taste of sugar coating his throat. Simon knew his own father had hoped to leave him without any foundation in life.

"Excuse me for a moment, Blake." Hugh touched his arm. "I just remembered, I need to check some invoices. Take a look around. I won't be long."

Hugh's footsteps on the oak planks echoed down the canyon of barrels as he walked toward the entrance of the warehouse. Simon watched him until Hugh turned at the end of the barrels, leaving him alone with his thoughts.

Weapons were being carried on Maitland ships in barrels of Maitland sugar. Who better to control the smuggling than the owner of the company? Hugh Maitland controlled the entire operation. And the man didn't try to hide the fact he thought the war should be ended.

Simon sighed as he walked down the passageway. There was nothing in Maitland's manner to betray him as a traitor. Still, Simon realized how very much he wanted the man to be innocent. He rested his hand on one of the barrels, where the sunlight streamed across the flat lid. Was there anything hidden inside? He needed to get a look at . . .

Wood scraped against wood. A tremor vibrated beneath his hand. He glanced up in time to see a barrel roll from the top of the stack. It took flight in a shaft of sunlight directly over his head. His muscles jerked with the sudden shock. He dove to one side, hitting the floor at the same time the barrel crashed.

The oak planks beneath Simon shivered with the impact. Oak stays splintered. One end of the barrel popped off, slamming into Simon. He groaned at the slap of wood against his thigh. Sugar sprayed in all directions, pummeling him like sleet. He rolled to his feet, coming up from the floor like a swimmer from water, shaking sugar from his hair, prepared to dodge another missile should it be dropped.

He stepped back, staring upward, searching for his opponent. Footsteps pounded on oak. A man rounded the corner at the far end of the canyon of barrels.

Through a powdery dust glinting in the sunlight, Simon saw Hugh rushing toward him. Maitland skidded on the sugar, careening into one wall of barrels. He gripped the shelf and stared at Simon. "What the devil happened!"

Simon waved sugar dust away from his face. "A barrel fell from the top shelf."

"Fell?" Hugh glanced up at the wall of barrels, then stared at Simon. "You could have been killed."

Simon rubbed his thigh, wincing at the pain. "So it would seem."

Hugh waded through the sugar and splintered oak to reach Simon. "Are you all right?"

"Fine." Simon looked up, studying the top shelf of barrels. They were stored on their sides, the ends facing the aisle. From what he could tell, the only way a barrel could roll into the aisle would be if it were turned and pushed. "It looks stable."

"It is. At least it has been in the past." Hugh coughed on the dust. "I'll talk to the foreman. One of the workmen must have stored a barrel incorrectly, with the side to the aisle. It's the only way it could have fallen."

Simon could think of another way. He walked to the end of the aisle. There was a ladder built into the rough oak shelves, easy access for a workman. Or an assassin.

"What are you doing?" Hugh asked as Simon began climbing the ladder.

Simon didn't reply as he ascended the ladder. If someone had pushed that barrel, he could still be there. When he reached the top shelf, he saw nothing more than the curved sides of stacked barrels. The man who had pushed that barrel had either escaped or . . .

"Do you see anything?" Hugh asked.

"Nothing." Simon glanced down at the fair-haired man standing near the foot of the ladder. The attempted murderer had escaped or he was in plain sight.

Still, it didn't make sense. Although he could think of several people who would want Simon St. James dead, he could only think of one person who would want to murder Sheridan Blake. And he seriously doubted that Miss Emily Maitland was capable of murder.

He supposed one of the workmen could have stacked the barrel incorrectly. Unless someone had discovered the truth of his identity, an accident seemed the most logical explanation. Still, the uneasy feeling in the pit of his stomach reminded him that logic didn't always provide the best answer.

Chapter Ten

Emily had always enjoyed fancy dress balls, until this evening. This evening she could find no appreciation of the elaborate costumes of the guests. No joy in their laughter. No amusement on the dance floor. This evening she felt as though something were alive inside her. Something restless. Something dangerous.

She felt the press of his hand against her waist. The heat of his palm radiated through the sapphire-blue silk of her gown as the scoundrel led her through the steps of a waltz. It was the first time he had touched her since that afternoon in her bedroom when she had nearly allowed him to make love to her.

He wore no gloves this night, no costume other than a black mask that matched his black coat and breeches. She stared for a moment at his hand, his long fingers curved around her bare hand. Dressed as a medieval lady, she also did not wear gloves. She imagined those elegant fingers stroking her cheek, her neck, the curve of her shoulder, and beyond. Her skin tingled with vivid memories. Heat shimmered across her breasts as she waltzed, shocked by her own wayward thoughts.

The man had humiliated her once. One should learn from one's mistakes. Yet here she was, longing to feel his touch once more. Was there any wonder the waltz was doled out sparingly by a proper host, like drops of the most potent liquor? It was an embrace set to music. A chance to plant illicit thoughts in a woman's mind. To waltz with a scoundrel invited all manner of wicked imaginings. To waltz with a scoundrel who had stolen her bed was utter folly.

"You're frowning." Simon led her through a series of turns, the gold trim at her hem swirling around her, brushing his legs.

"I'm wearing a mask." She stared up at him through her golden mask. "How in the world can you tell if I'm frowning?"

"I can feel it." He flexed his fingers against her waist. "You're as stiff as a poker."

"It comes from dancing with you, *Lord Scoundrel*," she said, smiling up at him.

He laughed, drawing her into a graceful turn, her unbound curls swaying against her back. The arrogant rogue sauntered through her life as though he belonged in it. She could scream when she thought of how casually he moved around her bedroom.

Every night he stripped off his clothes as though she weren't even there. Every night he slipped into her bed while she lay on the couch. And every night, time and time again, she caught herself staring at the stranger in her bed, remembering his touch. She couldn't help herself.

For some unholy reason she was mesmerized by the sight of his dark head upon her pillow, his broad shoulders kissed by moonlight, the long length of him stretched beneath a single white linen sheet slung carelessly across his slim hips. At times it was all she could do to keep from touching him. Dear heaven, she had to get rid of the man! "Why did you decide not to wear a costume tonight?"

"I don't care much for masquerades."

"Oh?" She cocked her head as she stared up at him. "You won't even tell me your name. Yet you say you don't enjoy masquerades."

He grinned. "One at a time is enough."

"I suppose that's true. Dressed as you are, I assume you are masquerading as a gentleman."

He laughed softly. "Dressed the way you are, I could imagine you presiding at a tournament."

"Can you?" She tried to keep a skeptical tone in her voice.

"You would slip the golden ribbon from your hair and give it to your champion. A token for the battle to come."

Emily stared up into the midnight eyes looking at her from behind a black mask. A warmth flickered inside her, a delicious heat that seeped into her blood and made her long for things too foolish to imagine. "And I would applaud as my champion planted his lance in your chest and knocked you from your charger."

His deep laughter melded with the bright sounds of strings streaming from the minstrels' gallery. "Ah, my lady, in another time and place I would fight to be your champion."

Emily stared up into his eyes, wishing they had met in another time and place, wishing they had a chance to be more than enemies. "What difference would another time and place make? You would still be the same scoundrel."

"Would I?" He led her into an elegant turn. "Am I completely beyond redemption in your eyes?"

Every time she looked at this man, she caught herself wishing for the illusions of her dreams to come true. Heaven help her, how could she protect herself from a man who threatened her very soul? "I don't understand how you can do it? How can you turn your back on everything you know? How can you walk away from your own life?"

Although he kept the smile on his lips, there was a change in him, a stillness, like a lake after the ripples of a tossed pebble have quieted. ''Have you ever wished you were someone else?''

''Yes, of course. At one time or another we all wish we were someone else.'' Emily looked up into his eyes, wishing she could see all the secrets hidden in the endless depths of midnight. ''But in reality, if granted the power to assume another life, I would refuse.''

''That's because you're still filled with promise, filled with your hopes and dreams and determined to make them come true.''

''And you?'' She stared up into his eyes, curling her fingers into the soft black wool covering his wide shoulder, wanting to strip away his mask. ''Have you abandoned your hopes and dreams?''

The music faded on a shivery note. Yet, Emily could not break away from his light embrace. She was drawn to this man in ways she was only beginning to understand. There was a darkness within him, a place where dreams lay in shattered pieces from a fall made long ago. She wanted to find those dreams. She wanted to fit together the pieces. She wanted to hold them up to the light. She had a strange notion those broken dreams once mended would resemble her own.

''Smile, my lady.'' He touched the tip of his finger to her nose. ''There is no need for sad looks. I'm hardly a lost lamb in need of your pity.''

''No. You aren't.'' She stepped back, needing some distance, fearing it was too late to search for it. She turned and marched away from the rogue. She couldn't afford to think of him in any way except as her enemy. She couldn't afford the risk of falling in love with him.

Emily stepped onto the terrace, escaping the crush of people in her uncle's ballroom. She needed air. She needed distance. But the restlessness persisted.

The music followed her through the open French doors. The lively notes of a country dance taunted her dark mood. A cool breeze drifted across the lawn, ruffling the sapphire blue silk of her gown, the full medieval fashion flowing around her legs. She took a deep breath, cleansing the mingled scents of countless perfumes and three hundred humid bodies from her nostrils. She had to quell this dangerous attraction to that man. If she didn't, she would do something foolish.

Absently she rubbed the taut muscles at her nape. A week of sleeping on a narrow couch had taken a toll, on her body and her nerves. The man had a way of chipping at her defenses, even when he wasn't trying.

The moon was smiling at her, a silver curve that mocked her and the longing she couldn't suppress. Was she destined to search all of her life for something that would forever remain outside her grasp? Was she destined to surrender her heart to a man who would destroy her dreams?

Lord help her, she had to escape this terrible fascination she had for that man. Still, she wondered if she ever would.

She closed her eyes, imagining the feel of his arms sliding around her. She pressed her hands against the solid stone balustrade, a poor substitute for the solid strength of his chest. This was how she had imagined meeting Sheridan Blake, at a party, in the moonlight. And he was here—at least the illusion of the man was here.

If this were her dream, he would follow her, he would take her in his arms and waltz with her in the moonlight. If this were a dream, he would kiss her and tell her how very much he loved her. She heard a footstep on the stone terrace, and in that instant, as her heart sprinted and her breath stilled, she realized she had been hoping he would follow her.

Emily turned, all the expectation collapsing when she saw Laurence Stanbury walking across the terrace.

"It's getting a little warm in there." Laurence removed the turban he wore and began fanning himself with the scarlet silk. He was dressed as a Turk, his patterned tunic of scarlet and black and gold belted at the waist, his loose-fitting black trousers tucked into knee-high black boots. "I hope you don't mind my joining you."

Emily managed a smile even though she wished to be alone. "Not at all."

"That costume suits you." Laurence passed his hand across his hair, smoothing the light brown strands that stood upward from the turban. "As I recall, even as a child you had a penchant for medieval lore."

"Yes." Emily stared across the lawn, where moonlight skimmed the smooth expanse of green. "I'm afraid my head was always full of romantic notions."

"And I was always far too practical. I suppose you were right to refuse my proposal."

Emily glanced up at Laurence, catching the frown that marred his brow before he smiled. "Laurence, you know as well as I do that I would have made you a perfectly terrible wife."

Laurence pulled his lips into a downward curve. "Perhaps."

Although Laurence had asked for her hand in marriage two years ago, she had never believed he held any deep affection for her. She suspected he had hoped for a marriage that would put Maitland Enterprises into his hands.

Laurence looked away, staring out across the lawn. "I trust you finally found what you were looking for in your intrepid major."

"Major Blake is everything I could have imagined." It was true, she assured herself. Since Sheridan Blake existed only in her imagination.

"I thought as much." Laurence rubbed his thumb over the scarlet silk of the turban he held. "I saw you earlier when you were dancing with your husband. It was obvious how very much you care for him."

Emily squeezed the balustrade. Dear heaven, was her attraction for the man so terribly obvious?

"Should I tell you something amusing?"

Emily glanced up at him. "What?"

"I was curious about Major Blake. It seemed odd that

no one had ever met him. No one had even heard of him. After all, town society isn't really that large. I must confess, until the day I saw Blake with my very eyes"—Laurence paused, chuckling deep in his chest—"until that night he walked into your father's ballroom, I wondered if Blake really existed."

His words hit her like a clenched fist. She fought to keep her face from betraying her shock, forcing her lips into a smile. "Now, why would you think of something so very . . . outrageous?"

"Is it really so outrageous?"

"Inventing a husband." Emily turned, staring through one of the open French doors to the ballroom. "It's hardly something that is done every day."

"It certainly isn't." He studied her a moment, smiling in a way that made Emily want to run and hide. "You have a vivid imagination. And I could understand how you felt as though you were obligated to marry. Even though you believed you had not met the man of your ideals. I can well imagine you would do something as daring as invent a husband."

Emily swallowed past the tight knot in her throat. "Obviously you were mistaken."

Laurence smiled. "Obviously."

"Please excuse me." She backed toward the nearest door. "I promised my husband the next dance."

"By all means." Laurence leaned back against the balustrade. "You mustn't keep your husband waiting."

Emily turned, forcing her legs to walk when every instinct screamed to run. Laurence was merely guessing. There was no means for him to discover the truth. Was there?

Chapter Eleven

Simon stood by one of the refreshment tables in Whitcomb's ballroom, staring at the French door where Emily had escaped after their waltz. He twisted the slender stem of his champagne glass in his fingers, staring at the doorway.

He wouldn't follow her. He couldn't. It would be a grave tactical error to follow Emily into the moonlight. She looked too much like a vision from a fairy tale this evening. Too much like the fine ladies he had dreamed about as a boy, when he had dared to dream he was a knight in King Arthur's court.

He sipped his champagne, but the cold wine did little to cool the fire that Emily had set in his belly. Damnation! He had to keep his distance. Still, even as the cautious thought formed, he was setting the wineglass on the table and starting for the door.

"There you are, Sheridan," Harriet said, approaching him.

Simon hesitated, staring at the doorway. Light from the

ballroom sliced a path into the darkness on the terrace, beckoning him to the lady waiting there in the moonlight. He drew a deep breath before turning to face Lady Harriet. She was dressed as a shepherdess in a bottle green jacket, a white patterned skirt covered in pink and green flowers, and a straw hat perched on her red curls.

"Are you enjoying the party?"

Simon smiled. "Now, what could there possibly be not to enjoy?"

Harriet lifted one brow as she looked up at him. "The crowd, for one thing. I can't imagine why Claudia believes she has to fill this place to overflowing to have a decent party."

The party was as crowded as any of the few he had attended in London. Men and women moved in steady streams to and from the adjoining dining room, where an elaborate supper was being served all evening. Most of the guests were in costumes. Yet he noticed that a few men had done as he had, simply donning a mask with their evening clothes. "I thought every party had to be a crush to be considered a success."

"Not in my opinion. But then, Claudia has never shared my opinions. On anything." Harriet crinkled her nose. "I never felt obligated to entertain so often or so lavishly as dear Claudia. But then, I was a mere countess. She fancies herself a queen."

"I gather you aren't overly fond of your son's wife."

"I had hoped he would marry a nice, responsible girl." Harriet sighed. "Unfortunately, he married someone with his own taste for extravagance."

Apparently Whitcomb and Claudia enjoyed entertaining often and on a grand scale.

"I noticed you and Emily dancing earlier." Harriet lifted a glass of champagne from a gold tray on the table. "Are you coming to some type of truce?"

"I'm afraid the lady would dearly love to murder me."

"Nonsense." Harriet smiled up at him, candlelight

sparkling in her eyes. "I'm certain she thinks death is far too painless a punishment for you."

"How comforting."

Harriet twisted the champagne glass between her fingers, the wine swirling against the cut crystal. "Do you have a plan for winning her over to your side?"

Simon lifted his glass from the table. "What makes you think I can?"

Harriet laughed, a soft feminine sound that made him realize how seldom he heard Emily's laughter. "Instinct."

Simon sipped his champagne, regarding Harriet over the rim of his glass. "I get the impression you are hoping Emily and I end this war between us."

"There is a good reason for that." Harriet sipped her wine. "I think it would be better for all concerned if you and Emily were to . . ." She hesitated, looking past Simon, her lips pulling into a tight line. "Oh, dear, here comes our hostess."

Simon turned as Claudia drew near. The lady cut a path through the crowd, men and women dodging the six-foot width of her court gown of white and gold brocade. She made a beautiful Marie Antoinette, her pale blond hair hidden beneath a tall white wig, the intricate ringlets adorned with a diamond tiara, her lovely face bare except for a dusting of powder and black beauty patch at the corner of her mouth.

"I do so love a masquerade." Claudia rested her gloved hand on Simon's arm. "Isn't it simply a marvelous party?"

He looked over the mound of Claudia's wig to Lady Harriet, catching that lady rolling her eyes toward heaven. "Lady Harriet and I were just discussing how much of a success the evening has been."

Claudia gave Lady Harriet a wide smile. "I think it rivals any ball in London, don't you?"

Harriet drew in her breath. "Oh, yes. You have definitely captured that crushed feeling popular with so many London hostesses."

"Oh, I'm so glad. Whitcomb so wants for our parties to always be top of the trees." Claudia giggled and turned her attention to Simon. "I wonder why we never met in London. Whitcomb and I are out and about every night during the Season. Neither one of us can understand why we had never even heard of you."

Harriet coughed, sending Simon a look of warning.

Simon sipped his champagne, the dry wine sparkling across his tongue. "I seldom had the opportunity to attend many social functions in London."

"Yes, of course." Claudia flicked open her fan. "What with the military keeping you busy with all that fuss in the Peninsula."

Simon smiled into her pretty face, wondering if there was anything besides hair beneath that elaborate white wig. "The war does tend to fill a soldier's social calendar."

"Pity." The small black beauty patch she had applied at the corner of her mouth tipped upward with her smile. "Although, I must say, I certainly do find regimentals most attractive. Don't you, Mama Harri?"

Harriet's smile looked brittle enough to break. "Yes. Considering the extremes to which some gentlemen have taken fashion, I find it a pity we couldn't dress them all in uniforms."

"Yes, some men look simply dreadful. Pity more of them don't have a sense of style, like my dearest Whitcomb." Claudia giggled, tapping her fan on Simon's arm. "Of course, you are quite a dashing figure even without all the braid."

Considering her appreciation for her husband's sense of style, Simon took her compliment with a degree of caution. "Thank you."

Claudia frowned, studying him over the gilt edge of her fan. "I simply don't understand how you and Emily could have carried on a courtship in London without me knowing anything about it."

"It all happened quite suddenly," Harriet said.

"Emily has said as much." Claudia shook her head. "Still, I find it all so very odd. One would think I would have caught at least a glimpse of Major Blake before he whisked Emily off into his arms."

"Claudia, dear, if I hadn't been friends with Major Blake's late mother, Emily would never have met him." Harriet sipped her champagne. "He was only in town for a few days, on leave, when he decided to pay me a call."

"How fortunate for Emily." Claudia flicked her white silk fan beneath her chin, smiling up at Simon. "I was beginning to think she would never find the man who could win her affection."

He noticed Emily moving toward him, easing her way through the crowd. "I consider myself fortunate to have been that man."

"Emily, dear," Claudia said as Emily drew near. "We were just talking about you."

"You were?" Emily glanced up at Simon. "And what were you discussing?"

Simon grinned. "How fortunate you were to have met me."

Emily smiled, far too sweetly, her eyes glittering like frozen gold behind her mask. "You can only imagine the true depths of my sentiments upon that subject, milord."

Simon touched the tip of her nose with his fingertip. "I think I can guess."

One corner of Emily's lips twitched, a sign of her growing agitation. "It's been a perfectly wonderful party, Claudia. I hope you don't mind if we retire early."

"No, of course not." Claudia glanced up at Simon and giggled. "I know what it is like to be newly married. Whitcomb and I have been married for three years, and we still like to retire early."

"Yes." Simon smiled at Emily. "We do enjoy the privacy of our chamber."

Emily cast him a dark glance.

Simon winked at her.

The smile Emily returned might have frozen boiling water. "Shall we go?"

"Anything for my . . ." Simon gasped at the sharp stab of pain ripping through his leg.

"Whitcomb!" Hugh Maitland shouted.

Simon pivoted, frowning through his mask at the two men standing a short distance behind him. George held a slender dress sword in his hand, Louis XVI prepared to turn back the mob, the polished steel glinting in the candlelight. He wore an elaborate white and gold brocade coat and breeches, white silk stockings, and a white wig perched on his empty head.

"Terribly sorry, Major." George slipped his sword into the white leather sheath hanging at his side. "Didn't mean to pink you."

Simon glanced at the back of his leg. Blood trickled from a small puncture wound in the middle of his calf. "What the devil?"

"Good God." Hugh stood beside George, dressed as a highwayman in black breeches and coat, black boots clinging to his calves, a black cape slung over his shoulders. "I can't believe you did that, Whitcomb."

"Well, I could have sworn old Blake padded his stockings." George frowned as he stared down at Simon's legs. "How many men have legs so well turned?"

"Whitcomb, darling, you didn't truly poke Major Blake with that silly sword?" Claudia asked, her blue eyes huge as she stared up at her husband.

"Now, pet, I didn't expect to do any harm."

Harriet made a strangled sound. "You stabbed a man with a sword and you didn't expect to do any harm?"

"Now, grandmama." Emily smiled up at Simon, her eyes filled with mischief. "I'm certain Uncle George had a good reason for stabbing Sheridan."

"Of course I did. We made a wager, you see. I bet fifty pounds Blake padded his stockings. Maitland said I was full of bluster." George looked up at Simon. "You don't by any chance pad your stockings, do you, Major?''

Simon drew in his breath, slow and steady as he reached for enough self-control to keep from strangling the man. ''No.''

Emily coughed, and Simon was certain the lady was hiding a giggle.

''The man is bleeding, Whitcomb.'' Hugh shook his head. ''How can you still think he pads his stockings?''

''Yes, well, there is that, I suppose.'' George turned, bending, attempting to get a look at Simon's calf. His dress sword arced, bumping Hugh's chin.

''Careful!'' Hugh said, batting aside the sword.

''Sorry.'' George turned, his sword smacking Simon's side. ''Terribly sorry.''

Simon backed away from his host, resisting the urge to snap that silly little sword of his. ''It's all right.''

''I'll have one of the servants fetch you a fresh pair of stockings. Been thinking I'll take a nod from good old Louis and have all my stockings done up with embroidery. I'm sure they'll be all the crack in London. Can't wait 'til Brummell lays his peepers on 'em.'' George turned his leg, showing off the clocks embroidered in gold down the side of his stocking. ''I've got a pair with peacocks I think you'll like.''

''Peacocks?'' Emily smiled up at Simon. ''I think the peacocks would suit you splendidly, *darling*.''

''Thank you, Whitcomb.'' Simon pressed his handkerchief to the back of his leg. ''But we were just leaving.''

''Invent a husband?'' Emily drummed her fingertips against the top of her vanity. She watched the scoundrel, who sat on an upholstered armchair beside the washstand, tending his wound. ''How could Laurence have imagined I would do such a thing?''

Simon glanced up at her, a grin tipping one corner of his lips. ''Shocking, isn't it.''

"This isn't amusing. Do you think he suspects the truth?"

Simon slid a damp cloth over his calf, wiping the blood from his skin. "I think he is curious."

Emily stared at his bare leg, tracing the sleek curve of muscle in his calf. "What shall we do if he discovers the truth?"

"What makes you think he will discover the truth?"

"*You* did."

"Yes, I did." He stood and walked to the washstand, where he began rinsing out the white linen cloth, frowning as he stared down into the water.

He had discarded his coat and cravat. His shirt was unfastened, the ruffled front hanging open halfway down his chest, revealing the dark curls that shaded sleek muscles. Strange, but a few days ago she would have thought it unimaginable to be sitting in her bedroom with a man in this state of dishabille. Now it seemed natural.

She drew in her breath, trying to ease the growing tension in her chest. She had to banish this man from her life. Soon. He glanced at her, smiling. Her heart tripped. Oh, yes, she had to get rid of the man very soon.

"People are curious." He folded the cloth and slipped it over the drying rack beneath the basin. "Even Claudia was asking questions about me and the reason she had never met me before last week."

"There was something more than curiosity with Laurence. It was as though he were testing a theory when he asked me about you."

He dried his hands on a towel hanging on the rack. "It could be that you are simply sensitive about this."

"I don't think so." Emily curled her hand into a fist on the vanity. "Laurence asked me to marry him once."

Simon frowned, a single line slashing between his black brows. "Any other suitors I should know about?"

She lifted her chin. "My past suitors are not your concern."

"I'm afraid I have to differ with you." Simon sank to the chair beside the washstand. He crossed his bare ankles, resting his elbows on the curved arms of the chair. "A man likes to know if the gentleman he is addressing happens to be a rejected suitor of his wife."

Emily pursed her lips. "I am not your wife."

He pressed his palms together, smiling at her over the steeple of his fingers. "To the world you are."

She crinkled her nose. "Thank you for the unpleasant reminder."

He studied her a moment, his eyes dark, his gaze warm and unsettling. "Every day I remember. And every day, I wonder."

The heated look in his eyes made her mouth grow dry. "Wonder?"

"What it might be like if we were truly wed." He lowered his eyes, his gaze sliding down the length of her, slowly, in a way that made her skin grow warm beneath the silk of her medieval gown.

The tips of her breasts tingled. A pulse flickered and throbbed in the secret recesses of her most feminine flesh. The way he could awaken within her these foreign sensations frightened her. It was as though only he could bring her fully to life. This man intrigued her. Beguiled her. Mesmerized her with this unspoken temptation. This man was dangerous.

He lifted his eyes, looking straight into hers with an intensity that touched her very core. There was a look in his eyes, flickering flames that made her wonder what it might be like to strip away her gown and stand naked before him. She wanted to feel his hands roam freely across her bare skin, absorb his touch of fire. Dear heaven, if she weren't careful she would make a fool of herself. Again. "You needn't waste your time wondering what it might be like if we were truly wed. It shall never happen."

He rested his chin on the tips of his fingers. "A man can dream."

"Stop talking such nonsense." It was too tempting to believe. "We have a problem to discuss. And you are trying to change the subject."

He grinned. "To a much more interesting one."

She released her breath in a ragged sigh. "Laurence is the type of man who will hold a grudge. He didn't love me. He only wanted to gain a part of my father's company. But, I don't think he has ever forgiven me for refusing him."

Simon studied her a moment, his eyes filled with a gentle understanding that made Emily want to toss a jar of cream at his head.

"Don't look at me that way."

"What way?"

"As though I were an orphan out in the cold without a soul to turn to."

He laughed, a dark rumble that coaxed her lips into an unwilling smile. "You certainly aren't an orphan."

"And I'm certainly not devastated over the fact that Laurence wanted me only for my father's money."

"What makes you so certain he wasn't simply captivated by you?"

Emily shook her head. "Laurence is hardly a man who would be captivated by any woman. He is far too practical. And methodical. He concerns me. If he suspects the truth, he just might start snooping about."

"I doubt Stanbury is going to go through as much trouble as I did."

"How did you discover the truth?"

He hesitated a moment before he spoke. "I was watching you, looking for a way to meet you."

An odd mixture of hope and dread assailed her. "Why did you want to meet me?"

A muscle flashed in his cheek as he clenched his jaw. "Emily, you're a very beautiful woman."

"But that isn't the reason you wanted to meet me, is it?" She stared at the book of sonnets resting on the corner of her vanity. She couldn't allow herself to look at this man and believe he had actually stepped from her dreams. "You knew I was an heiress."

"Yes." He stood and came to her, standing so close behind her she could feel the heat of his body radiate against her back. "Emily, under different circumstances, I wouldn't care if you had a single shilling to your name."

"I assure you, it doesn't signify." Emily drew her fingertip over the gold lettering on the cover of the sonnets, keeping her eyes hidden as she lied. "Under any circumstances, I am certain you and I would not be suitable for one another."

He rested his hand on her shoulder. The heat of his palm through the sapphire silk of her gown teased her. "Are you so certain?"

"Yes." She curled her shoulder away from him, rejecting the pity he offered. He withdrew his hand. The breeze drifting through the windows cooled the imprint of his touch.

Little sounds filled up the silence that stretched between them—the click of the ormolu clock on the mantel, the call of a raven on the ledge outside her window, the solid thud of her heart. She could feel him watching her. The heat of his gaze stroked her back like the warm rays of the sun.

She looked up, seeing his image in the mirror, a dark warrior who had stepped from the pages of a legend, his face reflecting an inner longing that stole the breath from her lungs. He met her look in the glass. For a moment she imagined seeing everything she had ever dreamed of in the endless depths of his eyes. For a moment he stood there, looking at her in the mirror as though he had been searching for her all of his life, before he turned and swept his dressing gown from the chair near the washstand.

"I'm going to take a bath before going to bed." He hesitated as he reached the door. He spoke without looking at her. "Take the bed, Emily. I'll sleep on the couch."

In the mirror, Emily watched him leave. In her heart she

felt a twisting, a silent protest as he left her alone. Dear heaven, she wanted to feel his arms around her. She wanted to believe he could look at her and see more than a bag of gold. She wanted to feel beautiful. Cherished. Loved by this man. Only this man.

She rested her elbows on the vanity and dropped her face into her open hands, despising the tears stinging her eyes. She couldn't live like this, with this man, knowing he cared nothing at all for her. She had to find a way to banish him from her life before he destroyed her.

A stone passageway led from the west wing of the house to a tropical paradise of white marble floors and walls, glass skylights, and potted plants. In this part of the house, Hugh Maitland's father had brought a piece of his former Jamaican home to Bristol. His builders had crafted two cavernous rooms upon the manse, separated from each other by a wide arched opening. One room housed a plunge pool filled with cold water, the other a pool fed by one of the many natural hot springs in the area.

Simon sat on a shelf built into the side of the pool. He sank down, allowing the hot water to swirl around his shoulders, easing the tension from his muscles. He stripped the condensation from his brandy snifter, beads of water dripping like tears down the cut crystal.

The brandy was doing little to ease the tight knot Miss Emily had tied in his belly. If he went to her now, if he took her in his arms, he knew he could have her. He could slip past the barriers. He could sink into her warmth. He could drown in her fire. And when the mission was over, he could try to live with the memories. He tightened his fingers around the glass.

"I sure wish there was a better place to be meeting, sir." Digby released his breath in a long sigh. "It's as hot as Talavera in July in here."

Simon stared through the steam rising from the water to the little man standing in blue livery beside the pool. "It's one of the few places we can be sure no one will overhear us."

"Aye, sir," Digby shucked his coat and draped it over his arm. "I heard some talk at a place called the Wayfarer last night. Some bloke bragging about how his captain has it fixed so his crew makes money without even taking out his ship."

Simon sat forward. "Sounds as if you could be on to something."

"Aye. I'm going to see if I can get him to tell me more about his captain."

"The smuggling captain is one big piece of the puzzle." Simon stared down into his brandy. "All the pieces are here. Our man in Maitland Enterprises buys the weapons from local manufacturers. His smuggler associates load them into legitimate cargo; that way they reduce the risk of being caught by one of our patrol ships. The cargo is shipped to Napoleon's agent in Tangier. Once there, it's a small matter to ship the weapons to Spain. It's all very neat."

"Is something bothering you, sir?"

Simon sighed. "I'm not sure. I suppose I'm a little surprised you could find one of the smugglers so easily."

"It wasn't that easy, sir," Digby said, his voice reflecting his wounded pride. "I've lost track of the number of slimy pubs I've crawled through in the past few days."

"I'm afraid I have a tendency to be skeptical." Simon lifted his glass to Digby. "Nice work, Sergeant-Major."

"Thank you, sir." Digby dragged his hand over his damp brow. "From what the lady told you about Stanbury, are you thinking he was the one who pushed that barrel at the warehouse?"

Simon rubbed the taut muscles at the nape of his neck. "His involvement with Emily might mean nothing."

"It might. I can't see how Stanbury would be knowing about you."

"Neither can I." Simon rested his elbows on his knees,

holding the glass above the water. He stared past the moisture beading on the cut crystal, looking into the amber liquid. "Still, I can't help thinking that incident this afternoon at the warehouse was a little too much of a coincidence. Perhaps Stanbury doesn't know about the mission. Perhaps he is simply a rejected suitor bent on getting rid of his rival."

"I doubt Miss Emily would be taking up with him if something happened to you. She didn't want him before you came. She won't want him after."

Candlelight from the wall sconces reflected in the brandy, shimmering like the fire in Emily's eyes. "Stanbury would never be able to handle that little hellcat. She would tear him to shreds."

Digby grinned. "How are you and the lady getting along, sir?"

Simon sipped his brandy, the liquor burning a mellow path down his throat. "Let's just say I'll be glad when this mission is over."

"Will you? And here I was thinking you and the lady make a fine pair."

Simon frowned. "Getting involved with the lady wouldn't be a good idea, Digby."

Digby shrugged. "No, sir, I suppose it wouldn't be sporting of you. But I must say, she's a tempting bit, she is."

Simon didn't need to be reminded of the lady's charms. "You better get out of here before you melt."

"Aye." Digby's lips wore a smug little grin. "And I guess you want to be leaving before you get scalded. By the water, that is, sir."

"Go." Simon skimmed his hand across the water, splashing the side of the pool, sending Digby scrambling. "And see what you can find out about that warehouse."

"Aye, sir." Digby tipped his wig to his major. "Be looking into it tonight, right on my way to the Wayfarer it is."

Simon stared into the brandy in his glass. He hoped Emily would be asleep when he returned to her bedroom. Lord help him, he wasn't sure he could resist the temptation of her if he saw desire flicker like flame in her eyes.

Chapter Twelve

"Emily, dear, you can't be serious." Harriet glanced up from her embroidery hoop, staring at Emily as though her granddaughter had declared she was the queen of Egypt. "You can't possibly do such a terrible thing to that young man."

Emily glanced out one of the windows in the drawing room. A summer breeze rippled across her mother's rose garden, blossoms of white and yellow and pink bobbing in the sunlight, dripping perfume into the warm current of air. "I can assure you, Grandmama, I am quite serious."

"Impossible." Harriet jabbed her needle through the white linen handkerchief held taut in her wooden loop. "I will not send that young man to such a fate."

"He deserves to be hanged for what he has done to me."

Harriet narrowed her eyes as she peered up at Emily. "Has he forced his attentions on you?"

"No." When she thought of how easily the man could ignore her every night, she wanted to scream. While she was aware of every breath he took, he wasn't even aware she existed.

Harriet lifted one finely arched brow as she stared at her granddaughter. "If I didn't know better, I would say you're angry because he hasn't."

"That's preposterous." Emily tugged on a tendril of hair that had fallen free of its anchoring pins, the red strands curling across the dark amber muslin covering her shoulder. "I can assure you, I certainly do not crave that scoundrel's odious advances."

"Of course." Harriet's eyes conveyed her true opinion.

"Grandmama, I don't find the rogue the least bit attractive."

"No?" Harriet smiled as she set a stitch in the muslin. "Well, I must say, I find him devilishly attractive. If I were forty years younger, that man wouldn't stand a chance of escaping me."

"Grandmama!"

Harriet glanced at Emily, a smile playing on her lips. "Perhaps you should stop fighting the situation and find the positive aspects."

"Positive aspects? What positive aspects?"

"Your parents adore him."

"Mother and Father are blinded by the scoundrel."

"It's a relief to your father to have a man as capable as Sheridan. Hugh is thrilled to have someone in the family help with his business dealings."

"That man is *not* in the family."

"I'm not blind to my youngest son's lack of abilities, mind you." Harriet turned her face toward the open windows, her eyes narrowing against the bright sunlight. "George is a charming man, but he never had any sense for business." She crinkled her nose. "Or women."

"Uncle George means well."

"Unlike his wife." Harriet curled her lips as though she had bitten into a lemon. "How he could marry that little social climber is beyond my comprehension."

"Claudia is beautiful, and really very nice."

"I always get the impression she works at appearing the

perfect little wet goose so that no one will realize how well she manipulates my son.'' Harriet shuddered with disgust. ''I took great pains to ensure that all of my children would have reliable investments. It's a miracle George and his little sapskull have not completely squandered his inheritance.''

Emily frowned. ''Grandmama, I believe you are trying to divert the conversation.''

''Oh?'' Harriet glanced at Emily, her brows arched in feigned innocence. ''As I recall, we were discussing the positive aspects of your marriage.''

''I am *not* married. You keep forgetting that I *invented* the man.''

''Hush, darling.'' Harriet glanced over her shoulder, staring at the closed door. ''Someone could decide to join us.''

''Not likely.'' Emily sank to the sofa beside her grandmother, her golden gown spilling across the burgundy velvet upholstery. ''The twins are in the schoolroom; Mother is shopping with Anna and Phoebe. And Father is at his office. With the impostor.''

''Emily, dear, I've been giving your situation a great deal of consideration.'' Harriet poked her needle through the white linen, drawing white thread into the pattern of a daisy petal. ''And I've decided it would be best if you married the man.''

''You can't be serious.''

''He might not have come to this family by legitimate means, but he certainly fits in well enough.''

Emily clenched her teeth when she thought of how well the man had insinuated himself into her life. It was as though he actually enjoyed spending each night surrounded by her family. The Sheridan Blake she had invented could not have fit more ideally into her life. Except, of course, for one small detail—he didn't love her.

''Every time I see the two of you together, I can't help think how right it is.'' Harriet smiled down at her embroidery. "I like him. And I think you would like him if you only gave him a chance."

Frustration rose inside Emily like steam building in a sealed kettle. "I'm certain I could never like the man."

"No?" Harriet glanced up from her embroidery, her eyes conveying her skepticism. "Well, you certainly enjoy playing chess with him."

"I do not enjoy playing chess with him."

"No? Strange, I believe you and Sheridan have played chess nearly every night since he arrived." Harriet smiled down at her embroidery. "Of course, he has beaten you every night."

Emily frowned, thinking of how the man managed to distract her thoughts when they played. How in the world could she hope to beat him, when her attention kept getting snagged by little things, such as the way he rubbed his fingertip over his lower lip when he was contemplating his next move—if the man took time to contemplate a move. His play was reckless. Yet calculated. Filled with cunning. Utterly ruthless. She would love to learn how to play that way.

"He has such a quality about him," Harriet mused. "Commanding, yet gentle. Have you noticed the way he tolerates Jayne and Olivia trailing after him like puppies?"

"The twins have some misguided notion he is a hero."

"Perhaps it isn't so misguided." Harriet rested her needle against the linen, staring off into the gardens like a young girl contemplating the prince from a fairy tale. "Have you noticed Sheridan is never overdressed, his clothes are all tailored with a subtlety of color and form that shows to perfection the width of his shoulders, the exquisite lines of his—"

"The man is a scoundrel," Emily put in, not wanting any reminders of his exquisite lines. "Nothing more."

"Poppycock! He is a man who saw an opportunity and took it. Given the life he has known, one can hardly blame him for that. And it isn't as if he intends to simply live off your income. He seems quite anxious to work with your father."

"He is using me!"

"I'm afraid you are saddled with him for life." Harriet smiled at Emily. "So you might as well marry him and make the best of the situation."

"I can't believe what I'm hearing. You still haven't forgiven Uncle George for marrying Claudia because you think she is a social climber. Now you want me to marry a man we know is a scoundrel."

"Emily, be reasonable." Harriet sighed as she drew the needle through the linen. "The man is here to stay. Everyone adores him. Everyone believes you are married. You might as well make it legitimate."

Emily rested her head against the back of the sofa and gazed up at the roundel painted in the center of the intricate scrolls and leaves crafted in the ceiling plasterwork. It depicted the goddess Diana with her javelin raised in the hunt. "I have a much better idea." She outlined her plan.

When Emily had finished, Harriet shook her head in disbelief. "I don't think you realize the dreadful conditions on board a man-of-war. Why, they flog men for no reason at all. And I understand there is very little to eat."

Emily smiled, imagining the scoundrel with nothing but stale bread and water to sustain him. "I'm certain he will survive."

"Perhaps he would. But, it would not be beneficial to his health."

"Grandmama, I must rid myself of that man."

"Emily, I've seen you around him. I've seen the way you look at him when you think no one is watching." She rested her embroidery in her lap. "No matter what you claim, you are attracted to him."

Emily clenched her hand into a red velvet pillow beside her. She didn't need to be reminded of how very much she was attracted to the dark-haired rogue. For the first time in her life she felt alive. Truly alive. As though she had been sleepwalking every moment of her life until the moment he had touched her.

"In time, I'm certain you could learn to love him."

"You don't understand. It isn't a matter of my learning to love him." Emily twisted her hand in the red velvet. Learning to love the rogue would be simple, like learning to breathe. "I will not give my love to a man who cares nothing for me."

"Emily, you are a lovely young woman. Stubborn, I'll admit. But I'm certain if you were to give him some encouragement—"

"You want me to beg the man for his affection, a man who is after nothing more than a comfortable position in life." A blade twisted in her chest when she spoke the words she wanted desperately to deny. Still, she couldn't deny the truth. He was here for money. Not for love. "That is something I shall never do."

Harriet pursed her lips. "There is a spark between you and that young man. A spark that burns so brightly a blind person could see the glow of it. I truly believe there is a chance this is the man you have been searching for all your life. If you don't take the time to get to know him—if you don't allow that spark a chance to catch hold and build into a fire, you will always look back to this moment of your life with regret."

"I can't allow him the chance to destroy me." Emily pounded her fist into the pillow. She was torn between anger, fear, and the longing for him she could not banish.

"Emily, do try to be reasonable."

"Reasonable? Don't you see? I can't trust him. How could I ever give him my heart if I can't trust him?"

Harriet cupped Emily's cheek in her palm. "Love is always a gamble, my darling girl."

"There is too much risk to this particular gamble." Emily held her grandmother's gentle gaze. "If you won't help me, I will do it myself."

Harriet folded her hands in her lap, shaking her head as

she stared down at her embroidery. "Something told me I should have gone back home the day after he arrived."

"Grandmama, please try to understand. I will not allow that man to stay here and ruin my life."

"Stubborn baggage," Harriet murmured. She stabbed her needle into the linen stretched in her embroidery hoop. "Very well. I suppose I shall have to assist you, or worry about you facing a press gang alone."

"Thank you." Emily gazed at the mythical goddess above her head, recalling the story of Diana and Actaeon, the arrogant young hunter who learned his lesson at the hands of the goddess. Soon the scoundrel would be in chains. Far at sea. Cursing the day he had ever crossed her path. She grinned, imagining the look on his handsome face when Lord Scoundrel discovered she had beaten him at his own game.

"How do you intend to explain the disappearance of your husband?"

"I have it all planned." Emily turned her head, smiling at her grandmother. "Do you recall the Landsdale boy? Two summers ago he fell from the cliffs above the gorge. They never found his body."

Harriet stared at Emily, her eyes wide. "You aren't seriously considering doing away with that young man?"

"Of course not. As I told you, I intend to ship him off to sea. Alive." Emily toyed with the curl that lay across her shoulder. "We shall tell people he slipped when we stopped to admire the gorge in the moonlight."

Harriet rolled her eyes toward heaven. "Lord help us, but I have a bad feeling about this."

"We shall need someone to help us. Someone strong enough to render the scoundrel unconscious. Do you think Beamish can be trusted?"

"Emily, I do wish you would reconsider."

"I have given this a great deal of consideration. This is the only way I can survive."

* * *

"A night at the theater?" Simon stared at her, searching her eyes as though he knew there were secrets she was fighting desperately to hide. "You want to go to the theater? With me? Tonight?"

Emily turned away from him, seeking some shelter from the intensity of his eyes. At times the man could read her mind. She couldn't afford to allow him that luxury tonight. "As you have pointed out on numerous occasions, it is important for people to believe we are enjoying wedded bliss."

"True. But you have a propensity for ignoring anything I say."

"I also can be made to see reason." She stood in front of her vanity, watching in the mirror as he approached her, his steps silent and sure, like a panther stalking prey. He paused close behind her. The heat of his body whispered against her back.

"Are you thinking we might be able to form a truce, my lady?"

She looked at him in the mirror, with an odd feeling of familiarity. He seemed to come to her from another place and time, a hero from an ancient legend. His hair, longer than the fashion, tumbled over his collar. His smile carved a dimple into his sun-darkened cheek. His eyes were as dark as midnight. A warrior from a time of chivalry. Her bold knight.

An illusion in a mirror.

She clenched the polished rosewood back of the vanity chair. "It would seem I have little choice but to try to get along with you in a reasonable fashion."

"Spoken like a true martyr." He rested his hand on her shoulder, his long, elegantly tapered fingers curled against ruby silk, the heat of his palm penetrating her gown. "I would like to think we could be friends, Emily."

Regret twisted inside her at his words. There was something terribly hollow in the idea of being only a friend to this man. Still, it was painfully clear that he felt no attraction for her. None at all.

Not that she cared. She would be a fool to care what this impostor thought of her. But, dear heaven, it hurt, like a wound carved into her chest.

She wanted to tell him she had no intention in this lifetime of ever being his friend. However, this was not the time for open warfare. She forced her lips into a smile. "Perhaps you're right. Life would be much less difficult if we could manage to live in some type of harmony."

He studied her a moment, something close to a frown etching his features, just a slight curving upward of his left brow. Something she might have missed if she weren't so intensely aware of him—every gesture, every subtle shift of his expression. "What time would you like to leave?"

Emily swallowed past the wedge of emotion lodged in her throat when she thought of what would happen to him. She was doing the right thing, she assured herself. He had left her no choice. None at all. "I've already changed. As soon as you're ready we can leave. We'll have dinner in town."

"All right." He smiled at her in the mirror. "It will take me a few minutes to get ready."

She grabbed her reticule from the edge of the vanity, feeling the solid weight of the pistol shrouded in ruby silk. "I'll be waiting for you in the drawing room."

He touched her arm when she started to leave. "Wait."

She froze beneath the warm touch of his fingers. "What is it?"

He grinned, mischief lighting his eyes. "Wait here and I'll show you."

Emily squeezed her reticule, forcing air past her tight throat as she watched him cross the room. He disappeared into the dressing room for a moment, then returned carrying a small package wrapped in silver paper.

"I saw this in town this afternoon. I thought you might like it."

Emily stared at the package he held out to her. ''You bought me a present?''

''A peace offering.''

''Oh.'' She stared at the package, fighting the guilt for what she had planned for this man. He had forced her into the war. Guilt had no place in battle.

''I promise there isn't anything in it that will bite.''

She didn't want the present, no matter what it was. She couldn't afford a single warm sentiment toward that man. Still, she couldn't risk piquing his suspicion. She rested her reticule on the vanity.

The package was warm from his hand. She stripped away the paper, anxious to be away from him. The silver paper tumbled from her trembling fingers, revealing a small box of polished wood. ''It's beautiful,'' she whispered, tracing with her fingertip the petal of one of the roses in the intricate marquetry pattern inlaid on the lid.

''Open it.''

She hesitated a moment before lifting the lid. The bright notes of a waltz drifted from the little box, tightening like a steel band around her chest.

''It's the waltz they played the first night we met,'' he said, his dark voice brushing against her cheek.

Her favorite waltz. The waltz her father had sanctioned for her first dance with her husband. If they were truly wed. Tears burned her eyes. Tears she refused to shed. Tears for a dream that couldn't come true.

She closed the box and placed it on the vanity beside the book of sonnets given to her by another scoundrel. This man was far more dangerous. This man could steal her heart, her pride, every ounce of her will. If he stayed, she would surrender. She would give herself completely to a man who didn't love her, a man who wanted a position not a wife. She couldn't survive that kind of torment. She had to banish him from her life before it was too late.

She lifted her reticule, her fingers curling around the pistol hidden inside the ruby silk. ''I'll be waiting for you.''

Chapter Thirteen

Simon shifted on the blue velvet carriage seat, his knee bumping Emily's leg. She flinched beside him, like a cat that had been dropped on hot coals. He saw her swallow hard, before she turned away from him and stared out the carriage window into the night.

He eased back in his seat, the nape of his neck prickling. The carriage swayed, throwing him against the side. Simon looked out the window. They were traveling on a narrow road winding along the cliffs. A partial moon cast a faint light across the countryside, turning the rugged stone face of the gorge to jagged chunks of silver. "We didn't go to town this way."

"No, we didn't." Emily glanced at her grandmother. "Beamish knows how much I like to see the gorge in the moonlight."

Simon frowned. "Then you should be sitting on this side of the carriage."

"Yes, well . . ." Emily squeezed her reticule. "I didn't think of it when we got in."

"Do you want to change places?"

"No. I'm fine." Emily sat pressed in the corner, looking as though she expected to be set upon by highwaymen at any moment. "You enjoy the view."

His muscles tensed. His instincts had kept him alive the past few years. At the moment they were screaming that something was wrong here.

"I do love a comedy. I thought it was a fine rendering of *She Stoops to Conquer*." Harriet flicked open her fan. "How about you, Sheridan?"

"I enjoyed the performance." He had a feeling that he was viewing one now. The ladies were up to something. He was certain of it. Emily and Harriet had barely touched their food at dinner. And, as he recalled, neither woman had found much amusement in the play. "Although, I have to admit, I have little to compare it to. I haven't had many opportunities to attend the theater."

"I can't imagine life in the military." Harriet studied him over the lace trim of her fan. "I can't imagine waking each morning knowing you must face the possibility of your own death." She looked at Emily as she continued, "I'm certain it's the same no matter if you are on land or sea. And to be cast into that life at the age of twelve, it must have been horrible."

Emily shifted on her seat, casting her grandmother a dark glance.

Harriet smiled, seemingly pleased with herself.

Simon rubbed the back of his neck.

"I assume his father had good reason for shipping him off to the military, grandmother."

"Oh." Harriet moved her fan back and forth beneath her chin. "I can't imagine any reason for shipping a child to war."

"No doubt the man was trouble even at the age of twelve." Emily glanced at Simon, her lips pulled into a tight line. "Did your father decide to ship you off to war? Or did you run away in search of glory?"

Memories Simon had long ago tried to bury peered at him like dark specters deep inside him. "I'm afraid a search for glory had very little to do with it."

"What did?" Emily asked.

Simon held her gaze, seeing the curiosity in her golden eyes, and something more—a need to understand him. She wanted him to surrender a part of himself. It was something he had never done. "It makes for rather boring conversation, I'm afraid."

"Another of your elusive replies." Emily's eyes narrowed as she stared at him. "I don't know why you even believed him when he told you he had taken a commission when he was twelve, Grandmama."

The intensity of her anger stunned him. It burned like a brilliant flame, so hot it could sear any other emotion that might try to breach her defenses.

"I doubt the man would recognize the truth if it spit in his eye." Emily tilted her head, glaring at him as though he weren't fit to share the same breathing space with her. "I wouldn't be surprised if he had never even been in the military."

"My father bought a commission for me when I was twelve because he hoped I would be killed on the battlefield." He heard Harriet's soft gasp. Yet he kept his eyes focused on Emily, watching her lips part, her eyes grow wide with shock.

He hadn't really expected to tell her the truth, wasn't really sure why he had. Perhaps he wanted to shock her. Perhaps he wanted more—to share some measure of truth with her.

Emily stared at him, her beautiful eyes brimming with outrage—either for a man who had lied or a father who had purchased his son a death sentence. "How can you say something like that?"

"Because you wanted the truth." Simon drew in his breath slowly, squeezing air into constricted lungs. Odd, how even now, after all these years, facing this particular truth could draw his muscles into knots. "And the simple truth is, my father decided he no longer wanted me."

"Why?" Emily stared at him, searching for answers that had eluded Simon most of his life. "Why would a man want his son to die?"

Simon leaned back in his seat, forcing his lips into a smile. "He had his reasons."

"Did he?" Emily held his gaze, persistent in her need to fully strip him of his defenses. "What reasons could a man have to justify something so terribly brutal?"

"It doesn't signify." He glanced out the window, avoiding the pity in her eyes. "I assure you, there is no need for sad looks. It all happened a long time ago."

"Is this all a lie?" Emily gripped his arm. "Is that why you can't give me a reason why your father would cast you away?"

He stared down at her hand, her slender fingers gripping his arm. The white kid of her glove glowed golden in the lamplight as she tried to drag him from the safety of the shadows shrouding the memories. He tried to breathe, but the air was too thick. Memories coiled around him, dragging him back to the day six months ago when he had faced his father for what could possibly be the last time.

He was in his father's study, staring across the expanse of a wide mahogany desk at the withering face of the man who had once personified all the power in Simon's world. Randolph St. James hadn't long to live. The disease he had was devouring him slowly from within.

"You've managed to defy me even in this, haven't you?" Randolph stared at Simon, his dark gray eyes filled with a lifetime of hate. "You've managed to survive, while I wither and die."

Simon swallowed past the tight knot of pain closing his throat. "If you taught me nothing else, you taught me how to survive."

"You think you're clever, just like she always thought she was so clever. You know I can't alter the entitlement.

You think you have triumphed over me at last. You think I will allow you and your tainted blood to inherit everything I own, to wear my title. Good God, how she would love to see it.''

Simon looked at this wasted shell of a man, searching for some way to mend wounds that had been carved long ago. ''I've never wanted your title or your lands or your money.''

''You're just like her. A liar. And just like her, I wish you to hell.''

Hatred. Simon had felt it as potently as a hand wrapped around his throat. The hatred that had never disappeared. No matter how hard he had tried to win his father's affection. No matter how hard he had tried to win his father's respect. He had failed. His father would go to his grave despising him.

Emily squeezed Simon's arm, her gloved fingers digging into his muscles, the sharp pinch dragging him back to this time and place. Simon looked up at her, and in that moment he wished with all his heart that he could take her in his arms. He wanted to hold her close against his aching chest. He craved her warmth, like a man banished forever to an icy realm. Yet she remained just beyond his reach.

''Tell me,'' Emily demanded. ''Is this the truth, or another of your lies?''

''Emily, there is no need to persecute the man,'' Harriet said. ''He obviously doesn't want to discuss it.''

''Fine.'' Emily released him, folding her hands over her reticule. ''I doubt we could believe him at any rate.''

Simon looked at Emily, seeing her anger in the thrust of her small chin, the determined tilt of her head. There was a barricade between them, built of lies constructed for the sake of duty. He realized he wanted to pound his fists against that barricade, put a crack in it, if nothing more. ''I was my father's only child by his first wife.''

Emily glanced at him, her eyes narrow and wary.

''I remember my mother was very beautiful. She was

French. Her hair was as dark as ebony, just as dark as her eyes.'' He hadn't lifted memories of his mother from that dark tomb inside him for a long time. Strange, but he could still remember her face, her voice, and so much more. ''She always smelled of roses.''

After a moment, when he fell silent, trapped by his memories, Emily spoke. ''You must resemble her.''

Simon sighed, wondering if his life would have been different if he had been born with his father's blond hair and gray eyes. ''I suppose.''

''It must have been painful for your father, seeing you after your mother's death.''

''My father would have been delighted if my mother had died.'' He glanced at Emily, seeing the distress in her beautiful eyes. ''My mother is still alive, living in America last time I heard, with her husband and their four children.''

Emily's eyes grew wide with understanding. ''Oh, I see.''

''When I was seven, my mother decided she wanted more out of life than my father could give her. He divorced her after she ran off with her lover.'' Simon smiled in spite of the pain from a wound that had never truly healed. ''Since his second wife had provided him with other children, my father saw no reason to keep me.''

''No reason to keep you?'' Emily shook her head as though she wanted to dismiss his words, but she couldn't. ''You were his son.''

''Yes. But I was also a reminder of his failure.''

Emily gripped the ruby silk bag in her lap, like a woman who was walking a narrow ledge, afraid of losing her balance. She caught her lower lip between her teeth, her gaze drifting to her grandmother.

Harriet leaned forward and rested her hand on his arm. ''I'm very sorry this dreadful thing happened to you.''

''It was a long time ago.'' Simon patted Harriet's hand, smiling into her concerned eyes. ''I've had time enough to understand why my mother chose to leave.''

"She wanted to spend her life with a man she loved." Emily lifted her chin. "Although I think what your father did was dreadful, it certainly didn't give you leave to invade my life."

"No doubt." Simon stared into the golden depths of her eyes, seeing the flame of anger burn away any trace of pity she might have felt for him. For once he welcomed that fiery shield.

The carriage slowed, swaying as it came to a halt. He glanced out the window. "Why do you suppose we've stopped?"

"I don't know," Emily said, her voice a little too eager.

Harriet lifted one brow as she gave her granddaughter a look full of reproach.

Emily held her grandmother's stare, her chin raised in determination.

Simon frowned as he looked from one woman to the other. Something stirred beneath the surface of their silent exchange, like a dangerous current waiting to drag an unsuspecting swimmer to his death.

He didn't like the feel of this. He leaned forward, slipping his hand into his pocket, his fingers gripping the smooth silver handle of his pistol as he reached for the door handle with the other. As his fingers grazed the cool brass handle, the door swung open, revealing the hulking figure of a man.

The man poked his head inside. Simon recognized the battered features of Lady Harriet's coachman, Beamish. The big man frowned, bushy dark brows knitting together over his flattened nose, his small dark eyes catching the lamplight as he looked at Simon. "Rest easy, sir. I be no highwayman."

Harriet gasped as she noticed the pistol in Simon's hand. "What are you doing with that?"

Simon rested the pistol on one knee of his buff-colored breeches. "You never know when you might need a little protection."

"Yes, well, it would seem you can put it away now," Emily said, clutching her reticule to her chest. "Before someone gets hurt."

"Trust me, my lady." Simon studied the woman sitting beside him. Emily's face was pale in the lamplight, her eyes wide as she stared at the pistol. "I know how to use it properly."

"Yes, I'm certain you do." Emily moistened her lips. "But unless you intend to shoot one of us, I don't see any reason for you to have it out like that."

Simon frowned, gripping the handle of the pistol, reluctant to put it away. He had a feeling he was being led into a trap. "What's the problem, Beamish?"

"Seems we got some problem with one of the rear wheels, sir." Beamish looked from the pistol in Simon's hand to Lady Harriet. "Begging your pardon, milady, but I'm going to need for you all to get out for me to be fixing the trouble."

"Yes, of course." Lady Harriet took Beamish's big hand and made her escape from the carriage. Emily followed, clutching her reticule in one hand as she allowed Beamish to help her with the other.

"I can manage," Simon said as Beamish offered him a hand. The big man nodded and walked toward the rear of the carriage.

Simon glanced out of the carriage door, searching for . . . what? Did he honestly believe Emily had hired a pack of ruffians to take care of her little problem—namely him?

He stepped down from the carriage. A cool breeze whispered through the few trees rising along the edge of the cliffs, birch and ash rustling in the breeze, moonlight rippling across the swaying leaves. An owl hooted somewhere to his right. He tightened his grip on the handle of his pistol, wondering if his instincts were overactive this evening.

Emily and Harriet were standing near the rear of the carriage, watching Beamish, who knelt on the rutted road beside the wheel, examining the axle. Simon slipped the pistol into his coat pocket and joined the women.

Emily and Harriet both backed away from him as he drew near, staring at him as though he were a highwayman holding them at gun point. Simon frowned as he looked down at the wheel. He didn't like the idea of having the ladies frightened of him. "What seems to be the problem?"

"Well now, as far as I can tell, it looks to be a bolt come loose." Beamish stood, shaking his head. "But my eyes ain't so good in this light. Mayhaps you could take a look, sir?"

Simon bent to look at the wheel, careful to keep his shadow from blocking the moonlight. He could see nothing wrong with the axle. "I don't . . ." As he spoke, he caught movement out of the corner of his eye.

Simon straightened. The fist Beamish had meant to plow into his jaw glanced off his shoulder. As Beamish rolled forward with the blow, Simon slammed his fist upward, catching the big man under his chin, snapping back his head. Beamish's teeth clicked together. Groaning, he staggered back. He shook his head like a dog shaking off water. A low growl escaped his lips as he charged Simon, wielding his right fist.

Simon dodged the blow, swinging with his left. He planted his fist into the larger man's diaphragm. Beamish's breath escaped in a whoosh of onion-scented air. He jerked forward, folding double at the waist. Simon slammed his right fist into Beamish's jaw. The brute gasped. He staggered a few steps before collapsing against the wheel, his deep moan ripping through the darkness. The carriage swayed beneath the impact.

Simon dragged air into his lungs. He rubbed his bruised knuckles, staring down at the unconscious man. It always paid to trust your instincts. The little tigress had actually . . . his thoughts froze as he turned to face Emily. She was standing a few feet away, moonlight glinting on the barrel of the pistol she held pointed at his chest.

Simon looked into the hard glitter of her eyes, and forced his lips into a smile. "Did anyone every tell you it's dangerous to point a pistol at someone?"

"I can assure you"—Emily steadied the pistol with her other hand—"I know how to use a pistol. Father taught me well."

An angry woman was dangerous when she *wasn't* holding a pistol, he thought. The problem was, you could never predict just exactly what a female was going to do. Still, he doubted this one was capable of cold-blooded murder. "Have you ever shot a man, Em?"

She moistened her lips. "Turn around."

He didn't know what she had planned for him, but he did know he wasn't going to like it. He took a step toward her. "You'll have a better shot if I face you."

The pistol bobbed in her hands. "Don't come another step closer."

"Aim a little lower." He placed his hand over his heart as he took another step toward her. "Right here. You'll put the ball straight through my heart."

"I told you not to move." She swallowed hard. "If you cooperate, the worst you will suffer is an extended sea voyage on a man-of-war, providing a service to the crown."

Simon frowned. "You plan to ship me off with a press gang?"

Emily nodded. "Precisely."

Simon stared at her, wanting to strangle her for putting him in this position, and at the same time admiring her pluck. Still, he didn't plan to spend the next few years of his life on one of His Majesty's men-of-war. "I don't think I would enjoy life at sea," he said, taking a step toward her.

Emily wagged the pistol at him. "Stay where you are."

"Emily, dear, perhaps you should reconsider," Harriet said as she stepped away from her granddaughter, seeking shelter against the side of the carriage.

"I see no reason to reconsider. I have the situation well under control."

"What do you have planned, Em?" Simon took another step. "How are you going to explain my disappearance?"

"You are going to fall over the cliffs. Your body will be washed down river and out to sea." She wagged the pistol at him. "Now, if you don't cooperate, I might just decide to make that part of the story come true. Turn around."

He smiled and stepped closer. "Give me the pistol, sweetheart."

"Stay right where you are," she said, stepping back. "I'll shoot, I swear I will."

"I don't think you will."

He advanced.

She retreated.

"Oh you are the most . . ." Her words dissolved in a gasp as she stumbled over a stone.

In a single beat of his heart, Simon saw the flash of powder, heard the explosion that ripped through him. A woman's scream sliced the still evening. Pain flared, a white-hot coal that seared through his head and died in darkness.

Emily gasped at the loud bark of the pistol that jerked in her hand. He flinched. A soft moan escaped his lips as he stumbled back away from her. And then he was collapsing, a slow dissolve of muscle and bone that delivered him into a heap at her feet.

Stunned, Emily stared at him. The pistol dropped from her limp hand, hitting the ground with a dull thud. He lay on his right side, right arm folded beneath him, the other curved on the ground, palm upward.

"Dear Lord!" Harriet grabbed her arm. "Look at what you've done."

"I didn't mean to shoot." Emily looked at her grandmother. "I slipped. It just happened."

"You've killed him," Harriet whispered, her voice strangled.

"No!" Emily pulled free of her grandmother's taut grasp. She sank to her knees beside him. "He has to be alive."

The half moon spilled a pale light over him, carving the left side of his face from the shadows. He looked as though he were sleeping, thick dark hair tumbling over his brow, black lashes still against his cheek, lips parted. She touched his cheek. His skin was warm, smooth beneath her fingertips.

"Is he breathing?" Lady Harriet asked.

"I can't tell." Emily touched his shoulder, pushing, rolling him gently to his back, his left arm settling across his waist.

Harriet gasped. "Oh, my dear heaven!"

A hard hand of fear closed around Emily's heart. Moonlight seared his image across her memory. The ball had hit him high on the right side of his brow, leaving a gash that wept his life's-blood. The dark liquid shimmered in the moonlight.

"I believe you've killed him."

"He can't be dead." Emily slipped her trembling hand inside his waistcoat, searching for the beat of his heart. The white linen of his shirt warmed her cold hand. She held her breath. Waiting. Praying.

"Emily, is he . . ."

Emily closed her eyes, nearly collapsing with relief when she felt the throb of his heart beneath her hand. "He's alive."

"Thank heavens!"

Emily snatched her handkerchief from the reticule dangling from her arm.

"Emily, dear, I hope you don't still plan to deliver him to the press gang. Do you? I truly believe the young man would not survive."

"No, of course we won't send him like this." Emily

dabbed at his cheek and brow with her lacy white handkerchief. "We'll take him back home."

"What do you suppose we can say to explain the rather obvious condition he is in?"

"We can . . ." Emily pressed the handkerchief against the gash in his brow. She frowned, searching for a plausible reason for bringing him back with a gash in his head. "We can say we were attacked by a highwayman."

"A highwayman." Harriet gave Emily a skeptical look. "Now, why didn't I think of that?"

"What would you suggest?"

"I would suggest not getting into this predicament in the first place."

"It appears to be a little late for that particular course of action."

Harriet shook her head, resigned to her fate. "I suppose a story of a highwayman shall have to do."

"Grandmama, do see if you can rouse Beamish." Emily gently smoothed the waves back from Simon's brow, the black strands curling around her fingers. "I think it would be best to get this man back home as soon as possible."

Chapter Fourteen

Emily gripped a post at the foot of her bed, staring at the surgeon as he examined his patient. ''Dr. Cheeson, why hasn't he awakened? It's been two days.''

Dr. Cheeson stepped back from the bed, shaking his head as though he were not pleased with his patient. He looked at Emily, his blue eyes solemn behind his round glasses, his thick white brows tugged together over the long line of his narrow nose. ''I always feel honesty is best in a situation like this. It saves grief in the long run of it.''

''Grief?'' Emily gripped the bedpost, her knuckles bleaching white with the strain. ''What do you mean?''

Audrey slipped her arm around Emily's waist, lending quiet support. ''He will be all right. Won't he?''

Dr. Cheeson slipped off his glasses and rubbed his nose. ''The truth is, I don't know.''

''You don't know.'' Harriet rose from the couch near the hearth. ''Why don't you know?''

''In cases like this, it's impossible to tell the extent of the damage. He might regain consciousness and be no worse for the incident. And then again''—Dr. Cheeson slipped on his glasses, carefully adjusting the wire frames over his ears—''he might never regain consciousness.''

''I see.'' Harriet looked at Emily, her eyes filled with silent incrimination.

Guilt struck like a knife in Emily's chest. ''He will awaken, Doctor. He must.''

''If he does awaken, you should realize that he might be drastically altered.''

''Altered?'' Emily asked.

Dr. Cheeson sighed. ''It's possible he won't even remember his name.''

''He might not know his own name?'' Emily whispered.

''You mean he could have amnesia?'' Harriet asked.

Dr. Cheeson nodded. ''At the very least. You might find yourself with the task of rebuilding his life, teaching him who he is.''

Emily nearly laughed. She stared at the man lying in her bed, his dark head on her pillow. How could she hope to teach him who he was when she didn't even know his name?

Dr. Cheeson lifted his black leather bag from a table. ''We should know more in the next few days.''

After the surgeon left, Emily sank to the chair beside the bed, resuming her vigil over the man she had nearly murdered.

''He's going to be all right.'' Audrey patted Emily's shoulder. ''I'm certain of it.''

Emily slipped her hand around his wrist, taking comfort in the slow, steady throb of his pulse. ''He has to recover.''

''Of course he is going to recover.'' Harriet tapped her fan against her palm. ''There is no question of it.''

Emily had to believe he would be all right. It was impossible to imagine that this man might never again open his beautiful midnight eyes.

Audrey rubbed her palm over the taut muscles in Emily's

shoulder. "You should get some rest, darling. I'll sit with Sheridan."

Emily shook her head. "I slept a little last night. I want to be with him when he awakens."

Audrey's hand tensed on Emily's shoulder as she looked at her mother. "Mother, if you don't get some rest, you're going to be ill."

Harriet sighed, her shoulders sagging as though burdened with the weight of the world. "I think I shall lie down for a little while. But I wish to be notified if there is any change."

"Of course," Audrey said. "You rest now. I'm certain we'll have good news for you today."

Harriet touched Emily's cheek, smiling when Emily looked up at her. "You must have faith that all will be well, my girl."

Emily managed a smile. "He is going to be all right, Grandmama."

"Of course he is." Harriet's smile didn't erase the doubts in her eyes. "He is a strong man. I'm certain he'll be fine."

Audrey crossed the room with her mother. The door closed with a soft click as they left Emily alone with Simon.

"You have to get well." Emily smoothed the thick black waves back from the bandage wrapped around his head, the white linen a band across his brow. Sunlight slipped golden light through the black strands that slid through her fingers like warm silk. "You must listen to me. I insist you awaken."

He didn't move.

"Please, wake up." She left her chair and sat on the edge of the bed, needing to be closer to him. "Please open your eyes."

Nothing. Not a flicker of his lashes.

"I want you to know I never meant this to happen." She smoothed the shoulder of the fresh nightshirt they had dressed him in this morning, easing a wrinkle from the white linen. ‘‘I only wanted you to leave before I did something foolish. You see, you have the most disconcerting influence on my emotions. I’m angry one moment. And the next I’m . . . Oh, you confuse me.’’

She smoothed her hand across his shoulder, absorbing his warmth. ‘‘You are a scoundrel. A fortune hunter. And yet, there is something about you. Grandmother was right. You have a quality, a way of making me feel as though you could take on all the evil in the world and win. No doubt the ability to create that type of illusion is important when you are a scoundrel.’’

She eased her hand across his shoulder, testing the strength of him beneath her arching fingers. His warmth radiated against her palm, a teasing reminder of the smooth skin beneath the soft cloth.

‘‘I’m certain you would think it amusing if you knew that you have the most infuriating way of invading my dreams. I catch myself thinking about you at the oddest moments. She allowed herself the illicit pleasure of recalling the few moments when he had held her in his arms. The warmth of his body wrapping around her. His lips brushing her skin. ‘‘Since you came, my thoughts are far from those a proper young woman should have. Of course, most proper young women don’t have a man residing in their bedrooms.’’

She held her breath as she slid one finger into the collar of his nightshirt. She eased back the white linen, parting the nightshirt to the center of his chest, revealing the hollow at his throat, and those starkly masculine black curls. She stared at him, watching the steady rise and fall of his chest, her own breath growing taut in her lungs.

Without understanding her own need, she leaned forward. She pressed her lips to the inviting depression of his throat. Soft chest curls tickled her chin. His warmth bathed her face, tempting her to rub her cheek against him. She breathed deeply, absorbing the tangy scent of his skin rising with the heat of his body. And deep inside, she felt the flutter of an open flame. She leaned back, her face warm with the rush of her blood.

"Do you know what I wish? I wish you were really Sheridan Blake. I wish you would open your eyes and look at me as though you really loved me." She pressed her lips to his, his breath warm and soft against her cheek, his lips firm and still beneath her touch. Tears burned her eyes. Tears that came from wanting something she could never have. She slid her fingertips across his cheek, absorbing the scrape of dark whiskers. "I suppose I'm still reaching for a dream. Foolish of me, isn't it?"

He turned his head on the pillow, following the gentle stroke of her fingers.

Emily's heart bumped against the wall of her chest. "Can you hear me?"

His lips parted on a sigh. His lashes fluttered against his cheeks.

Emily tried to swallow, but her mouth had turned to parchment. "Listen to me. Open your eyes."

He moaned, deep in his throat. The sound of a wounded lion.

"Please, wake up." Emily rested her hand on his shoulder and shook him gently. "You must wake up."

His lashes fluttered and lifted.

She cupped his face in her hands, staring down into his dark, unfocused eyes. "Are you all right?"

He blinked, frowning as he stared up at her.

"Emily, what is it? Has something happened?"

Emily glanced over her shoulder. Her mother was rushing across the room, clutching her white muslin knitting bag to her chest, a pair of wooden knitting needles peeking out from the top.

"Mother, he's awake!"

"Oh!" Audrey dropped her bag. A ball of blue yarn spilled from the white muslin, rolling across the floor. She rushed to Emily's side. "This is wonderful. Simply wonderful."

Simon looked from Emily to Audrey and back again, a curious expression in his dark eyes.

Emily touched his face, tears misting her vision. "You're going to be all right."

"Sheridan." Audrey grasped his hand. "My dear young man, you gave us a most frightful turn."

"Sheridan?" He moistened his lips. "Why did you call me Sheridan?"

"Oh my goodness." Audrey glanced at Emily, then back at the injured man. "Sheridan, please think for a moment. You know who you are."

He frowned. "You called me Sheridan."

A sudden fear sank sharp talons into Emily. She couldn't afford to have the man start rambling. Especially if he couldn't remember Sheridan Blake, but he could remember his real name. She sprang to her feet and took her mother's arm. "Mother, please send for the doctor."

"The doctor? But I . . ." Audrey sputtered as Emily ushered her toward the door.

"Please, hurry. Dr. Cheeson will have some idea of how to handle this situation."

"Oh. Of course. I'll send someone for him straightaway."

Emily closed the door. She sagged back against the solid oak. Stay calm, she told herself. She must keep her wits about her if she was going to get out of this tangle. She looked at the bed, where a dark-haired stranger was staring at her with eyes as black as midnight. Would he remember that she had shot him?

Simon stared at the beautiful red-haired woman as she approached the bed. Before she reached him, she hesitated in a column of sunlight slanting through an open window. Poised in the sunlight, she seemed to come from another realm. Bathed in golden light. Fire flaming darkly in her hair. She was an avenging angel come to claim him.

Through the pounding in his head, he sought to gather his scattered wits. Images flickered in his brain. This woman. Staring at him. Anger and fear in her eyes.

Where was he? This was not one of the hospitals where he had found himself time and again over the long bloody years. He was in bed with ivory silk and lace dripping at all four corners. A woman's bed.

Sheridan. For some reason that name had significance. Even though he knew it wasn't his name.

Think.

He had to slice through the pain fogging his thoughts. He had a mission. He was certain of it. He had just misplaced the details.

The redhead moved closer. She paused beside him. Her hands clenched into fists at her sides. A look of apprehension in her eyes. "Do you remember me?"

As he stared up into those huge golden eyes, his memories crashed through the fog in his brain, breaking over him like a wave beating against the shore. The last time he had seen Miss Emily Maitland, there was moonlight in her hair. And a pistol in her hand. He released his breath, fighting the moan that crept up his throat as he tried to pull himself into a sitting position.

"Easy," she said, pressing her hands against his shoulders.

He fell back beneath her gentle prodding, appalled to find he was too weak to fight her. Beneath the white linen of his nightshirt, his body broke out in a cold sweat. His head throbbed. His right arm felt as though someone had rammed him with a red-hot poker. He couldn't place why his arm was on fire. But he remembered all too well why his head felt as though a regiment had used him for target practice. The beautiful little hellcat had shot him.

"The doctor said you might suffer some memory loss."

"Memory loss?" No, he was reasonably certain he remembered everything. Including Miss Emily Maitland's plan to ship him off with a press gang.

She gnawed her lower lip, studying him with wary eyes. "Do you remember your name?"

It was always important to trust one's instincts, he thought. Right now his were telling him a wise man might not be quick to reveal the truth. "My name?"

Emily nodded. "Do you remember who you are?"

He closed his eyes, trying to think past the pain that throbbed with each beat of his heart. He sensed there was an opportunity here. A distinct advantage to be found in losing his memory. And he was going to need every advantage against his beautiful enemy.

"My name is . . ." He stared up at her, hoping he looked as dazed as he felt. "What is my name?"

Her eyes grew wide. "You don't remember?"

"I don't remember anything."

"Really?" she asked, her voice filled with sudden excitement.

"Who am I?" Simon glanced around the room, trying to look suitably disoriented. With the pain pounding in his head, he found the role easy to fill. "Where am I? Who are you? What happened?"

"Easy." She sat beside him and rested her hand on his shoulder. "You must not exert yourself. You've been injured."

"Injured? How?"

"You were shot." She lowered her eyes, staring at the base of his neck. "By a highwayman."

"A highwayman." Simon fought to keep the smile from his lips. The lady certainly had a vivid imagination.

"Yes." She fiddled with the satin ribbon laced through white eyelets at the high waist of her bottle green gown. "We were attacked while on our way home from the theater."

"We were coming home from the theater together."

She nodded, keeping her eyes lowered.

"Then we know each other?"

"Yes." She moistened her lips. "We know each other."

He studied her a moment, wondering how far she intended to take this maneuver. "Are we brother and sister?"

She shook her head. ''No.''

''Cousins?''

''No.'' She met his eyes, a frown etched between her brows. ''Are you certain you don't remember anything?''

He looked up at her with as much innocence as he could manage. ''Not a thing.''

''We are''—she took a deep, steadying breath—''married.''

''Married.'' He smiled. He couldn't help it. Not when he realized the trap the little tigress had set for herself. He cupped her cheek with his left hand, her skin smooth, her rising blush warm against his palm. ''I should have guessed we were husband and wife.''

She stared at him, an uneasy blend of curiosity and anxiety in her eyes. ''Why?''

''Because when I opened my eyes and saw you, I knew I had always loved you.''

She parted her lips, but nothing escaped except a startled rush of air.

He smoothed his thumb over the corner of her mouth. ''Never in my life have I felt this way,'' he said, surprised at how easy the words came to him.

''Oh.'' She stared down at him, her beautiful eyes wide with shock.

If the hellcat wanted to play this game, she would find he had a few tricks of his own. He slid his hand into the soft hair at her nape, his fingers curving beneath her ear. ''My darling, what you must have gone through, not knowing if I would live or die.''

''Yes. It's been quite harrowing.'' She planted her hands on his chest, resisting as he tugged her near.

''I'm back, sweetheart.'' He cupped her breast in his right hand, sliding his thumb over the tip.

She gasped, lashing her arm against his. Pain flared in his arm, dragging a moan from his lips. She shot to her feet, glaring at him, her breath coming in uneven gasps. ''How dare you!''

He dragged air into his lungs, trying to clear the darkness that threatened to drown him in a wave of pain. When his vision cleared, he stared up at the indignant beauty. "Mind telling me why you did that?"

"You have no right to maul me."

"No right?" He frowned, resting his palm over the crook of his right arm, trying to ease the fire burning there. "But, sweetheart, I'm your husband."

"Oh." She caught her lower lip between her teeth. "Ah . . . what I mean is, you're in no condition for this type of sport. You must take more care. I won't have you doing yourself any harm."

He pressed his head into the pillow, pain stabbing his temples like hot steel. In this condition he was hardly a match for the lady. The battle would wait for another day. "What happened to my arm?"

"The doctor bled you yesterday."

He released his breath in a ragged sigh. Far too many times he had watched a leech drain the life from a man. It would be the last time he allowed one of those quacks near him with a silver bowl and lancet.

She started backing toward the door. "You should rest."

"Tell me something."

She bumped into the bedpost. "What?"

He smiled, taking pleasure in rattling the lady's composure. "What is my name?"

"Oh." She fiddled with the satin ribbon at the high waist of her muslin gown. "Sheridan. Sheridan Blake."

"Sheridan Blake." He contemplated the name for a moment. "I wonder why it doesn't sound at all familiar."

She shrugged. "I wonder."

He smoothed his palm over the crook of his arm, trying to ease the burn left from the surgeon's knife. "Please forgive me, my love, but I don't seem to remember your name."

"Emily. Emily Maitland."

"Don't you mean Emily Maitland *Blake*."

"Yes. Of course. You'll have to forgive me." She glanced down at the ribbon she held clenched between her fingers. "We haven't been married very long."

"No? How long have we been married?"

"Nearly two months. But you only just arrived here. At my father's house. A little over a week ago." She slid the satin ribbon through her fingers. "After you retired from the army."

"So we are still getting to know each other."

"You might say that."

A slow smile curved his lips as he thought of just how well they were going to know each other.

She stepped back, away from the bed, a doe with the scent of a lion in her nostrils. "I'm going to see what is taking Dr. Cheeson so long."

"Hurry back, sweetheart." He pressed his hand to his heart. "I miss you already."

She stared at him as though he were a fire-breathing dragon about to turn her world to cinders. She turned and ran toward the door.

He swallowed his laughter as he watched her dash from the room in a swirl of green muslin. If the little witch thought she could play games with him and walk away unscathed, she had a few things to learn. And he was just the man to teach her.

Chapter Fifteen

"Did I hear you correctly?" Harriet sank to the pale yellow chaise longue near the fireplace in the sitting room that adjoined her bedroom. "You mean to say he actually believes he is Sheridan Blake?"

"He couldn't remember his name when he awakened." Emily paced the length of the room, turning when she reached the hearth. "So I told him he was Sheridan Blake. I didn't know what else to say."

"Now the young man who has been pretending to be your husband actually believes he *is* your husband?"

Emily rubbed her fingertips against her throbbing temples. "Yes."

"I don't know why I should be surprised. Not after everything that has happened in the past few weeks."

"I thought it was for the best at the time. At any rate, I think he will be less dangerous if he believes he really is Sheridan Blake."

"Dr. Cheeson would not agree with you." Harriet shook her head with a wry smile. "I doubt the good doctor will ever come near that young man with a knife again."

"I can't say I entirely blame the scoundrel for threatening to turn one of those awful little knives against Cheeson." Emily crossed the room, pausing in front of a window. "I shouldn't like to awaken in pain and have a surgeon want to drain more of my blood."

"Surgeons are all only guessing at what to do." Harriet paused a moment. "The question is, what are you going to do now?"

Emily stared out the open windows. In the distance she could see Ravenwood Castle, stone walls rising like a dark gray phantom from the lush green hills. "Exactly what I planned to do the other night."

"You can't mean you still intend to have that young man hauled away by a press gang?"

Emily hugged her arms to her waist. An odd chill gripped her even though a warm summer breeze swept through the windows, bringing the scent of roses from the gardens. "He has left me little choice."

"That young man nearly died at your hand."

"I know." A raven soared from the copse of trees near the far edge of the rose garden. She watched the bird ride an invisible current of air, black wings stretching, shining in the sunlight. "I intend to wait until he is quite recovered."

"Oh well, that makes all the difference, doesn't it?"

Emily turned to face her grandmother. "You make it sound as though I'm sending the man to the gallows."

Harriet pursed her lips. "I understand more than a few men have died aboard a man-of-war."

Emily shuddered deep inside, guilt competing with some other emotion, one she wouldn't even try to identify. "He is a military man. He is accustomed to war."

"Yes." Harriet clasped her hands in her lap. "The man has been at war since he was twelve."

"That isn't my concern," Emily said, trying to convince herself it was true.

"No." Harriet studied Emily a moment, her expression revealing every bit of her displeasure. "You have other concerns. Such as a virile young man who will no doubt want to enjoy all of the charms of his beautiful young wife."

The hot tide of her blush rose in Emily's cheeks. Beneath the soft muslin of her gown, her breasts tingled from the memory of his touch. "I can handle the man."

"Can you?"

"Yes." She would have to be cautious around him, that was all. Very cautious. "As soon as he is healthy enough to become a problem, I intend to see him shipped off to the other side of the world."

"He may recover much quicker than you think."

Emily fiddled with the ribbon at the waist of her gown. "I assure you, I can handle the man."

"Perhaps. But I must tell you, I don't approve of this." Harriet frowned, her lips drawing into a thin line. "I don't like to think of that young man brutalized in the name of king and country."

"What would you have me do?"

"Marry him."

"Impossible!"

"No. I believe it is quite possible." Harriet tilted her head, a smile on her lips. "I'm quite certain my solicitor could arrange all the details."

Emily paced the length of the room, feeling like a tigress newly trapped and caged. "I cannot marry that scoundrel."

"Emily, you are presented with a most interesting opportunity."

Emily paused near a small rosewood pedestal table that held a pale yellow urn filled with a rainbow of roses. "What opportunity?"

"That young man has no memory, no thought of who or what he once was. You can shape those memories. You can create a past for him. You can create Sheridan Blake."

"Create Sheridan Blake." The breath stilled in Emily's

lungs at the possibilities presented by the prospect. Could she spin dreams into reality?

"The man is a marvelous block of clay, my darling. Sculpt him into the man of your dreams."

Sheridan Blake. Living. Breathing. The embodiment of her every dream. "And if he remembers who he is?"

"Then you really aren't in any worse position than you are right now."

Emily shook her head. "You're mistaken, Grandmother."

Harriet lifted one brow as she looked at Emily. "In what way?"

"I could be in a much worse tangle." Emily drew her fingers over the soft petals of a pink rose. "The man has the most unsettling influence over me."

Harriet frowned. "What frightens you?"

"I'm not frightened." Emily stared down at the pink blossom, the petals unfurled, revealing all its secrets. "I simply do not intend to allow misguided emotions to develop within myself."

"Ah. You're frightened of falling in love with the man."

The truth in those words stiffened her spine. "I doubt that would happen, but I don't intend to take any chances."

Harriet sighed. "Then, as soon as he regains his health, off he goes to lose it."

"The man is quite resourceful." Emily frowned, trying to dismiss the image her grandmother's words had conjured in her mind—her scoundrel lying ill on some dirty pallet, with no one to tend him. No one to care if he lived or died.

He had spent his entire life alone, without a family, without anyone to care for him. A fist tightened around her throat when she realized how much she wanted to give him all he had never had. Still, she knew she couldn't afford the luxury of such tender emotions. "He will survive."

"You do realize it's quite possible the young man will never regain his memory. Which means you would be sending him away while he believes he is your loving husband.'' Harriet regarded Emily with a look of censure in her eyes. ''Can you imagine what he will think of you?''

''I imagine it would be quite confusing for him.''

Harriet nodded. ''I would imagine.''

''Then I shall tell him the truth. Once he is bound and ready to be taken aboard the ship, of course.''

Harriet rolled her eyes toward heaven. ''Emily, my girl, I fear you are even more stubborn then I was at your age.''

''He has left me no choice.'' Emily paced the length of the room, pausing at the windows. She held her grandmother's steady stare. ''This is war, Grandmother. I'm fighting for my future, and I don't intend to lose.''

''If you truly wish to win, then you will reconsider your course of action.'' Harriet studied her a moment, a single line digging into the smooth skin between her brows. ''That young man has qualities, Emily. Don't throw him away as though he were rubbish. Seize this opportunity. Make your dreams come true.''

Emily turned toward the windows. She stared at the dark gray walls of Ravenwood, sensing a stirring inside her, a flutter of hope, like the flexing of wings by a bird that has forgotten how to fly. All her life she had dreamed of sharing one special love. Could she make that dream come true with a man who made her heart soar each time he looked at her?

The man was a fortune-hunting scoundrel. He wanted her for one reason, and it had nothing to do with affection. Still, if a man were to forget his sins, would he still be guilty?

Sheridan Blake, alive and in her arms. Warmth seeped into her blood at the memory of his arms around her. There was so much to be gained.

So much to risk.

So much to lose.

The man calling himself Sheridan Blake could destroy her if she gave him her heart. She could imagine how he would manipulate her if she ever gave him the type of power that came from complete surrender.

"I don't believe I can take the risk, Grandmother. I think it would be best for everyone if Sheridan Blake took a sudden fall from the cliffs."

"Emily, I feel you are being—"

"Grandmama, please." Emily turned to face Harriet. "I've made up my mind."

Harriet pulled her lips into a tight line as she stared at Emily. "Then I suggest you return to your husband's side. If you are going to pretend to be his wife, do try to make a good show of it. I wouldn't care to have people talk about how you neglected your husband when he was in need."

Emily's cheeks grew warm under her grandmother's disapproving glare. "I will do my best to play the role of devoted wife."

"I certainly hope you will." Harriet smiled, her eyes filling with a light that gave Emily the uneasy feeling she was being manipulated in some way.

"I don't intend to change my mind, Grandmama."

"Of course you don't, my girl. Now run along." Harriet waved her hand toward the door. "I don't wish to have anyone think my granddaughter is a heartless little rattlepate who treats her husband as though he were a foundling. You know how the servants devour gossip."

"I shan't give them anything to chew."

Harriet nodded, seemingly satisfied. Yet, as Emily left the room, a sense of impending disaster settled around her like an icy shroud.

"It's odd." Hugh rested his shoulder against one of the posts at the foot of the bed, frowning as he looked at Simon. "There hasn't been a report of a highwayman in this area in the past three years."

"I wish I could help with a description." Simon rested his palm over the wound in his arm, trying to ease the throb of pain centered there. "But I don't remember anything."

"Don't concern yourself about it." Hugh smiled. "You

just concentrate on getting well. I need you back in the office.''

''As if that were his main reason for getting well.'' Audrey slipped her arm around her husband's waist, smiling up at him. ''He needs some rest. Which means you need to leave, before you start filling his aching head with shipping schedules.''

''Termagant.'' Hugh kissed her, a quick brush of his lips across hers that left little doubt of how very much he loved his wife.

''I'm going to sit with Sheridan awhile, until Emily returns.''

Hugh stroked his fingers across her cheek. ''Where is she?''

''I imagine she is lying down. She hasn't had much sleep in the past two days.''

Hugh glanced over Audrey's head, smiling at Simon. ''I leave you in capable hands.''

Simon watched Hugh and Audrey. He felt himself a stranger with his nose pressed against the window, staring in at all the warmth and affection he had never experienced. Perhaps he never would. He only prayed he wouldn't have to tear this couple apart.

Emily paused in the hall outside her bedroom, squeezing the tray she held close against her waist, preparing for battle. She could handle the man, she assured herself. She could play the role of devoted wife and keep the beast at bay.

Still, she hesitated.

She took a deep breath, filling her senses with the aroma of hot tea, warm bread, and beef broth rising from the tray. She gathered the tattered edges of her defenses around her and entered the room.

Sunlight poured through the open windows, painting pale streaks across the ivory and mint-green stripes in the silk wall covering. Her mother was sitting on an upholstered armchair near the windows, knitting socks that would be donated to the poor. She stuffed her knitting into a white muslin bag when she saw Emily.

"I think he is finally sleeping," Audrey whispered, rising to greet her daughter.

"In that case, he won't need this." Emily glanced down at the tray she was holding. "I'll take it back to the kitchen."

"Why don't you just set it on the table near the bed? He might awaken soon." Audrey glanced toward the bed. "He has been terribly restless. I imagine he is still in a great deal of pain."

Emily clenched the tray, hating to admit she had caused that pain.

"Don't worry, Emily. I do believe he has come through the storm." Audrey squeezed Emily's arm. "And I'm certain he will regain his memory. It's only a matter of time before he is your dear Sheridan once again."

Emily had the terrible urge to confess everything as she watched her mother leave the room. She didn't, of course. To do so would be complete disaster. Her mother would be horrified to discover that "Sheridan" didn't exist.

She approached the bed slowly, like a hunter approaching the lair of a lion. Only this lion was asleep, his head turned away from the windows and the late afternoon sunlight, thick black lashes still against his cheeks. She stood beside his bed a moment, holding the tray close to her waist, looking down at her enemy.

Strange, he didn't look like a scoundrel. Not while he slept. Sleep eased the lines that flared from his incredible dark eyes. It softened the curve of his parted lips. He looked younger. More approachable. Far too vulnerable.

He lay cradling his right arm across his waist, as though it gave him pain even in his sleep. The sheet was tangled around his thighs, kicked there in his uneasy slumber. Beads of perspiration glistened on his neck and above his lip.

She eased the tray to the table by the bed and leaned over him. He seemed overly warm, an unnatural heat burning beneath her palm when she touched his cheek.

He opened his eyes.

Chapter Sixteen

Emily jumped back, bumping the table, rattling the dishes on the tray. "I'm sorry," she said, righting the cup she had overturned. "I didn't mean to disturb you. I just brought you something to eat. But you probably want to sleep. Yes, I'm certain you need your sleep."

He smiled, a sleepy curve of his lips that made her wonder what it might be like to awaken beside him each morning.

"I'll let you rest." She turned, intending to make a hasty retreat.

"Please wait."

She hesitated, staring at the door. "What is it?"

"I'm thirsty. And I don't think I can manage the pitcher."

She moistened her dry lips and turned to face him. He was lying back against the pillows, his right arm over his waist.

"Would you help me?"

"Of course." She hurried to the table by the bed where

a porcelain pitcher and glass had been left for him. She snatched the pitcher and sloshed water into the glass, appalled at how her hands were shaking. This was not the way wars were won, she told herself. She took a deep breath and turned to face him.

He was watching her, a curious expression in his midnight eyes. And for one brief moment she had the impression he found her amusing.

She crossed the short distance between them, trying to steady the glass in her hand. When she offered him the glass, he tried to draw himself into a sitting position, and failed. He fell back against the pillows, breathing hard, fresh beads of moisture appearing above his lip.

"I don't seem to be able to manage."

"Let me help." She eased her arm around his shoulders, cradling his head against her shoulder as she pressed the glass to his lips.

He drank deeply, as though the water were the nectar of the gods, draining it dry. When he was done, he leaned back against her, his breath escaping in a contented sigh. "Thank you."

She gazed down at the man cradled against her side. The heat of him radiated through her gown, bathing her breast, filling her with an odd sense of protectiveness. And something more. Something dangerous. She yanked her arm from beneath him, spilling him back against the bed.

A groan escaped his lips. His face twisted into a grimace of pain.

Emily flinched. "I'm sorry."

After a moment, he opened his eyes, smiling as he looked up at her. "It's all right, sweetheart."

Longing leaped inside her at the soft endearment. He spoke with such easy familiarity, as though they had been married a hundred years. And somehow, in some strange way, it felt right.

He tugged on the sheet, struggling to untangle it from his legs.

"Let me." She took the lace-trimmed edge from his weak grasp, tugging on the sheet, settling it over his waist.

"Thank you." He turned his head on the pillow, glancing at the tray. "Something smells good."

"Are you hungry? Would you like to eat something? There's broth and bread and tea. I can help if you like." It was the least she could do, wasn't it? She could at least help the man she had nearly killed. It had nothing at all to do with the way he made her feel.

He gave her one of his smiles. The kind that made his eyes sparkle, and her heart tumble. "If you could prop me up a bit with these pillows, I think I could manage not to drown in the broth."

"Of course." She grabbed one of the thick down pillows and slipped her arm around his shoulders. She tried not to notice the way his black hair curled at his nape as she slipped the pillow behind his shoulders. But it was impossible. Just as it was impossible not to notice the solid shift of muscles against her side when he struggled to push himself into a sitting position.

He leaned back breathing as though he had just climbed a mountain. He frowned as he looked up at her. "I didn't mean to lean against you so heavily."

"It's all right." She brushed the hair back from the bandage wrapped around his brow, the damp strands curling around her fingers. It was a simple gesture. A wifely gesture. One that suddenly seemed far too intimate. She sat back, stunned by her own reaction to this man, the warmth that flared deep inside her.

"I'm certain that in no time at all you will be up and about and as good as new." And headed for the sea, she thought, picking up the spoon and bowl from the tray.

"I'm certain I owe the condition of my health to you."

There was something in his voice, a note that made her wonder if he had suddenly remembered who he was and what had happened. "What do you mean?"

He smiled. "Your gentle care, of course."

"Oh." Emily stirred the broth, peeking at him from the corner of her eye. He certainly wouldn't be smiling at her that way if he knew she had been the one who was responsible for his condition, she assured herself.

When she was satisfied the broth was not too hot, she lifted a spoonful to his lips. He allowed her to feed him as though he were a child, or a man who had been drained of the strength that had always seemed so much a part of him.

Emily fed him the broth, alternating at times with the warm bread and tea, watching him—the rise and fall of his thick black lashes, the shape of his lips as she slid the spoon into his mouth, the dark beard that had grown on his cheeks.

She dipped the spoon into the broth, glancing to where his collar spilled open, exposing the hollow of his neck. No doubt he would feel better if he were bathed, his skin looked so warm, so damp, so very tempting. An image stole into her mind, an image of him as she had seen him so many nights in this bed—his bare shoulders kissed by moonlight, his naked chest rising and falling with each breath.

She imagined what it might be like to draw a soft damp cloth over his skin. She remembered the few times her father had been ill. As she recalled, her mother had always tended him in his every need.

She slipped the spoon between his lips, parting her own as he accepted her offering. Her heart crept upward in her chest until each beat throbbed in her throat when she thought of his shoulders, bare and damp. If they were truly wed, she would bathe the dampness from his skin. If they were truly wed, she would lie beside him and hold him until he fell asleep in her arms. But they were not truly wed.

Regret tightened around her heart when she faced the truth: this was only a role she was playing, an illusion that would soon end. She had to remember to separate truth from the lies.

When the last of the broth was gone, she set the spoon and bowl on the tray and glanced at the man lying in her bed. The man who believed he was indeed her husband.

"Tell me something," he said, smiling up at her.

She pressed a linen napkin to one corner of his lips, dabbing away a drop of broth she had spilled. "What?"

"How did we meet?"

"Oh." She folded the napkin in her lap, thinking of the way she had once imagined meeting the man of her dreams, the story she had invented for the sake of her family, of how she had met Sheridan Blake. "We met at a ball, at my grandmother's town house in London."

He touched her wrist, a warm slide of long fingers across her skin. "And did I ask you to dance?"

"Not exactly." She moistened her lips. "It was a warm night, late in April. I had gone onto the terrace for some air. I was standing by the balustrade looking into the gardens when you stepped up behind me."

"I must have followed you." He brushed his fingers across her wrist.

"I wanted you to follow me." Emily closed her eyes, heat tingling across her breasts. In her mind she conjured up that evening that had occurred only in her dreams, imagining this man in the moonlight. "There was a waltz playing, the only one my grandmother had sanctioned for the evening. You touched my shoulder. And when I turned toward you, you took me in your arms."

"I didn't ask permission?"

She smiled. "No."

He slipped his fingers around her hand and turned it, resting the back of her hand against his thigh. "And you didn't think me overly bold?"

"Yes." She opened her eyes, watching his long, elegant fingers drift across the pale skin of her inner wrist, aware of the heat and strength resting beneath her hand. "I thought you were incredibly bold."

"Were you looking for a bold warrior, Em?" he asked,

and she could hear the smile in his dark voice.

"I suppose I was. When you walked into the ballroom, I thought you were a hawk who had suddenly descended into a covey of doves," she said, recalling the first time she had seen this man, this stranger who could make her blood sing with the simple touch of his fingers upon her wrist. "I thought you were the most attractive man I had ever seen."

He hesitated in his gentle stroking, his sun-darkened fingers resting against the delicate blue veins in her wrist. After a moment that seemed to expand with the breath she held in her lungs, he lifted his hand and touched her face. He rested his fingers below her chin and coaxed her to lift her head.

When she looked into his dark eyes, her breath caught in her throat. There were fires in his eyes, flickering flames in the black depths that both tempted and threatened her.

He brushed his fingertips across her cheek, a soft stroke of warmth. He touched the lobe of her ear, caressed the curve of her neck before slipping his long fingers into her hair, tunneling through the dark red curls, cradling her head. "I must have fallen in love with you when first I looked at you," he said, his voice a husky whisper.

Dear heaven, how she wished that were true. A fantasy lay at her fingertips. A fantasy she had always dreamed would come true. A fantasy she did not dare try to make reality. Did she?

He drew her toward him with a gentle pressure she might have escaped. But she could not escape the longing lingering in his eyes.

He kissed her, a soft slide of his lips against hers, bringing to life all the feelings she had tried so hard to destroy. She returned his kiss, emotion unfurling inside her. Filling her. Warming her. This was all she had ever imagined. This man was all she had ever wanted. This was an illusion. Such a sweet illusion.

She pulled back until she could look into his eyes, his

beautiful dark eyes that were looking at her with such terrible confusion. She stroked his cheek, absorbing the rasp of his beard, fighting the tears in her eyes.

"I think you'd better rest. You've had enough company for the moment." And she'd had far too much of a truth she didn't want to face.

She lifted the tray and escaped the room, but she couldn't escape memory and longing. She had never in her life felt this unsettled. This taut inside, as though every muscle were drawn to the breaking point.

She paused in the hall, her heart pounding so violently the blood swam before her eyes. The man in that bed believed he was her husband. He actually believed he was in love with her. And she was going to send him away. Forever.

She forced air into her tight lungs. She should march right back into that room and tell him the truth. She should end this charade before it got out of hand, before reality and fantasy became so tangled she couldn't tell one from the other.

Her grandmother's words echoed in her head: *That young man has no memory, no thought of who or what he once was. You can shape those memories. You can create a past for him. You can create Sheridan Blake.*

Could she?

Dare she?

Dear heaven, she had a terrible feeling she was about to do something foolish.

Simon turned his head on the pillow, staring into the sunlight, trying to sear away the compelling image that lingered in his brain—Emily looking at him, a wealth of longing and need in her eyes. It was bloody hard to think of duty and country when he looked into her eyes and glimpsed a future just beyond his grasp.

From his bed, Simon stared into the rose garden that stretched out from the back of the house. The flowers formed a colorful carriage wheel with a stone fountain planted in the middle. Water spilled from the urn held by a smiling nymph, sunlight transforming the liquid into glittering crystal. Even from a distance he could hear the splash as the water tumbled into the basin of the fountain. It was a relaxing sound, which he had listened to every night since coming to live here. But it couldn't relax the turmoil inside of him.

It was all a fantasy, he reminded himself. The beautiful lady was playing a game with him. Yet, he had a feeling there was something beyond the threads of deception she was weaving around them. Something that shimmered like the gold in her eyes. A thread of truth she hadn't expected to spin. Or was it simply that he wanted to see some truth in her lies?

He glanced to the door, sensing someone there. Digby was standing just inside the room, looking at him with apprehension in his brown eyes.

"Begging your pardon, sir," Digby said as he approached the bed holding a porcelain pot decorated with red tulips in his rough hands. "I've come to bring you a clean chamber pot."

"Just as I suspected, Digby." Simon smiled at his friend. "We have finally found you an appropriate position. Though I thought that particular duty would be handled by one of the housemaids."

Digby's shoulders sagged as he released his breath. "I was expecting you to have windmills in the head, sir. They told us you had lost your memory."

Simon rubbed his fingertip over the bandage wrapped around his brow. "I'm lucky I didn't lose more than my memory, Digby."

Digby frowned. "By the looks of Beamish, you got a few licks in yourself, sir."

Simon smiled. "A few."

"To hear him tell it, 'The thatch-gallows that set upon me was a true out-and-outer with his fives.' He said the highwayman gave him a facer he won't soon forget." Digby rocked back on his heels, smiling like a father proud of his son's first steps. "And Beamish has milled with Jackson and Belcher, sir."

"Beamish was the least of my troubles."

"Aye." Digby shoved the chamber pot under the bed. "The pretty redhead is the one who laid you low, isn't she?"

"To be fair, I don't think she meant to shoot me. Only deliver me to a press gang."

Digby whistled softly. "That's one devil's daughter, that is. How do you plan to keep her from having you dragged off to sea while you investigate her papa?"

Simon rested his hand over the wound the doctor had carved in his arm, seeking to ease the nagging throb of pain. "I intend to become Sheridan Blake."

Digby's bushy brows lifted to the edge of his white wig. "You mean she actually believes you don't remember who you are?"

At times Simon found himself forgetting who he was. "So it would seem."

"And you think that will do the trick?"

"I think it might keep her off balance for a while. I hope long enough to catch a traitor."

Digby nodded. "I have to admit, sir, I've got a real hope it isn't Mr. Maitland. I've come to like the family. There's not a cross word ever said about any of them below stairs, and that's a true sign of quality."

"I know how you feel. But I can't eliminate the man as a suspect. At least not yet."

"We had a dispatch last night, sir. And it ain't good." Digby drew his lips into a tight line, his bushy brows drawing together over his crooked nose. "Seems there was a traitor in the ministry, one of Lord Pemberton's aides by the name of Hazelitt. The man's been selling information to the enemy. And it's possible our mission was one of the parcels he sold."

Simon released his breath between his teeth. "Did Hazelitt give any clues to the identity of the head of the smuggling operation?"

Digby shook his head. "He swore he knew nothing about the smuggling. And, since he hanged himself soon after he was arrested, it doesn't look like we're going to find out more."

"So we don't know who he is, but the blackguard we're after might know who we are."

"Aye, sir. 'Tis a snake's nest, it is."

"Then we can assume the incident at the warehouse was not an accident."

"Aye, sir, and I think we can also assume the blackguard will try again. I'm thinking we might need to withdraw before you get yourself killed."

Simon frowned. "No."

"But, sir, you don't know what direction he'll be coming from."

"If he comes at me, he might reveal himself."

"And he might well kill you."

"I'll take that chance."

"But, sir—"

"I intend to keep Sheridan Blake alive long enough to catch a traitor." Simon stared into the ivory silk of the canopy over his head, refusing to dwell on the other reasons he might have for wanting to keep Sheridan Blake alive. "Have you been able to discover anything of importance?"

"Well, sir, I got a look into that warehouse." Digby released his breath in a sigh. "And I didn't see any weapons."

"It's too early. From what I was able to learn, Maitland has three customers in Tangier. Two of them have been dealing with the company for years. The third, Mr. Alberto Ramirez, started doing business with Maitland Enterprises five months ago."

"He has to be the one, Napoleon's agent."

Simon nodded. "The next shipment to Ramirez is scheduled for the last week of August."

"It would make sense for the smugglers to wait until close to the shipping date. Less chance of someone getting a look at what is really being shipped."

"I need to get a look at Maitland's private files." Simon drew a deep breath, the scent of roses spilling through the open windows mingling with the delicate fragrance of lavender in the room. "I need to see if there is anything linking him to Ramirez."

"Aye. Let's hope the good man is as innocent as he seems."

"Any progress with your smuggler friend?"

"Not much, sir."

"I need to gain access to that gang." Simon rubbed his fingers over the throbbing in his temple. "Tell him you know a man who is interested in finding a crew who can help him deliver certain items to a customer outside of England. Tell him this is very special cargo. Imply it might be of the explosive type."

Digby stroked his chin. "If they know who you are, they'll kill you as soon as you get within sight of them."

"I'll deal with that when the situation arises."

Digby shook his head. "It be an awful chance you're taking, sir."

"Don't look so worried." Simon smiled in the face of Digby's worried frown. "You'd better go, before someone wonders why you're spending so much time delivering a clean chamber pot."

"Aye, sir." Digby turned to leave.

"And Digby." Simon grinned as the little man turned to face him. "Don't forget to take the old one."

Digby winced. "Aye, sir."

Simon turned his head toward the windows as Digby left the room, his gaze snagged by a young woman in the gardens. Emily sat on a stone bench, staring off into the distance, as though she were waiting for something, or someone.

The breeze ruffled across the rosebushes, setting flowers bobbing, as though paying tribute to the beauty in their midst. That same breeze stirred the dark red curls framing her face and carried the fragrance of roses into the room. He breathed deeply of the fragrant air that had touched her face, feeling his chest tighten with an emotion he didn't try to identify.

He saw the longing in her face as she stared into the sunlight and contemplated dreams. He recognized that longing. Understood it without question. He too had dreams. He looked in the direction of her gaze.

In the distance, gray stones rose, shaping the tower of a Norman castle, the ancient structure crowning the emerald slope of a nearby hill. It was as if it stood in another time and place, separated from this century by a rolling sea of misty green.

He glanced at the table beside the bed, studying the watercolor framed in carved rosewood. It depicted the same castle. And for the first time he noticed the name signed in black at one corner of the canvas: *E. Maitland.*

He turned his head on the pillow, watching Emily, wondering what dreams she had spun around those ancient stones. He should stay clear of the woman. It was far too dangerous to get involved with her. Foolish, really. Yet, he had no choice but to continue this masquerade.

He leaned back against the pillow and closed his eyes, shutting out the image of Emily surrounded by a thousand worshiping roses. Still, he couldn't evade the woman. She haunted his memories. And his dreams.

Chapter Seventeen

There was a full moon, but Simon didn't open the drapes in Hugh Maitland's study. Even though it was well past midnight, he couldn't take the chance of anyone seeing him there. Light from a single taper flickered along the slender wire he slipped into the lock of Maitland's desk. He turned the wire, easing open the mechanism. A soft click echoed in the silence of the room. And beyond the walls of the study he became aware of another sound. Footsteps.

He snuffed the candle between his thumb and forefinger. He held his breath, listening as the footsteps approached the study. It was a woman, her slippered footsteps light on the polished oak parquet lining the hall. The door to the library opened and closed. A few moments later, light glowed beneath the connecting door.

One of the Maitland ladies was making a midnight raid on the library. Phoebe, no doubt. She seldom had her pretty little nose out of a book. At fifteen she lived her adventures between leather-bound covers. He had done the same until he was twelve. Then the adventures had become far too real.

He remained crouched behind Maitland's desk, listening to the soft sounds from the library, feeling like the traitor he had been sent to catch. He was getting too close to these people. He was getting too close to Emily.

In the past week, since the shooting, he had chipped his way through her defenses. Only to find his own defenses breached by the beautiful red-haired tigress. He wanted her. Not just for a moment. But for the rest of his life.

He rested his brow against Hugh Maitland's desk. Men were being lost because of a traitor. The blackguard had to be stopped. Even if it meant tearing this family to shreds. Even if it meant destroying any chance he might have of winning his lady.

Emily wasn't certain what had awakened her. Since the accident, her slumber was never deep, never truly sound. Each night as she slept on the little chaise longue in her room, a part of her remained alert, listening for any signs of distress from the man she had nearly killed.

With each passing day her scoundrel grew stronger. Soon she would have no excuse for not sleeping in the same bed with him. Today he had even spent most of the day out of bed. Playing chess with her. Winning every game. The man might not be able to remember his name, but he certainly remembered strategy. Still, each day Dr. Cheeson had taken great pains to caution her against becoming overly cheerful. In the case of a head wound one never knew if the patient would suffer a relapse.

She glanced toward the bed. Moonlight from a full moon spilled through the open windows, spreading across the bed like cream poured from a pitcher. The covers were tossed aside, revealing a white sheet rumpled from a restless sleeper.

He was gone.

Emily sat up, the counterpane tumbling over the side of the couch. Dr. Cheeson's words pounded in her brain: *Watch him closely. His behavior could be erratic. He could wander off, searching for clues to his identity.*

She came to her feet, her heart pounding with fear. She checked the dressing room. He wasn't there.

What if he had wandered away from the house?

Into the night.

Alone.

She snatched her robe from the arm of the chaise and rushed toward the door, the white muslin of her nightgown flinging out behind her. Where would he go? She stuffed her arms into the sleeves of the robe. Oh, she was going to strangle the scoundrel when she found him.

She swung open the door. She plunged into the hall, plowing into six feet three inches of solid male strength.

"Easy," he said, slipping his arms around her, stepping back with the impact.

Emily turned her cheek against the emerald silk that covered his chest. The dressing gown spilled open, offering her the crisp scent of herbal soap and man. His warmth wrapped around her, easing the chill of fear. She looked up at him. The bandage was gone. His hair was slicked back from his wide brow, revealing the small wound high on the right side. Red, but healing.

Standing like this, in his arms, she perceived a shaking inside her that quivered along her every nerve. A trembling that had nothing to do with her earlier fear. That fear had disappeared, dissolved into this new emotion, this far more frightening feeling.

"Where were you?" She broke free of his light embrace, bumping into the door frame. "Your hair is wet."

"I couldn't sleep." He smiled, his dimple peeking at her from his right cheek. "I thought a long, hot soak would help."

She caught herself staring at his chest where the dressing gown had spilled open. Black curls glistened in the light of the wall sconces. The pale yellow light stroked smooth skin still damp from his bath. Such warm-looking skin. Golden. Tempting.

A Special Offer For
Leisure Romance Readers Only!
Get
FOUR
FREE
Romance
Novels
A $21.96 Value!
Travel to exotic worlds filled with passion
and adventure —without leaving your home!
Plus, you'll save $5.00 every time you buy!

Thrill to the most sensual, adventure-filled Historical Romances on the market today...

FROM LEISURE BOOKS

As a home subscriber to Leisure Romance Book Club, you'll enjoy the best in today's BRAND-NEW Historical Romance fiction. For over twenty-five years, Leisure Books has brought you the award-winning, high-quality authors you know and love to read. Each Leisure Historical Romance will sweep you away to a world of high adventure...and intimate romance. Discover for yourself all the passion and excitement millions of readers thrill to each and every month.

Save $5.00 Each Time You Buy!

Each month, the Leisure Romance Book Club brings you four brand-new titles from Leisure Books, America's foremost publisher of Historical Romances. EACH PACKAGE WILL SAVE YOU $5.00 FROM THE BOOKSTORE PRICE! And you'll never miss a new title with our convenient home delivery service.

Here's how we do it. Each package will carry a FREE 10-DAY EXAMINATION privilege. At the end of that time, if you decide to keep your books, simply pay the low invoice price of $16.96, no shipping or handling charges added. HOME DELIVERY IS ALWAYS FREE. With today's top Historical Romance novels selling for $5.99 and higher, our price SAVES YOU $5.00 with each shipment.

AND YOUR FIRST FOUR-BOOK SHIPMENT IS TOTALLY FREE!

IT'S A BARGAIN YOU CAN'T BEAT! A Super $21.96 Value!

LEISURE BOOKS *A Division of Dorchester Publishing Co., Inc.*

"And your bandage." She sought protection behind a shield of anger. "Dr. Cheeson didn't say it was all right to remove your bandage."

"Dr. Cheeson is too frightened to come close enough to take a look beneath the thing. That's why he has asked you to change it every day."

"You can hardly blame the man for being frightened to come near you." She marched back into the room, seeking distance. But he followed her, as she knew he would. She tilted her head, staring up at him. "You did threaten to slice his throat if he tried to bleed you."

He winked at her. "It did the trick."

"I'm certain you're the most difficult patient the man has ever had." She watched as he closed the door, her legs shaking like aspic. It seemed so intimate, watching a man close a bedroom door. This man. This door. It sparked all manner of thoughts. All of them dangerous. She reached for her anger, clinging to it like a shield. "Did you give a thought as to what I would think when I found you gone?"

He moved toward her, each long stride filled with a predatory grace. "I didn't expect you to awaken."

The warmth of his body radiated through his dressing gown, reaching for her. She hugged her arms to her waist, trying to ignore the shaking inside her. "Dr. Cheeson has said over and over again how dangerous a head wound can be."

"I'm sorry, Em. I didn't mean to frighten you."

She knew he wore nothing beneath his dressing gown. A single veil of emerald silk teased her. It stroked the width of his shoulders. It brushed his chest, his waist, his thighs, shading sleek muscles, hiding dark masculine curls.

She wanted to touch him. She wanted to feel his arms slide around her. She wanted his hands on her skin, his lips touching her, his tongue hot upon her breasts. A pulse flickered in the heart of her feminine flesh.

She looked up at him, trying not to think wicked thoughts. But it was impossible. Not with the moonlight tangling in his damp black hair. Not with flames flickering to life in his midnight eyes. It was impossible not to wonder what it would be like to lie with him in her bed.

"I thought you might have wandered away from the house. I thought you might have . . ." The words tangled in her throat when she thought of harm coming to this man. "You have to take care."

"You mustn't worry about me." He lifted a lock of her unbound hair, sliding the dark red strands through his fingers. "I'm fine."

"You are, aren't you?" She touched him. She couldn't help herself. She ran her hand down the length of his arm, from his shoulder to his wrist, sliding along emerald silk warm from his skin, her fingers curling around sleek muscles. "You are truly going to be all right?"

"Truly." He brushed the back of his fingers over the crest of her cheek. "It will take more than this scratch to put me in the grave."

He was well. She should be thinking of sending him away. Forever. She certainly shouldn't be thinking what she was thinking. She shouldn't conceive of slipping that emerald silk from his shoulders. She shouldn't think of stepping into his arms. She shouldn't imagine pressing her body against the heat and strength of his naked flesh.

Sheridan Blake. Alive and in her arms.

She shouldn't try to make dreams come true. Yet she was already reaching for the belt cinched around his lean waist. She could no longer hide from this man or the desire he ignited inside her. She could no longer ignore the longing that simmered like embers deep in her flesh and burst into flames each time he touched her. She could no longer deny the emotion that had taunted her with each passing day.

She loved this man. She loved him by any name. Beyond dreams. Beyond reason. Beyond hope for redemption.

He drew in his breath, holding it deep in his chest as she unfastened the belt. She let it fall. The emerald silk parted, teasing her with a glimpse of smooth skin and dark curls.

There was time to stop this. Time to return to her life. But, dear heaven, she didn't want to turn back to that life. She wanted this man. Now and forever.

"Sheridan," she whispered, sliding her fingers over the face of the dragon emblazoned on the dressing gown. His muscles tensed beneath her touch. Every muscle was rigid, as though he were poised for battle in a war his mind could not remember, but his body could.

She smiled as she slipped her hands inside his dressing gown. There would be no battle tonight. Tonight the war ended. Tonight a lady surrendered to her bold warrior. Tonight she would claim a dream.

She slid her hands upward, across his chest, absorbing the feel of crisp curls, the heat of smooth skin, peeling the emerald silk from his shoulders. The dressing gown fell in a soft whisper, spilling in a dark pool on the carpet at his feet.

Pale light stroked the curve of his shoulder, tangled in the curls on his chest, and streamed lower.

Emily hesitated a moment before she lowered her eyes, looking to where moonlight etched potent masculinity from the shadows. Moonlight transformed flesh to marble. He stood before her, a magnificent sculpture crafted by a master. She was breathless, staring at him, awed by his dark masculine beauty.

"Emily," he whispered, his voice taut as though he were straining against invisible bonds.

"I've been waiting for you all my life," she said. She touched him, a tentative brush of her fingers across the tip of his arousal. The powerful organ bobbed in response, a sculpture coming to life at her touch. She reached for him, mesmerized by the bold masculine flesh.

"Emily." He grabbed her wrist, pulling her hand away when she would have held him. "Don't."

The harsh sound of his voice shaped that single command into a finely honed blade of rejection. She looked up at him, her eyes full of hurt and confusion. "What is it? Have I done something wrong?"

He squeezed her wrist, his features a taut mask of pain.

She stared up at him. All of the doubts she had ever harbored about herself crept from the shadows within her. "You don't want me."

"Emily, I—"

"It's all right." She tugged free of his grasp, stumbling back, hitting a post at the foot of the bed. She turned away from him. She gripped the carved mahogany bedpost, fighting the urge to curl up and cry.

What was wrong with her? Dear heaven, what was wrong with her? Even this man, the man who thought he was her husband, even he didn't want her.

"Emily." He rested his hand on her shoulder. "Please don't cry."

"I'm not crying." Emily gripped the bedpost, fighting against the humiliating tears burning her eyes. She sniffed, her shoulders trembling. Tears spilled in hot streams down her cheeks.

"God, I didn't mean to make you cry." He slid his arms around her waist, pressing against her. "I want you, Em. I want you so much I ache."

She could feel the hard thrust of his arousal against her lower back. It was proof of his desire. Wasn't it? "Did I do something wrong?"

"Nothing." He pulled aside her hair, dropping the heavy mass of curls over her shoulder.

"You don't want me to touch you?" Emily wiped her tears with her fingertips. "Is that it?"

"No." He pressed his lips to her neck, breathing against her skin. "I want your touch. The brush of your fingers. Your lips. Your skin. Everywhere."

Emily gripped the bedpost as he slid his hands upward along her ribs, the heat of his palms seeping through sapphire satin and white muslin, bathing her skin. She held her breath as he crept upward slowly, inching closer and closer to her breasts. He slid his hands under the plump curves, his long fingers gliding over the tips, setting fire to a fuse that sizzled and sparked to the very core of her.

She moaned low in her throat. "I need . . ." She hesitated, unsure of herself.

"I know, my love." He tugged the pale blue ribbon at the top of her nightgown. He slipped his fingers inside the round neckline, loosening the gathers, sliding the gown and robe from her shoulders. "I need you too."

Emily sighed, releasing her tight grip on the bedpost, allowing him to slide the gown and robe down her arms. White muslin brushed her breasts, her belly, her thighs, her skin tingling, every nerve coming alive. Muslin and satin pooled at her feet, leaving her bare in the moonlight. She shivered in the warmth of his body, feeling deliciously wicked standing like this, naked and aroused with his hands on her heated skin.

He slid one arm around her, holding her close. "Beautiful, so very beautiful," he whispered, sliding his hand over the curve of her hip, spreading his long fingers, massaging gently.

She leaned back against him, reaching for him, sliding her hands against his thighs, crisp curls tingling her palms. "I've dreamed of this moment."

"You've bewitched me," he whispered, rocking his hips forward. "You fill my dreams, my every waking thought."

Emily moaned at the feel of his hardened flesh sliding between her thighs.

"God, you're so wet." He slid his arousal against her, easing across damp feminine petals. "Soft and wet and hot. I imagined you would feel like this."

She smiled, his husky words filling her with a wondrous sense of power. "There is nothing soft about you."

"Because of you." He pressed his lips to her neck, opened his mouth, touched her with the tip of his tongue.

Her breath escaped in a long shudder at the scorching touch. Instinct drove her, and she arched back into him, sliding intimately against his hard staff. Sensation flared, a sudden burst of sparks that shimmered through her at the touch of his flesh sliding against some mysterious point low on her body. "Oh my goodness!"

"Yes." He smiled against her neck. "It is good."

She curled her fingers against his thighs, needing something. Not knowing how to express her desire. Not in words. But he knew. He understood. As though he could look into her mind, unravel secrets that even she did not know existed.

He slid his hand down her belly, his fingers sinking into feminine curls, searching beneath, sliding against her weeping flesh, finding the place where pleasure dwelled, locked like a captured bird trapped deep within her. He stroked her there, cupping her breast in his other hand, squeezing her nipple as he unlocked the chains.

Emily clenched her fingers against his thighs. He pressed his lips to her neck, stroking her low, teasing her breasts with his fingertips. Pleasure surged within her, fluttering, rising. She shuddered in his arms. She clutched his thighs, soft sobs of pleasure slipping from her lips as sensation soared.

He lifted her in his arms. She trembled in his embrace. She clung to him, throwing her arms around his shoulders, pressing her face to his neck, breathing in the musky scent of his warm, damp skin.

"Easy, love," he whispered as he carried her to the bed.

Cool white linen touched her back, absorbing the dampness from her skin. Her hair spilled across the pillow. She gazed up at him. Moonlight tangled in his thick black lashes, stroked the sharply etched features of his face. He was smiling, his eyes filled with a warmth that rivaled the heat of his body as he covered her.

"I never thought I could feel this way." He brushed his lips against hers. "I never imagined I would hold a dream in my arms."

She trembled at the passion in his dark voice. She tightened her arms around him, holding him close, dark curls teasing her breasts and the inside of her thighs where they cradled his thighs. The heat of his skin radiated like the sun against her. She lifted into him, needing more than the brush of his skin. "Make love to me."

"I want nothing more than to make love to you. But we must not rush." He lowered his head, brushing his lips against her breast, making her writhe and moan beneath him. "It's like our first time together, isn't it?"

Emily nodded, her voice trapped by desire.

"And the first time should be slow and easy." He flicked the tip of his tongue over her nipple, dragging a low moan from her lips. "We'll make a memory here tonight. I want it to be one we will cherish."

Memories to cherish. Emily closed her eyes, tears stinging her eyes. Tears for the man who held her, the man whose memory she had destroyed.

"I want to taste you. All of you." He flowed down her body, kissing her, flicking his tongue against her as though she were the most exotic spice in the world.

She was stealing this moment. Stealing his love. It was all an illusion with one exception: the feelings she had for him. "I love you," she whispered.

He sighed at her soft words, his breath streaming warm and moist against her belly. "I love you," he whispered.

If only it were true. She held a fantasy in her arms. Yet, fantasy had blended with the reality of his hands on her skin, of his mouth hot against her belly, kissing her, nipping her, swirling his tongue lower and lower, until . . .

She clenched the sheet in her hands. Dear heaven! Never in her wildest dreams had she imagined this intimate kiss, this absolutely delicious caress of lips and tongue.

She arched against him. Her dreams could not compare to this man, to this moment and the magic he conjured inside her. She lifted her hips, offering him all she possessed, receiving so much more in return. Soft sobs spilled from her lips as the pleasure ripped through her, so intense she thought she might die.

He surged above her, holding her, absorbing her shivers. He pressed against her moist entrance. The tip of his aroused flesh slid inside her. "Tell me you love me."

She stared up into his midnight eyes, seeing his need, so very much like her own. "I love you."

He closed his eyes as if on a silent prayer. "Say it again."

She smiled, relieved to give him at least this small measure of honesty. "I love you."

He slid his fingers over her damp feminine curls, finding the taut bud where sensation flared. "Tell me as I come into you."

"I love you." She arched as his arousal slid deeper inside her. For a fleeting moment she wondered what he would say if he realized she was untouched. How could she explain that his *wife* was still a virgin? Yet she couldn't stop. Not now. "I love you," she whispered, coaxing him deeper. "I love you."

"My own beautiful tigress." He eased his way inside her, as though he realized she had never before felt the slow stretch of a man's body filling her. He kissed her, opening his mouth over hers, dipping his tongue into her, retreating, plunging, in a hypnotic rhythm that mirrored the thrust and withdrawal of his sex within her.

He stroked her with his fingers, banking the fires that shimmered inside her. She clutched at his shoulders, arching her hips as he rocked forward, filling her. Pain flickered as he plunged past her maiden barrier, a spark that flared before succumbing to the flames of pleasure pulsing within her.

Such sweet pleasure. A part of her knew it could never be like this with another man. This was what she had waited for all her life. This man was the missing part of her soul. A dream shaped into living flesh and blood.

She moved with him, countering each thrust of his body,

holding him, kissing him, sensing the rising flames of pleasure inside him. He lifted his head, looking down at her, fires leaping in the depths of his beautiful eyes. She saw his pleasure, a mirror of her own. And the pleasure grew, filling her, expanding inside her, until she could not contain it, until she was shuddering, clinging to him, taking him with her in this wondrous release.

"Emily!" He thrust once, holding her tight against him as he spilled his very essence into her.

She held him with her arms and legs, her face pressed against his neck, her every breath filled with the tang of his skin. He eased in her embrace, his heart pounding hard and fast against her, each beat an echo of the pulse pounding in her ears. She slid her hand down his back, gliding her fingers along the deep valley between sleek muscles, his skin hot and moist beneath her touch.

Perhaps she was stealing this moment. But he didn't seem to mind. Not in the least. And for now, she wouldn't consider the possibility that one day he would remember who and what he was. For now, she wouldn't think of the consequences she might face.

She touched his neck with the tip of her tongue, tasting the salt of his skin. He was real. He was here in her arms. And it was all that mattered.

He stirred in her arms, raising himself onto his forearms, looking down into her eyes. There were doubts in his eyes, confusion in the endless depths. She held her breath, wondering if he would question her now, demand to know why she had never before taken his body into her own.

"I love you, Em." He brushed the damp waves back from her cheek. "Promise me you will never doubt my love. No matter what happens."

There was an edge in his voice, a subtle note of desperation, an icy current curling within the warmth they had forged together. She sensed it had nothing to do with curiosity about her virginity.

He rested his hand against her cheek. "Promise me you

will never doubt my love for you."

It was the confusion of his memory, she thought. That was all, the only reason for the desperation she saw in his dark eyes.

"Promise me," he whispered, his fingers curving against her cheek. "Promise you will always remember this moment, and know how much I love you."

His words slid around her like an icy wind, bringing with it a sense of impending disaster. "It's only your confused memory that has you so tense, my love."

A muscle flickered in his cheek as he clenched his jaw. "Promise me."

She swallowed hard, forcing back the tight knot of fear in her throat. "I promise."

"I've been searching for you all my life." He drew in his breath. "I never want to lose you."

"You aren't going to lose me." She refused to think of what would happen if his memory returned. She slid her fingers through the black hair curling at his nape, feeling desperate suddenly, frightened of losing him. "Hold me, my love."

He held her close, burying his face against her neck. She clung to him, feeling his muscles grow tense, his body harden against her.

"I want you." He turned his head, kissing her as he brushed his fingers across her breast, his touch a breeze whispered across the smoldering embers of desire. "I can't get enough of you."

"Take all you want." She slid her hand down his back, searching for his warmth to chase away her fear. "Love me."

"As long as I live," he whispered, sealing his vow with a slow slide of his body into hers.

Moonlight streamed across the bed, tangling in the dark red curls spilled across his chest. He brushed his fingers over Emily's skin where the moonlight kissed her pale cheek. She stirred in her slumber, rubbing her cheek against his shoulder, her sigh warming his skin. She snuggled close against him, her arm slung over his waist, her thigh nestled over his loins, as though she were afraid he might slip away from her in the night.

He had dreamed of holding her like this. Only in his dreams there were no lies between them. In his dreams no deceptions threatened to rip them apart. In his dreams she loved him for who he was, not for who she wished he might be.

"I don't want to lose you," he whispered, pressing his lips to her brow. Still, he knew these moments with her might be the only ones they would ever share.

A future could not be built on lies. And he could not give her the truth. He could not tell her he had crept out of their bedroom this night to explore her father's study. He could not tell her he had examined her father's papers, searching for signs of treason. And he could not tell her what he had found.

He drew in his breath, trying to ease the tightening in his chest. He had come here looking for a traitor. He had found the woman he wanted for the rest of his life. And he knew in his heart, he would lose her.

Chapter Eighteen

"Are you feeling all right, sir?" Digby dropped an armful of towels on a marble bench near the hot water pool. "You're looking a bit done in."

Simon leaned back against the side of the pool, hot water lapping at his chest. "I'm tired, that's all. Were you able to meet with your smuggler friend last night?"

"Aye, sir. I told him about this man I know who wants to be doing business with his captain." Digby shucked off his coat, dropping the heavy blue wool over the bench. "He tried to hide his interest, but I could see his eyes sparkle at the mention of easy gold. He said he would ask around, see if there was any smugglers interested in a new customer."

"Good work." Simon rolled his shoulders, trying to ease the kinks from his muscles. "Now all we have to do is wait until he takes the bait."

"I'm only hoping you aren't the one reeled in."

Simon smiled. "I can take care of myself, Digby."

"Aye, sir. I've no doubt you can in a fair fight. Still,

they might know what you're about. They might kill you before you have a chance to defend yourself."

"I appreciate your concern, Digby. And I can assure you, I shall take care."

"Aye, sir." Digby wiped the back of his hand across his brow. "Were you able to get a look at Mr. Maitland's private files last night?"

Simon curled his hands into fists against his thighs. "Yes."

Digby frowned, thick brows tugging together over his crooked nose as he peered through the steam at Simon. "You found something?"

Simon stared through the steam to the skylight above. "I found letters from Ramirez. It seems Mr. Ramirez is most satisfied with the quality of Maitland sugar."

"Do you think this could be a different Ramirez?"

"Both of them residing in Tangier? Both of them dealing with Maitland Enterprises?"

Digby removed his white wig and slowly rubbed his hand back across his damp hair. "It don't look good."

Simon took a deep breath of the steamy air. "No."

"I can't think of any reason why Maitland would have letters from one of Napoleon's agents."

Steam collected against the arched ceiling, falling like tears into the pool. "Someone could be trying to cover his own trail."

"Did you find anything else?"

Simon stared up through the steam, considering the other letters he had found in Maitland's desk, letters from Randolph St. James concerning lead mines in Dartmoor. Apparently ten months ago Maitland had withdrawn his support from the venture, causing its failure, according to Randolph. It was typical of Simon's father to point the finger of blame. Even more typical of him to react with anger. Anger was a vengeful man's most powerful ally.

Although Simon found the connection ironic, it certainly wasn't surprising for his father to be involved with Hugh

Maitland. Both men prided themselves on creating financial empires. Simon only hoped Maitland hadn't turned to smuggling to expand his own. "I didn't find anything else of significance."

"Still, the letters combined with everything else we know make a strong case against Mr. Maitland." Digby sighed, his breath stirring the steam into eddies around his face. "What are you going to do?"

Simon wasn't willing to convict Hugh Maitland. Not yet. Not until he had exhausted every possible chance to prove the man innocent. "I'm going to return to Maitland Enterprises tomorrow. I want to see if I can find more evidence."

"I have to say, I'm hoping you find something to prove Maitland innocent. Even if he looks guilty as the devil right now."

"So do I, Digby." Simon closed his eyes as Digby left the pool chamber. He rubbed the taut muscles in his shoulders, trying to ease the tension that had been building for days. Maitland had to be innocent. Simon could well imagine the devastation that would be wreaked upon this family if Maitland were sentenced to death as a traitor. He could imagine the hatred he would see in Emily's eyes when she realized he was the man who had delivered her father into the hands of the executioner. Dear God, Maitland had to be innocent.

The door leading to the passageway opened and closed. Someone locked the door. The slide of the metal bolt echoed in the cavernous chamber. Even before he opened his eyes, Simon knew who he would see. He sensed her presence. Still, he wasn't prepared for the swift tide of desire that swept over him when he looked at Emily.

She stood in the arched entrance to the hot pool chamber, watching him. Steam rose between them, a shifting barrier he knew she would penetrate. The way she had penetrated his defenses.

She dropped her blue satin robe on a marble bench near the entrance and moved toward him. Steam swirled around her, spinning the white muslin of her nightgown into a transparent veil. It hugged the lush curves of her breasts. He could see the shape of her nipples—round and pink and drawn up into tight little buds. And lower, damp white muslin clung to her thighs, outlining the shadow of feminine curls. Blood pumped hard and fast into his loins.

She paused beside the pool, smiling at him, all the warmth of summer shining in her eyes. "Once again I awaken only to find you gone."

"I needed a bath."

Sunlight spilled through the skylight above her, shimmering in the rising mist. He had the strangest sensation looking up at her. It was as though she came to him from another time and place. A goddess of light and warmth come to bewitch a mortal male.

She tugged the satin ribbon at the top of her gown. "I suppose you don't remember this, but you like company when you bathe."

"Do I?" White muslin spilled open, revealing the tempting valley between her breasts. "Anyone in particular?"

"You tell me." With the slow grace of a cat stretching in the sunlight, Emily peeled the damp white cloth downward until it dissolved into a pool at her feet.

Steam curled upward along her long legs, phantom arms reaching for heaven. His breath thickened in his lungs.

"So tell me." She smiled, teasing him, a budding temptress testing her power. "Who would you like to join you?"

He shouldn't allow this. Not when he knew that one day he might well betray her. Yet, he could no more ask her to leave than he could deny the next beat of his heart. He lifted his hand toward her, water trailing from his arm. "Only you."

She sighed as though her breath had been suspended, awaiting his response. She stepped into the pool, descending wide white marble steps, swinging her hips provocatively, until the water lapped at the top of her thighs. There she paused, smiling at him, a woman content in exploring the sensual power she held over her man. "And tell me, will you scrub my back?"

"If you wish, my lady, I will bathe every delectable part of you." He brushed his fingertips over the curve of her hip. "With my hands. My lips. My tongue."

"Oh." She slipped on the bottom step. Her feet slid out from under her. She tumbled back, water pluming all around her as she sank like a stone.

Simon flinched as the water splashed into his face. She broke the surface, coughing, flinging water in every direction with her arms. So much for the temptress. He laughed, he couldn't help it.

She pushed wet hair from her face. She frowned, glaring at him through narrowed eyes. "So you think this is amusing, do you?"

He nodded, his deep laughter reverberating against the white marble walls. God, she had the power to make him laugh, the magic to make him feel as though the world were a wonderful place, warm and welcoming. He couldn't remember ever feeling this way before he had met her.

"Oooooh!" She dragged her arm across the surface of the water and sent a wave toward him.

Simon gasped as the heated wave crested over him. He coughed. He blinked the water from his eyes. Her laughter rippled over him, bright and shining as a summer rain.

She stood a few feet away, a beguiling mermaid, water lapping at her breasts, dark red hair clinging to the pale curves, pink nipples peeking at him, tempting him. And lower, through a provocative veil of mist and water, he caught a glimpse of the dark curls crowning her thighs.

He leaned back against the pool. "I'm afraid you've done it now."

"What?"

"There's a dragon living in these waters, my lady. And I'm afraid you've awakened him."

She cocked her head, giving him an impish grin. "Really?"

He nodded. ''At this very moment you're in danger of being devoured. Of course, you could try to negotiate with the beast.''

''Negotiate?'' She moved toward him, long strands of red silk swirling around her. ''What do you suppose this beast would want from me?''

He slipped his hands around her upper arms, his fingers sliding against her wet skin. ''Everything you have to give.''

He yanked her against him. Her startled shriek dissolved into a heated gasp when he pressed his arousal against her belly.

She swallowed hard. ''The dragon certainly seems hungry.''

''Ravenous.'' He slid the tip of his tongue along the curve of her jaw, sliding upward, taking the lobe of her ear gently between his teeth.

Emily gasped, clutching his shoulders. ''There seems only one thing to do.''

Simon circled the delicate shell of her ear with the tip of his tongue. ''What?''

Emily leaned into him as though she were melting in the heated pool. ''Surrender.''

Simon released his breath in a long sigh against her shoulder. He slid his hands down her back, over the curves of her hips, lifting her. She came to him, floating like an angel on a summer breeze.

The sleek skin of her thighs brushed his as she straddled him. She knelt on the shelf, her softness poised above the tip of his hardened flesh. Yet when he tried to thrust upward, his flesh craving the snug feel of her skin closing around him, she lifted herself, teasing him.

She sank her hands into the wet waves at his nape and tipped back his head, smiling as she looked down into his eyes. ''Surrender to me, my beautiful dragon, and I'll keep you well fed for the rest of your days.''

He lifted his hand, touching a pink nipple with the tip

of his finger. She bit her lower lip, but she couldn't halt a whimper. "Do you wish to cage me, my lady?"

"Nay. I wish only to tame the dragon. I want him by my side for all time."

"For all time." Simon closed his eyes, pressing his cheek against the plush softness of her breasts. Fear assailed him, fear such as he had never known, the sharp unyielding fear of losing this woman. God, there had to be a way to stay by her side. Now and always.

She rocked her hips, brushing soft curls against his hard flesh. Simon moaned with the exquisite torture. "What say ye, my powerful dragon? Shall ye be my ally, my protector, my lover for all time?"

"I shall never turn away from you." He looked up into her eyes, praying she would never turn away from him. "My heart, my soul, my body, all I have to give, I give to my lady."

Tears mingled with mist in her eyes. "For all time," she whispered, pressing her lips to his.

"For all time." He slid his arms around her, holding her close as she sank slowly against him, taking him within the sanctuary of her body. Joined with her, feeling the delicious heat of her, he understood the true meaning of heaven on earth. And in that moment he understood hell as well, knew it for the threat lurking in the shadows.

Emily licked at a sticky spot on the tip of her forefinger, cleaning away a lingering trace of sugar and cinnamon from a roll she had eaten for breakfast. She had never before gone on a picnic for breakfast. She glanced at the man lying on the quilt beside her, smiling when she thought of several other things she had never done before last night.

Simon smiled, his dark eyes filled with understanding. "You look like a kitten that has just polished off a dish of cream."

She stretched her arms toward the sky, reaching for the thick white clouds rolling above Ravenwood. She felt like a kitten. All cozy inside. So contented she could purr. "My mother and father met here at Ravenwood."

"They did? This seems a rather unusual place for them to have met."

"I always like to think it was destiny."

"Crafty thing, destiny. Tell me, how did it work to bring them together?"

The edge of the quilt rippled in the cool breeze sweeping across the bailey, white cotton flipping upward, folding over one of the pale yellow tulips her mother had embroidered in the fabric. Emily smoothed the quilt back against the thick grass. "My grandfather Whitcomb once owned Ravenwood and the land where my father's house now stands. The castle had been in his family since it was built. In fact, one of my grandfather's titles was Baron of Ravenwood."

"So your mother is a descendant of the first Lord and Lady Ravenwood."

"Yes." She stared up at the castle keep. The sun peeked out from the clouds overhead, streaking golden light across gray stones, touching the castle as it had for the past four hundred years.

In the misty sunlight she could almost see Lord Ravenwood's banners perched high on the towers, whipping in the wind. In this place of ancient footsteps, she could almost hear the people—talking, laughing, going about the business of life. In her lifetime, she had always hoped to share this magical place with one special man. And now he was here.

"When he was young, my grandfather Whitcomb had a passion for gambling. To cover his vowels, he sold Ravenwood and the land to my grandfather Maitland when my father was still a child."

Simon plucked a long blade of grass and began twisting it around his forefinger. "Did it cure of him of gambling fever?"

"My grandmother said he never again placed a wager

on anything. But he always resented my grandfather Maitland for buying Ravenwood, even though it was Grandfather Whitcomb's fault it left the family. I believe it was one of the reasons he was so set against Mother's marriage to Father.''

Simon's eyes sparkled with his smile. ''But destiny had brought them together.''

''And destiny would not be denied.'' Emily looked up at the ancient stones. ''My mother lived with her family in Castleleigh Park just outside Bath. She had come to explore Ravenwood one day when my father was here. They were attracted to one another, and agreed to meet another day. That one day turned into another, and another. After three weeks of meeting here, my father took my mother into the chapel inside the keep and asked her to marry him.''

''Now Ravenwood is once again in the hands of an ancestor.''

''You see, it was destiny.'' She turned toward him, smiling with the sheer joy of being near him. ''And it wasn't the first time lovers met their destiny at Ravenwood.''

The breeze ruffled his hair, flinging an ebony wave over his brow. ''When did destiny first touch Ravenwood?''

''The first Lord Ravenwood kidnapped his lady on the day she was to be married to another man. The lady had been betrothed to Ravenwood when they were both children, but over the years her father had changed his mind, seeking what he thought might be a stronger alliance.''

''Ravenwood was simply a man doing what needed to be done.'' Simon drew the tip of his finger down her arm, from the edge of her short dark gold sleeve to the delicate bone of her wrist. That soft touch sent an army of tingles skittering along her every nerve. ''But I wonder what the lady thought of being a pawn?''

''According to the story, she was furious at first. She thought Ravenwood a scoundrel for kidnapping her.''

Simon lowered his eyes to where he held her wrist. Emily looked at him, fascinated by every detail of his face.

The thick black lashes at the corners of his eyes. The fine straight line of his nose. The secret place in his cheek where an intriguing dimple lay hidden, awaiting his smile. Strange, to look upon a man and think him beautiful.

He stroked his thumb over her wrist. "Tell me, did the lady change her mind about Lord Ravenwood?"

"Yes." Emily stared down at his long, sun-darkened fingers curving around her pale wrist. In spite of the warmth of the day and the heat of his hand, she shivered, wondering what might happen should he ever regain his memory.

"When her father came, she refused to leave her lover. They say she stood on the highest wall of the keep and threatened to jump to her death if her father didn't withdraw his army. No one, not even Lord Ravenwood, could dissuade her from her intent. There is a cross etched into a stone in the wall, near one of the towers. It's said that is where she stood."

He tightened his fingers around her wrist. "Did she jump?"

"No. Her father withdrew and acknowledged her marriage to her scoundrel."

He lifted her hand and pressed his lips against her wrist, releasing his breath in a heated stream against her skin. "You have her spirit, my lady."

"I understand her. I know why she would defy an army to stay at her beloved's side."

"I hope you always retain that spirit, my lady." Simon turned her hand over, staring down at the lines on her palm as though he were looking for her future.

She touched his cheek, sensing his sudden sadness. "Is anything wrong?"

He looked up at her, his smile lighting the shadows in his eyes. "I was simply thinking how very much I love you."

"I like that kind of thinking." She leaned forward and dropped a quick kiss on his cheek. "Come with me. I want to show you Lady Ravenwood's stone."

He glanced up at the tall castle walls. "That's at the top of the castle?"

"That's right." She got to her feet anxious to share Ravenwood with him. "When you pass through the entrance of Ravenwood, it's like stepping back in time."

He stared at the castle walls. "Yes, I can imagine it is."

"Come with me. You'll love the view from the top." She lifted her skirts and ran toward the entrance to the keep.

The door had long ago disappeared. Yet most of Ravenwood survived. The air was cool within the thick stone walls, even though no roof sheltered this place. Her half boots tapped against the stone floor as Emily walked into the center of what had been the great hall.

Only the rooms built into the corners of the castle keep, those fashioned with stone floors, remained intact. Thick beams projected from the walls above her, marking two floors that had once existed. Black streaks etched the stones above each hearth, all that remained of fires that had died long ago. Yet she could imagine Ravenwood in all its former glory.

Although his footsteps were silent upon the stones, she sensed him enter behind her. He approached as silently as a phantom. He paused, so close she could feel the warmth of his body against her back.

"There is something magical about this place," she whispered. "Can you feel it?"

"Yes. You can almost see them, Ravenwood and his lady sitting at the far end of the room on a raised platform. Acrobats, jugglers, jesters entertaining the guests at long tables below them."

She leaned back against him, smiling as he slipped his arms around her. She closed her eyes, allowing the magic to sweep her back in time. She could hear the voices lifted in conversation and laughter. She could smell the bread, the mead, the roasted meat of the feast. "At times I wonder if it is possible we once lived in another time and place. From the very first moment I saw Ravenwood, I felt I had come home."

He rested his cheek against her hair. "I had that feeling the first moment I saw you."

She tilted her head and looked up at him. "Perhaps we once knew each other, in another time, another place. Perhaps that's why I felt drawn to you when I didn't even know your name."

A frown touched his face like a shadow, so fleet she nearly missed it.

"What is it?" She turned in his arms, resting her hands against his chest. "What's wrong?"

"Nothing."

She touched his cheek, absorbing the warmth of him, hoping it might chase away the icy doubts within her. The chill of reality. The painful knowledge that he was only an illusion she had created. "You were thinking about all the memories you've lost, weren't you?"

"Let's not talk about it." He kissed the tip of her nose. "Not today."

She smiled, in spite of the cold specter lurking just beyond the light of her happiness. "We shall simply have to make new memories to replace all the old ones."

He wiggled his eyebrows at her. "The ones we've made so far have been most enjoyable."

She laughed, the bright sound echoing on the stone walls, wrapping around them as she stepped back and took his hands in hers. "Explore the past with me. Let me show you the stone at the top of the castle."

He frowned. "At the top of the castle."

She tugged on his hands. "They say that to those who love with purity of heart, a wish will be granted upon touching Lady Ravenwood's stone."

"Do they?" He walked with her to a stone stairway winding up through one corner of the keep. There he paused, holding her hand, anchoring her to the ground floor.

She turned and looked up at him. "I know it looks like a bit of a squeeze, especially for a man your size, but I'm certain you'll have no trouble at all getting to the top."

He moistened his lips. "Lead the way, my lady."

Chapter Nineteen

Simon stared at Emily's back, following her up through the narrow stairway. Each step was a wedge carved from stone. Each step lifted him toward the top of the castle. Three stories high. Anxiety squirmed low in his belly, an old serpent awakening once again. He despised the weakness within him. Despised even more the memories that lingered, lifting ugly heads—Medusa captured in a thousand mirrors.

He stared at Emily, watching her dark red curls sway against the soft golden muslin of her gown. He thought of her smile, her joy, hoping to anchor himself here to this time and place. Yet memories wrapped around him, dragging him into a dark pit where demons from his past lurked like vipers.

Blood pounded in his temples. He was eight years old again, a child who had broken a vase. By accident. Dear Lord, it had been an accident. And the other times, what terrible crimes had he committed? The details of his youthful mistakes had faded with time. Yet, the years had not dimmed the punishment. Even now he could feel them, sweaty hands gripping his ankles. He could hear his father's voice, commanding the footmen.

Throw the little bastard over the side!

And they had, thrusting him over the balustrade on the second floor, holding him out above the white and black marble squares lining the hall below, sweaty hands slipping on his ankles. It was always the same. Each time Simon pleaded, the blood pounding in his head until he thought it would explode. Each time his father stared at him, smiling, gray eyes filled with all the hatred in Simon's young world. His father had wanted those sweaty hands to slip. He had wanted to see his son broken on the marble below.

In time Simon had come to understand his crime. It was simple enough. It was his blood. His flesh. For even though he was his father's son, it had never been enough to cleanse him of his mother's guilt.

Simon paused at the top of the winding stone stairs. Wind swept across the crenellated walls, licking at the moisture beading on his face. He was shaking, fear spiraling outward through his arms and legs. He wanted to turn, to sink back down those stairs away from the dizzying height, away from the memories.

Emily's gown whipped out behind her, dark golden muslin flapping like a sail as she walked along the narrow stone rampart walkway wrapping around the inside walls of the keep. She paused and gazed down at a stone in the wall. "Here it is. Lady Ravenwood's stone."

Simon squeezed his hands into tight fists. He was no longer that frightened little boy. He refused to allow his father to control him. Yet, he couldn't quell the anxiety in his stomach. He glanced over the edge of the walkway where the roof had once covered the heart of the castle keep at Ravenwood. His palms grew slick with sweat as he stared at the stone floor three stories below.

"Come," Emily said, offering him her hand. "Let's make a wish."

Simon drew in his breath, trying to ease the steel band wrapped around his lungs. He stepped away from the relative safety of the stairway, fighting to ignore the gaping hole where the roof of the keep had once been. He gripped her hand. Too tightly. She frowned, and he realized she could feel the dampness of his palm.

"What should we wish for?" he asked, hoping to divert that concerned look in her eyes.

"Are you all right? Is your wound troubling you?"

He forced his lips into a smile, trying to disguise the humiliating weakness within. "I'm fine."

She stared at him a moment, understanding dawning in her eyes. "I didn't realize you would remember your fear of heights."

He stiffened. "It's not a fear exactly."

The sun peeked through the clouds, capturing Emily in a shaft of golden light, illuminating her frown. "What is it, exactly?"

"It seems as though"—he glanced past her, staring at the stones shaping the wall—"heights make me dizzy."

"Why in the world did you come up here?"

"I don't believe in being a prisoner to my defects."

"I see." She gripped his hand. "Let's go down."

Simon shook his head. "The only way to defeat your demons is to face them."

"Are you certain?"

"We came up here to make a wish."

She smiled, pride in him shimmering in her eyes. "Let's each make a silent wish."

"You want to keep yours a secret?"

She glanced down to their clasped hands. "Only until the day it comes true."

Simon had abandoned his belief in wishes a long time ago. Yet, looking at her, he found he desperately wanted to believe in wishes and dreams and hopes that wouldn't turn to dust.

"When our wishes come true, then we'll share our secrets with each other."

"All right." Simon lowered their clasped hands to the cross etched deep in the stone. The gray stone was warm to the touch, oddly so, as though it had sat for hours in bright sunlight. Yet the day was cloudy.

He watched as Emily closed her eyes, wondering what wish she would make. She squeezed his hand, her face solemn, her body rigid, as though her very life depended on the wish she made on the lady's stone.

Simon stared at their clasped hands. His stomach churned with a sick feeling that had nothing to do with the dizzying height and everything to do with the lady he might one day lose.

Emily stood beside the fireplace in her grandmother's sitting room. She stared down at the blackened bricks beneath the polished brass andirons, doubts shadowing her joy. "This morning when we were at Ravenwood, he remembered his fear of heights."

"He is frightened of heights?" Harriet's voice betrayed her surprise. "My goodness, I never would have suspected such a thing. Why, the young man didn't hesitate to climb that tree to rescue you."

Emily frowned as she looked at her grandmother. "How he deals with the fear isn't the point."

"What is the point?"

"I wonder if his memory is all going to come back one day."

Harriet considered this a moment, her expression growing serious. "I think you must face the fact that he very well might regain his memory."

Emily squeezed her hands into fists at her sides. "What shall I do if he remembers who he is?"

"Emily, he is the same young man whether he remembers his name or not."

"How can you say that? Right now he believes he is in love with me."

"Perhaps because he is in love with you."

"No." Emily sank to the pale yellow chaise longue beside her grandmother. "It's all an illusion. And it could vanish with a snap of his fingers."

"Poppycock! I don't believe it for a moment." Harriet slipped her arm around Emily's shoulders and held her close. "My darling girl, don't tell me you haven't felt the spark that glows between you and that virile young buck."

Emily rested her head on her grandmother's shoulder. "I love him, grandmama. I love him so much I ache."

"And do you believe you shall love him less if he remembers his name?"

"No." Emily stared at the afternoon sunlight streaking across the gold and ivory urns stitched into the carpet. "But he might have other thoughts. Especially if he remembers I'm the one who shot him."

Harriet squeezed Emily's shoulder. "Yes, well, I'm certain he will understand that was only an accident."

"I wish I had your certainty."

Harriet smoothed the curls back from Emily's cheek. "I truly believe time will prove that the love you share with that young man is strong enough to weather the most violent storm."

"I hope you're right." Emily wasn't certain how she would survive if she lost the illusion of his love.

Simon never truly surrendered to the depths of slumber. Instincts honed by years of war, by an eternity filled with false identities and concealed danger, remained alert even when he slept. He sensed the moment Emily slipped quietly from their bed. It was more than the soft shifting of the mattress beneath him as it surrendered her weight. It was more than a sound. It was the loss of her warmth.

Without moving, he watched as she slipped into her robe, veiling the beauty of her naked body. She lifted her hair, freeing the heavy curls from the robe, her breasts swaying softly beneath blue satin. She walked toward one of the windows as though drawn to the moonlight. His body warmed with memory as he watched her.

It had been only a few hours since he had held her, since he had plunged into the heated core of her, since she had taken him with her to the far side of heaven. Their lovemaking had been wild, explosive, edged with the silent desperation of lovers who shared the same fear—the fear of losing all they had found in each other's arms.

Without words, he knew she was frightened that he might remember who and what he was. And he wished he could share the truth with her. If only he weren't certain it would bring even greater disaster.

She stared at a point in the distance. He knew what she saw. A Norman castle rising like a ghost in the moonlight, a place filled with romance, legend, and wishes. She looked like a child lost and longing for home, yearning for a place to keep all her dreams safe and sound. And he wished deep in his heart to give her that home. If only fate would grant him the honor of living the rest of his days with her.

"Emily."

She jumped at his soft whisper. "I'm sorry," she said, pressing her hand to her heart. "I didn't mean to awaken you."

"I don't mind. I like the way you look in the moonlight, like a fairy princess."

She smiled, a pale blush rising in her cheeks. "I was just thinking of this morning and how you remembered you didn't like heights. Have you remembered anything else?"

His chest tightened with the longing to sweep away the lies between them. "I remember I love you. That's enough for me."

She moved toward him, her robe flowing around her long legs. "I hope you always remember that. No matter what other memories come back, I hope you always remember this love we share."

He folded back the sheet and blanket, providing a space for her beside him. She slipped the robe from her shoulders, sapphire-blue satin falling in a whisper to her feet. She stood beside the bed, moonlight spilling across her skin, caressing each soft curve. She stared down at him, the heat of her gaze like sunlight on his skin, seeping into his blood.

"Come lie beside me," he said, stroking his hand across the linen sheet. He needed some affirmation that they had a future together. And for now, that affirmation could come only in the physical joining of his body with hers.

She stretched out beside him, so close the warmth of her flesh brushed his skin. "I used to dream of lying beside you like this," she said, brushing her palm over the curve of his naked hip.

"Dreams could never compare to the reality of you, my lady." He reached for her, curving his fingers around her arm.

"Not yet," she whispered, breaking free of his gentle grasp. She came to her knees beside him, her hair spilling around her shoulders, covering her breasts. She stared down at him like a tigress eyeing her prey. "It's my turn to learn every inch of you, my beautiful dragon."

Simon's breath caught in his chest. She pushed against his shoulder. He fell back, surrendering without a fight.

She smiled, triumph glittering in her eyes. Her hair tumbled across his chest as she leaned over him, silky strands brushing his skin. Her breasts grazed his chest, taut little nipples teasing him. He growled deep in his throat as she brushed her warm hands over his shoulders and down his chest.

"Was that a purr, my dragon?"

He grinned up at her. "The closest a dragon can come to a purr, my love."

"I like the sound." She pressed her lips to the hollow at the base of his neck, tasting him with the tip of her tongue. "I like the taste of you."

He slid his hands upward along her arms. "I like the taste of you."

She giggled as she pushed aside his hands. "I have noticed. And I must say I'm certainly glad you do. But you must play by the rules this night."

"Tell me, princess. What are the rules?"

"I want you to lie there without touching me until I grant you permission." She nipped the sensitive curve at the joining of his neck and shoulder. "Do you agree to my terms, dragon?"

"I'll try, princess."

"Here." She tugged on the sheet on either side of him, until she released the edges from the bed. "Take hold of this and don't let go."

Simon wasn't accustomed to relinquishing control to anyone, especially in a situation this intimate. Yet, he couldn't deny her, or the sensual promise he saw in her eyes. He gripped the sheet in his hands, feeling strangely vulnerable.

"Relax, my dragon." She dropped a soft kiss on his lips. "I won't hurt you, I promise."

She touched his scars—the puckered flesh of his shoulder, the thin saber wound across his ribs, the various smaller reminders of war etched into his flesh—softly, reverently, as though she wished she could erase the ugliness that had touched him. She slid her hands down his chest, flexing her fingers against his taut muscles, pausing against his belly just above the flesh that pulsed and throbbed, hungry for her.

He held his breath, waiting for the first touch of her fingers on his arousal. It didn't come. She slid her hands over his hips, along his thighs, his calves, her palms soft and warm, like the touch of rose petals warmed from the sun.

"You are such a wonderful collection of textures, dragon. Smooth in places, rough in others."

She pressed her lips to his chest, flicking the tip of her

tongue over the tiny nub of his nipple. He moaned at the unexpected rush of sensation.

"Hummm, you like this."

"Yes," he whispered.

"When you touch me like this, with your lips and tongue, I feel as though lightning is running loose inside me. Sparking in all directions."

He tipped back his head, gripping the sheet between his hands as she flowed downward, kissing his chest, his belly, flicking her tongue against his skin. He had never been with a woman so intent on pleasuring him. He had never been touched like this, as though she loved every inch of his body.

Her hair tumbled over his aching sex, silky strands sliding between his thighs. He stared at her, fighting every instinct to take her. Now. Yet he wanted to see how far she would take the game. He wanted to experience this sweet torture of her hands and lips upon his flesh. He twisted the sheet in his hands, watching her, waiting.

She lifted her hand. Every muscle in his body went rigid. She touched him, a soft brush of her fingers across the tip of his arousal. He groaned with pleasure.

"Do you feel the lightning?" she whispered, stroking him with her fingers as though he were a kitten.

"Yes. God, yes."

"Strange, I feel it too. An ache low inside me, pulsing with need. And you haven't even touched me."

"Release me from bondage, princess. Let me touch you."

She looked up at him, a knowing smile curving her lips. "Take what you want, my dragon."

He surged upward, taking her in his arms, pulling her down to the bed beneath him. He kissed her lips, her cheeks, her neck, pressing the tip of his tongue against the pulse pounding wildly there. She stirred beneath him, stretching, brushing her skin against his as though she wanted to touch every bit of him.

He gazed at her breasts, rising and falling with each soft breath, moonlight kissing the soft curves, the taut peaks. He lowered his lips, drinking moonlight from her skin. She sighed softly as he closed his mouth over one rosy tip. He celebrated the little bud with his tongue and teeth, drawing sweet sounds of pleasure from her lips.

He slid lower, spreading kisses across her belly, plunging into the soft tangle of curls, absorbing the hot musk of her arousal. She whimpered, gripping his shoulders. He loved her until she shuddered with pleasure, until her sweet song of release lifted like the soft ringing of a bell. And still he lingered, tasting the warm honey of her pleasure.

She tugged on his shoulders. "I want you, dragon. Inside of me. Now."

Her soft words rippled upon the desire pooling low in his loins. He looked up at her. "Anything, princess."

She smiled, tugging on his hair. "Now, my precious dragon. Come into my arms."

He covered her, brushing his hair-roughened chest against her soft breasts, capturing her moan beneath his lips. She arched her hips in silent demand. He obeyed, sliding into her, moaning against her lips with the sheer pleasure of her hot flesh closing tightly around him.

They moved in perfect counterpoint, one to the other, finding a rhythm that was theirs alone, banishing doubts and fears, ignoring everything except the love burning like pure fire between them. And as the moon made its lazy arc across the evening sky, they settled into slumber, sated, at peace in each other's arms.

Chapter Twenty

Simon sat behind his desk in his office at Maitland Enterprises, looking up at the man standing in the doorway. ''I'm going to stay for just a while longer. I want to review a few of the reports on the Jamaican runs.''

Hugh pursed his lips as he glanced at the papers scattered across Simon's desk. ''Blake, this is your first day back. You shouldn't push yourself.''

''I'll be home in time for dinner.''

''Emily and my wife will hang me up by my thumbs if they think I'm overburdening you.''

''I'll explain to Emily.''

Hugh shrugged. ''All right. If you aren't home in time for dinner, promise me you'll cut me down when you do get home.''

''I'll be there.'' Simon rested his forearms on the desk, listening to Hugh's footsteps tap against oak planks as he walked down the hall. Hugh's deep voice rumbled in the hall as he said good night to a clerk in one of the offices. Stanbury and Whitcomb had already left. In a few minutes the offices of Maitland Enterprises would be deserted.

Simon pivoted in his chair, staring out the open window behind his desk. Light from the setting sun touched the river, setting it ablaze with scarlet and gold. Square-riggers rocked in the breeze, their tall masts empty of sails.

God, he hated this. He felt like a thief, waiting for everyone to leave before he crept into Maitland's office and searched for evidence. His only salvation was the knowledge that he was searching for evidence to prove Maitland's innocence. He intended to take a look into Stanbury's files as well as those in Whitcomb's office.

Maitland. Stanbury. Whitcomb. One of them was guilty of treason. He didn't like any of the choices.

The wall sconces in his office chased away the shadows as darkness slowly crept over the river. Simon pulled his gold watch from the pocket in his pearl-gray waistcoat. The last clerk had left a few minutes earlier. If he intended to get back to Maitland's in time for dinner, he would have less than an hour to search the files. Time enough.

He glanced up when a sound disturbed the silence in the hall. Footsteps? Yes, footsteps. Soft, nearly soundless. Had one of the clerks returned? The man who stepped into his office was someone he had never seen before. The man was tall, heavyset, and in his right hand he held a pistol aimed at Simon's chest.

"Now ye won't be makin' any sudden moves, will ye, guvnor?" The man waved the pistol at Simon. "Ole Bess here can put a hole in ye the size of me fist."

From the looks of his dirty brown coat and breeches, he was a dock worker. Or smuggler. Or both. Looking into the dark slits of his eyes, Simon had no doubt the man had killed before. "What do you want?"

He smiled, revealing chipped teeth, brown and rotting. "Me captain wants a few words with ye, he does."

A few words that would end in Simon's death. "Who is your captain?"

"I ain't here to answer none of yer questions." He lowered his eyes, staring at the watch in Simon's hand. "But ye can hand that fine gold watch over 'ere. Ain't no reason why poor ole Billy can't be taking a bit of the spoils now, is there?"

Simon slowly unhooked the chain from his waistcoat, glancing at the desk, searching for something to use as a weapon. The silver handle of a letter opener peeked at him from beneath a stack of papers. He moistened his lips, feigning a look of terror as he stared at the smuggler. With any luck he could lure the smuggler into a sense of false security. "You won't shoot me, will you?"

Billy thrust out his massive chest. "Ye do as ole Billy tells ye and I won't be spillin' yer claret. Now come over 'ere and hand over that fine piece o' gold."

Simon stood, resting his hand on the desk as though he needed support. "Please don't shoot me."

Billy smiled, obviously pleased with himself. "Move yer bleedin' ass or I'll shoot, I will."

"Yes, sir." Simon dangled the watch out at his side. Billy's eyes followed the piece of gold for an instant. It was long enough. Simon grabbed the letter opener, hiding the blade behind his wrist.

"Move it, we ain't got all night." Billy waved the pistol. "The captain don't like te be kept waitin."

Simon stepped around the desk. He flicked his wrist and flung the letter opener. It hit the mark, plunging into the smuggler's chest.

Billy stumbled back, gasping. "Bastard!"

Simon dove to one side as Billy fired. The shot exploded in Simon's ears. Fire streaked across his upper arm. He hit the floor, rolled, and came to his feet.

Billy was leaning against the desk, pulling a second pistol from the waistband of his trousers. Simon surged forward. He hit the big man. They tumbled back against the desk. Simon grabbed Billy's wrist, trying to wrench the pistol from his hand.

"I'll kill ye!" Billy shouted.

Simon slammed Billy's wrist against the desk. The pistol clattered to the floor. Billy swung his arm, slamming his fist into Simon's cheek. A burst of sparks filled Simon's head. He staggered back, snatching for his breath.

Billy dropped to his knees and reached for the pistol. Simon swung out with his foot, catching Billy beneath the chin. The big man groaned and fell back, oak planks shuddering beneath his weight.

Simon dropped to his knees. He gripped the wooden handle of the pistol and turned to face the smuggler. Billy lay on his back, hands flung out at his sides, eyes closed.

The door slammed behind him. Simon turned, swinging the pistol. No one was there. Footsteps pounded in the hall. He struggled to his feet. Pain throbbed in his temples. Ragged streaks of pain shot along his arm. He staggered to the door. He grabbed the brass handle and twisted. It was locked.

"What the devil?" Why had someone locked him in his office? In the next heartbeat he had his answer. Smoke drifted beneath the door, like dark gray serpents curling upward along the solid oak panel. In the hall, flames lapped against the door with a soft sucking sound.

Simon stumbled back, stuffing the pistol into the waistband at the small of his back. It wouldn't take long for the ravenous flames to eat through the door. In minutes the entire floor would be consumed. He staggered to the window, coughing as smoke swirled into every corner of the room. Moonlight reflected on the cobblestones two stories below. He squeezed the windowsill in terror. He was trapped.

Something was wrong. Emily paced the length of the drawing room, pausing at the fireplace, staring at the crystal clock on the mantel. "Where is he?"

"He must have lost track of time," Hugh said. "He said he would be home in time for dinner. He still may."

Emily cast her father an accusing glance. He sat on one

of the Sheraton sofas beside her mother, who was giving him an icy stare.

Hugh frowned as he looked from his wife to Emily. He glanced around the room to his other daughters and his mother-in-law, a man staring into the face of an angry mob. "Blake is, after all, a grown man."

"I'm not at all certain you should have allowed him to return to work so soon," Audrey said.

"Audrey, my love, Blake insisted."

Audrey crossed her arms at her waist, glaring at her husband. "The poor man can't even remember his name and you're filling his head with all manner of shipping nonsense."

Hugh raised his hands in surrender. "All right. If it will make you feel better, I shall . . ." Hugh hesitated at a sharp knock on the door. A moment later, Redcliffe the butler entered the room.

"Sir, a man from town is here. He says your offices are on fire."

"Fire!" The word ripped through the room.

Emily hurried to her father, who had risen and started across the room. She grabbed his arm as he reached the door. "You don't think . . . dear heaven, Sheridan could still be there."

Hugh squeezed her hand. "I'm certain he's fine, Emmie."

"I'm going with you."

"No. You stay here."

"Sheridan might be hurt. I'm not about to sit here and wait to find out what has happened to him."

"And neither am I," Audrey said, joining Emily. "We shall stay out of the way, Maitland, but please don't ask us to sit here and wait."

He stared for a moment into his wife's determined face before he spoke. "All right. But stay in the carriage."

* * *

Emily leaned out the carriage window, watching as her father shouldered his way through the crowd at the end of the quay. The Maitland carriage could get no closer to the fire. Spectators and the fire brigade filled the street from this point to the place where several buildings had ignited into a terrible inferno.

A bright orange light glowed at the end of the quay, illuminating fire engines and men fighting desperately against the blaze, pumping water, sending tiny streams into the blaze. In the face of those spiraling flames, their efforts seemed futile.

Smoke billowed toward the evening sky, blotting the stars from the heavens. Each breath Emily took filled her nostrils with the acrid flavor of burning wood. "Where is he? Mother, you don't think Sheridan could still be in there, do you?"

Audrey sat at the window across from Emily, her face turned toward the blaze, a red gold light illuminating the concern etched upon her features. "I'm certain he is all right."

Ashes drifted on the breeze, fluttering like gray snow from the sky. "I can't just sit here," Emily said, reaching for the door handle.

Audrey grasped her hand. "You will accomplish nothing by going out into that crowd. Except perhaps getting yourself injured."

"But he could be hurt."

"And he could be just fine, already on his way home." Audrey squeezed Emily's hand. "How would he feel if he discovered you had gotten yourself killed trying to rescue him?"

Emily shook off her mother's hand. "I have to find him."

"Emily!"

Emily was already out of the carriage. She plunged into the crowd of spectators. With the determination of a tigress protecting her young, she pushed through the crush of bodies, fighting her way toward her father's offices. The crowd grew thinner the closer she came to the blaze. Heat radiated against her, like a giant fireplace blazing light and warmth into the night. In the light of the fire, she saw her father, standing near the edge of the quay, staring up at the blaze.

"Father!" she shouted, fighting to be heard above the roar of the flames.

Hugh turned, frowning when he saw her. "I told you to stay in the carriage," he shouted.

"Sheridan—have you found him?"

Hugh's lips flattened into a tight line. "Not yet."

"Did anyone see him leave?"

"No."

Emily turned, staring up at the building. Tongues of flame licked out of the windows. Smoke billowed from every portal. Wood groaned under the voracious flames devouring everything in their path with a whooshing sound that filled the night. "He could be in there."

"Emily!" Hugh grabbed her arm when she started for the door. "Damnation, just what do you think you're doing?"

Emily twisted trying to break free. "Let me go! I have to find him."

Hugh gripped her shoulders, shaking her hard enough to make her teeth clatter. "Emily, think, girl. Nothing could survive in there."

"No!" Emily fought against her father's powerful hands. "Please let me go to him."

"You wouldn't last a minute in that blaze."

Emily stared through her tears into her father's face. "I can't lose him," she whispered.

"I can't lose you."

She felt so helpless, so totally useless. "Papa, help me."

Hugh pulled her into his arms, holding her close against him. "We don't know for certain he was in there when the fire started. He could be home, wondering where you are."

Emily clung to her father and the slender thread of hope

he offered. "He could be, couldn't he?"

Hugh stroked her hair. "Yes. Now, come on, sweetheart. We can't do anything here. Let's go home. Blake is probably waiting for you."

After depositing Audrey and Emily safely at home, Hugh returned to town. There was nothing left for Emily but to wait and hope and pray he was alive. Audrey, Harriet, and Anna shared Emily's vigil. They sat in the drawing room, quiet except for an occasional encouraging remark. Yet, as the minutes gathered into hours, and the hours drifted into a new day, the encouragement waned, as did Emily's hopes.

It was dawn by the time Hugh Maitland returned home. He entered the drawing room without changing his soot-covered dinner clothes, without washing the grime from his face. He brought the scent of ashes into the room.

Emily rose from her chair. But the solemn look on his face kept her rooted in place. "Sheridan?"

Hugh glanced away from Emily, looking at Audrey a moment before he spoke. "There is no easy way to say this."

The blood slowly drained from Emily's limbs as she stared at her father and saw the truth in his eyes.

Audrey slipped her arm around Emily's waist. "Did you find him?"

Hugh nodded. "We found his body in the rubble."

Emily moved toward her father, her legs shaking violently. "I have to see him."

"Emmie," Hugh whispered, resting his hands on her shoulders. "He was badly burned. You don't want to see him. You wouldn't recognize him."

Emily clenched her hands at her sides. "It could be someone else."

Hugh held her tortured gaze. "Everyone else is accounted for."

"But he . . ." Emily stared at a streak of soot on her

father's neck. There were no words. No thoughts. Only pain. A pain that rose inside her, displacing strength and hope, leaving her empty. When her father slipped his arms around her, she fell against him, allowing him to take the weight of her body.

"I'm sorry, Emmie," Hugh whispered. "I'm so sorry."

Chapter Twenty-one

A carriage plunged through a puddle where the cobblestones had dipped in front of Lord Pemberton's London town house, spraying gray water against the wrought-iron fence enclosing Portman Square. Simon stood by a window in the library. The storm had stolen the light from the day, turning afternoon into dusk. Rain driven by the wind tapped against the panes, sliding in serpentine rivulets down the glass, reminding him of Emily's tears.

Before leaving for London, Simon had attended his own funeral, from a distance, of course. Yet close enough to see Emily's tears. She had leaned against her father's sturdy shoulder, weeping as the casket bearing a smuggler's remains had been carried into the family tomb. It had taken every ounce of his willpower to maintain his distance when all he wanted to do was take her in his arms and kiss the tears from her cheeks.

"Your father was at the Ministry yesterday, making inquiries about you," Lord Pemberton said.

Simon's smile reflected in the glass, a sardonic twist that

portrayed every bit of the sarcasm filling his deep voice as he spoke. "I'm certain he was most anxious about my welfare."

"In the past your father has made discreet inquiries, Simon. I think he wanted to keep track of what you were doing. He must be very proud of you."

Simon swirled the brandy in his glass, candlelight rippling in the liquid. No doubt his father had kept track of him with every hope that Simon's next assignment would be his last.

Lord Pemberton's image reflected in the window glass. The old soldier sat on the edge of his mahogany desk, bushy gray brows tugged together over his Roman nose as he regarded Simon. "You're a hero, for God's sake. I shudder to think of the number of times you've risked your life for your men. Any man would be proud to call you son. I know I would."

Simon smiled. "Thank you, sir."

"I understand your desire to see this mission through to the end, but I must say it isn't necessary." Pemberton paused for a moment, as though choosing his words carefully. "Your father hasn't long to live. You will inherit an immense fortune as well as the title, Simon. That's a great deal to risk."

Candles burned behind glass along the mahogany-lined walls, casting their light over elegant opulence—brass and mahogany bookcases filled with leather-bound volumes, finely crafted mahogany chairs, Sheraton sofas covered in emerald velvet. Such opulence awaited Simon upon his father's death. Yet, it meant nothing to him. "We have only a few days until the next shipment of weapons is scheduled. If we don't find the traitor before we stop that shipment, we'll lose him."

"You said yourself, it's possible the head of this operation might realize it was his man's body they found in the rubble, not yours."

Simon's palms grew damp with the memory of the narrow ledge he had crossed to reach the next office and an unlocked door. ''I doubt he will recognize me in this disguise.''

Pemberton shifted, crossing his arms over his narrow chest. ''But he might see past the fake whiskers and the dye in your hair. And if he does, the entire operation would be jeopardized. I'm not certain I can take that risk.''

Simon turned to face the older man. ''There isn't time to bring another man on board.''

Pemberton stroked one thick white side whisker as he studied Simon. ''I believe there is enough evidence to bring charges against Hugh Maitland.''

''No.''

Pemberton arched a bushy white brow at the vehemence of Simon's reply.

Simon eased air into his lungs, forcing control over his emotions. ''Maitland is innocent. If we arrest him now, the real traitor will make good his escape.''

''I hope you aren't allowing Miss Maitland's beauty to distract you.''

''I can infiltrate that smuggling ring, sir. I have to go back.'' He had to prove that Hugh Maitland wasn't guilty, and the only way to do that was to catch the real traitor.

Pemberton pursed his lips. ''You do realize that Miss Maitland might not be easily fooled by your disguise.''

''I don't plan to see the lady.''

Pemberton studied Simon, his brown eyes as sharp as a hawk's beneath his bushy brows. ''Seeing her would be a grave tactical error.''

''No doubt.''

Pemberton sighed. ''I wish I had someone else as capable as you ready to send on this mission. But I don't. And we don't have time to waste.''

''I can leave this evening.''

Pemberton studied Simon with a look that tore away all pretense. ''You have until the seventh of August. If you haven't uncovered other evidence, we shall take Maitland into custody. And I'm afraid that with the evidence we already have, and the climate in London these days, it won't go well for him."

"I'll find the traitor, sir."

Pemberton lifted his brandy snifter from the desk and raised it to Simon. "Good fortune, my lad. You shall need it."

Simon sipped his brandy, the slow burn of the potent liquid easing the chill in his chest. God, he hoped he wasn't deceiving himself in his belief in Maitland's innocence. When this mission was over he had every hope of walking back into Emily's life. Yet he knew she would never accept him if he were the man responsible for sending her father to the gallows.

He stared down into his brandy, where candlelight reflected golden in the amber liquid, reminding him of Emily's eyes. He was about to embark on a mission that could very well get him killed. And all he could think about was a golden-eyed temptress who had ignited a fire in his heart.

Easy, old man. He had to stay clear of the lady. There was too much at stake. Yet, as his mind demanded caution, his heart rebelled. He had to see her. If only from a distance.

Emily awoke with a start, a sudden wrenching from slumber that sent her heart slamming into the wall of her chest. She sat up in bed, dragging air into her lungs, shaking with the terror of her dream. Sheridan surrounded by flames. Reaching for her. Calling her name. She couldn't reach him. Dear God, she could only watch him die.

She hugged her arms to her chest, rocking slowly, trying to ease the pain. Sheridan was gone. They had buried the pitiful remains of his body in the family tomb, enclosed him behind a slab of white marble engraved with a name that wasn't his. Yet the memories wouldn't go away. The memories were with her every waking hour. Memories that worsened at night.

At times she awakened, holding his pillow close against her, imagining his arms around her, warm and content until reality ripped her from the sanctuary of dreams, filling her with a stark emptiness and a longing so potent she thought she might die. At other times the nightmares came.

She threw aside the covers and rose from the bed. Her legs trembled as she walked to the window. A cool breeze heavy with the scent of damp roses swept through the window as she threw it open, billowing the ivory brocade drapes. She leaned against the window frame, taking deep breaths of the moist air.

It had rained most of the day, but the skies had cleared, allowing moonlight to pour from a waning moon. Ravenwood stood like a pale gray ghost in the distance, a specter of wishes that hadn't come true. She lifted the lid of the small marquetry music box on her vanity. The bright notes of a waltz drifted on the cool evening air, stirring memories.

Longing pressed against her heart, the lifeless weight of dreams frozen in the midst of summer. Moonlight rippled across the rustling leaves of the oak tree standing near the house. It seemed a lifetime ago that a man without a name had stood high above the ground, rescuing his damsel in distress.

Something moved beneath the tree. Emily stiffened, staring into the darkness, wondering if her mind were playing tricks with her. Moonlight spilled through the leaves, defining a shape in the shadows. Someone was there. A man, standing beside the wrought-iron bench.

She held her breath, her heart pounding so loudly she was certain the figure in the shadows could hear it. That shadowy form was so familiar. She leaned forward, straining to see through the shadows. He was tall, lean. The way he stood—proud and arrogant—reminded her of. . . .

It couldn't be.

She tried to fill her lungs and failed. Emotion choked her throat until only a trickle of air could pass. Moonlight rippled with the swaying leaves, touching one broad shoulder, grazing his narrow hip. She knew that man. She knew every inch of his splendid body. Yet she knew he was dead. Still, moonlight and shadow mocked a reality she wished with all her heart was a lie. For one breathless beat of her heart, she wondered if she were staring at a ghost.

"Who are you?" Her voice was choked by an odd sense of expectancy. Yet he heard. She saw the shifting of his stance, the hesitation before he stepped back into the darker shadows cast by the tree. "Wait!"

Emily turned and ran from the room. Her nightgown billowed in the evening breeze as she stepped from the house. Damp grass chilled her bare feet as she ran toward the oak tree. Yet even before she reached it, she knew what she would find—an emptiness filled only by shadows.

"Is everything all right, madam?"

Emily jumped.

"Sorry, madam," Digby said, emerging from the shadows near the house. "I didn't mean to startle you."

Emily pressed her hand to her throat, staring at the footman. "What are you doing out here?"

Digby glanced up at the stars, moonlight falling across his smiling face. "I like to gaze at the stars, I do."

"How long have you been out here?"

"Oh, going on the better part of an hour, I would say."

"An hour." Emily twisted the soft linen at her neck. "You must have seen the man who was standing here. Who was he?"

Digby pursed his lips. "I'm not sure what you're meaning, madam."

"The man who was standing beneath the tree. You must have seen him."

Digby frowned. "I'm sorry, but I didn't see anyone."

She hugged her arms to her chest, shivering with more than the chill of the evening. "Are you certain?"

"Yes, madam."

She had seen someone, she was certain of it. Still, a part of her wondered if her tortured mind had only conjured the image of a man she would never again see in this lifetime. She retreated to her room. But there was no comfort waiting for her there. Only memories and an awakening fear that she was quite possibly losing her wits.

The next morning, Emily fingered the garments hanging along one side of her dressing room. There was no sense in keeping these things. They were merely wool and cloth, fashioned for a man who would never again wear them. The vicar could put them to good use clothing the poor.

This was the right thing to do, she assured herself. For the sake of her sanity she had to stop living in the past. "So tell me, why do I feel as though I'm betraying you by giving away your things?" she whispered to herself.

She brushed her fingers over the dragon stitched in gold and scarlet on his emerald robe. "My Lord Scoundrel," she whispered, her voice catching on a ragged edge of pain, "you would think it amusing to know I fell in love with you before you lost your memory. I fell in love with the bold warrior who charged into my life and turned everything upside down."

Tears pooled in her eyes, blurring her vision. She lifted the robe into her hands, the emerald silk cool against her skin. A scent lingered on the soft silk. His scent. She pressed her face to the cool silk, breathing the intoxicating spice into her lungs.

"I miss you." Tears spilled down her cheeks, falling against the emerald silk. "Dear God, how I miss you."

She began to shake uncontrollably, the silk absorbing her tears. All her strength drained away with her tears. She leaned back against the wall. Yet her legs refused to hold her. She sank to the floor, dissolving in a puddle of black muslin and tears.

Days had passed, and the pain was still as sharp as the moment she had learned he was dead. It hurt. Never in her life had anything hurt this terribly. Caught in the bitter tempest of her pain, she didn't hear her grandmother enter the room.

"My dear girl," Harriet whispered, touching Emily's shoulder.

Emily gulped for breath, hating the humiliating tears streaming from her eyes. "I'm sorry," she whispered. "I don't know what's wrong with me."

"There now, my poor darling child." Harriet knelt beside her and slipped her arm around Emily's trembling shoulders. "If you didn't cry over losing him, I would think something was wrong with you."

Emily rested her head on Harriet's shoulder, taking comfort in her warm embrace. "I miss him."

"I know, child." Harriet rocked Emily softly, as though she were a child. "I miss him too."

"I keep thinking there are people we should notify. His family. But we never even knew his name."

"We were his family, Emily."

"I thought I was done crying." Emily wiped the tears streaming from her eyes. "Tears don't help. They don't take away the pain."

"Only time will help," Harriet whispered. "Give yourself time to heal."

She stared down at the robe she clenched in her hands, the dragon staring up at her with golden eyes. "We had so little time."

Harriet stroked the damp curls from Emily's face. "Try not to think of all the time you were denied. Try to think of how fortunate you were to have met him, to have loved him, if only for a little while."

"I know I have to stop living in the past." Emily dragged air past the tightness in her throat. "Grandmother, last night, I thought I saw him, standing beneath the oak tree outside my room."

Harriet rested her hand against Emily's shoulder. "Who did you think you saw?"

Emily licked the tears from her lips. "Sheridan."

Harriet was quiet a moment, her hand taut against Emily's shoulder. "It was a dream."

"No." Emily looked up into her grandmother's eyes. "I awakened from that terrible dream I keep having."

"The fire again?"

Emily squeezed the robe in her hands. "He was in the middle of flames and I couldn't get to him. I awakened. I got out of bed. I went to the window. That's when I saw him."

"Emily, you couldn't possibly have seen him."

"I saw something, I know I did. But when I went outside, one of the footmen was there. He said he hadn't seen anyone."

"Well, that's the answer, isn't it?" Harriet dabbed her handkerchief to Emily's cheeks, the sweet scent of gardenias clinging to the soft white linen. "The footman was your ghost."

"No. The man I saw was tall and lean. That hardly describes Digby."

Harriet squeezed the handkerchief in her palm. "It must have been a trick of the moonlight."

"I saw someone. I know I did."

"Oh, my darling girl." Harriet hugged Emily close. "You haven't been sleeping well. Last night you were upset from your dream. You saw nothing more than moonlight reflecting through the branches. That's all."

She felt so tired, so confused. "I suppose it could have been the moonlight."

"Of course it was. You'll be fine. All you need is a little rest."

Emily managed a watery smile. "I'm glad you're here."

"I'm glad I can be here for you." Harriet kissed Emily's brow. "I'm taking Anna and your mother into Bath. There is nothing like a shopping expedition to raise one's spirits. I thought we could start assembling a new wardrobe for Anna."

"Poor Anna. Just when she is about to enter society, the

family is plunged into mourning.''

''Anna understands. And in a few months, when our deep mourning has past, I promised to open my town house in Bath and take her to the Assemblies. It will help prepare her for London. She is a bit nervous about it all.''

Emily smiled. ''I understand how she feels.''

''You must come with us.''

Emily sniffed. ''I'm not certain I would be very good company.''

Harriet patted Emily's shoulder. ''You could use a little diversion.''

''Yes, I suppose I could.''

''Come along.'' Harriet rose and reached for Emily. ''I won't take no for an answer.''

The weight of Emily's mood lightened later that day. Bath glowed golden in the sunlight. The town was filled with fashionable men and women, there to extend the social season. Anna was thrilled with it all, radiating with the promise of her first dip into society, even though it was months away.

Strange how things always seemed easier to handle in the daylight. As Emily sat with her family in the tea room of the Assembly Rooms, bathed in sunlight spilling from the tall second-story windows, listening to Mozart played by a string quartet, all the confusion from the night before slipped away like a dark cloak. By the time they left the tea room, Emily had convinced herself the ghost from the night before was merely a trick of the light. It was much easier to accept than the possible alternatives.

''Emily, do you think I should choose bold colors, like you wear?'' Anna asked as they approached Grantham House, one of the finest linen-draper's in Bath.

Emily smiled. ''I'm certain we shall find a style right for you.''

Anna turned to her mother. ''I do hope to be considered an *original*, like Emily.''

Audrey slipped her arm through Anna's. "My darling, you shall be quite the toast of the town."

Emily hesitated as her mother and Anna entered the shop. The back of her neck prickled as though someone were staring at her. She glanced around.

People strolled along both sides of the street, promenading past the golden stone walls of tea rooms and shops. Ladies carried parasols against the sunlight, pale gowns rippling in the warm summer breeze. Gentlemen swung walking sticks at their sides, lifting quizzing glasses to eye the ladies, sauntering with a practiced air of boredom. And in the crowd of faces, Emily noticed one man.

He stood near the entrance of a tea room across the street. He was tall, broad-shouldered, dressed in a dark gray morning coat such as many of the other gentleman wore. Yet there was an air about him, an aura of purpose the other men lacked. And he was watching her with eyes as dark as midnight. Her heart stumbled, then surged, sprinting into a rhythm that stole the breath from her lungs.

It couldn't be Sheridan. The truth of his death had been scrawled across her mind with the same intensity as the flames that had ripped him from her side. Sheridan was dead. What was left of his mortal body lay encased in white marble in the Maitland tomb.

This man had hair the color of polished mahogany. This man had a beard. Not at all like Sheridan, she assured herself. Yet she couldn't deny the compelling sense of familiarity gripping her.

"Emily, what is it?" Harriet touched her arm. "You look as white as a ghost."

"The man across the street." Hardly had the words left her lips before he disappeared into the crowd streaming along the walkway.

"What man?"

"He's gone." Emily started for the street.

"Emily!" Her grandmother grabbed her arm, staying her when she would have stepped out in front of a carriage.

Emily stepped back, pressing her hand to her racing heart as the carriage rumbled past on the cobblestones.

Harriet's fingers pinched Emily's arm as she led her to the entrance of the shop. She paused in the arched foyer, standing close to the leaded windowpanes where dress fabrics and trimmings were displayed. "What in the name of heaven has gotten hold of you?" she whispered.

"Someone was watching me."

"Who?" Harriet asked.

Emily moistened her dry lips. "A man."

Harriet looked across the street. "Which man?"

"He disappeared the moment he realized I had noticed him." Emily rubbed her arms, chilled in spite of the warmth of the day. "Grandmother, he seemed so familiar."

Harriet stared into Emily's eyes. "Who do you think you saw?"

Emily shook her head. How could she explain seeing a ghost? "It doesn't matter."

Harriet drew a deep breath, as though she were gathering her strength. "What did he look like?"

"He was tall." There had been something in his eyes when she had caught him staring at her—a hunger she would remember until the day she died. Dear God, it couldn't be Sheridan. Her mind was simply playing some horrible trick. "He had a beard. His hair was reddish brown," she said, taking cold comfort in a description that didn't resemble her lost love.

Harriet smiled at two ladies as they left the shop. "Well, I must say that description doesn't sound like anyone I know."

"It doesn't sound like anyone I know, either." Emily managed a smile in spite of the uneasiness twisting low in her belly. "I'm sorry for the fuss. I'm afraid I've turned into some nervous ninny."

"Nonsense. You are simply tired, that's all. A bit done in from all that has happened." Harriet slipped her arm through Emily's and smiled. "Now come along. Let's find something extravagant to buy."

He was getting careless, Simon thought. And in his position a careless man soon became a dead man. He should never have followed Emily to Bath. She had recognized him. He was certain of it. She had seen straight through his disguise. And he realized that a part of him had wanted her to see the man beneath the mask. He wanted to believe that the bond between them was strong enough to reach beyond deception. Strong enough to survive every lie that had passed between them.

Reckless fool. He had to stop thinking about Emily and start concentrating on his mission. He drew a deep breath, his senses flooding with the pungent stench of the pub. Smoke drifted in the room like a treacherous fog, rising from pipes and cigars, melding with the scent of stale ale, spilled rum, and unwashed bodies. Any of the men crowding the pub could be an enemy. All it would take would be one who recognized him.

"Can I get anythin' else fer ye, sir." A flaxen-haired barmaid leaned close to Simon, pressing soft, plump breasts against his shoulder as she placed a tankard of ale on the table. She smiled down at him, lowering her brown eyes, her gaze dipping to his shoulders, his chest, and finally his lap. Her breath escaped in an exaggerated sigh. "It'd be a real pleasure, sir."

Simon tossed a coin on her tray. "Maybe later."

She winked at him. "I'll be waitin', han'some."

Feminine laughter punctuated the low drone of male voices, the sound of barmaids hoping to make a few extra coins by allowing a quick fondle here and there. In one corner of the room, a barmaid sauntered down the stairs. Simon had noticed the same barmaid lead a drunken sailor up those stairs when he had entered the pub ten minutes ago. No doubt she had emptied his pockets before leaving him sprawled on a dirty bed.

After seventeen years in the army, Simon was accustomed to pubs like the Wayfarer. His first time with a woman had been in a place like this, when he was fourteen. The experience had left him with scratches on his rump, fleas in his uniform, and a lot more sense in his head. It was an important lesson in refining his tastes.

Simon leaned back in his chair, studying the man across from him as Grady drained a tankard of ale, his second since Simon had met the man a few minutes ago. In spite of the tension coiling like a viper in the pit of his stomach, Simon managed to betray none of his thoughts or feelings. He had learned a long time ago how to mask every emotion.

"Ahhhh." Grady plunked his empty tankard on the scarred oak table top and dragged the back of his dirty hand across his mouth. "Damn fine ale."

"Grady, I told my friend here you could help him." Digby leaned forward, resting his arms on the table. "Can you?"

"Mayhaps." Grady sniffed, rubbing his hand over his stubbly chin, his attempt at nonchalance spoiled by the expectation glinting in his eyes. "Me captain says he'll meet with ye."

Simon curved his lips into a lazy smile. "When?"

"Tomorrow." Grady rubbed his tongue over his teeth, crinkling his crooked nose as he eyed Simon. "Where ye stayin'?"

"The Red Lion Inn."

Grady nodded. "Fancy."

That was the reason Simon had picked the expensive establishment. He wanted the smugglers to believe he was a wealthy American, with a desire to purchase weapons for his cause.

"Ye come walkin' out the door at ten sharp. And I'll take ye te 'im." Grady stood, his chair scraping on the rough wooden planks. "Come alone. Me captain don't want to see none of yer friends. Understand?"

"Yes." Simon rubbed his thumb over the smooth handle of his tankard as he watched Grady walk toward the door, the little man insinuating his way through the crowd like a terrier through a tight rabbit hole. How many of the men here were part of the smuggling gang that were his prey? Predator and prey. At times it was impossible to tell the difference. If any of the smugglers recognized him, Simon knew he might not walk out of the pub alive.

"I don't like the smell of this," Digby said. "Why does he want you to come alone?"

"I suppose he's worried I might be an excise officer." Simon sipped his ale, the strong brew biting his tongue.

"I don't know how you manage, sir. You aren't the least bit nervous, are you?"

Only a fool faced danger without a care. Simon knew the risks that came with the search for justice. He had no death wish. Never had. Inside him, anxiety blended with excitement, like contrasting threads in a tightly twisted strand of yarn. Both had kept him alive all these years. "It's not the first time we've been in a tight spot."

"Aye, sir. It's just . . ." Digby frowned, his thick, sandy-colored brows meeting over his crooked nose. "If it weren't for you, sir, I would have died on that bloody field in Coruna, along with most of our regiment. I keep thinking how you stood up and warned us, trying to fight back the French single-handed, giving us time to defend ourselves. And I keep thinking of how you took a ball in the shoulder. Then there was that time in—"

"We aren't going to review my entire military career, are we, Digby?"

Digby shook his head. "No, sir, but I have to tell you, at times, you don't have the proper amount of fear a sane man should have."

Simon grinned. "Are you trying to say I'm crazy?"

"I'm trying to say, this is far too dangerous to be handled this way. It could be a trap. You could be walking straight to your death."

"Yes." Simon grinned at his friend. "And there is only one way to find out for certain."

Chapter Twenty-two

Emily paused on the top step of the Maitland tomb, a prickly sensation creeping up her spine. She glanced around, certain someone was nearby. Watching her. Yet she saw no one lurking about the granite monuments or marble tombs, no one near the thick trunks of the oak and ash trees that shaded the resting places of the dead.

She shook her head, dismissing the odd sensation. She needed rest. For three nights she had gazed out her window, watching, waiting for the return of the ghost. Three days, and she hadn't caught another glimpse of that shadowy specter.

It was strange. In some perverse way she couldn't quite understand, she was disappointed. Perhaps she wanted to believe that Sheridan's spirit had returned. Perhaps she wanted the assurance that some part of him would remain with her for all her days. Without him all the rest of her days stretched out before her, one blending into another, each as empty as the day before.

The breeze whispered through the leaves of the tall oak

standing like a sentinel beside the white marble tomb. It was a beautiful day, soft and warm and gentle. A day for picnics and walks along the bluffs. A day to share with the one you love. Perhaps that was why she had come here today, as she had every day since they had brought the man she knew as Sheridan Blake to this place, to be near him, in the only way remaining for her.

Emily tugged on the brass handle. The oak door creaked on its hinges, releasing a cool, damp scent into the summer breeze, like freshly tilled soil. Sunlight rushed through the open door, carving a golden wedge in the shadows. She followed that golden light to his resting place. A shelf enclosed from the world. A name carved into marble. All that remained of the man who had stepped from her dreams.

Her great-grandparents rested in this place. Her infant brother who had died soon after his birth twenty years ago slept in this quiet place. And in time she would lie here, beside a man she had loved without ever knowing his name.

She rested her hand against the marble that encased his mortal remains, touching cold stone, longing for the warmth forever beyond her reach. Her throat tightened with the reality she still found so difficult to accept. It seemed impossible that she would never again see his face. Never again hear his voice. Never again feel the touch of his hand. Even now, she found herself awakening each morning expecting to see him lying beside her.

There were so many years left of her life, so many mornings to awaken from empty dreams, so many hours to fill. And all the years to come, all gathered and distilled, could never amount to the few short days she had had with him.

She arched her fingers against the unrelenting marble. "We had such a short time together, you and I. Yet, in those few moments with you, I lived a dream. I shall never forget you. And I shall never, never stop loving you." She closed her eyes against the sting of tears. Tears were useless against the pain.

* * *

Simon stood beside a granite monument, hidden in the shadows of a tall ash tree. He watched as Emily left the Maitland tomb. She looked so fragile, an ethereal wraith, pale skin against black muslin, dark circles beneath her beautiful eyes. From a distance he could sense the weight of her sadness.

For one tortured heartbeat he considered revealing himself. He fought the urge to run to her, to take her in his arms. Yet he knew Emily's first loyalty would be to her father, especially when she realized how completely Simon had deceived her. If Maitland discovered the purpose of Simon's mission, he might inadvertently spoil any chances Simon had of finding the real traitor.

He clenched his fist on the granite monument, thinking of all the young men facing death on a distant battlefield. He couldn't jeopardize the mission. What's more, he couldn't walk back into Emily's life when he was still in the middle of a dangerous mission. He could be killed. The lady didn't need to grieve for him twice.

Duty dictated his course of action. Duty might very well cost him the only woman he would ever love. If it didn't cost him his life.

Instead of retreating to her room after visiting the cemetery, Emily rode to Ravenwood. In this place she had always felt a sense of peace, as though the spirits of Lord and Lady Ravenwood guarded this ancient dwelling, as though they welcomed her like a lost child.

She climbed the twisting stone stairs that had felt the tread of Lord and Lady Ravenwood, allowing her imagination to sweep her back in time. She stepped onto the rampart walkway, lifting her face to the warm breeze. This was the first time she had come here since the fire. The first time she had faced the lady's stone after her dreams had been shattered. She rested her hands on Lady Ravenwood's stone, absorbing the warmth hidden there. Sunlight peeked through the clouds overhead, casting Emily's shadow over the cross carved into the stone.

Lady Ravenwood had stood upon this stone, prepared to die rather than watch the man she loved be killed by her father's army. Emily had never really understood the lady and her courageous stand, until now. Now she knew the lady had realized that life without her beloved was not worth living. It had taken courage and conviction to end that war. Courage and conviction to risk her life for the man she loved.

How had Lady Ravenwood felt, standing here, facing her own death? Without conscious thought of what she was doing, Emily climbed onto the flat stone. Slowly she came to her feet, holding the raised stonework on either side of the embrasure. One step and she would die. Her heart thudded with the confrontation of her own death. Her palms dampened the stones beneath her tight grip.

A warm breeze swept across Ravenwood, rippling the hem of her gown. It flickered above the lady's stone, like the tail of a black cat. Far below her, the breeze whispered across the thick grass of the bailey. She imagined Lady Ravenwood standing here, looking beyond the stone wall guarding the castle, seeing her father's army poised to attack.

Emily closed her eyes, imagining people crowding the bailey below. Through the mists of time she could hear their voices, shouting for her to step away from danger. Lord Ravenwood stood on the walkway a few feet away, as close as the lady would allow. His deep voice sliced like a sword through the noise as he pleaded with her to step back from the edge: *Come back, my love. By all that's holy, please come back to me.*

Lord Ravenwood hadn't understood. None of them had understood the lady's conviction. But Emily understood. She knew the lady's fear, her resolution.

There was no reason to continue living.

Not if he was gone.

One step and the lady would have died.

One step . . .

Someone grabbed her arm. Emily jumped, startled from her daydream. Her foot slipped on the edge of the stone, upsetting her balance. She pitched forward. The bailey loomed in her vision. Her heart lurched with the certainty of her own death. A scream ripped the air. Her own. She clawed at the stone wall, seeking purchase against the fall.

A strong arm whipped around her waist. One moment she was teetering on the brink, the next she was crushed in a powerful male embrace, her back flush against a solid chest. A pitiful whimper escaped her lips as he lowered her to the relative safety of the narrow walkway. She might have fallen, her legs too shaky to hold her, if he hadn't gripped her shoulders and forced her back against the stone merlon.

''What the devil were you doing up there?'' he demanded.

''I was . . .'' Her voice faded, stolen by the sudden pounding of her heart as she stared up into a pair of furious black eyes.

He squeezed her shoulders, holding her as though the wind might carry her away if he didn't serve as her anchor. ''What could have possessed you to climb onto that wall?''

Emily stared up at him, confusion undermining the certainty she had felt upon looking up at this man. On first glance she had been certain this man was Sheridan. It couldn't be, of course. Sheridan was gone. This was the same man she had seen in Bath. ''A lady once ended a war by standing on this stone and risking her life. I wanted to understand how she must have felt.''

He stared at her as though she had told him she could fly. ''So you climbed up on that stone?''

''Yes.'' Even in the stark light of logic, she trembled beneath the hard hands gripping her shoulders, as though her body recognized his touch even as her mind dismissed the possibility. It was absurd to imagine this man could be Sheridan. He was dead. She had to accept the fact.

This man was a stranger. Still, emotion refused to surrender to logic. There was something about him that whispered to the childish hope lingering deep inside her, a hope that had been planted by a ghost carved of shadows and moonlight.

"Damnation, woman. Haven't you got a wit in that lovely head of yours? I would expect a ten-year-old child to have more sense."

The harsh tone in his voice struck her like a hand across her cheek. She stared up at this stranger, confusion dissolving in the hot tide of her rising anger. "I would have been perfectly fine if you hadn't startled me."

He frowned, dark brows meeting above the thin line of his nose. "Perfectly fine? Lady, you could have been killed."

"Nonsense." She struggled against the powerful hands still gripping her shoulders, resenting the perverse trick of nature that made her believe in miracles. Sheridan was gone. "Take your hands off me."

"Calm down." He lifted his hands. "This isn't a good place for childish tantrums."

"Childish . . ." She stared up at him, stunned by the impertinence. "How dare you speak to me in that manner?"

He smiled, and she caught herself looking at his right cheek, wondering if a dimple was hiding beneath that close-clipped beard. The breeze ruffled the dark mahogany waves falling over his brow, as thick and silky as the hair of another man, but the wrong color. "Fiery little vixen, aren't you?"

She stared up at him, stunned by his powerful awareness rippling through her just from being near this stranger. Her skin tingled. A pulse flickered in the tips of her breasts. For some dreadful reason she couldn't separate memory from reality, hope from despair. "Who are you? Why are you following me?"

"Following you?" His voice was husky, rough where Sheridan's had been as luxurious as black velvet, and this voice was colored with an accent that marked him as an American. ''I don't know what you're talking about.''

''Oh, really?'' She curled her hands into fists at her sides, disguising the tremble she couldn't prevent. He was like a puzzle in which the pieces didn't quite fit. Her mind registered one thing when she looked at him, her instincts recognized another. ''You were in Bath a few days ago. I saw you.''

''Yes.'' He rested one broad shoulder against the wall, his smile positively dripping arrogance. ''I see I made an impression on you, sweetheart. 'Course, I've always had a way with ladies.''

''Why, you . . .'' She stared up at him, her body growing rigid with her soaring animosity. She wanted to punch him. Lord help her, in that moment she hated him. For his arrogance. For everything he was and even more for everything he was not.

He had no right to look at her that way, with eyes the color of midnight, eyes that should be filled with desire instead of mocking laughter. He had no right to be so tall, his shoulders so broad. He had no right to barge into her life and remind her of everything she had lost.

She started shaking from the terrible war between emotion and logic raging inside of her. Sheridan was gone. Her misguided attraction to this arrogant buffoon was caused by nothing but her agitated nerves and his unfortunate resemblance to another man. She pivoted, needing to put as much space between them as possible. Preferably an ocean.

In her anger, she forgot exactly where she was. Her foot caught the edge of the walkway. She tripped, her balance shifting, her weight spilling toward the gaping hole where the roof had once been. She gasped, her heart slamming against the wall of her chest.

''Careful!'' He grabbed her arm, yanking her back to safety. Fear stripped away her anger. She threw her arms around his waist, trembling in his powerful embrace as he held her close against his chest.

"You're safe," he whispered, stroking her back. "I won't let you fall."

His voice softened into a haunting familiarity. His words teased a poignant memory of a broken limb and a tarnished hero. *Sheridan.*

It can't be.

Emotion ambushed logic as a scent curled around her with the warmth of his skin, an intoxicating blend of wool and leather and man. Recognition struck her with such force it nearly buckled her knees. This man couldn't be Sheridan. It was impossible. Wasn't it?

She pulled back in his arms, staring up into his midnight eyes. "Who are you?"

He didn't answer, but stood with his arms around her, flames flickering in the depths of his eyes. The moment stretched and expanded, forcing everything from her world except this man. For all the impossibility of it, she wanted to believe in miracles. With his arms around her, with the warmth of his body seeping through her gown, she wanted with all her heart to believe this was her one and only love returned to her.

"Who are you?" she whispered again.

A flicker passed across his features, an instant of pain before all expression drained from his face, as though a mask were sliding into place. Although he smiled, his eyes remained impassive, as if all emotion had been carefully washed from the dark depths. "Simon Richardson, at your service."

"Simon Richardson," she whispered. It was a lie. She didn't care one whit about logic. She knew this man was her scoundrel. She stepped away from him, shivering as she left his warm embrace. "What are you doing here?"

"I've been taking in the sights. I heard this castle was a fine example of fourteenth-century architecture."

She crossed her arms below the high waist of her gown, drawing a deep breath she hoped would ease the trembling of her limbs. Why would he lie to her? Why would he come here in disguise? Nothing made sense. "You're American?"

"Yes." He leaned one shoulder against the stone merlon rising between the embrasures of the battlement, his dark head rising above the peaked stones. Emily had the absurd notion of how vulnerable he would have been in battle, his height lifting him above the castle defenses. "I was here on holiday when our two countries decided to declare war. I haven't quite found a way to get back home."

She noticed the way he stayed close to the wall, as far away from the gaping hole of the missing roof as possible. The way a man who was frightened of heights might behave. "Are you staying with friends?"

"No. I have a room in an inn."

"Which one?"

He grinned. "Are you planning to come visit me?"

She chose to ignore the bait, sensing he wanted to stir her anger, use it to keep her off balance. She rested her hands on Lady Ravenwood's stone. The river Avon meandered past the rugged slopes of the gorge far below the lofty perch of the castle. A single square-rigger floated on the dark gray water, white sails billowing in the breeze. "The view is magnificent from here, isn't it?"

"Yes." He kept his gaze focused on her, and she wondered if he was simply flirting, or frightened of the height.

She studied him a moment, mentally peeling away the beard, darkening his hair. Could she be wrong? "Won't you come and look?"

He hesitated a moment before moving to her side. She watched him, taking heart in the way his hand curled into a fist against the wall as he stared through the embrasure out across the gently sloping land toward her father's house.

"You know, it's strange, but you remind me of someone."

He glanced down at her, a slight tensing of his brow the only trace of his anxiety. "Who is that?"

Emily held her breath. "My husband."

He held her gaze, revealing nothing in his eyes or his expression. ‘‘Your husband is a lucky man to have such a beautiful wife.’’

‘‘My husband is dead.’’ Emily swallowed past the tight knot of emotion in her throat. ‘‘At least, we think he died in a fire. His body was too badly burned to identify him properly.’’

He stretched his hand against the gray stones. ‘‘I should think he would have found his way home if he hadn’t died in the fire.’’

Emily turned her face into the breeze, fighting the tears rising in her eyes. She couldn’t be wrong. This man had to be Sheridan. ‘‘Perhaps he had a reason to disappear. Perhaps he was in trouble, and that trouble caught up with him.’’

‘‘Your husband wasn’t a criminal, was he?’’

‘‘I don’t know. I don’t care.’’ She looked up at him, knowing she revealed her love for him in her eyes. *Please tell me the truth. Please drop this masquerade.* ‘‘I only know I love him. I want him back. No matter what.’’

His lips parted, and for one fleeting moment she believed he might confess. Instead he looked away from her, staring out across the countryside, where ash and oak trees rose from the lush green hills, poised like scattered soldiers from an ancient war. Slowly he drew his hand into a fist against the wall. ‘‘If he did survive that fire . . . if he is still alive . . . you have to believe there is a good reason why he can’t be with you.’’

‘‘Why?’’ she whispered, her voice betraying her anguish.

He hesitated a moment before he looked at her, his face betraying not a trace of emotion. But his voice was softer as he spoke. ‘‘I feel sure he’ll tell you when he comes back to you.’’

A single tear slid down her cheek. ‘‘Do you think he will come back to me?’’

Simon touched her cheek, wiping away the tear with his thumb, his rough skin serving only to enhance the gentleness of his touch. ‘‘If he is alive, I would wager that the devil himself couldn’t keep him from your side.’’

Chapter Twenty-three

Emily paced the length of her grandmother's sitting room, pivoting at the windows, yellow brocade drapes swaying in her wake. "It's Sheridan, Grandmama. I'm certain of it."

Harriet turned her head, watching Emily's progress as she paced back toward the fireplace. "Why would Sheridan fake his own death?"

"I'm not certain, of course." Emily turned at the white marble hearth, pacing back toward the windows. "But what if the man who came here as Sheridan Blake was in trouble with someone? Perhaps over a gambling debt, or some such thing."

Harriet frowned, her eyes gentle as she looked at Emily. "We found a body after the fire," she reminded her.

"Yes. A body we couldn't identify."

"No one else is missing."

"No one we know."

"Come here, my dear girl." Harriet patted the cushion beside her on the chaise longue. "Come sit beside me."

Emily crossed her arms at her waist, her dignity pricked

under Harriet's patronizing gaze. "Grandmother, you mustn't look at me that way."

Harriet lifted one finely arched brow, giving Emily a look filled with cultivated innocence. "What way?"

"As though I were a pitiful creature in danger of losing my mind."

"Nonsense." Harriet patted the pale yellow silk brocade beside her. "I'm simply getting a stiff neck watching you pace back and forth. I fear you are going to wear a rut in the carpet."

"Well, I wouldn't want you worrying about the carpet. Not when I'm discussing the most important thing in my life." Emily marched to the chaise and sank to the cushion beside her grandmother.

Harriet pursed her lips, studying Emily a moment before she spoke. "You want to believe Sheridan is still alive. That's why you have convinced yourself this American is a man returned from the grave."

"If you had been there today, if you had seen this man, you would understand my certainty."

Harriet sighed. "It doesn't make sense."

"Perhaps it does." Emily leaned forward, fighting the urge to stand and pace. Hope and expectation swirled inside her, sparking an energy that overcame any attempt to contain it. "What if Sheridan was being followed by some man? What if this man confronted him that night in his office? They might have struggled, knocked over an oil lamp. Sheridan could have escaped. The body we found could have been the other man."

Harriet stared at Emily, her eyes wide in astonishment. "Emily, my child, you have always had much too active an imagination for your own good."

Emily groaned, her frustration rising like steam in a boiling kettle. "Simon Richardson is Sheridan Blake. I know it."

Harriet rested her hand against Emily's forearm. "Stay calm."

Emily squeezed her hands together in her lap. ''I am calm,'' she said, her voice far too bright.

''Right.'' Harriet tapped her closed fan against the black silk covering her knee. ''Let's say, for the sake of argument, that what you described happened. Why wouldn't Sheridan come to us? Why would he allow us to believe he is dead?''

''I have an idea.''

Harriet rolled her eyes to heaven. ''I knew you would.''

Emily ignored her grandmother's lack of enthusiasm. She had enough for both of them. ''Sheridan could be afraid he would be arrested if he came forward. A man died. He could be held responsible.''

Harriet considered this a moment. ''Not likely. He could always say the man was a brigand out to steal his money.''

Emily sat back, frowning at the logic she couldn't deny. ''That's true. But suppose there are others after him. Suppose the man who confronted him was part of a gang.''

Harriet blinked. ''A gang?''

''Yes.'' Emily rubbed her palms together, warming to her new theory. ''They could be out there now, looking for him. Because they know it was one of their men who was killed, not Sheridan.''

Harriet snapped open her fan and began flicking the painted silk beneath her chin, fluttering the curls framing her face. ''Do you mean to say you believe Sheridan was involved with smugglers or some other type of miscreant?''

''Smugglers! Of course!'' Emily clapped her hands, thrilled to fit together this piece of her puzzle. ''Why didn't I think of it?''

''Oh, I don't know. Perhaps because it is so perfectly bizarre.''

''No. It makes perfect sense.'' Emily twisted on the cushion, looking directly at her grandmother. ''Don't you see? That's why he can't return to us. It would mean exposing the family to a horrible scandal, or worse. I'm sure he means to spare us any danger.''

Harriet shook her head. "He didn't even remember his name when the fire occurred. How would he know he was involved with smugglers?"

"They told him, of course."

"They told him?"

"When that brigand confronted him the night of the fire, he must have told Sheridan everything." Emily drew a deep breath, her chest tightening with the pain she knew he must be feeling. "Think of what he must be going through. His memory gone. Murderers on his trail. No one to turn to."

"Emily, you really mustn't upset yourself this way."

"I understand now why he has been following me. He wants to see me, but he thinks he has to keep his distance. He doesn't want to expose me to any danger."

Harriet closed her eyes. For a moment her lips moved, as if in silent prayer. When she looked at Emily, her eyes were filled with an equal measure of pity and concern. "Emily, you need rest."

"No. I need to find him." Emily sprang to her feet. "We must send Beamish into town. I want him to check all of the inns."

Harriet stared up at her. "And if you find him?"

Emily turned toward the windows, staring at the ancient castle rising on a distant hill. Perhaps wishes did come true. "When I find him, I'm going to wrap my arms around him and let him know I shall stand with him through anything."

Harriet groaned. "Emily, you mustn't get your hopes up this way. This Simon Richardson might be everything he said he is."

Emily smiled, experiencing the same ripple of excitement as she did when she placed a chess opponent in check. "I can prove he is Sheridan."

Harriet stared at Emily, her eyes wide and wary. "How do you plan to prove it?"

"I don't know why I didn't think of it this morning. All I had to do was push back his hair."

"Push back his hair?"

"Yes." Emily pushed back the curls from her own brow. "Sheridan has a scar right here. From where I shot him."

"Oh." Harriet carefully closed her fan, spine by spine. "I'm certain Mr. Richardson will understand when you ask to push the hair back from his brow. All you need say is you want to see if he has a scar where you shot your husband."

Emily frowned. "I would find another way to ask him, of course."

Harriet nodded. "Equally persuasive, I'm sure."

"Grandmama, please." Emily sank to the cushion beside her grandmother and took Harriet's left hand between both of her own. "You must help me. I have to know if this man is Sheridan."

"Emily, you can't go chasing after every man who reminds you of Sheridan."

"I have to know."

Harriet stared down at their clasped hands for a moment. "Have you considered the possibility this man could be Sheridan's brother?"

"His brother?"

"He is an American." Harriet looked up at Emily, her expression as gentle as her fingers as she squeezed Emily's hand. "He told us his mother was living in America, with her husband and their children."

"No." Emily shivered with a possibility she refused to accept. "This man is Sheridan. And if you won't help me prove it, I shall simply find him on my own."

Harriet sighed. "Yes. I'm certain you will."

Emily squeezed her grandmother's hand like a lifeline. "Will you help me?"

Harriet rested her palm against Emily's cheek. "My darling girl, I do hope you can live with the truth once we find it."

Emily smiled, realizing her grandmother would stand beside her in this, as she had stood beside her all her life.

"There is nothing I want more than to live with the truth, Grandmama. Because the truth is, the man we know as Sheridan Blake is alive."

Simon stood in front of the mirror in his room at the Red Lion Inn, pressing one edge of his fake whiskers into place. Emily had seen through the disguise. She had looked up at him, her eyes filled with pain and a silent demand for the truth. A truth he couldn't give her. Lord, when this was over, he prayed she would forgive him.

"Not meaning any disrespect, sir, but do you think it was wise, allowing Miss Maitland to get a close look at you?"

Simon looked past his reflection in the mirror to where Digby stood near the big four-poster bed behind him. "At the time I thought she was about to jump off a rather high ledge."

Digby released his breath in a loud sigh. "Aye, sir, she's been taking on terrible since you passed away. I hate to see it, I do."

A tight band of guilt squeezed his heart when Simon thought of the pain Emily had suffered. With any luck, when this mission was over, he would be allowed to spend the rest of his life making sure she never lost her smile again.

"What do you think Miss Maitland will do now?"

Simon folded the edges of his neckcloth as he considered Emily and her active imagination. The woman had invented a husband. God alone knew what she would do next. "I wouldn't be surprised if she tracks me down just to tell me to go to blazes for putting her through this grief. Let's hope this mission is over by the time she finds me."

"Sir, if Miss Maitland saw through your disguise, there's a good chance the smugglers will too."

Carefully he eased the starched white silk into an elegant but simple fashion favored by Americans. "Miss Maitland knows me a little better than the smugglers, Digby."

Digby's lips pulled into a tight line. "Smugglers be a mighty suspicious lot. They'd sooner slit your throat than take a chance."

"I intend to offer them an opportunity to make a large profit. I don't think they will slit my throat."

"Unless they realize you're an agent for the ministry. Which they already did once. This time you might not be so lucky to walk away with your skin."

"I don't have a choice." Simon lifted his watch from the washstand, his skin tingling with the expectation of the coming contest. For the first time in his life, he had something very precious to lose if things did not go well—Emily. Still, if he didn't find the real traitor, Hugh Maitland might very well face the hangman. He snapped his watch closed and slipped it into the pocket of his pale blue waistcoat. "It's time."

"Sir, I don't like the feel of this." Digby lifted Simon's black coat from an armchair and held it up for him. "You could be walking straight into a trap."

Simon slipped into the elegantly tailored coat, the superfine wool fitting him as closely as a glove. With any luck the smugglers would see a rich American when they looked at him. If not, he could easily end up as fish bait. "Digby, if you have a better idea for discovering the identity of our traitor, I'm more than willing to listen."

Light from the oil lamp burning on the wall near the door fell across Digby, illuminating the deep lines creasing his full face. He stared up at Simon like an old bulldog reluctant to let go of his bone. "If you don't mind me saying so, sir, at times you're a mite too reckless with your own neck."

Simon smiled, seeing the affection behind Digby's gruff facade. "It isn't only my neck at stake. If we don't come up with some evidence to the contrary, Pemberton is going to arrest Hugh Maitland."

Digby nodded. "I'll be watching your back, sir."

"No. I want you to return to the Maitland house."

"But, sir—"

"You said yourself, smugglers are a suspicious lot. They'll be watching. If they see I've brought a friend along, they just might decide to get rid of both of us."

Digby's shoulders sagged with his slow sigh. "I'd feel better if I could take a hand in this."

Simon gripped Digby's shoulder. "If something goes wrong, there won't be time for a rescue."

Digby nodded. "You take care, sir."

"I will. I have no intention of attending my own funeral again for a very long time."

Emily squeezed the reins so tightly her horse tossed his head, his high whinny piercing the night air. "Sorry, Arthur," she whispered, patting the chestnut gelding's neck. "I'm afraid my nerves have me a bit ham-handed tonight."

She stared across the street at the Red Lion Inn, safe in the shadows of an alley, feeling like a rabbit hiding in a hole. Perhaps she should have followed her grandmother's advice and waited until morning to complete her quest for the truth. She didn't even want to imagine what her grandmother would say if Lady Harriet knew her granddaughter had slipped out of the house like a thief to confront a man in an inn. Emily shivered at the thought.

What would she do if someone saw her here? The street was quiet. The shops were closed for the evening. If she was going to confront the man, she should do it now. Still, she hesitated in the shadows. What would she say to him? Dear heaven, what if she was wrong? What if Simon Richardson really was an American on holiday?

The rattle of carriage wheels on cobblestones interrupted her thoughts. She sat back in the shadows, watching as a black town coach pulled by a pair of matched bays stopped beneath a streetlamp in front of the Red Lion. Lamplight shimmered on the polished lacquered doors, unadorned by heraldic arms or any ornamentation even though it was obviously a private vehicle.

She frowned, staring at the driver, his figure painted starkly by the flickering lamplight. For such an elegant coach, she expected to see a coachman in livery sitting on the box. Small and wiry, dressed in a baggy brown coat and striped breeches, the driver looked more like a sailor than a coachman. Why in the world would anyone allow a coachman to dress in that unfortunate manner?

As she contemplated this little mystery, a man walked out of the inn, a tall man dressed in black. Emily's heart tripped when he stepped into the pool of light cast by the street lamp. The golden light spilled across his face, illuminating features that had haunted her dreams. It was Sheridan.

"Get in," the driver said, gesturing toward the door, his sharp voice slicing the cool evening air.

Emily bit her lower lip. That was certainly not the behavior she would expect from a coachman, even one dressed like a sailor. The man calling himself Simon Richardson didn't seem to take offense. He climbed into the carriage.

The wiry little driver glanced around, flicking his head like a rat with the scent of a cat in his nostrils. Emily held her breath, afraid for a moment that he might actually be able to catch her scent on the cool breeze. The driver flicked the ribbons, starting the horses at a trot. She pulled on the reins, easing Arthur farther into the shadows as the carriage rattled past her hiding place.

"I have a bad feeling about this," she whispered, stroking Arthur's neck, watching the swaying carriage as it rattled down the road toward the docks. If Richardson really was Sheridan, and Sheridan really was involved with criminals, then he could be in trouble.

"I think we should find out where they are going," she whispered.

Moonlight glittered on the river, casting the reflections of buildings and square-rigged ships on the water, tall masts shimmering beside church towers. Simon glanced about as he followed Grady upward along the short gangplank leading from the dock of Bristol's Floating Harbor to the smugglers' ship. As far as he could see, only two men were on guard, both on the main deck. Either the captain didn't think Simon was a threat or he wanted to keep him off balance.

The two guards glanced at Simon, then returned to their conversation as he stepped on board. They leaned against the railing at midship, appearing lazy and unconcerned. Much too calm for men on guard. The back of Simon's neck prickled.

Grady stopped at the door of the cabin beneath the quarterdeck. "Ye ain't carryin' no weapons, are ye?"

Simon smiled. "I'm a businessman, Grady. I have no reason to be carrying a weapon."

Grady's brow wrinkled in a frown. "I'll just be seein' to that meself. Put out yer arms."

Simon did as directed, lifting his arms to his sides. Grady patted Simon's sides, explored his pockets, checked the waistband of his breeches, and dug his fingers into the tops of his boots. When he was satisfied that Simon was unarmed, he turned and rapped on the cabin door. At a gruff command from inside, Grady opened the door and ushered Simon inside.

Grady snatched his dirty hat from his head as he faced a man who sat in a high-backed chair in a corner of the spacious cabin. "Captain Trench, sir, I brought 'im like ye says."

"Ain't nothin' wrong with me eyes, Grady. Wait outside."

"Aye, sir." Grady scrambled to do the captain's bidding, closing the door softly as he left.

Captain Trench sat in a wingback chair covered in scarlet velvet, his ample hips testing the width of the seat, his booted feet propped on a small footstool covered in delicate needlepoint. He had the look of a predator, the kind that devoured all the flesh of his prey, then sucked the marrow from its bones. He chewed on a cheroot, his dark eyes narrowed against the smoke that rose and curled like a gray sea serpent around his dark head. He stared at Simon for a space of twenty heartbeats before he spoke. "Yer American?"

"That's right." Simon held the captain's steady stare, aware of Trench's intimidation tactics, careful to betray none of the uneasiness he had felt since boarding the ship. "I own a shipping business in Boston."

Trench grinned, his thin lips pulling back from stained teeth. "And what would a rich American be wanting with the likes of a poor sea captain like me?"

Simon surveyed his surroundings, the scarlet velvet drapes tied open at the portholes, the oil paintings in ornate gold frames on the mahogany-lined walls, the Persian carpet in shades of scarlet and ivory stretching to all four corners of the room. The cabin might have graced a duke's yacht. "It looks to me as though you do fairly well for yourself, Captain Trench."

Trench chuckled, the cheroot bobbing between his stained teeth. "Aye, that be true. So tell me what it is ye think ye can do fer me?"

Simon strolled to a Chippendale armchair across from Trench. "May I?"

Trench's eyes glittered like a cat with a plump mouse in sight. "I always like me guests to be comfortable, I do."

Simon sat and crossed his legs, forcing muscles tense with apprehension into a casual pose. He had the uneasy feeling this man knew exactly who he was. Still, there was nothing for him to do but to play out the game. "I represent a group of businessmen who would like to enter into a partnership with you."

Captain Trench removed the cigar from his mouth and picked a piece of tobacco from the tip of his tongue, taking his time to examine the brown fleck. The lamp suspended from the ceiling swayed like the pendulum of a clock with the gentle rocking of the ship, creaking on its chain, chipping away the seconds of Simon's life.

Trench looked at Simon, a cat playing with its prey. "Now, what type of business would ye be lookin' te start with me?"

Simon rested his elbows on the arms of the chair, gazing at his opponent over the steeple of his fingers, taking as much time to reply as Trench had. "I understand you have access to black powder, gunshot, and rifles. All the finest England has to offer."

Trench clamped the cigar between his teeth, his dark eyes sparkling with humor. "Now, what would rich businessmen want with all that nasty stuff?"

"I've heard you have a safe way to transport weapons in legitimate cargo. If that's true, we can do business. If it isn't, I won't waste any more of your time."

Trench tossed back his head and laughed, a man enjoying a private joke. Simon pressed the tips of his fingers together, keeping his emotions in check.

"I'm afeared yer a bit too late. Ye see, I already got a partner. And he told me all about ye." Trench slipped his hand into the crevice between his hip and the chair, withdrawing a pistol as he spoke. "Yer an Excise man come here to catch poor ole Captain Trench and his men."

The air froze in Simon's lungs. He glanced at the pistol, then looked up, meeting the deadly glare in Trench's eyes with an icy calm that belied the churning of emotion within him. If he was going to get out of this alive, he would have to keep his wits. "Obviously your partner has mistaken me for someone else."

"Has he? I'm thinking there is one way to be . . ." Trench paused as someone rapped on the door. "What is it?"

Grady opened the door and poked his head inside. "Sir, we found someone sniffing around the ship."

Trench grinned at Simon. "One of yer friends. Bring him in, Grady."

Simon silently cursed Digby's loyalty. He turned, his heart slamming against his chest when he saw Emily standing in the doorway.

Chapter Twenty-four

At the sharp prodding of a pistol in the small of her back, Emily stepped into the cabin, hoping no one noticed the trembling of her legs. She flinched at the sound of the door closing behind her, like the solid thud of a cage door slamming shut.

She looked at the man who called himself Simon Richardson, seeking a measure of reassurance. The fury flaming in his dark eyes only served to strengthen her resolve. This man had to be her Sheridan. And he was in trouble, just as she had suspected.

The big man sitting in a wingback chair in the corner grinned at her. ''Prime little bit of muslin,'' he muttered, lowering his eyes and leering at her in a way that made her stomach turn over in disgust.

Emily lifted her chin. ''I demand you release me this instant.''

The big man laughed at her, *laughed*, as though he found her outrage amusing. Light from a lamp suspended from the paneled ceiling shifted to and fro with the soft rocking of the ship, carving the burly man from the shadows, reflecting on a piece of metal he held against his thigh. Emily swallowed the gasp rising in her throat as she recognized the metal for what it was—a pistol aimed straight at Simon's heart.

She glanced at the wiry man standing beside her, who was staring at her like a hungry mongrel eyeing fresh meat. At least she knew for certain that she had been correct about the smugglers. Still, one question remained: How in the world were they going to get out of this tangle?

"Your men are a little jumpy, Trench." Simon planted his elbow in the arm of his chair, resting his chin in his palm, as casual as a guest at afternoon tea. "The lady was obviously simply looking at the ships in the harbor. I suggest you let her go before her companions come looking for her."

Trench frowned. "Companions?"

"A respectable lady doesn't go anywhere without a companion." Simon glanced at Emily. "Tell the good captain you were only out seeing the harbor by moonlight, Mrs. Blake."

Emily stared into his midnight eyes, taking her cue from the cold sense of calm radiating from him. "That's right. I became separated from my friends. I'm certain they must be looking for me."

"I'm thinking the lady came looking fer ye." Trench dropped his cigar into a brass cuspidor by his chair, the smoldering tip dying with a sizzle. He stood, floorboards groaning beneath his weight as he moved to stand in front of Simon. "Being yer her husband and all."

Simon stared up at the man, unwavering in his nonchalance. "You're mistaken."

"Am I now?" Trench grabbed one corner of Simon's beard and slowly peeled the fake whiskers from his face.

Emily stared at features that had haunted her dreams, pure joy pumping through her veins like liquid sunlight, banishing the last of her doubts. "You're alive. I knew it."

Simon looked at her and regret passed across his face. "I couldn't tell you, Em."

"It's all right," she whispered. Yet, her joy at having her wish fulfilled withered with the realization they both might soon be dead.

"So you didn' even tell yer wife ye be alive." Trench dangled the whiskers from his fingers like the pelt of a slaughtered animal. "Me partner will be real happy to be seein' the likes of you. He doesn' much like ye. I'm thinking he has somethin' interestin' planned for yer death. Said he wants to watch ye take yer last br—"

Simon surged to his feet. He wrenched the pistol from Trench's hand, his movements as fluid as a panther as he wrapped his arm around the big man's neck and held him like a shield in front of him.

Before Emily could react, Grady whipped his arm around her waist. She groaned at the sharp stab of a pistol jammed into her ribs.

"Let 'im go," Grady demanded, prodding Emily with the pistol. "Or I'll kill 'er."

Simon's lips pulled back from his teeth, his smile as cold and deadly as a demon. "Step away from the lady, Grady."

Grady shook his head. Emily bit her lower lip, fighting the urge to scream as he pressed that cold pistol into her ribs. *Calm and steady.* She had to remain calm.

Simon kept his cold gaze pinned on Grady as he spoke. "Tell your man to step away from the lady, Trench."

Trench sucked air between his teeth. " 'E'll kill her, 'e will."

"Oh no, I don't think he will. Not if you want to live, Captain." Simon tightened his arm around Trench's neck. "Do you understand me?"

"Aye." Trench looked at Grady, his fear naked in his eyes. "Let 'er go."

Grady hesitated, looking from his captain to Simon and back, all the while forcing the pistol tight against Emily's bruised ribs. She held her breath.

Simon tapped the muzzle of the pistol against Trench's temple. ''Seeing your man point a pistol at my wife has me a little nervous, Trench. Tell him to move before my finger slips on the trigger.''

''Move, man!'' Tench demanded, his voice choked to a whisper by Simon's forearm across his windpipe. ''Release 'er!''

Grady obeyed, stepping away from Emily as though she had the pox. Emily's knees threatened to buckle. She gripped the back of an armchair, steadying herself.

Simon smiled at her, a man in complete confidence of his own prowess. He actually looked as though he were enjoying himself. ''Would you mind taking the pistol from him, Em?''

He might have been asking her to serve the smuggler a cup of tea. Emily managed a smile, finding her own strength in the light of his. She glared at the little man who had poked that pistol against her side. Without a word she held out her hand, a queen silently demanding the surrender of a peasant. Grady licked his lips, hesitating a moment before thrusting the pistol into her trembling hand.

''Take a seat, Grady.'' Simon gestured with the pistol toward the armchair beside Emily. Grady obeyed, backing up until his knees hit the chair and he tumbled back into the seat.

''Good boy. Emily, tie him to the chair and stuff something into his mouth. I don't want any interruptions from the guards. I might have to shoot the captain if they decide to barge in uninvited.''

Trench cast a worried glance at Simon, who returned a smile.

Emily rested the pistol on a small desk that was built into one wall. She stripped the gold braided tiebacks from the drapes at the portholes and tied Grady to the chair, binding his arms to the arms of the chair, his legs to the front legs. She took particular pleasure as she stuffed the man's dirty handkerchief into his mouth. When Grady was secured, Simon released his hold on the captain.

''Please have a seat,'' Simon said, gesturing toward the armchair he had recently occupied. ''I wouldn't want you to be uncomfortable.''

Trench sank into the chair, the wood groaning beneath his weight. He rubbed his throat, staring up at Simon, an uneasy sinner sitting before his final judgment.

''Emily, would you be so kind as to tie the captain to his chair? I wouldn't want him to leave before our interview was complete.''

Emily glanced around, looking for something to use as rope. She pulled the scarlet counterpane from the bed built into one wall, crinkling her nose at the stench of human sweat clinging to the yellowed sheets below. She tugged one of the linen sheets from the bed and proceeded to tie the captain to the chair, wrapping the linen around his chest and the chair. When she was done, she tugged at his starched neckcloth, intending to stuff it into his mouth.

''There's no need to gag the captain,'' Simon said. ''At least not yet.''

Emily glanced at the door. ''Shouldn't we be leaving?''

''In a moment. After I get a few answers from the captain.''

''Oh.'' Emily retrieved the pistol, taking comfort in the solid feel of the weapon in her hand. ''I don't like to rush you, but I wonder if you could hurry a bit?''

Simon smiled. ''Did you hear the lady, Trench? She would like to be on her way.''

Trench pursed his lips, giving Simon an obstinate look. ''What do ye want?''

''The name of your partner.''

Trench glanced to the pistol Simon held. ''That pistol 'ill make a loud enough pop to bring me men.''

''You're right.''

Trench smiled, thin lips pulling back from yellowed teeth. ''I'll make ye a deal. Let me go, and I'll see yer death is quick. Not that slow painful end me partner has in store for ye.''

``You know, Trench, I've always been fascinated by knives.'' Simon bent, drawing a knife from the captain's boot. He held it in front of Trench's face, turning the dagger, capturing the lamplight in the shiny blade. ``Oh, and this is a lovely dagger. Nice balance. And the blade looks sharp enough to peel the skin from a man.''

Trench leaned back in the chair, straining to get as far away from the tall man and that knife as possible.

``I'll make you a deal,'' Simon said, his voice as dark and soft as black velvet. ``Tell me what I want to know, and I won't slit your throat before I leave.''

Trench considered this a moment, his small dark eyes darting from Simon's smiling face to the blade and back, obviously weighing loyalty to his partner against the certainty of his own death glittering in Simon's eyes. ``He calls hisself Smith.''

Simon rested the flat edge of the blade against Trench's cheek. ``And I suppose you have no idea what his real name is.''

Trench swallowed hard. ``I ain't never seen his face.''

``But you are partners, aren't you?''

``He wears a scarf over his lower face. A hat pulled over his eyes. He keeps out of the light.''

Simon frowned, easing the blade upward across Trench's cheek, slicing away the stubble of his beard and one thick black side whisker. ``You wouldn't lie to me, would you, Trench?''

Trench clenched his eyes shut. ``No. I swear.''

After a long moment, Simon lifted the blade. ``Where do you meet him?''

Trench gulped the air, like a flounder on the deck of a ship. ``It changes. He sends a message.''

``Where were you going to meet him tonight?''

Trench shook his head. ``He said he'd be watchin' the

ship. If he thought everythin' was all right, he'd send a message."

Simon swore under his breath. "Your partner is a very cautious man."

Trench nodded. "Aye, that he is."

Emily held the pistol between her hands, watching the interchange between the two men, her fear of the cutthroats fading in the light of a fresh concern. She stared at the man she had held in her arms, seeing a menacing stranger who could turn a hardened smuggler into a quivering mass of fear.

Fear curled the edges of her stomach. She shivered with a doubt she couldn't dismiss. Had he regained his memory? If he had, she might already have lost him. Sheridan Blake might be as dead as the man they had buried in the family tomb. And in his place might stand the scoundrel who had stolen her heart, a man she could never trust. Simon looked at her and winked. In spite of everything, she managed to give him a smile. It was Sheridan, she assured herself. It had to be.

Simon moved to stand behind Trench's chair, resting the flat edge of the blade against the smuggler's thick neck. "When I give you the word, I want you to call in your guards."

Emily stared at him. "You want him to call in the guards?"

Simon smiled. "Duck down behind Grady's chair. I want you out of the line of fire. His body should stop any stray lead."

Grady moaned.

Emily glanced at the door. "I suppose we can't just leave?"

"I doubt it." When she hesitated, Simon continued. "Trust me, Em."

"Fine." She marched to his side, ignoring the commanding look of displeasure molding his features. "We are in this together, sir."

Simon's mouth flattened to a narrow line. "Emily, I—"

She rested her fingertips against his lips, absorbing the warm exhale of his breath upon her skin. "I intend to stand at your side, no matter what. Please, don't fight me."

The harsh lines of his face softened, and for a moment she glimpsed the man beneath the hardened mask, a man filled with a need that mirrored her own. He touched her face, a soft brush of his fingers across her cheek, a touch filled with an aching tenderness. "God, I've missed you."

She smiled, her heart filling with hope, pushing away all her doubts. "When we get out of here, I'm going to insist you show me just how much."

"With pleasure." He brushed his lips across hers.

Emily leaned toward him, needing his arms around her. But he pulled away, leaving her craving his warmth.

"If anyone starts shooting, I want you to take cover behind me or behind this chair. Agreed?"

Emily nodded, her throat too tight to reply.

"All right." Simon pointed his pistol toward the door. "Let's invite your men to the party, Captain."

At Simon's command, Trench called to his men on deck. Emily bit her lower lip, listening to the footsteps pounding on the oak planks. At last the door to the cabin opened. She held the pistol between her damp palms, pointing it in the direction of the two smugglers who entered and froze when they saw their captain and his captors.

"Gentlemen, do come in." Simon pressed his pistol against the captain's temple. "And drop your weapons."

"Do as 'e says," Trench shouted. "And be quick about it."

The two men dropped their pistols, the heavy weapons falling with soft thuds on the carpet. Simon shoved the captain's dagger into the top of his own polished black Hessian, then collected the pistols, shoving them into the waistband of his breeches. At his order, the smugglers sat on the floor, back to back. After binding them together with the remaining sheet from the captain's bed, he gagged them and returned to the captain.

Simon leaned over the burly man until he could stare directly into Trench's eyes. "Tell your partner I won't stop until I see him swinging from the gallows. No matter what happens, he will not escape me."

Trench flicked his tongue over his lips, like a nervous lizard. "One of ye will die, there's no doubt of that."

Emily tapped Simon on the shoulder. "I really hate to interrupt you, but I thought we might leave."

Simon pulled the neckcloth from Trench's collar, rolled it into a ball, and stuffed it into the smuggler's mouth. "Let's go."

Masts creaked with the soft rocking of the ship as Simon walked with Emily toward the gangplank. He held her arm, keeping her at a slow, steady pace when she would have bolted.

"I suppose there is a reason you are creeping along," she whispered, glancing up at him, moonlight glittering in her eyes.

"There are three gentleman standing on the forecastle who might think it a little odd if we started running."

She glanced to where three sailors were standing in the shadows cast by moonlight against the masts. "Do you think they suspect anything?"

"They are probably only curious. Of course, that will change if one of the gentlemen we left tied in the captain's cabin finds a way to alert them."

Her hand tightened against his arm. "Yes, I suppose it would."

Simon glanced around as they crossed the narrow gangplank leading to the dock. Was the traitor still out there, in the shadows, watching them? Where would he hide? Another ship? One of the buildings lining the quay?

Emily drew in her breath, a slow easing of air past her lips, when they reached the cobblestone-covered quay. "I never realized the harbor was so empty at this time of night. No one would hear if we shouted for help.''

Someone might, Simon thought. A man calling himself Smith. He wanted to search every building standing along the quay, every alley, every ship. Yet he knew it wouldn't accomplish a bloody thing. The blackguard was too smart to stick around.

The captain's coach and horses stood where Grady had left them, tethered to a hitching post beside the road that curved along the edge of the harbor. The threat of Trench and his men gnawed at his stomach as Simon approached the coach.

He glanced over his shoulder. The three men who had watched them leave the ship were standing by the railing of the upper deck, watching them. One loud noise from the captain's cabin could turn them loose like a pack of hounds after a fox.

''Wait here,'' Simon whispered as they drew near the horses. ''I want to make sure Trench didn't post a guard.''

She stared up at him with wide eyes.

He touched her cheek. ''Try to look as though nothing is wrong. We don't want our friends on board to wonder what we're doing.''

She gave him a smile that was far too bright. ''Be careful.''

Simon squeezed the pistol in his pocket as he gripped the door to the coach. He took a deep breath and pulled open the door. Empty.

He turned and smiled at Emily. ''Your coach is ready, my lady.''

Emily bit her lower lip. ''We can't leave without Arthur.''

''Arthur?''

''My horse. I left him in the alley across the street.''

Simon glanced back at the ship fifty yards away. The three smugglers stood at the railing, dark shadows carved from the moonlight. In his mind he saw an hourglass, sand streaming away, marking the seconds until Trench and his men broke free. One wrong sound and . . .

Emily touched his arm. "Please. I can't leave him here."

"All right. I'll get him." Simon took her arm and helped her into the carriage.

He ran across the street, his heart pounding with the sound of his boots on cobblestones. He found Emily's chestnut gelding near the entrance of the alley. The horse followed him like a big puppy as Simon led him toward the coach. He was tying Arthur's reins to the back of the coach when he heard the first shouts. The sound ripped through him like a bolt of lightning.

Emily poked her head through the open window. "Are you all—"

"Get down on the floor. Lie flat!" Simon shouted as he dashed for the front of the coach. Ahead of him, he saw men streaming down the gangplank of Trench's ship.

He scrambled to the box and grabbed the ribbons. Leather slapped horse flesh. Shots cracked the night air. A lead ball whizzed past his cheek, so close the heat sizzled across his skin. The coach lurched against the sudden surge of the horses. He pulled on the ribbons, guiding the horses into a wide arc, veering away from the men who were running toward them.

Blood pounded in his ears, drowning out the clatter of horse shoes on cobblestones and the shouts of men intent on murder. He ducked low on the seat, trying to minimize the target he made in the moonlight. He had to get Emily out of this mess. He had to find a safe place, a place to confront his beautiful lady and the lies lurking between them.

Chapter Twenty-five

A full moon hovered in the midnight sky above Ravenwood, casting silvery light on the ancient stones and pathways, creating an oasis in the night. Simon knew the Red Lion wouldn't be safe. He knew he couldn't take Emily home. Not with the tattered shreds of deception still clinging to him. He wasn't certain how to explain the lies. He wasn't certain how to balance duty with emotion. He was only certain he had to try.

He led the horses through the arched entrance of the gatehouse, thinking of how Ravenwood's defenses still stood after four hundred years. Odd, he wondered if this was how Lord Ravenwood had felt the night he had brought his captured lady to this place—heart pounding with the anticipation of holding his lady again, skin tingling with anxiety at what would follow.

The horses tossed their heads, harnesses jangling in the quiet night, as he pulled them to a stop in the bailey. He jumped from the seat and jogged through the thick grass toward the coach door Emily was already opening.

''Are you all right?'' he asked, slipping his hands around her waist, the black silk of her gown warm from her skin.

''Fine.'' She threw her arms around his neck. ''Are you hurt?''

''Not a scratch.'' He lifted her, taking the plush weight of her against him, her breasts soft against his chest.

She stared into his eyes as though she had too long been denied the pleasure. ''I was frightened half to death you would be shot.''

Slowly he lowered her, absorbing the lush softness of her body sliding against his hardened flesh. Desire surged through his veins, curling into a fist that pounded low in his belly. ''When I saw you walk into that cabin I wanted to slip my hands around your neck and strangle you. What were you thinking?''

She touched his cheek, her palm soft and warm against his skin, her eyes filled with moonlight. ''I knew you were in trouble. I had to help.''

Her simple confession closed around him like comforting arms. She cared enough to risk her life to ride to his rescue. And in that moment, as he looked down into her face and saw her love for him shining in her eyes, he embraced all the hope that lay battered inside him, all the tarnished dreams.

''I knew the man in the fire must have been after you, because of something in your past. I came to the inn to tell you it didn't matter. Nothing that came before mattered. Nothing could keep me from loving you.''

''My brave lady.'' He slipped his arms around her, holding her close as she curled her arms around his shoulders and clung to him. She loved him. Through all the deceptions, her love had survived. ''My reckless, foolish, beautiful lady.''

''You're alive,'' she whispered, her voice broken by the tears falling hot and slick against his neck. ''I almost can't believe it. I prayed for a miracle, some wonderful event that would make the harsh reality of your death disappear. And here you are.''

''I'm sorry, Em.'' He turned his face, pressing his lips to her damp cheek, tasting her tears. ''I wanted to tell you the truth. I couldn't.''

''It doesn't matter.'' She gripped his face between her hands, looking up at him through her tears. ''Nothing matters except the fact you're here. Warm and alive and in my arms. Nothing else matters.''

The pure beauty of her love humbled him. He lowered his head, meeting her as she rose in his arms. He trembled like a callow lad at the first touch of her lips against his. All his life he had hungered for this moment, when he would hold this woman in his arms and taste her love. He had lived a lifetime lost in the cold depths of loneliness. A lifetime without the simple truth of honest affection. Until this moment in time. ''I love you, Em. Dear God, how I love you.''

''Show me.'' She tugged at his coat, stripping the black wool from his shoulders. ''I need your arms around me. I need to feel the warmth of your skin. I need your heart pounding against mine, each beat reassuring me over and over again that this is real.''

Love and desire pounded through him, so violent he shook. He lowered his arms, allowing the coat to fall to the grass. Emily was already tugging at the buttons of his shirt, tearing white linen in her haste. He helped her remove his clothes, sensing her need to strip away the barriers between them, just as he wanted to strip away his mask.

Finally he stood before her draped only in moonlight, as naked and vulnerable to this woman as the day he was born. She touched the puckered scar on his shoulder, a smile curving her lips. ''It really is you. I knew it the moment I saw you standing beneath my window.''

A cool breeze lifted her gown, brushing black silk against his legs. His skin tingled in response to the silky caress. He thought of all the lies scattered like shattered glass between them. All the pain he had caused her. He pledged in his heart he would erase the scars, ease the pain, with the love he had for her.

He fell to one knee before her, a knight before his lady. And in a distant part of his mind he wondered if the man who had fashioned the stone walls that sheltered them had once knelt like this, ready to pledge his heart, his soul, all he possessed to his lady. "I await your pleasure, my lady."

Emily smiled, her lips tipping into a mischievous grin. "Yes, I see you are offering me your sword. And I must say it really is quite impressive, my lord."

Simon grinned. "But I need a sheath, my lady. One soft and supple, fashioned for my sword alone."

"I think I can accommodate you, my bold warrior." Emily tugged the satin ribbon at the high waist of her gown, loosening the gathers. She slipped open the three jet buttons lining her bodice. Slowly she slipped the black silk from her shoulders, sweeping away her gown and the flesh-colored shift beneath. Moonlight poured over her pale shoulders, sliding downward across her breasts, her belly, the sleek curves of her legs, touching her the way he longed to touch her.

His blood thickened with the need to take her down upon the soft cool grass and plunge deep into her fire. Yet he forced control where primitive forces would rage. He wanted to love her slowly. He wanted to show her how much she meant to him. He wanted to give the very best of himself to this woman who had dragged him from the shadows of his lonely prison.

He slid his hand upward along the dark silk covering her leg, exploring the shape of her ankle, her calf, toying with one of the black silk garters adorned with pink rosebuds that held her stockings above her knees. "Let down your hair for me."

Emily lifted her arms, the soft swells of her breasts rising with the motion. She slipped pins and combs from her hair, curls tumbling around her shoulders in a riot of burgundy silk.

Simon stared up at his lady of moonlight and fire, savoring her beauty. The delicate fragrance of her feminine flower drifted to him on the breeze, a lush, exotic spice intoxicating his senses. "I've caused you pain, my lady. Let me heal the wounds."

"Touch me, my bold warrior. Let me feel the warmth of you, the strength of you."

"My lady," he whispered, leaning toward her, drawn to her fire.

Emily sighed as he pressed his lips to the smooth skin of her inner thigh just above her garter. He slid his palm upward, along the back of her thighs, the curves of her hips. She shifted in his hold, a soft whimper escaping her lips as he blazed a heated trail upward along her thigh, kissing her, tasting her.

He slipped his arms around her hips, pressing close against her. He brushed his lips against her soft feminine curls. He breathed in her scent, taking the spice of her arousal deep inside his lungs.

The pulse of his lifeblood pounded low in his belly, hungry flesh straining for a taste of her honey. Yet he lingered, teasing his own starving flesh, finding the secret place where her passion flared, feeding her pleasure with his lips and his tongue.

She trembled in his hold, soft agitated sounds slipping from her lips. She kneaded his shoulders with her hands, grasping and pushing, while she rocked against him, dancing to the ancient rhythm that mirrored the way he wanted to move inside of her. Never had he imagined a woman more responsive in his arms, as if she had been fashioned for him.

She shivered against him, shattering with the sudden surge of a pleasure too powerful to contain. He absorbed every shiver, tasting her pleasure, his every breath filled with her fragrance.

"I feel I've been granted a gift more precious than anything in this world," she whispered, sliding her hands through his hair. "Come into my arms, my bold warrior. Let me share with you this gift of our love."

He rose slowly from the ground, kissing her belly, her breasts, lifting her trembling body in his arms. She curled her arms around his shoulders, nestling her cheek against the curve of his neck, her breath hot puffs against his skin. For a moment he did nothing but hold her, absorbing her shivers, savoring the potent expectation of becoming one with her, before he lowered her to the thick cushion of grass. Each pulse of his heart throbbed in his loins, his need for her pounding like a clenched fist in his belly.

She touched his cheek, smiling up at him. "My sheath is well oiled, my lord. Pledge to me your sword."

"For my lady," he whispered, pressing his aroused flesh against that secret, silky place, where desire flowed from her. "Only for my lady."

She arched to receive him, sighing as he became a part of her. He kissed her, slanting his lips over hers, slipping inside to taste the sweetness of her mouth, a man long famished presented with a sumptuous feast. He forced a tight rein on the desire that demanded hard thrusts and quick rewards. He moved within her, deep slow strokes, savoring the desire awakening once more within her. She closed her arms around his shoulders, lifting her hips, meeting his every thrust.

On and on they moved, one into the other, friction sparking flames, until the very moonlight touching their skin turned to fire. Simon felt her shimmer, her body tightening all around him. She arched beneath him, singing the sweetness of her feminine release. And in the next heartbeat, he found his own release, a prolonged pleasure that streaked along every nerve, tightened every muscle, so intense he felt he might shatter.

He eased against her, pressing his lips against her neck, feeling the throb of her pulse against his skin. He breathed in her fragrance, the musk of their lovemaking teasing his senses.

Contentment. He had never really understood the meaning of that word until this moment. She slid her hands down his back, flexing her fingers against his skin. He smiled against her skin, drowsy, wanting to sleep in her arms.

"I thought I would die for missing you." She brushed her hand across his shoulder. "When I saw you beneath the tree outside my window, I was afraid I had gone mad for missing you."

"I needed to see you, Em. Even if from a distance."

"It must have been terrible for you." She pressed her lips against his neck. "Those dreadful men after you, without your remembering anything about them."

Her words whispered like frost across his damp skin. His breath froze in his lungs. She couldn't still believe his lie. Could she? He lifted his head, looking into her eyes, seeing a truth he wanted to deny.

"What is it, Sheridan? What's wrong?"

Sheridan. It had never occurred to him she might still believe in that fantasy. He closed his eyes, but he couldn't shut out the truth. She still believed he was Sheridan Blake, a man she had invented.

She cupped his cheek in her palm. "You mustn't think of those men. You mustn't dwell on anything from your past."

He pulled away from her, the breeze chilling his damp skin. He rolled to his feet, standing naked in the moonlight, feeling lost suddenly, as though he had been swept up by a storm and thrown to some distant place far from home. He had imagined all of it. Forgiveness. Acceptance. Love. He had imagined there was a place for him here, with this woman.

Emily got to her feet behind him. He felt her draw near, the warmth of her body reaching out to him. "What is it, my love?"

How ironic, to be trapped in a cage of his own making.

Every touch of hers had been meant for another man. Every kiss. Every caress. All of her affection. He had only stolen a few moments with her. And now he must face a truth that would cost him everything he wanted most in this life. He lifted his face to the breeze, fighting the urge to howl in pain.

She slipped her arms around his waist and pressed against him, warm and soft. She was every smile he had ever been denied, every touch, every warm embrace. She was everything he wanted, and everything he couldn't have.

"You must believe I will stand beside you no matter what you did before coming into my life. That was all in your past. You can't be held responsible for things you don't even remember."

But he could and would be damned for all he did remember, he thought.

She kissed his back, a warm brush of breath and lips that rippled along his spine. "I love you, Sheridan."

Sheridan. He didn't move. It was as though the moonlight had turned him to stone, his muscles tense and hard, while inside he was breaking into pieces. He wanted to turn. He wanted to take her in his arms and hold her, allow the fantasy to continue.

She pressed her cheek hard against his back. "I don't care if you were a smuggler. You have to believe me, I'll love you no matter what."

God, he wanted to believe her. Yet he knew that all of her compassion was for another man. He swallowed past the tight knot of emotion lodged in his throat. "I'm not a smuggler, Em. I'm an agent for the ministry."

She stiffened, her hands flexing against his waist. "An agent for the ministry?"

"I was sent here to stop a band of smugglers. The head of the operation found out who I was and decided to eliminate me. The man they sent to take me to Trench died in the fire."

She pulled away from him, the breeze cooling the skin

she had protected from the evening chill. ''You're an agent for the ministry?''

He turned to face her. Doubts shimmered in her eyes as she stared up at him. And he knew those doubts were born of concerns about what he knew and when he had learned the truth. ''Would it be easier to accept the fact if I were a smuggler?''

''No. I just . . .'' She studied him a moment, her eyes wide and wary. ''I wonder why you never told me you were working for the ministry.''

He realized she was still clinging to the hope he would remain Sheridan Blake, a man without a memory, clay for her to mold. And it was tempting to allow her to believe in a fairy tale he wished could come true. Yet he couldn't. He could no longer hide behind deception.

''Why didn't you tell me the truth? Why didn't you tell me you were working for the ministry?''

''I couldn't tell you the truth for fear of jeopardizing my mission.''

''I see.'' She shivered, hugging her arms to her waist, suspicion etched on her face.

He retrieved her gown, the black silk she had worn to mourn another man's death. ''You'd better get dressed.''

She took the gown, keeping her distance. While she dressed, he tugged on his clothes, slipping back into a disguise that could never shield him from the truth he now must face. When she was dressed once more, shrouded in black, she turned to face him. Her unbound hair rippled in the breeze that whispered across the bailey. Moonlight filled the empty space between them, a pale wall of light his lies had made as impenetrable as stone.

''How did you discover you were working for the ministry?'' she asked, her voice barely rising above a whisper. ''Was it Trench and his men? Did they tell you?''

The hope in her eyes taunted him. She wanted to keep Sheridan Blake alive. ''Trench knew who I was and why I was here.''

''Have you remembered anything else?''

He looked into her eyes, knowing for certain he would never love another woman the way he loved her—with all his heart and soul. And he prayed that he could salvage what they had shared. ''Emily, you have to believe me—when I took this mission I never meant for us to become involved. I never planned to hurt you.''

''You know.'' She pressed her hand to the base of her neck. ''When did your memory return? How long have you known the truth?''

He held her gaze steadily, a man unflinching in the judgment he knew would come. ''I never lost my memory.''

She stumbled back a step, as though his words had been a physical blow. She stared at him, a look so open in its pain that he could see the death of her dreams. She shivered, her breath escaping in a ragged groan.

''Emily,'' he whispered, moving toward her, reaching for her.

''No!'' She lifted her hand to keep him at bay. ''I don't want you to touch me.''

He stared at her, feeling utterly powerless for the first time in his adult life. ''You didn't feel that way a little while ago, Em.''

''How dare you remind me of my foolishness!''

''I know how you feel.''

''Do you?''

''Betrayed.''

She laughed, the sound carrying the bite of her bitterness. ''You're very good, aren't you? A wonderful deceiver. But then, I wanted to believe you.''

''Look at me.'' He opened his arms, wanting only to hold her, to take her close against his chest and ease the hurt he had inflicted. ''I'm still the same man who made love to you a few moments ago. I haven't changed simply because I wear a different name.''

''You lied to me.''

''Not about everything.''

"You used me. You used my dreams against me."

He stared into her tear-filled eyes, allowing all his defenses to drop away from him like tarnished armor. "I love you."

"Liar!"

Simon flinched, the single word piercing him like an arrow. "I didn't want to fall in love with you. It was a bloody foolish thing to do. But you a have a way about you, Miss Maitland, a way of penetrating the best defenses a man can erect."

She stared at him, suspicion naked in her eyes. "What do you hope to gain by these lies?"

"I hope to save what we have together, my lady."

She shook her head, dismissing his words. "Why did you come into my life? Why did you pretend to be Sheridan Blake in the first place?"

Simon turned away from her, realizing that any chance they might have for salvaging a future together would hinge on what he would now say. He rested his arm on a part of the wall where the stones had tumbled away, staring down at the river flowing like liquid silver in the moonlight. He could lie to her. Perhaps he should. Still, to what end would the lies lead them? He had three days to find a traitor or watch Hugh Maitland be arrested for treason. "A gang is smuggling weapons to Napoleon's forces in the Peninsula. While I was investigating the operation, I learned of your fake marriage."

"How in the world is my private life connected to a smuggling operation?"

Simon turned to face her, resting his back against the ancient stones. "Someone is using your father's ships to transport the weapons. I became Sheridan Blake to infiltrate your father's company."

Emily stared at him a moment, realization dawning in her eyes. "You think someone in my father's company is a traitor?"

"It has to be someone who can control the shipments."

Emily shook her head. "How do I know what you're saying is the truth? How do I know you aren't involved with these smugglers? You could have become Sheridan Blake to gain access to my father's company."

"Emily, I could have continued lying to you about my memory. That's what you wanted. But I wanted to end the lies."

"You're talking about my Uncle George or Laurence Stanbury."

He refused to add her father to that list. "It's possible one of them is a traitor."

"I can't believe . . ." Emily turned away from him, pacing a few feet into the bailey. She stood for a moment, staring up at the castle, before turning to face him. "It has to be Laurence."

"It's possible."

Emily pursed her lips. "It can't possibly be Uncle George."

"Emily, I need your help."

"My help? You expect me to help you?"

"If I can't find the traitor in three days, an innocent man could be sent to prison."

Her eyes grew wide. "Who?"

"It doesn't matter. It's better if you don't know."

"What do you want of me?"

"Your silence. No one must know I'm alive. No one must know about my mission."

She curled her hands into tight balls at her sides. "Do you have any idea how much pain you've caused my family? They grieve for you every day."

"I know. And I wish I could ease that pain. But I can't."

"No. It seems all you're really good at is causing pain."

Simon stared into her eyes, his own dreams withering beneath the icy tempest of her fury. "Three days. That's all I'm asking for, Em. Three days to catch a traitor. Three days to save an innocent man from the gallows."

Emily looked away from him, staring at the castle rising

in the moonlight, a pale ghost of another time and place. When she looked at him, her eyes were as cold and unyielding as gold in winter. ''All right. It's better if my family believes you're dead. Because as far as I'm concerned, Sheridan Blake died in that fire.''

Simon held her icy stare, wondering if he had forever lost the warmth he had found in her arms. ''Sheridan Blake is dead, my lady. But the man who loves you with all his heart is still alive.''

Pain flickered across her face. ''I've already agreed to keep your secrets. There is no more need for lies, Mr. Richardson, if that is your name.''

''It isn't.''

She released her breath in a long sigh. ''Somehow I didn't think it was.''

''It's St. James. Simon St. James.''

''St. James. Such a saintly name for a scoundrel.''

He managed a smile. ''I never said I was a saint, Em.''

''No. I never had any illusions about your sainthood.'' She turned away from him, staring at the gatehouse, her shoulders stiff with wounded pride. ''How do you expect to catch this traitor?''

''I don't want you to become involved in this.''

Emily pivoted to face him. ''You suspect someone in my father's company, perhaps even my uncle, of shipping weapons to the French. I would say that involves me.''

Simon studied her face, noting the militant thrust of her chin. If he wanted her cooperation, he would have to share a measure of the truth. ''The traitor ships weapons to a French agent going by the name of Ramirez. I need to find some evidence linking Ramirez to the man in your father's company.''

''How are you going to do that?''

''I'm going to see if I can find some documents in the man's possession linking him to Ramirez. Unfortunately, the records at Maitland Enterprises were destroyed in the fire. And I can't be certain the traitor would keep documents in his home. If I can't find anything linking one of the suspects to Ramirez, I'll have to set a trap."

"Set a trap?" Emily frowned. "That sounds dangerous."

"Worried about me?"

She stiffened. "I'm concerned about my uncle. If you make a tangle of this, he might very well go to prison."

"I'll do everything in my power to make certain the traitor is caught."

She smiled, a tight twisting of lips that left her eyes glittering with ice. "How very comforting to know that someone of your sterling character is hard at work."

Simon held her stare, the weight of his deception pressing against his heart like frozen lead. "When this is over, perhaps we could begin anew."

She shook her head. "When this is over, I never want to see you again."

Chapter Twenty-six

''An agent for the ministry.'' Lady Harriet paced the width of her bedroom, pivoting when she reached the carved mahogany fireplace. ''What the devil was he doing masquerading as your husband?''

Emily stood beside a window in her grandmother's bedroom, watching as the rising sun chased away the darkness from the sky above Ravenwood. After Simon had brought her home, she had come directly to her grandmother's room. She didn't want to be alone with her memories. ''He was investigating me, looking for a way to get close to Father when he discovered the truth about my marriage.''

Harriet crossed the room, turning when she reached the windows. ''And he believes Laurence Stanbury is a traitor?''

''Yes.'' Emily had neglected to tell her grandmother that the other man St. James suspected was her Uncle George. There was no reason to upset her grandmother over a complete impossibility. ''He has three days to discover the truth, or an innocent man will go to prison.''

"Who?"

Emily sank to an upholstered armchair near the vanity, weary suddenly, as though she were carrying a lead weight upon her shoulders. "I don't know."

"Smugglers. Traitors. Escapes into the night. I should have realized you were too impatient to wait until morning. I do recall telling you I would accompany you on your visit to Simon Richardson. But no. You must go off in the middle of the night." Harriet pivoted at the fireplace, the gold satin of her wrapper swirling around her legs. "What could have possessed you to do such a reckless thing?"

"I needed to know the truth. I never expected to walk into a tangle of smugglers and traitors."

Harriet shoved her lace-trimmed cap back from her brow. "You might have been killed."

"We escaped without a scratch."

Harriet marched toward the windows. "To think of my granddaughter in the company of smugglers. Good heavens!"

"Grandmama, please sit beside me." Emily smiled, hoping to ease her grandmother's anger. "I fear you might wear a rut in the carpet."

Harriet froze at the windows, casting Emily a stern look. "Young lady, I am not amused by your attempt at levity."

"Grandmama, please. I need your counsel, not your scolding."

Harriet sat in the vanity chair, her back as stiff as a bedpost. "I'm not at all certain why you want my counsel, you certainly don't intend to take any of my advice. If you would only—"

"I've lost him, Grandmama. I've lost Sheridan."

Harriet stared at Emily, the anger draining from her face. "Emily, he is alive. You have a second chance with him."

Emily squeezed her hands together until her knuckles blanched and her fingers ached, trying to hold together the frayed edges of her emotions. "Simon St. James never loved me. It was all a deception."

Harriet touched Emily's chin, soft fingers urging her to lift her head. She smiled when Emily looked at her. "I suspect that young man fell in love with you the first moment he looked at you."

Emily shook her head. "I was nothing more to him than a means to infiltrate my father's business. Perhaps his motives were different from those of a typical fortune hunter, but the result was the same. He used me."

"You can actually keep them separated, Sheridan Blake from Simon St. James?"

Emily smiled, a sad twisting of her lips that she knew lacked any joy. "I created Sheridan Blake. And like Pygmalion, I fell in love with my creation."

"But he is the same man, regardless of his name."

"No. The man who barged into my life was a man who wanted only to use me. Sheridan Blake loved me. Of course, that love wasn't real. Sheridan wasn't real."

Harriet rolled her eyes toward heaven. "There are times when I wish you had not inherited my stubborn streak."

"I'm not certain how I'm going to explain all of this to father and mother."

"I suppose it is inevitable that you tell them the truth."

"They deserve the truth."

"Yes. Of course they do." Harriet cleared her throat. "Unless you have a plan."

Emily had a plan, but it had nothing to do with telling her parents the truth and everything to do with proving her uncle innocent. Still, she knew her grandmother would never sanction the activities she had planned for this evening. "When this is over, Grandmama, I'm afraid we shall each face our own reckoning."

A cool breeze drifted through the two arched windows of the chapel at Ravenwood, brushing Simon's face with the scent of damp grass. He leaned his shoulder against a stone wall and stared out across the bailey where he had made love with Emily. The first rays of the awakening sun sparkled against the dew-covered grass, chasing away the shadows of the night. Simon wished his own doubts and fears would vanish in the sunlight.

"This reminds me of the time our regiment camped in that ruined church near Coruna," Digby said as he dropped an armload of blankets on the stone floor. "Can't say I envy you, sir."

Simon smiled. "At least it's only for a few days."

"Aye." Digby rubbed his chin, staring down at the provisions he had stacked in a corner of the room. "We have three days to find the traitor. I'm hoping you have a plan."

Simon leaned back against the wall. "I'm going to take a look at the private files of both Stanbury and Whitcomb tonight."

"And if you don't find anything?"

"Then we are going to set a trap, and hope our man is frightened enough to walk into it." Simon rubbed the stiff muscles at his nape. "Meet me here tomorrow at dawn. If we need to, we'll work out the details then."

Digby frowned. "I was thinking I would be going with you tonight, sir."

"I want you to keep an eye on Emily. I have a feeling she might try something foolish."

"But, sir, you'll be needing someone to watch your back."

"I'll be fine."

"Sir, if you don't mind me saying so, you're being a mite too reckless again."

Simon smiled. "All I'm going to do is break into two houses, Digby. I think I can manage."

Digby sighed. "Aye, sir. I'll keep my eye on Miss Maitland. You won't need to be worrying about her. I'll make sure she doesn't get into any trouble."

Emily pulled her shawl closer around her head and shoulders, hoping the black lace would help her blend into the shadows in the gardens of Laurence Stanbury's townhouse on Queen's Square. She had slipped out of her house soon after eleven, certain no one had seen her leave. She intended to search the desk in Laurence's library for any evidence linking him to the smugglers, but the man seemed intent on staying up all night. It was close to midnight, and Laurence showed no signs of retiring.

She eased closer to the library window, careful to stay clear of the golden light spilling into the gardens from the wall sconces and table lamps glowing in the room. Laurence was sitting at his tiered mahogany desk, which stood against an oak-paneled wall, perpendicular to the windows. Papers were scattered across the desk in front of him. Several ledgers were propped open. Emily wondered if anything dealt with Ramirez.

A branch of a yew poked her in the ribs. Emily flinched, bumping into the rosebushes planted below the library windows. The sharp prick of a thorn in her thigh dragged a startled gasp from her lips. She stepped back, slapping her hand over her mouth. But it was too late. Laurence had heard her.

She ducked beside the yew. Through the thick branches of the bush, she saw Laurence rise and walk toward the partially open windows. She held her breath, hoping he would think the noise had come from the street, or perhaps the alley behind the house.

He stood staring into the moon-swept gardens, his hands plunged into the pockets of his russet-colored coat, a frown carved into his brow while Emily prayed he couldn't hear the pounding of her heart in the quiet night. After a moment, he turned away from the windows. Emily released her pent-up breath. Laurence paused in front of his desk, as if debating the rewards of returning to work.

Go to bed. Emily silently willed Laurence to leave the library.

As if he had heard her, he closed one of the ledgers and locked it in a drawer before extinguishing the candles and lamps. Emily's heart crept upward in her chest as she watched Laurence leave the room. Why would he lock only that one ledger in his desk? Perhaps because that one ledger contained information he couldn't afford to allow anyone to see. Information implicating him with the French.

Emily waited a few moments, until she saw a light glow at the windows of a second-floor room. She took a deep breath and crept toward the windows. She eased her way around the rosebushes, pushed one of the windows open wide, and hopped onto the windowsill. After swinging her legs inside, she eased to the floor, aware of the loudness of her own breath and the pounding of her heart.

Moonlight spilled through the windows, lighting her way as she hurried to the desk. She ignored the papers scattered across it, and the open ledger. She was more interested in the ledger and other papers that were locked in those drawers. The question remained, how could she get the blasted desk open?

She began shifting papers, searching for something to pry open the lock, settling on a silver letter opener. She was bending over the lock when she felt a presence in the room. Good heavens, someone was there, in the darkness.

Fear whispered like frost over her skin. The fine hair on her arms tingled. She gripped the letter opener and turned toward the windows, hoping to escape before the intruder caught her.

Before she could take a step, a man whipped a strong arm around her waist and clamped a hand over her mouth. She struggled, twisting in his grasp, slamming her elbow into his hard belly. He grunted. A dark curse rumbled near her ear. But he didn't release her.

"Damnation, Emily, stop struggling before you have Stanbury and the servants upon us."

Emily nearly collapsed at the sound of that familiar whisper. She sank back against Simon's chest, dragging air into her lungs as he pulled away his hand. "I thought it was Laurence."

"What the devil are you doing here?"

Emily turned to face him. With his dark hair and his black shirt and breeches, he blended into the shadows. Still, the moonlight through the windows revealed his face, and the anger etched upon his features. "I thought I might find some evidence."

"And I thought you promised to stay out of this."

Emily lifted her chin. "I never said anything of the kind."

He closed his eyes and dragged a deep breath into his lungs. When he looked at her, she flinched at the fury blazing in his eyes. "I want you out of here. Now."

"But I can—" Emily gasped as he grabbed her arm and started hauling her toward the windows. "I must say I don't care to be dragged about like a bone in the clutches of an angry dog."

Simon paused at the windows. "I must say I don't care to have my orders disobeyed."

"Orders!" Emily glared at him. "How dare you believe you can . . ." Her whispered words dissolved in a rush of air as he lifted her into his arms. "What do you . . ."

Simon thrust her out the window, released his arm from beneath her knees, and deposited her into the rosebushes.

Emily yelped as a thorn pricked her bottom.

Simon frowned. "Quiet. Stanbury's bedroom window is open."

Emily planted her hands on her hips, glaring up at the man. "If you hadn't thrown me into the roses, I wouldn't have—"

"Go home," he whispered, his dark voice filled with command.

"But I—"

He shut the window and disappeared, sinking back into the shadowed library.

"Of all the high-handed . . ." She eased open the window and poked her head inside, her anger at his brutish behavior dissolving into fear for his safety.

He was kneeling in front of the desk, inserting a small

piece of wire into the lock. A heartbeat later, she heard a soft click as the lock opened.

"You're very good at that," she whispered. "But then, I'm certain breaking into homes is only one of the abilities scoundrels find advantageous."

He cast her an angry glance. "I thought I told you to go home."

Emily lifted her chin. "You will find I do not obey orders as readily as a green recruit."

Simon shook his head. "Even a green recruit usually has enough sense to be frightened of battle."

She crinkled her nose at him. "I thought you should know Laurence locked a ledger in the bottom left-hand drawer."

Simon pulled open the drawer and retrieved the ledger. He tipped it toward the moonlight, glanced at one page after another, putting it back in the drawer when he was done. Deftly he searched the other drawers, shuffling through papers, holding them out to the moonlight, moving like a panther in the shadows. He was going through the last drawer when footsteps echoed on the oak planks of the hall outside the room.

Emily looked at Simon, intending to warn him. He was glancing toward the door. Obviously he had heard the sound, but there was no time to reach the windows. He gestured for her to duck before he headed for cover, crouching behind a settee near the fireplace.

Emily sank down into the roses, drawing her black shawl up over her head. She held her breath as the library door opened and closed. A light flickered in the window above her, the faint light of a single taper in a darkened room. Would it be enough to betray Simon? she wondered. And then she remembered the unlocked desk. If Laurence had returned to retrieve something from that desk, they were lost.

Footsteps crossed the carpet. She ducked her head, huddling close to the brick wall below the window. The window! Dear heaven, would he notice the open window? Her heart pounded. Her skin dampened with fear. Inside the room the soft shuffle of a book being drawn across an oak shelf rumbled like thunder to her heightened senses. *Please go back to bed. Please don't look around.*

It seemed a lifetime before she heard the soft sound of footsteps moving across the carpeted floor. The library door opened and closed. Footsteps echoed on oak. Emily collapsed against the wall, limp from the sudden release of tension.

A few moments later Simon slipped through the window. He dropped to the ground without a sound. After closing the window, he grabbed her arm and hauled her to her feet. When she opened her mouth to speak, he pressed his fingers to her lips. He gestured upward toward Laurence's room.

Emily nodded, realizing they still had to get out of the garden without being seen. He gripped her upper arm, leading her toward the gate that opened to the alley. If Laurence chanced to look out his window, would he recognize the two shadowy figures racing from his house? If he raised an alarm, would they be caught?

Dear heaven, she could just imagine what her grandmother would say. Worse, if she were tossed into prison she would have to confess everything to her parents.

Still, Laurence did not see them as they slipped through the gate and into the dark alley. Simon's hand was like a vise around her upper arm as he dragged her to the place near the entrance to the alley where her horse stood beside a tall black stallion. Arthur tossed his head when he saw her, whinnying as though he too wanted to scold her.

"Of all the foolish, pig-headed . . ." Simon ran his hands through his hair, plowing furrows in the thick dark waves. "Woman, do you ever tire of your own reckless behavior?"

His sharp words pricked her pride. She lifted her head, meeting his anger with defiance. "I was doing quite well before you barged into the library."

Simon grabbed her shoulders. "What the devil would you have done if Laurence had caught you in there?"

"He didn't."

"But he bloody well could have."

Emily twisted under his tight grasp. "I was only trying to help."

"What the devil am I going to do with you?"

"I don't intend to allow my uncle to be accused of something he didn't do."

Simon released his tight grip on her shoulders. "I don't want anything to happen to you. Do you understand?"

"Pity you didn't have those noble sentiments a few weeks ago."

His lips pulled into a tight line as he stared down at her. "This isn't a game, Emily. The men involved in this operation are willing to betray their country. They certainly wouldn't hesitate to murder one headstrong female."

"I'm not as incapable as you seem to think I am."

"I don't think you're incapable." He studied her a moment, the anger draining from his features, replaced by a warmth that threatened her more than smugglers ever could. "I think you're intelligent, resourceful, and far too brave."

Heat unfurled inside her, like a bright blossom opening in the rays of the sun. She stepped back from him, appalled at her own treacherous reactions to this man. "And I think I shall never again believe a single word you have to say."

"Emily, this is my mission. Trust me when I say I can deal with it on my own."

"I have discovered that trust is a fragile commodity."

Simon released his breath in a sigh. "Emily, if you don't stay out of this, if somehow you alert the real traitor to our suspicions, there is a very good chance you could help send an innocent man to the gallows."

"Oh." Emily pressed her hand to her throat, her fingers brushing the pulse racing there. "I only meant to help."

"Promise me you will stay out of this."

"Very well. I shall leave the housebreaking to the experts."

He smiled, a shadow of the smile she had come to love. "Thank you, my lady."

She stiffened with the memories conjured by his soft endearment. "I would prefer that you not call me that."

"And I would prefer that you could understand why I lied to you."

"I do understand. You had a mission to complete." She stepped back when he lifted his hand to touch her face. "But it certainly doesn't alter my feelings toward you. I despise you."

He hesitated a moment, his hand outstretched, his fingers slowly curling toward his palm. He lowered his hand, all expression draining from his face until all that remained was a handsome mask. "I'd better get you home."

Emily turned away from him, hiding her pain, afraid he might glimpse her weakness. If he knew her weakness, he would take advantage, of course. Predators knew how to take advantage of their prey. She had to face reality. She could no longer rely on illusions. For a few moments she had held a dream. A dream that couldn't survive the light of reality.

Chapter Twenty-seven

Moonlight was fading. Outside the chapel walls of Ravenwood, birds sang to the awakening day. Simon stood by a window, thinking of Emily, wondering if her night had been as restless as his own. Lord, he couldn't close his eyes without seeing her. She taunted him during the few hours he had slept, coming to him in his dreams, warm and soft and willing in his arms.

Digby paced the floor behind him. "I'm wishing you had found something last night, sir."

"Whitcomb doesn't have a single paper related to Maitland Enterprises in his desk. Stanbury looks as though he brings half of his office home every night. Nothing concerned Ramirez."

Digby paused beside Simon, the gray light of dawn illuminating the deep lines carved into his face. "I was afraid of that, sir."

Simon rubbed the tight muscles in his neck. "When you get back to Maitland's I want you to write and deliver a note to Stanbury. Address it to Mr. Smith. The note should read: 'We got trouble. Meet me at St. John's Gate. Midnight tonight.' Sign it 'Trench.' "

Digby rubbed his chin. "What if the man doesn't know anything about Trench? What do you think he'll do?"

"I suspect he will think the note was delivered to the wrong man and ignore it."

"You don't want me to deliver a note to Whitcomb?"

Simon shook his head. "I doubt Whitcomb is involved. And I can't be certain he wouldn't tell someone about it. He could spoil our chances with Stanbury."

"What if Stanbury doesn't show tonight?"

Simon rested his hands on the stone sill of the window and stared out at the bailey. "Then tomorrow I'll try Whitcomb. If that doesn't work, I'm afraid I'm out of ideas."

"And Hugh Maitland is out of luck."

Simon's muscles tensed at the thought. "I'll keep looking for evidence to clear him, Digby."

Digby was quiet a moment. "I want to come with you tonight, sir."

Simon smiled, realizing that asking Digby to watch Emily was a waste of time. Even if the lady broke her promise to him, which he hoped she wouldn't, Emily had a way of slipping past the guard. "I'm expecting you to watch my back, Digby."

Digby grinned. "Aye, sir, I'll be there."

Simon drew a deep breath, hoping Stanbury would also be there.

Emily sat on a sofa beside her grandmother in the Maitland drawing room, watching as her father, her Uncle George, and Laurence Stanbury entered the room. The gentlemen had apparently finished their after-dinner brandy and decided it was time to join the ladies. Emily twisted the stem of her sherry glass between her fingers, watching Laurence as the men greeted her along with Harriet, Audrey, Anna, and Claudia. She had known Laurence most of her life. Was the man truly a traitor? She had to discover the truth. She had to find a way to be alone with him.

''Emily, I really must say you look delightful in black. You should wear it more often.'' Claudia sipped her sherry, oblivious to the startled stares she received from the other ladies.

Audrey and Anna, who were sitting on the sofa across from Emily, both cast worried glances in her direction. Her parents and sisters treated her as though she were made of porcelain, in danger of breaking if not handled gently. And Emily recognized the truth—she had been that fragile before learning Simon was still alive. Her family was in mourning for a man who was very much alive. It was all Emily could do to keep from telling them the truth.

Harriet cleared her throat. ''Claudia, I doubt Emily would care to be presented with a reason to wear mourning more often.''

Claudia's huge blue eyes widened as she looked at Harriet. ''Why, no, of course not. It really was a terrible shame about poor dear Major. Wasn't it, Whitcomb?'' She looked up to where George stood beside her chair.

''Yes, Blake was a true out-and-outer.'' George rested his hand on the back of her armchair, the white lace of his cuff spilling across the lyre-shaped rosewood. ''Pity, the way he went.''

''He was such a lovely man, so incredibly dashing.'' Claudia smoothed the black silk of her skirt. ''But it's good to know that if one is forced to wear mourning, one looks so delightful in it. I sometimes fear it is a trifle too severe for me.''

''No need to fear, pet.'' George pulled a red enameled snuff box from his coat pocket, the rubies and diamonds adorning the trinket sparkling in the candlelight. ''You look like a diamond, sparkling against black silk.''

Claudia smiled up at George. ''Why, sir, you do flatter me.''

George lifted his chin, obviously pleased with himself. Emily watched as he crossed the room to where Laurence and her father were standing near the open French doors. It was insane to even imagine that her uncle could be involved with the French. Wasn't it? It had to be Laurence, she assured herself.

George flipped open his snuffbox and held it out to Hugh. "I'm trying a new blend. Mixed for me exclusively by Fribourg and Treyer, Prinny's favorite tobacconists, you know. Care for a pinch?"

Hugh raised his hand. "No, thank you."

"I'm told that Prinny actually drops the stuff before he takes a sniff. If you can imagine that." George shifted the box, holding it toward Laurence's face. "I find this blend particularly pungent. Clears the head."

Laurence shook his head. "I'm afraid it gives me a headache."

A breeze swept through the open French doors, ruffling the burgundy velvet drapes, sweeping across the open box, tossing snuff into Laurence's face.

"Sorry, old man," George said, withdrawing the snuffbox, but the damage had been done.

Laurence blinked. He passed his hand over his face, trying to brush away the fine tobacco powder, to no avail. His features screwed up. He sneezed so hard his hair stood on end, oiled brown strands poking up like a porcupine's quills.

"Oh, I say, I am sorry, old man. Let me help." George whipped a white linen handkerchief from the pocket of his black coat and made to wipe the snuff from Laurence's face.

Laurence sneezed, jerking forward straight into George's outstretched hand.

"Bad luck, that," George muttered.

Laurence reeled back, lifting a hand to his cheek, tripping over a footstool near the hearth. He fell, whacking the carpet. The impact rattled the crystal decanter of sherry and glasses on a lion-footed pedestal table.

Laurence groaned. The ladies gasped. Hugh rushed to Laurence's side.

George frowned as he stared down at the man sprawled on the carpet. "I say, old man, are you injured?"

Laurence sucked in his breath. He stared up at George as though he faced a demon straight from hell. "I'm . . . fine."

Emily poured sherry into a glass as Hugh helped Laurence to his feet. "Here, sip this," she said, moving to Laurence's side. "It might help clear your head."

Laurence stared down at her, his eyes wide with shock. "Thank you," he said, taking the glass.

"Why don't we go out on the terrace?" Emily said, taking Laurence's arm. She looked up at her father. "I think he could use some fresh air."

Hugh slanted a glance at George. "I suspect it will be safer out there."

"I say, Stanbury, I do hope the snuff doesn't give you a headache," George said as Emily led Laurence toward the French doors.

Laurence smoothed his hand over his ruffled hair, grimacing as he touched a tender spot near the back of his head. "I shouldn't worry about that, Whitcomb. I doubt the *snuff* will give me the headache."

"Glad to hear that, old man."

A cool evening breeze bathed her face as Emily stepped onto the terrace. She walked with Laurence toward several white wicker chairs standing a few feet away, her heart pounding as she realized she had her chance to question Laurence.

He eased into one of the chairs, the wicker creaking under his weight. "I do believe I shall be sitting lightly for the next few days."

"Are you all right?" Emily asked.

Laurence drew in his breath. "Yes. Thank you."

Emily leaned against the stone balustrade, looking down at him, uncomfortable with the idea he might be a traitor.

Still, presented with only two options, she had to believe her uncle was innocent. "I thought you seemed distracted tonight at dinner."

Laurence stared down into his sherry. "I was thinking of business, I'm afraid. The Americans are quite a nuisance. They are wreaking havoc with our trade to the Indies."

"I would hope our other markets are secure."

"The Mediterranean runs have had little trouble."

She needed to catch him off guard, make him slip and reveal his connection to Ramirez. "Yes, well, Father has mentioned he believes Ramirez will remain satisfied with our shipments."

Laurence looked up at her, failing to disguise his surprise. "I didn't realize you were so interested in your father's business dealings."

"Oh, I find it fascinating." She toyed with the black satin ribbon at the high waist of her gown. "Have you ever met Mr. Ramirez?"

Laurence frowned. "No, I can't say I have. Why do you ask?"

"He seems to be quite an important customer. I thought you might have had dealings with him."

Laurence sipped his sherry. "Your father handles Ramirez. I can't say if he has met with him directly."

Emily shivered with a sudden, disturbing thought. "Father deals with Ramirez?"

Laurence nodded. "He usually handles the new customers until he is well satisfied they will remain with the company."

"I see." If Simon suspected Laurence and Uncle George, did he also suspect her father? It was a preposterous idea, of course. Her father would never betray his country. Still, the thought of Simon investigating her father left her strangely unsettled.

"Is something wrong? You look pale suddenly."

Emily forced a smile to her lips. "I was simply thinking of how precarious shipping during a time of war can be."

He pulled his lips into a tight line, his brown eyes glittering like ice in the moonlight. "You needn't worry. The shipping business is only a small part of your father's empire. You wouldn't end up a pauper if all of the shipping concerns were sunk."

Emily studied him a moment. "You're still very bitter about your father, aren't you?"

Laurence drained his glass. "I intend to be wealthy again. One day soon."

Emily suspected that a man could become very wealthy shipping weapons to the enemy. "Have you made some wise investments?"

Laurence sat back, studying her as though she were a prize mare up for auction. "I can assure you, I would be able to provide for you if you ever decide to accept my offer."

"It's not exactly appropriate to be discussing marriage when I've only just become a widow."

"I realize you are in mourning now. But the time will come when you will be looking for companionship. I only wish you to know, I am still interested."

Emily cringed at the thought of this man ever touching her. "I shall keep that in mind."

Laurence rose, grimacing as he straightened. "It's getting late. I have some work I wish to complete this evening. Good evening."

"Good evening." Emily watched him leave, wondering what business he had to attend to. In spite of his insistence that he had nothing to do with Ramirez, Emily couldn't believe him. The alternatives were too terrifying.

She turned and stared out across the garden. Bright blossoms swayed in the evening breeze. Yet, she couldn't appreciate their beauty. A nagging suspicion gnawed at her belly.

It has to be someone who can control the shipments. Simon's voice rippled in her memory. The traitor was someone in command at Maitland Enterprises. Did Simon suspect her father? Was that the reason he had been investigating her? Had he been looking for a way to get close to her father?

If I can't find the traitor in three days, an innocent man could be sent to prison. Simon's words taunted her. Emily pressed her fingers to her lips, trembling with a terrible suspicion. She stared past the flowers to where Ravenwood stood in the moonlight. Simon St. James had a few questions to answer. And she intended to get those answers tonight.

Moonlight glowed on the hands of the clock in the steeple of St. John-on-the-Wall. The stone church rose like an ancient sentinel from the medieval gateway to the city. Simon stood in a narrow alley across from St. John's Gate, watching, waiting as the clock clicked away the minutes of the new day.

Where was Stanbury? Simon stared into the shadows, searching for a shifting of light that might betray a man hidden in the recesses of shop entrances, or the alleys in between the rows of wooden buildings. Smith was an intelligent opponent. If Stanbury was indeed Smith, he might very well see the note as a trap. He might send some of his men to deal with the threat.

Something rustled in the alley behind Simon. His muscles tensed. He pivoted, lifting the pistol he held at his side. In the faint glow of moonlight filtering into the alley, he saw a man approach.

" 'Tis only me, sir," Digby whispered.

Simon leaned back against the wall, some of the tension draining from his taut muscles. "It's not a good idea to sneak up on a man who is waiting for a murdering cutthroat, Digby."

"You always keep your wits about you, sir. I knew you wouldn't be shooting unless you were sure of your target." Digby paused beside him, brushing against his arm in the narrow space. "It don't look like our man is going to be showing his face tonight."

Simon wanted to deny the truth of those words, but he couldn't. It was half past midnight, and Stanbury hadn't put in an appearance. He slipped his pistol into his coat pocket and rested his head back against the brick wall at his back. "I still can't believe Whitcomb is involved in this."

Digby rubbed his chin. "I hate to say this, sir, but do you think we were wrong about Maitland being innocent?"

The weight of that possibility pressed against Simon, like a carved marble tombstone marking the demise of his future with Emily. "I honestly don't know. But I do know I'm not satisfied with the evidence. Until I've explored every possible alternative, I refuse to believe Hugh Maitland is guilty."

Chapter Twenty-eight

It was after midnight when Emily passed the gates of Ravenwood. She left Arthur in the bailey and entered the castle keep. Moonlight spilled through the phantom roof, silvery light sliding down the stone walls, guiding her through the great hall to the chapel. Simon's few provisions sat nearby. But there was no sign of him.

Was he in danger?

Emily thumped her palm against the stone wall of the chapel. Lord, she hated this. The emotions she couldn't bury. The horrible need to wrap her arms around him and lock him to her side—forever.

Forever.

She closed her eyes, bitter bile etching a path upward along her throat. She hated this most of all, the dreadful reality she couldn't deny. Simon St. James didn't love her. He had only used her. "Forever" for them had been no more than a fleeting dream. She curled her hand into a fist against the ancient stone. Dear heaven, reality was far from kind.

Footsteps echoed in the great hall of the castle, booted heels clicking against stone. She pivoted, her heart bumping against her ribs in a rush of excitement. Simon was here.

A man appeared in the threshold of the chapel. Moonlight carved his dark shape in the arched doorway, casting his face in shadows. Yet Emily didn't need to see his face to know that this tall, terribly slender man was not Simon. She stepped back, flinching with sudden fear.

"I've always had remarkable insight into the human mind." He stepped into the room, pausing in a shaft of moonlight slanting through one of the arched windows. "Take you, for example. I knew you would lead me to his lair. All I needed to do was follow you."

An involuntary shudder rippled through her. His hair was as white as his skin, slicked back from a face awash in moonlight. His skin stretched tautly over bone. His eyes sank into shadows so dark they seemed no more than twin hollows in a skeleton's skull. "Who are you? What are you doing here?"

He laughed low in his throat, a sound more akin to bitterness than to joy. "Why, my dear Miss Maitland, do you mean to say you don't recognize me?"

"No. I don't." Emily stepped back, seeking escape, finding only a stone wall. The only way out was behind him. And she had the feeling he didn't intend to let her pass.

"I'm afraid I have changed a bit since last we met." He ran his hand over his cheek, as though he were touching delicate porcelain. "I was once quite handsome. But, alas, the illness has taken a rather severe toll on me. I shudder each time I glance in a mirror."

Emily edged toward the door, fighting her fear of him. "This is my father's property. I don't know what you're doing here, but I want you to leave."

"You aren't thinking of leaving, are you?" He lifted his hand, bringing the pistol he held into the moonlight. "I'm afraid I must insist you stay a while."

Emily pressed back against the wall, her heart hammering against her ribs. "What do you want?"

"I thought you might have guessed by now, you are such a clever girl."

Emily stared at the glittering steel in his hand. "You're Smith, aren't you?"

"When it suits me."

"You're Trench's partner."

"Not exactly. Trench works for me. At least he did, until I realized he had outlived his usefulness. I killed him."

Emily pressed her hand to her lips, unable to catch the frightened gasp escaping her tight throat.

His lips curled into the slow, satisfied smile of a predator reliving a kill. "It was the first time I ever killed a human being. Though I must admit, Trench was barely human. Still, I was amazed at the sense of power I felt as I watched him die. One does feel so powerless facing one's own demise. It was really quite exhilarating to experience the divine power of life and death."

She had little doubt the man wouldn't hesitate to kill her. She shivered at that stark reality. "Are you working with Laurence Stanbury?"

"So Stanbury is at the top of your list of suspects, is he?" He laughed, as though enjoying a private jest. "I suppose that is where Simon is at the moment, trying to catch the traitor."

Emily swallowed past the fear lodged in her throat. "You know Simon?"

"Oh, yes. I know him well. Although I suspect not half as well as you know him."

In spite of her fear, Emily's cheeks grew warm at the man's suggestive tone.

He rested his shoulder against the wall near the narrow window, smiling at her. "I rather suspected you might fall in love with Simon when I chose your father to play a role in my little drama. It only makes everything that shall follow all the more enjoyable."

"What does my father have to do with any of this?"

"Your father made the mistake of betraying me. No one betrays me and walks away unscathed. No one."

There was an icy calm about this man, an aura of evil that spilled into the air and coiled like tendrils of fog around her. Emily hugged her arms to her waist, trying to ease the chill of fear. "I can't believe my father would ever do anything dishonest."

"Oh, I never said he was dishonest. Quite the contrary. You see, a few months ago I invited your father to join me in a mining venture. At first he agreed. But when he discovered the condition of the mines, he withdrew his support. You see, he thought it was too dangerous for the miners. At his urging, other investors withdrew. Within two weeks, the venture collapsed."

"Mines? You were involved in that mining venture in Dartmoor?"

"That's right."

She studied his face a moment, trying to reconcile his face to a face in her memory. "You can't be Lord Blackthorne."

He bowed his head in a graceful affirmation. "You see, my dear, what terrible destruction time and illness can wreak upon a man."

"How could you, the Marquess of Blackthorne, be involved with smugglers?"

"You would be surprised at the number of peers involved in a little smuggling here and there. How do you suppose we keep our wine cellars well supplied?"

"But to ship weapons to the French. That's treason."

He smiled. "I thought it rather appropriate to involve your father with treason. Considering the fact he betrayed me."

"My father is not a traitor."

"No. But I made it appear as though he were swimming up to his neck in treachery."

"What do you mean?"

"I can't stand here discussing every detail of my plan.

I'm certain Simon will return shortly. Now come along, my dear, let's wait for him on the battlements."

Emily thought of that narrow rampart walkway high above Ravenwood, and Simon's fear of heights. "Why wait for him up there?"

"Because it's always important to face one's enemy on one's own terms."

This man knew of Simon's fear. He planned to take advantage of that fear.

He gestured toward the door with the pistol. "Let's not dawdle. I've waited a long time for this moment, and I don't plan to allow you to spoil it."

Emily hesitated, unwilling to climb to the dangerous walkway with this madman.

He smiled. "I should tell you, I won't hesitate to kill you."

Emily clenched her hands into fists at her sides. "You're going to kill me whether or not I go with you."

"Nonsense. I intend to give your lover a chance to rescue you. You would like Simon to rescue you, wouldn't you?"

Simon. She had to find some way to warn him. She couldn't do that if she was dead. She walked toward the door.

Blackthorne stepped aside as she drew near. "After you, my dear. And do refrain from any sudden movements."

She walked out of the chapel into the pale moonlight flooding the great hall. She sensed him behind her, his footsteps slow and steady across the stones, a demon of death stalking his prey. Her knees trembled. Her palm left damp smudges against the stone wall of the stairway as she climbed the tower steps. She had to get away from this madman. How?

Her half boots tapped on each wedge of ancient stone. Think. She had to think. No room for fear. Fear would only get her killed. And Simon. Dear heaven, she had to warn Simon.

When they reached the roof, Blackthorne paused, sagging against the stone wall. He dragged air into his lungs, as if each thready gasp for breath might be his last. Emily seized upon his weakness. She turned, running for the opposite tower. If she could just make it to the other stairway . . .

"I'll shoot!" he shouted.

Emily froze, trembling with the pounding of her blood. She held her breath, afraid that any movement might cause him to shoot. A cool wind swept across the crenellated walls of the castle, licking at the moisture beading her upper lip. His footsteps dragged against the stone walkway, a slow shuffle that grated along her spine.

"That was very foolish, my dear." He poked the pistol against the small of her back.

Emily closed her eyes, waiting for the explosion of the pistol.

"You might have missed Simon's arrival. Have a look, my dear. Your lover is riding to your rescue."

Emily stared through the embrasure above the lady's stone. A horse and rider were crossing the bailey, a tall man sitting upon the back of a black stallion, headed straight for danger. She was aware of the man standing beside her, aware that any sound could cause him to shoot. Yet she knew she had to warn Simon.

"Go back!" she shouted. "Simon, it's a trap!"

Simon pulled up on the reins. He tilted his head, staring up at the battlement where she stood. Moonlight illuminated the startled look on his face. He stared for a moment at the man standing beside Emily, as though he were staring at a ghost risen from the grave.

"I see you've caught his attention." Blackthorne grabbed her arm and pulled her close to his side, pressing the cold barrel of the pistol against her cheek. "We must let him see just how things stand."

Emily bit her lower lip, appalled at the horrible whimper escaping her throat. The horse pranced beneath Simon, sensing the tension that Emily could see in his face.

Blackthorne rubbed the steel barrel against Emily's cheek in a chilling imitation of a lover's caress. "Won't you come up and join us?" he shouted.

"Simon don't!" Emily tried to shout, but fear strangled her voice. "He'll kill us both."

"You really don't know Simon very well if you think he would leave you in my clutches," Blackthorne said, lifting his voice to carry to the man in the bailey below. "He has spent his entire life pretending to be a hero. He won't tarnish his image now. Will you, Simon?"

The horse pranced in a circle, straining against the tight reins in Simon's hand. Simon brought the animal under control, staring up at Blackthorne with murder in his eyes. "Harm her and I'll kill you with my bare hands."

Blackthorne laughed. "Come up and join us. Let's see what you're really made of."

Simon jumped from the saddle and ran for the entrance of the keep.

"No!" Emily strained in Blackthorne's grasp, trying to break free.

"Easy now, my dear Miss Maitland." Blackthorne pressed the pistol to her temple. "You wouldn't want to miss the show, would you?"

Emily closed her eyes, praying for a miracle.

Moonlight slipped through the narrow slits of the windows at each floor Simon passed, silvery slats of light guiding him upward to his reckoning. His footsteps were silent against the stone wedges of the stairs. There was no sound in this curving stairway. Nothing except the wind breathing past the windows and the pulse pounding in his ears. Yet in his head he heard a voice, harsh with rage.

Throw the little bastard over the side!

His father's voice.

His father's hatred.

Anxiety slithered in his belly, vipers filled with the poison of old fears. He could feel them, phantom hands slick with sweat gripping his ankles, thrusting him out over the banister. In his mind he could see the squares of black and white marble of the floor where he had imagined his body lying broken and bleeding. Blood pounded in his temples.

Simon paused below the top step, staring up at the entrance where moonlight beckoned him to the blossoming of a confrontation whose seeds had been sown years ago. God, of all places. Why here? Three stories of ancient stone and cold angry memories. But he knew why Blackthorne had chosen this place. He wanted his enemy weakened by fear.

Throw the little bastard over the side!

The man had Emily. Simon knew Blackthorne wouldn't hesitate to kill her. Somehow he had to keep her safe. No matter what the cost.

Simon drew air into his tight lungs and took the remaining steps. The wind whipped across the top of the castle, pushing against his face, tugging at the tails of his black coat, as though it tried to force him back to safety. Emily stood with Blackthorne near the lady's stone. Her face was pale in the moonlight, her eyes wide and pleading.

Blackthorne smiled, a man sure of his prey. "How nice of you to join us."

"Let her go." Simon pushed against the wind, moving toward Emily and the demon who held her. "She has nothing to do with this."

"That's close enough." Blackthorne forced the pistol against her cheek. He had one arm around her waist, holding her like a shield in front of him. "One little slip of my finger, and a piece of lead will rip away part of your lady's lovely face."

Simon froze on the walkway.

"That's better. Do toss your weapon over the ledge. I wouldn't want to take the chance of a stray shot hitting Miss Maitland."

Simon slipped the pistol from his pocket and tossed it over the edge of the walkway.

"Aren't you going to watch it fall?" Blackthorne asked.

Simon didn't watch it fall. He couldn't. Instead he looked into Emily's eyes, seeing the fear there, wishing he could take her in his arms. Metal smashed against stone three stories below, the sound twisting along his spine.

I'll keep you safe. Silently Simon made a pledge that he would give his life to keep.

"Tell me, Simon, are you surprised to see me?"

Simon tore his gaze from Emily, concentrating on his enemy. "What are you doing here?"

Blackthorne laughed. "I've been very clever. I've enjoyed watching you dance to my tune, though I must say, I expected you to arrest Hugh Maitland long ago. I gave you enough evidence."

"How are you involved with this?"

"Why, Simon, this is all my creation. A smuggling operation shipping weapons to the French. An agent for the French in Tangier. I invented all of it, and I made certain you had all the right information."

With the moonlight full upon his face and hair, Blackthorne looked like some horrible phantom risen from the grave, a demon from his past.

"There never was a smuggling operation, was there?" Simon asked.

"Exactly."

"And Trench?"

"I hired him to play the role of a smuggler captain. Wonderful casting, don't you think?"

Simon stared, barely able to absorb the enormity of this man's hatred. "You wanted me to help you destroy Hugh Maitland because of the mining venture in Dartmoor. You created this scheme as some elaborate trap for both of us."

Blackthorne inclined his head. "That's right."

"Why Simon?" Emily asked, staring up at Blackthorne. "What has he ever done to you?"

One corner of Blackthorne's lips twitched. He stared at Simon, his eyes filling with a hatred that reached across the distance, brushing Simon's skin with ice. "He is the spawn of a witch. He mocks me with his very existence."

Emily looked at Simon, her lips parted, her eyes filled with sudden understanding.

"He wishes to take all that is mine." Blackthorne eased the pistol from Emily's cheek, pointing it at Simon. "But I won't allow it. I will send him back to hell where he belongs."

"No!" Emily twisted in his hold.

Blackthorne held her tighter, quelling her struggle. "I've waited a very long time to see you dead, Simon. The war failed me. Trench failed me. But I won't be denied again."

Simon glanced at the weapon held in Blackthorne's skeletal grip. After Blackthorne killed him, he would kill Emily. There would be no one to stop him.

"Stay where you are," Blackthorne shouted as Simon surged toward him. "I'll shoot."

Emily had one chance. Simon had to stop Blackthorne. Now.

A metallic click cracked the air. Simon dashed toward Blackthorne and Emily, hoping he could take Blackthorne over the edge before the bullet took his life.

"No!" Emily slammed her elbow back into Blackthorne's chest.

Blackthorne groaned. A gunshot exploded in the quiet night. Simon flinched with the sudden blaze of pain searing his side. He stumbled, pain sucking the strength from his limbs. A few feet away, Emily struggled with Blackthorne. Close to the edge. Too close.

Emily kicked the man's shin. Blackthorne lost his balance. Simon forced his feet to move. He reached Emily as Blackthorne teetered on the edge of the walkway.

"Help me!" Blackthorne screamed, clawing at Emily's arm.

Simon whipped his arm around Emily's waist, flinging her against the wall beside the lady's stone. Blackthorne fell backward over the edge. His scream rose as he fell.

Simon watched, helpless to look away, the last few moments of this man's life searing across his memory. Blackthorne flayed the air, fighting right until the moment he hit the stones three stories below. The solid thud of his body hitting stones vibrated in Simon's soul.

Throw the little bastard over the side!

The words echoed in his mind over and over again as Simon stared over the ledge. Blackthorne's image faded in the moonlight. He saw a young boy lying bloody and still upon squares of black and white marble. Images from his nightmares.

"Simon."

As though she called to him from a distance, Simon became of aware of Emily's voice.

"Simon, don't look down. Don't look."

He felt her hand against his cheek, her fingers digging into his skin as she forced him to look at her. She seemed a stranger to him, a woman standing outside the circle of memories engulfing him.

She pulled aside his coat, a soft gasp escaping her lips as she stared at his blood-soaked shirt. "Come down the stairs with me. Let me tend your wound."

He allowed her to take his arm, to lead him across the narrow walkway and down the winding stairway. Only when they reached the ground did he resist her gentle lead. He pulled away from her, moving toward the man lying on the stones. Moonlight fell with brutal clarity upon the twisted body of Randolph St. James, Marquess of Blackthorne. He lay staring up at the sky, his lips parted on a silent scream. Yet Simon could hear it echoing in his head.

He stared down at this man whose seed had given him life. He should feel something. Regret perhaps. Anger. Pain. Yet, the reality of his father's death trickled through his consciousness like a flake of snow sliding down a frozen windowpane. He felt nothing.

"Simon, you're hurt." Emily touched his arm. "We have to get you home."

He lifted his gaze from his father to the woman standing beside him. She was so beautiful, a vision from his dreams. "Home?"

"Simon, please," Emily whispered, touching his arm. She stared up at him, moonlight revealing the concern in her face. "We should stop the bleeding. Come with me. Let me tend your wound and then we'll go home."

"I have no home."

She took his arm, tugging him toward the entrance of the chapel. He followed her, his legs growing heavier with each step. She took him into the chapel, where moonlight slanted through arched windows, illuminating the small chamber.

"Sit," she said, pointing toward a stack of blankets.

He didn't want to sit. He didn't want to surrender to the lethargy creeping into his muscles. Instead, he leaned against one of the stone walls, staring up at the arched ceiling while she rummaged through a portmanteau in one corner. Vaguely he wondered about all the prayers that had been spoken within these four walls. Had any been answered? He shivered, the warmth draining from his body.

Emily moved toward him, rolling a white linen shirt in her hands. "This will have to do until I can get you home."

She looked like an angel, standing before him in a shaft of moonlight. Celestial light slipped into her unbound hair, finding fire in the darkness. He felt her warmth reaching out to him, brushing his skin.

"Lift up your arms just a little, so I can bind your wound."

His arms felt like lead as he lifted them to his sides. Lavender rose with the warmth of her skin, a soft mist of scent drifting over him as she bent near him, wrapping linen around him. Pain flickered from his side, a bright spark that skittered along his nerves, dragging a moan from his lips as she pulled the linen tight around his waist.

"I'm sorry," she whispered, looking up at him. "I've never done this before. We need to get you home. We need to have Dr. Cheeson tend you.''

Simon shook his head, the blood swimming before his eyes. ''Don't let him bleed me.''

''No. I won't let him bleed you. I promise.'' She touched his cheek with the warmth of her palm.

He was tired. So very tired. He wanted to lie with her, to sleep in the warmth of her embrace. But she was tugging on his arm once more, urging him toward the door.

''Simon, please come with me. We have to get you home.''

He tried to follow, but his legs wouldn't obey. Darkness filled in the edges of his vision. Emily seemed to stand at the long end of a tunnel, pale light shimmering around her. He wanted to touch her. He needed to touch her one last time. He lifted his hand, reaching for her as his legs crumpled beneath him. Darkness engulfed him. He hit the ancient stones of the chapel floor without feeling the fall.

Chapter Twenty-nine

"All the young man needs now . . ." Dr. Cheeson lifted a lancet and a silver bowl from the black bag he had placed on a chair by the bed in Emily's bedroom. He looked at Simon, a smile on his lips, a measure of triumph glittering in his eyes.

Emily stepped in front of the surgeon as he approached the bed. "I believe he wouldn't care to be bled."

Dr. Cheeson lifted one white brow. "He is hardly in a position to . . ."

Emily sidestepped when the doctor tried to go around her. "I shall not allow it, Dr. Cheeson."

Cheeson pursed his lips. He looked to where Hugh Maitland was standing near the foot of the bed. "Mr. Maitland, if we don't bleed the young man, the poisoning will set in and he will die."

Hugh frowned. "The young man has bled a great deal already."

"He may still have poisons within him. We must bleed him. Now. Before he awakens."

"You mean before he is able to come at you with one of your own knives?" Emily asked.

Cheeson cleared his throat. "The young man does prove to be a most difficult patient."

Hugh looked at Emily, a smile tipping one corner of his lips. "I'm afraid I have to agree with my daughter. I'm certain Blake would definitely not wish to be bled."

Cheeson glanced at the man lying unconscious in the bed, a look of disappointment passing over his features. "Very well. I shall not be held responsible."

Emily smoothed the sheet over Simon's chest as the doctor closed his bag and left the room. She glanced at her mother and grandmother sitting on the chaise longue by the hearth. Audrey was staring at Simon, her lips parted, her eyes filled with bewilderment. Harriet was staring at Emily as though she expected the sky to fall at any moment.

Emily's stomach tightened when she realized what she must now do. The time for deception had passed. It was time to face the truth and all the consequences awaiting her.

"Emily, I must say I'm delighted to see Blake alive." Hugh rubbed the back of his neck as he looked at Emily. "But I am more than a little confused."

"With good reason." Emily held her father's befuddled gaze, praying he would forgive her for everything she had done. "Please, would you all mind waiting for me in the drawing room. I want a few moments alone with . . . Sheridan. Before I explain everything."

Hugh studied her a moment, frowning, looking as though he wanted to explore the matter further.

"Please, Father. Give me just a few moments."

Hugh came around the bed. He slipped his arms around Emily, holding her close against his chest. "Whatever you are about to tell us you must know we are all grateful to have Blake back in our lives. No matter what difficulties lie ahead, you must know we will face them together."

Emily closed her eyes, the beauty of her father's affection serving only to heighten the ugliness of her deception. Tears burned her eyes as she watched her father walk to her mother's side. Together, they left the room.

Harriet stood, facing Emily, her face pale and drawn. "Are you planning to tell them the truth tonight?"

"Yes," Emily whispered, regret squeezing her throat.

Harriet nodded. "It's for the best. I suspect they will understand why we went to such extreme measures. At least I certainly hope they do."

"So do I."

"In the worst case, we shall have each other, my girl."

"Thank you, Grandmama, for always being here for me. You can't know how sorry I am for involving you in all of this."

"Poppycock!" Harriet lifted her chin, her lips curving into a smile. "We've had a marvelous adventure, my girl. And without it, you would never have met your young man. All things will be as they should, in time."

Emily glanced down at the man sleeping in her bed. "I would like to think that's true."

"It will be. You must have faith, Emily."

Emily watched Harriet leave the room, wishing she could find a measure of the optimism her grandmother possessed. She sank to the edge of the bed. Light from the oil lamp on the table beside the bed fell across Simon's face.

"I never really had a chance to say good-bye." She leaned over him and touched his cheek, dark pinpoints of beard teasing her skin. She kissed his brow, the crests of his cheeks, his lips, the damp warmth of his breath brushing her cheek. A single tear fell from her eye, dropping softly against his cheek. "Good-bye, Sheridan Blake. I shall always remember what we shared, even if it was no more than an illusion."

She leaned back and stared down into his sleeping face, emotions warring within her. "As for you, Simon St. James, I wonder if you realize what your deception did to me. Oh, I understand why you came into my life and forced me to pretend you were Sheridan Blake. It was duty. You had your responsibilities. Your mission.''

She closed her eyes, a sudden shaft of pain slicing through her heart. ''But I don't understand how you could have allowed me to believe you had lost your memory. You stripped me bare. You left me with nothing, not even my pride.''

Tears pricked her eyes. Tears born of shame, of humiliation, of the pain of knowing she had acted the fool. ''How could you allow me to parade my dreams before you? How could you allow me to throw myself into your arms like a beggar seeking a few crumbs? How could you deceive me so completely? I truly believed you loved me.''

She stood and hugged her arms to her waist, feeling lost suddenly, as though she had been dragged from her home and tossed into a dungeon where everything was cold. ''I didn't realize it was possible to love someone so much, and to despise that person with equal measure. But I do love you. And I despise you for destroying my dreams.''

Hugh sank to the sofa beside his wife, hitting the burgundy velvet hard enough to bounce Audrey on the stiff cushion. He stared at Emily, his eyes as wide as his wife's. ''You mean to say Sheridan Blake never existed?''

Emily swallowed past the anxiety that had formed a tight knot in her throat. ''I thought it was an excellent solution to my problem. You wanted me to marry, and I didn't know of anyone I wished to marry.''

Audrey pressed her hand to the base of her neck. ''So you simply invented a husband?''

Emily shifted on her feet. ''I wanted Anna to have her chance. If I had only known you intended to allow her to have her first Season this coming year, I certainly would never have dreamed of inventing Sheridan Blake.''

Audrey glanced at her mother sitting in a wingback chair near the open French doors. ''You knew of this?''

Harriet tilted her chin, regarding her daughter like a

queen. ''It appeared to me as though you and Maitland had provided Emily with little choice but to marry or see her younger sisters become spinsters.''

Audrey flicked open her fan and began fanning her face, tiny brown curls fluttering in the breeze. ''But, Mother, to invent a husband . . .''

''Emily did not wish to marry except for love.'' Harriet pursed her lips, pinning first Audrey, then Hugh, in her icy glare. ''Both of you should understand her sentiments better than most.''

Audrey lowered her fan to her lap. She glanced at Hugh, her expression growing sheepish beneath her mother's glare.

Hugh released his breath in a sigh as he looked at Emily. ''Perhaps I can understand why you refused to marry a man you didn't love. Knowing your imagination, I suppose I can even understand why you would invent a husband. But it certainly doesn't explain the young man in your bed.''

Emily's face warmed with the implication behind his words. ''It's rather a long story.''

Audrey groaned. ''Emily, that young man has been staying in your bedroom, and you aren't married. Or are you married?''

Emily rested her hand on the back of her grandmother's chair. ''Not really.''

Hugh leaned back against the sofa. ''I think I should like to hear how that young man happened to masquerade as your husband. Before I shoot him.''

Emily squeezed the burgundy velvet beneath her hand. ''Father, please, there has been enough bloodshed this night.''

Audrey rested her hand on her husband's arm as though to stay him. ''Emily, why did you hire him to act as your husband?''

''Oh, no, I never hired him. Simon—that's his real name—found out about my fake marriage when he was investigating a smuggling operation he believed was shipping weapons to the French.''

Hugh frowned. ''A smuggling operation?''

''Yes. Simon is an agent for the ministry, you see. He had information that someone in Maitland Enterprises was involved in shipping weapons to the French.''

''He suspected someone in my company of treason?''

Emily nodded. ''Only there never was a smuggling operation. Lord Blackthorne, who was actually Simon's father, invented the smuggling operation. He was angry over the mining venture in Dartmoor last year. He wanted revenge. And I'm afraid he also wanted to kill Simon.''

''I've suddenly realized that young man is a St. James.'' Harriet sat forward in her chair. ''Simon St. James. The eldest son of the Marquess of Blackthorne.''

''Yes,'' Emily whispered, a chill rippling along her spine when she thought of the consequences of his identity.

''Now that his father is dead, that makes him the new Marquess.'' Harriet tapped her finger against her lower lip. ''I always knew that young man was quality.''

''Oh, dear.'' Audrey flicked her fan beneath her chin. ''The new Marquess of Blackthorne is unconscious in my daughter's bed. How in the world shall we ever live down the scandal?''

''There needn't be a scandal,'' Simon said.

Emily pivoted at the sound of his dark voice. Simon stood at the threshold of the room, leaning heavily against the door. His face was as pale as the fresh white linen shirt tucked into one side of his buff-colored breeches; the tail of the other side dangled to his hips. His hair looked as though the breeze had whipped the dark mass into waves around his face. His feet were bare against the burgundy and ivory roses in the Aubusson carpet.

''You should be in bed,'' Emily said, rushing to his side. ''Dear heaven, you could have fallen down the stairs in your condition, and broken your neck.''

Simon touched her cheek, smiling into her eyes, before looking past her to her father. ''There are things I need to discuss with your father, Em.''

Emily glanced over her shoulder at her father, sensing the anger simmering behind Hugh's calm mask. ''I'm certain what you need to discuss with Father can wait. You are, after all, injured,'' she said, hoping her father wasn't inclined to shoot an injured man.

Simon resisted when she tried to tug him from the room. ''This can't wait.''

''Emily,'' Audrey said, resting her hand on Emily's arm. ''I believe we should allow the gentlemen a few moments of privacy.''

Emily hesitated, certain she would be one of the topics discussed. ''But I—''

''Come along, dear.'' Harriet took Emily's arm. She cast Simon a look full of meaning. ''I suspect there is much Simon and your father need to discuss.''

''If part of the discussion has to do with me, I believe I should stay.'' Emily lifted her chin as she looked at her father. ''Forgive me, Father, but I shouldn't like to be discussed as though I were a child incapable of making decisions about my future.''

''Forgive me, Daughter, but in the past few months you have managed to demonstrate a true propensity for getting yourself into trouble.''

Emily bit her lower lip, feeling the sting of her father's words as sharply as a slap across her face.

''Since your behavior has placed the reputations of your sisters at risk, it is not only your future I am considering.''

''Of course, I only . . .'' The icy look in her father's eyes froze the words in Emily's throat.

Hugh's shoulders rose beneath the black cloth of his coat—the deep inhalation of a man trying desperately to control his rising anger. ''I would care to have a few moments of private conversation with Lord Blackthorne. Do you believe you are capable of demonstrating this small measure of respect?''

Emily nodded, her cheeks burning. She turned and escaped the room, catching a glimpse of Simon's face and the pity in his eyes. Dear heaven, the last thing she wanted from this man was pity.

Simon leaned back against the door. His heart ached for Emily. She had looked so embarrassed, so vulnerable, so incredibly appealing. He had wanted to come to her defense, but he sensed that intervening between father and daughter at this juncture would only cause more harm.

He met Hugh Maitland's angry glare. The blood pounded in his head. Beneath the linen shirt, his skin was damp. He wanted nothing more than to curl up in bed and fall asleep, with Emily in his arms. But he couldn't. Not until the last traces of deception had been swept away.

"I suggest you sit, young man, before you fall."

Simon drew in a breath that sent a splinter of pain spiraling upward from his side. He eased away from the door, forcing each step as he walked toward the nearest chair.

"Emily was right, you know. You should be in bed," Hugh said, taking his arm. He helped Simon into the wingback chair Harriet had recently occupied, then stared down at him, his lips a tight line. "Although I must say, I'm not altogether pleased to have you in my daughter's bed."

Simon sagged against the stiff chair back. "Under the circumstances, I can well understand your sentiment."

"Can you?" Hugh turned away from Simon. He paced to the French doors, looking into the gardens a moment before turning to face him. "From what I gather, you came into my home to spy on me. Is that correct?"

Simon held Hugh's steady gaze. "We had reason to believe that someone in your company was involved in shipping weapons to a French agent in Tangier. A Mr. Alberto Ramirez."

"Ramirez? I've corresponded with this man."

"Ramirez doesn't exist. He was merely part of a scheme concocted by Randolph St. James to destroy you. He made certain there was enough evidence to convict you of treason. I was supposed to uncover that evidence, and in the process be killed by one of the smugglers."

Hugh studied him a moment. "St. James was your father?"

"Yes." Simon rested his hand against the wound in his side, the pain a pale reflection of the ancient wound throbbing deep in his soul.

A breeze drifted in from the gardens, fluttering the burgundy velvet drapes. "You say he left enough evidence to convict me. Why didn't you arrest me?"

"Because I believed you were innocent. I've been searching for proof. Lord Pemberton gave me until this morning to find it." Simon glanced at the ormolu clock on the mantel. It was the fifth hour of a new day. "If I couldn't find evidence to prove your innocence, I was ordered to arrest you."

Hugh cocked one golden brow. "How many people in the ministry know of this?"

"Only Pemberton knows all the details."

"I'm certainly glad to hear that. I would like to spare my family as much scandal as possible." Hugh drew in his breath, his lips drawing into a tight line. "That brings us to the issue of Emily. You used her rather badly."

A tight band squeezed Simon's chest when he thought of Emily. "I never planned to hurt her."

"If the truth of this ever becomes public, not only will Emily suffer, but the rest of my family as well. As you well know, I have four other daughters."

Simon thought of his father and his family, brothers and sisters he scarcely knew. The truth could destroy them as well as the Maitlands. "I'm certain Lord Pemberton will agree to keep the details of my mission private. The truth would have far-reaching consequences."

"And what about Sheridan Blake? What about Emily?" Hugh stared straight into Simon's eyes. "Do you mean to walk out of her life?"

"It's the last thing in the world I want to do."

"I suppose I can understand why you assumed the role of Sheridan Blake when you saw the opportunity. But I want to know if you came into my house planning to seduce my daughter."

Simon met Hugh's look, seeing the anger in the smooth lines of his face. "No."

Hugh's eyes narrowed. "Are you going to tell me you never touched her?"

Simon held his angry look. "No."

A muscle flashed in Hugh's cheek. "I trust you plan to do right by my daughter."

"I hope to marry her. If she will have me."

Hugh huffed. "From what I've seen, she will have you, all right."

"I'm not altogether certain that's true. She fell in love with a man she invented."

Hugh frowned. "I don't see what difference a name might make."

Simon rested his head back against the chair, staring up at the roundel painted in the center of the intricate scrolls and leaves crafted in the ceiling plasterwork—the goddess Diana with her javelin raised in the hunt. He thought of Actaeon, the young hunter Diana had destroyed for spying upon her. He wondered if Emily would destroy him for his transgression. "I hope you're right."

"Of course I am. Still, the question is, how the blazes are we to explain the fact that Sheridan Blake is actually Simon St. James?"

Simon smiled. "I have an idea."

Chapter Thirty

Hugh rested his arm on the mantel in the drawing room. "Simon has assured me Lord Pemberton is the only one in the ministry who knows the details of his mission. He is quite certain Pemberton will keep everything private. The last thing the ministry needs is a scandal involving Lord Blackthorne."

Emily squeezed her hands together on her lap. She resisted the urge to stand. She fought the need to pace like a caged animal as she sat beside her mother on a sofa, listening as her father outlined the course of the rest of her life.

"We can simply say Simon was on a mission to investigate a suspected smuggling ring working out of Bristol. I was helping him. During the course of the mission, Emily and Simon met, fell in love, and were married. But because of the sensitive nature of his work, we decided to keep his identity a secret."

Emily glanced at the man sitting nearby. Simon was watching her, all expression washed from his face. He sat in the wingback chair near the open French doors, looking elegant in spite of his attire. He seemed totally relaxed, his long legs crossed, his arms resting casually along the arms of the chair, as though her father were discussing the details of his latest shipping venture instead of the details of their coming marriage. Oh, she wanted to grab those broad shoulders and shake him until his teeth rattled!

"What about the fire?" Audrey shifted on the sofa beside Emily, glancing up at her husband. "How do we explain Sheridan's death?"

"One of the smugglers attacked Simon while he was working. The smuggler was killed. We decided it was safer for Simon to allow Sheridan Blake to be buried." Hugh lifted his hand from the mantel, planting his elbow against the white marble, rubbing his finger along his chin as he continued. "The beauty of my plan is that, for the most part, it's the truth."

Audrey glanced at Simon, a frown tugging her smooth brow. "All except for a few minor details."

Emily squeezed her hands together until her fingers ached. She watched Simon, who refused to betray his emotions in words or gesture or expression. She wanted to scream. She refused to have her life planned for her.

Harriet rose from the sofa across from Emily. "I shall contact a friend of mine who lives in Bath, a magistrate. I believe I shall have little trouble convincing him to perform the ceremony and alter the dates by a few weeks."

Hugh propped his chin on his fist. "Would this be the same magistrate who forged the marriage papers for Emily and Sheridan Blake."

Harriet gave Hugh a proud smile. "As a matter of fact, he is."

Hugh shook his head, a smile tipping one corner of his lips. "Countess, you never fail to amaze me."

Harriet inclined her head, a queen addressing one of her noblemen. "I believe we should have this entire tangle under control in a few days."

Emily could stand it no more. She fixed Simon with a

hard stare. "Have you actually agreed to this scheme?"

Simon returned her steady regard, failing to betray any of his emotions. "It seems the best way to prevent a scandal."

A scandal. Of course. He would be wary of scandal. "Mother, Father, Grandmama, I beg you to leave us, please. I would like a few moments alone with Lord Blackthorne."

Audrey rested her hand on Emily's arm. "Is something wrong, dear?"

Emily managed a smile. "I simply need to discuss a few details with Lord Blackthorne."

Audrey stood and glanced at Hugh, her huge eyes filled with uncertainty.

Hugh regarded his daughter a moment, his expression growing wary. "Emily, everything has been decided to the best advantage of everyone involved."

"Since you have determined the course of my future, I would hope you could allow me a few moments alone with the man you *expect* me to marry."

Hugh glanced at Simon, as though looking for reinforcements in a campaign he feared might be lost. Simon offered no support. He had lowered his gaze to the arm of the chair, as though fascinated suddenly with the texture of the velvet beneath his hand.

Hugh cleared his throat. "Emily, I—"

"Father, please. I would like a few moments of privacy."

"Yes. Well . . ." He offered Audrey his arm, a man making a judicious retreat. "I'm certain there are a great many things you and Blackthorne need to discuss. You have your entire future ahead of you."

Emily stared at Simon as her parents and grandmother left the room. Odd, she had slept in this man's arms, she had felt the power and strength of his body deep inside her, and now she felt as though she were facing a stranger.

He glanced up from his contemplation of the arm of the

chair, looking straight into her eyes, revealing nothing in his direct look. "I take it you're unhappy with the arrangement?"

The arrangement. She tried to draw a deep breath, but the weight of her emotions pressed like lead against her chest, compressing her lungs. "I don't see any reason why we should both be forced to carry on this masquerade any longer."

"Can you think of no reason?" he asked, his voice as calm and scrubbed of emotion as his expression.

She could think of only one reason—her love for him. A love that had taken root even when she believed the man was nothing more than a scoundrel. A love she refused to nourish now that she knew she could never trust him.

She rose to her feet, her restlessness refusing to be contained a moment longer. She paced to the French doors, seeking the words that would release them both from this prison of their own making. Words that wouldn't betray her heart. Beyond the terrace the shadows of night were fading into the radiance of dawn. Yet she felt trapped in the depths of darkness. "Tell me, how could you lie to me the way you did? How could you let me believe you had lost your memory?"

"As I recall, I thought it was the best way to keep from being shot, again."

Emily folded her hands at her waist, staring at him in prim disdain. "I didn't actually mean to shoot you."

He smiled. "No. You intended to ship me off with a press gang."

"You left me little choice."

"As you left me, my lady."

"It isn't at all the same thing."

"Isn't it? We both did what we needed to survive."

"Ooooh." She shook with frustration. "You lied to me first."

"Yes." He came to his feet, but he made no move toward her. "I came here in search of a traitor. Perhaps that doesn't excuse my methods, but it should at least explain them."

"And does it explain the way you manipulated my emotions?"

"Emily, you have to believe me, when I assumed the role of Sheridan Blake, I never meant for us to become involved. I never planned to hurt you."

Emily shook her head, denying the sincerity in his voice and in his eyes. "I suspect you're a wonderful spy for the crown. You're so very good at deceiving people. But then, I wanted to believe you. I wanted to believe you really could be that one special man I have waited for all my life."

"I haven't changed simply because I have a different name."

Emily's cheeks warmed with the shame of all she had revealed to this scoundrel. "I'm certain you found me terribly amusing, with my silly little dreams."

He smiled, his eyes filling with a beguiling warmth. "I found you enchanting."

The man could lie with the ease of a hawk taking flight. It would be far too easy to believe those tempting lies, to throw herself into his arms, to surrender to her own terrible weakness. "Please, the game is ended. You've won. There really isn't any need to continue the performance."

"I could have lied about my memory. I could have continued this game, but I didn't want to build our life together based on a lie."

"You *did* lie to me."

"Not about everything."

"You used me."

He stared into her eyes, and all of his defenses seemed to drop away from him. The mask was gone, and in its place was the face of a man in pain. "I love you, Em."

Emily shook her head. "Please, don't do this. I'm not some pitiful creature in need of your tender and all too false declarations. I shall survive quite nicely with the truth."

"The truth is I love you. When I fell in love with you, I knew the day would come when I would stand before you and face your outrage. My only hope is that our love is strong enough to survive."

Tears burned her eyes. She stared at him, refusing to blink, to allow a single tear to betray her. "Why not be honest for once? Why not simply say you find yourself in a situation that demands you make amends for what you and your father have done to this family? After all, scandal would be a terrible thing for the new Marquess of Blackthorne, wouldn't it?"

He rested his hand on the back of the chair, as though he needed support. He looked weary, a fallen angel pushed to the brink of hell, trying to fight his way back to heaven. "I do want to make amends. I want to erase all the ugliness of the past few weeks. All the ugliness that has been my life. I want a chance to begin anew. To build a life. With you."

"Perhaps in some strange fashion you do care for me. But if this is the way you show your love, if you can lie to me, deceive me, manipulate me into revealing my most precious secrets, then I don't need your kind of love." She turned away from him, her legs trembling beneath her as she plunged through the French doors into the gray light of dawn. She crossed the terrace, wanting to run, knowing there was nowhere to hide from her own foolishness.

Dear heaven, she wanted to throw her arms around him and hold him until her last day on earth. But she couldn't. She refused to allow her heart to be trampled on once again. She pressed her hands against the stone balustrade, fighting the tears burning her eyes.

Although his movements failed to betray him, she sensed him approach, felt the warmth of him brush against her back before he rested his strong hands against her shoulders. "You can't believe that what we share is a lie."

She curled her shoulders, rejecting his gentle touch. He lifted his hands, but remained standing behind her, so close his warmth wrapped around her. "You aren't the man I fell in love with. You're a stranger to me."

"I'm the same man who held you in his arms. The same man who made love to you. The same man who pledged my heart, my soul, my body, all I have to give, to my lady."

She pivoted to face him. "How dare you remind me of my foolishness!"

"Look at me." He cupped her face between his palms, holding her when she would pull away from him. "Do you truly see another man when you look at me? Can't you see I haven't changed? I'm the man you love. I'm the man who loves you. I am your Sheridan Blake."

"Sheridan Blake would never have deceived me."

"You pledged your love to me. Does it really matter what my name is?"

"You're a scoundrel who—"

He lowered his head, cutting off her words with the slide of his lips over hers. Emily remained impassive. She had no intention of participating in this kiss. No intention of allowing him the knowledge of how very much she wanted him. She would show him exactly how unmoved she could be. But the heat of his kiss conspired against her determination, lulling her into a languor that came with the drugging power in his kiss.

She tried to break away, seeking sanity in distance. He slid one strong hand around her nape, holding her as he plied her lips with a magical elixir that seeped into her blood like liquid fire. He slipped one arm around her, holding her close to the heat and power of his body. Memories awakened within her, flickering like a thousand candle flames, desire and passion reflected in the blaze, her body melting against him. Against the best of her intentions, she parted her lips beneath his, drinking in the taste of his mouth.

"Tell me this isn't real, Emily," he whispered against her lips.

He pressed against her, forcing her back against the balustrade, allowing her to feel the hard thrust of his arousal through the soft silk of her gown. Emily trembled with the promise pulsing in his powerful body.

"Tell me you don't want me. Tell me I wouldn't feel the damp heat of your desire if I lifted your gown and slipped my hand between your thighs."

Emily pulled back, dragging air into her lungs like a drowning woman. She *was* drowning, in his warmth, in the desire he conjured up inside her. "The man I want no longer exists."

He stared down at her, his lips pulled into a tight line, his eyes filling with the same anguish crowding her chest. "Was it all make-believe, Emily? When you made love with me, were you making love to a fantasy that lived only in your imagination?"

She stared up at him, needing to deny the emotions she could no longer trust—the desire in his eyes, the longing for him deep inside her. He dealt in lies. And lies were all she had to give him. "When I looked at you I saw only Sheridan Blake. A man I invented. A man I loved. A man you could never be."

Simon stepped back from her, as though her words had struck a physical blow. "You once said you would stand beside me no matter what I had done before coming into your life. You were willing enough to forgive Sheridan Blake. Can't you find a small measure of forgiveness for Simon St. James?"

A demon of pain drove her on, crushing tenderness. "Simon St. James is a scoundrel far past redemption in my eyes."

"I suppose Sheridan Blake is perfect."

Sheridan Blake was an illusion. But she couldn't quell the need to lash out at this man. She couldn't quell the need to hurt him as much as he had hurt her with his deception. "Sheridan Blake is honest. Loyal. Brave. And always a gentleman."

"A paragon. But then he has a distinct advantage. He isn't real. You see, real people make mistakes. I've made mistakes. One of the biggest was falling in love with a woman who prefers fantasy over reality."

"I prefer honesty over treachery."

He released his breath, his shoulders sagging as though under a great weight. He glanced past her, staring into the garden a moment before he looked at her, all expression carefully scrubbed from his face. "I realize now I could never make you happy. I could never live up to that ideal you carry around inside you. I've spent my entire life trying to live up to an ideal. And I failed. I know I would fail you also. You see, I could never maintain that level of perfection."

A breeze swept in from the garden, swirling the scent of flowers around them, ruffling his dark hair. Emily leaned back against the balustrade, fighting against the instincts that demanded she fling herself into this man's arms.

He touched her cheek, a soft brush of his fingers, as gentle as the breeze. "I hope you find your paragon, Em. I hope he makes you happy."

She watched him turn and walk away from her. If she didn't say something now, he would walk out of her life. Still, she stood paralyzed by her demons, her head demanding one thing, her heart another. Through the open French doors, she watched him walk across the drawing room. She took a step.

What could she say to him? Dear heaven, could she believe him? How could she ever trust him? The man could lie to her while he made love to her. How could she make a life with a man who could deceive her with such ease? Such cunning?

He opened the door at the far end of the drawing room. Her heart pounded against her ribs. He stepped across the threshold, closing the door behind him. She lifted her hand to her lips.

"Simon," she whispered, knowing it was too late. It had

been too late the moment he lied about his memory. He wouldn't be coming back this time. This time she would lose him forever.

Forever.

How strange to think she had once contemplated a lifetime with a man whose name she hadn't even known. It was better this way, she assured herself. The man had deceived her time and time again. He had used her. It was better not to live with a man she couldn't trust. Still, it hurt.

She began to shake, a trembling that spiraled from the very core of her being. She turned, leaning heavily against the balustrade, the gray stone preventing her collapse to the terrace. Regret she could no longer deny shook her. She fought against the humiliating sting of tears, losing a battle as the scalding proof of her weakness spilled down her cheeks.

Foolish woman, chasing after a dream. Foolish still, for the doubts she couldn't banish. Doubts that sank like thorns into her heart, taunting her with the possibility that she had just thrown away her one chance for happiness.

"Emily, what have you done?"

Emily stiffened at the sound of her grandmother's voice. She wiped her tears, hoping to hide the stain of her shame, as her grandmother approached.

Harriet's footsteps tapped against the terrace, slow and steady, giving Emily a few precious moments to compose herself. "Simon is preparing to leave."

Emily swallowed hard, clearing her throat of the tight band of emotion. "I hope he has a safe trip back to London," she said.

"You can't let him leave."

"I don't want him to stay."

Harriet gripped Emily's chin, forcing her granddaughter to look at her. "Are these tears of joy, my girl?"

"They are tears for a foolish young woman who allowed herself to believe in a fantasy."

Harriet pursed her lips. "If you don't walk back into that

house and convince that young man you want him in your life, then you are truly a foolish young woman."

"Grandmama, I have no intention of marrying that scoundrel."

"Good heavens. What am I to do with you?" Harriet rested her hands on the balustrade and stared out across the garden. "You're in love with him."

"I'm in love with an illusion."

"That illusion is the new Marquess of Blackthorne."

"I wouldn't care if he were King of England."

Harriet drew in a steady breath before she inclined her head and pinned Emily in an icy glare. "He loves you. Does that mean nothing to you?"

"I don't need the type of love he offers."

"Emily, there are times when I wonder how a woman as intelligent as you could be such a mutton-headed dolt."

Emily flinched with the sting of her grandmother's words. "How can you expect me to marry him after all the lies? How could I ever trust him? The man can lie with the ease of breathing."

"I know you well enough to realize that anything I say to you now will not alter your opinion. But I should like to know how you intend to reconcile yourself to the fact that you will be plunging your family into a terrible scandal if you don't do as your father has asked."

"I have a plan."

Harriet rolled her eyes to heaven. "I rather suspected you might have a plan."

"Grandmama, please. I need support, not mockery."

"You need that young man who is about to walk out of your life." Harriet raised her hand when Emily started to protest. "But since you refuse to believe that, please do tell me your plan."

"It's simple, really."

Harriet flicked open her fan. "I was afraid of that."

Emily pursed her lips, casting her grandmother a dark glance. "We can follow Father's plan, with one exception.

Instead of that nonsense about falling in love and marrying, we can say I only pretended to be his wife to help catch a traitor.''

Harriet stared at Emily a moment. ''You can't be serious.''

''I assure you, Grandmama, I'm quite serious. We shall have the word of Lord Pemberton and the Marquess of Blackthorne.''

Harriet tapped her fan against her chin. ''I suppose it could work.''

''It shall have to work. I have no intention of marrying that scoundrel.''

Harriet studied Emily a moment before she spoke. ''Have you considered the possibility that you could be with child?''

Emily pressed her fist against her waist, the blood draining from her limbs.

''I see you haven't.'' A smug smile curved Harriet's lips. ''Perhaps you should reconsider your decision to banish that young man from your life.''

Emily closed her eyes, fighting the urge to scream. ''We should know in a week. If God has mercy on me, I shall never again set eyes on that scoundrel St. James.''

''I only wish I knew you wouldn't come to regret this day. But you will.''

Emily glanced away from her grandmother's perceptive gaze. She stared out across the garden, trying not to think of Simon St. James.

''One day you will look back to this moment in time, and realize you allowed the man of your destiny to walk out of your life.''

''Sometimes it's better to live with a dream than to watch that dream ground into dust by a scoundrel.''

Harriet sighed. ''One day, when your wounds are healed, perhaps you will meet Simon again. Perhaps you will look past the memory of your own pain and see the love he has for you. I only hope it isn't too late.''

"Too late." The words slid through Emily like jagged pieces of ice. "What do you mean?"

Harriet smiled. "Didn't you notice, my girl? Simon St. James, the handsome young Marquess of Blackthorne, has just become one of the most sought after bachelors in all of England. With his looks, his wealth, his title, every mother with an eligible daughter will be stalking the young man. Every starry-eyed chit will be dreaming of capturing his heart. It's only a matter of time before he finds some lovely young woman to help heal his wounds."

Emily curled her hands into fists on the balustrade, jealousy flaring inside of her at the thought of Simon with another woman. "What Simon St. James does with his life is none of my concern."

Harriet patted Emily's arm. "I hope that's true, my girl. I hope you don't find yourself one night in a crowded ballroom watching Simon and his lady, thinking of things that might have been."

In her mind Emily imagined Simon holding another woman in his arms, smiling into her eyes, touching her cheek. A tight band of jealousy and longing clutched her chest. A part of her demanded that she run to him. Yet she refused to surrender to that shameful weakness. Even if fate forced her to marry the scoundrel, she would never deliver her heart into the keeping of a man without honor.

Candles burned behind glass along the mahogany-lined walls of the library in Lord Pemberton's London townhouse. Simon sat on one of the Sheraton sofas, swirling the brandy in his snifter. He felt strangely detached, like a ship cut from its mooring, drifting on an open sea, with nothing but a gray expanse before him—his future.

"What a diabolical scheme. Blackthorne could have destroyed you and Maitland." Pemberton turned from the windows, regarding Simon with troubled eyes before he continued. "If not for the other lives it would harm, I should like to tell the world what a complete scoundrel

Randolph St. James truly was.''

Simon squeezed the crystal globe of his snifter. ''I wouldn't like to see more injury done, sir. The Maitlands have suffered. The truth would destroy my father's wife and their children.''

''You don't imagine Gilbert is involved, do you? With you gone, he would inherit everything.''

Simon thought of the dandified young man who was his father's firstborn son by his second wife. Gilbert had demonstrated the supreme good sense to possess his sire's fair hair and gray eyes. He was everything Randolph St. James had ever wanted in a son, everything Simon was not. ''I doubt Randolph would have involved Gilbert in his plans. He wouldn't want to put him at risk.''

Pemberton nodded. ''And so Randolph St. James shall be laid to rest in the family tomb without a breath of the truth. I suppose it is the best way.''

''He did enough damage while he was living.''

Pemberton studied Simon a moment, his expression growing thoughtful. ''How are you, my lad?''

Simon shrugged, avoiding the questions in Pemberton's eyes by looking down into his glass. ''The wound wasn't serious.''

''The pistol wound wasn't what I meant. This must have been a terrible trial for you. Discovering your father was the man behind a scheme to murder you.''

''I never harbored any illusions about my father's affection for me.''

''I find it poetic justice that you will now take over his title, Blackthorne Park, the other estates, all he possessed.''

Simon thought of Blackthorne Park, the country home where he had been born, the place he had lived until his father had packed him off to war. It was a place of memories. None he wanted to remember. ''The dowager Marchioness can have Blackthorne Hall. I have no intention of living there.''

''Where will you live?''

Simon sipped his brandy, the aged liquor warming his throat, easing the chill in his chest. "I don't know. I'll find a place."

"Have you any thoughts of returning to Bristol?"

Simon swirled the brandy, keeping his gaze fixed on the amber liquid. For a few short days the possibility of a baby had kept him in Emily's life. But that possibility had died two days ago, along with his dreams. "There is nothing for me in Bristol."

Pemberton sighed. "I was rather afraid this business might have spoiled your relationship with Miss Maitland."

Emily.

Emotion twisted inside him, a glimmer of pain seeking to burn away the icy walls Simon had carefully constructed around his emotions. He drew in his breath, slow and steady, tamping down the flicker of pain. He and Emily had shared a moment's illusion. Nothing more.

"Miss Maitland and I never became involved." He looked up at Pemberton. "It's important that people believe the lady and her father were aiding the ministry in this mission. I want to make certain that her reputation doesn't suffer because of me."

Pemberton nodded. "I shall make sure that the lady and her father are suitably recognized for heroism."

"Thank you, sir."

Pemberton patted Simon's shoulder. "I know it was merely business with you and the lady, but if you had lost your heart to Miss Maitland, you could take comfort in knowing there are women enough who would love nothing more than to erase the lady from your memory. This coming Season, you will no doubt feel like a lamb tossed to the lions. Every huntress in town will try to leg shackle you to some pretty little chit."

Simon frowned at the prospect. How would the Marquess of Blackthorne ever know if a woman wanted him for more than his fortune and title? The travesty of a loveless marriage—was that what lurked in his future? Empty hours.

Endless nights. A life filled with nothing more than the illusion of passion, a pale reflection of a lost love.

He stared down into his brandy, watching the shifting mirrors of light in the amber. Perhaps his father had had his revenge after all. A vengeance Randolph had never planned. His father's machinations had brought the woman of Simon's dreams into his life for one splendid moment in time. A love built on deceptions. A love that would forever remain a memory.

Chapter Thirty-one

An icy wind swept in from the sea, whipping the capes of Simon's greatcoat, numbing his cheeks as he climbed the winding path from the beach to his home on the top of the cliffs. Although early spring had touched the southern coast of England with warmth, here in the wilds of northern Yorkshire, winter still ruled.

Afternoon mist swirled around the base of his immense house, curling upward along the gray stone walls. The crenellated walls of the fourteenth-century Norman keep soared toward the gray sky in odd harmony with the gables and chimneys of the manor house grafted to its ancient stones. Ivy clung to the walls like thick brown spider webs, withered, waiting for spring to breathe life into them. The long-neglected gardens were no better.

Simon had purchased the house and land seven months ago from a peer who preferred his comfortable manse in Kent to this ancient pile of stones. Wynden Castle had stood unoccupied for twenty years, and it bore the stain of neglect.

It was hardly a beautiful house, Simon thought as he walked toward the rambling pile of stones. And the restoration of its 87 rooms would take another year at best. No doubt his family thought him a fool for buying the place. Still, he cared little what people thought of him. The ancient walls, the wild untamed country so far removed from the crush of London society, suited him. As did the name he had bestowed on his home—Dragonwyck.

Digby opened the door as Simon climbed the wide stone stairs leading to the front door. The sergeant-major had retired from the army to assume the role of Simon's major-domo. But the expression on Digby's face made Simon wonder if they were about to be attacked by the enemy. "Ah, but I'm glad to be seeing you back, sir."

The scent of wet paint and sawdust swirled around Simon as he entered the manse. Hammers striking nails in the gallery and the music and dining rooms echoed through the halls. Scaffolding stood in one corner of the cavernous entrance hall, where a man lay on his back finishing the murals on the plastered ceiling—scenes from Greek mythology. "You look as though Napoleon were waiting for me in the drawing room, Digby."

"Not exactly Napoleon, sir. But you do have a visitor."

Simon frowned, wondering if his brother had come to visit. Again. For some reason the young man had taken the notion that his older brother was a hero. When in the vicinity of his sibling, Gilbert trailed after Simon like an adoring puppy. "Who is it?"

"Lady Harriet Whitcomb, sir."

For a space of a dozen beats of his heart Simon forgot to breathe. Lady Harriet brought with her all the memories he had tried so hard to bury these past months. Memories that surged with the pounding of blood through his veins. *Emily.*

He had moved to the far end of England, trying to escape her and the memories. Yet, he could not deny the fact that Dragonwyck was a monument to those few moments he had shared with her. A distant castle for a man exiled from the warmth he had once sought to possess.

He stripped away his greatcoat and handed the damp black wool to Digby, his movements mechanical as his mind churned with possibilities. Why had Lady Harriet come? What news would she have of her granddaughter?

"Have tea prepared, Digby."

"I've already served the lady, sir."

"Good." Simon crossed the hall, the hammering of his heart drowning the clatter of the workmen. Lady Harriet was standing near one of the long-mullioned windows in the drawing room, looking out at the tangled brown heaps of dead leaves and withered bushes of his garden.

He paused on the threshold, aware of the contrast between her pale yellow gown and the shabbiness of the room. Faded tapestries depicting Arthurian legends covered the dark, oak-lined walls. The emerald green silk covering the Queen Anne chairs and settee were frayed at the corners, the seats shiny from overuse. No doubt he appeared an eccentric recluse hiding away in his tattered lair. He sighed, realizing he was in danger of becoming just that.

She turned when he entered, her lips curving into an impish grin. "It will take a great deal of care to bring that garden back to life, young man."

"I warn you, Lady Harriet, my family has already exhausted the arguments against buying this huge pile of stones." He managed a smile as he walked toward her, resisting the urge to pummel her with questions about Emily. "I'm quite beyond redemption from my folly."

"I always knew you were a man of conviction." Lady Harriet set her cup and saucer on a mahogany tea cart that had been drawn up beside one of the wingback chairs. She lifted her hands to him, meeting him near the center of the huge room.

"And I always knew you were a beautiful lady of rare insight." He took her long, slender hands in his, kissed her cool fingers, and smiled down into her eyes, the golden depths reminding him too poignantly of the lady who still haunted his dreams.

She squeezed his hands. "How have you been, my dear young man?"

"Fine." He took her arm and led her to the settee by the stone fireplace, where a fire crackled, casting an oasis of warmth and light in the gloomy room. "I've been busy sorting through my father's business affairs as well as trying to put this place in some type of order."

She glanced around. "I can see how this place alone would keep you busy."

Simon grinned. "I intend to hire someone to do the interior, once the workmen have finished putting the structure back together."

"I can see now why you haven't come to London."

The house and business were excuses he used to stay away from London. He had other reasons for clinging to the sanctity of his castle. "I've never cared much for town society."

"Do you realize you have become the talk of the town? War hero. Spy. They are calling you the Mysterious Marquess. Every hostess in town is hoping to be the first to have you attend one of her parties."

"Did you come all the way up here simply to tell me I've become the latest rage?"

"No." She folded her hands on her lap. "I came all the way up here to invite you to a party."

Simon stared at her a moment. "A party?"

"I have a ball planned for Anna on the twenty-sixth of this month. And I want very much for you to attend."

Simon lifted one dark brow. "You want me to attend a ball for Anna?"

"That's right. If anyone is going to be the first to boast of having the Mysterious Marquess attend one of her parties, it should be me."

Emily's words echoed in his memory: *We met at a ball at my grandmother's town house in London*. A lifetime ago she had shared that bit of fantasy with him. It was tempting, the idea he might bring that fantasy to life. And dangerous. Far too dangerous. A life together could not be built on a foundation of fantasy. "I'm not at all certain that would be a good idea."

"But why not?"

"It wouldn't be wise to resurrect stories of Sheridan Blake," he said, appalled at the bitterness in his voice as he spoke of his rival. "It might prove embarrassing for your family."

"Poppycock. Because of Lord Pemberton, Emily has become the darling of the Season. Everyone wants to know of her exploits as a spy for the ministry."

Simon smiled. "I am glad Emily's reputation remains unblemished."

"You and Lord Pemberton came to the rescue."

Simon dismissed her words with a wave of his hand. "I'm the man who nearly caused the scandal."

"It wasn't your fault."

"I'm only glad no one was hurt in my father's scheme."

"Come to London, Simon. Come to my party."

Simon looked into the fire, watching red-gold flames lick at the blackened logs, thinking of a woman with fire in her hair. There would be no escape from Emily in London. Town society was too small. It had taken months for the ragged wound she had carved across his soul to heal. He didn't intend to allow her to rip it open again. "I appreciate the invitation, but there is nothing for me in London."

"Nothing? I rather thought there might be something. Or someone."

Simon glanced at her, careful to mask his emotions. "Tell me, dear lady, what scheme is brewing in your beautiful head?"

She shrugged. "I thought it was time for you and Emily to make peace."

Simon felt a twisting in his chest, hope and need conspiring to betray him. "Does Emily know you're here?"

Harriet pursed her lips. ''I told her I intended to visit a friend for a few days.''

He tipped his lips into a smile he didn't feel. ''I doubt the lady would appreciate it if she knew you were trying to convince me to come to London. I'm one of the last people she wants to see.''

''She misses you.''

''She told you that?''

''Not in so many words.''

Simon released the breath he had been holding. He stared into the fire, concealing the disappointment that came from longing for things that could never be. ''The lady had no trouble finding words when last we met.''

''She is far too stubborn to admit she made a mistake in sending you away.''

''I'm not at all certain she made a mistake.''

''Of course she did. You and Emily are perfect for each other. You need only to come to London and prove it to her.''

Simon drew in his breath, dragging the smoky scent of burning wood into his lungs. ''There are times when it's wise to know when a battle is lost, Lady Harriet. I'm not the paragon Emily wants. I'm afraid if I tried to become Sheridan Blake, it would eventually destroy both of us.''

''Poppycock! Emily fell in love with you when she thought you were a fortune-hunting scoundrel.''

Simon lifted his brows. ''She has a rather strange way of demonstrating her affection.''

''If you're referring to that incident with the press gang, I must tell you she wanted to ship you away because she was frightened of her feelings for you. Falling in love with you terrified her.''

Falling in love had terrified *him*. Still, he had been willing to risk everything for her. He had offered up his heart with all the innocence of a foolish child. But it hadn't been enough. Not nearly enough. ''She managed to find a cure for her fear.''

Harriet rested her hand over the tight fist he held clenched against his knee. "Simon, you still love her. Don't try to deny it, I can see it in your eyes."

"Yes, I love her. I've tried to forget her, but I can't."

"She loves you. I know it. I can see it in her face, as she watches for a glimpse of you at every party and ball she attends. I can hear it, in the soft sparkling notes of a music box she plays every night in her bedroom." Harriet squeezed his hand. "You must go to her. Tell her how you feel."

Memories coiled around his heart. Memories of a young boy who had tried to be everything his father wanted. Memories of a man who had risked his life to win honor in the hope it might win a father's approval. Still, he had failed. "Love isn't always enough. I won't spend my life trying to be someone's ideal. I can't do it. Not again."

"Simon, you must give your love a chance to flourish. Go to London. Talk to her. Spend time with her. See if what you have together is real."

Simon thought of his parents and the disaster they had made of their marriage. The truth was, he had no idea how to make a marriage work. He only knew he didn't intend to awaken one morning and find that his wife didn't think he measured up to the fantasy who lived in her imagination. "What we shared was an illusion. In time that illusion will fade."

Harriet was quiet a moment. Simon kept his gaze focused on the fire, keeping her in the periphery, where she sat and studied him, a frown marring her brow.

She drew in her breath and sighed. "I suppose this means you won't be coming to my party?"

"I'm sorry." Simon smiled as he looked at her. "I think it would best for all concerned if Emily and I allow the past to die."

She cupped his cheek in the palm of her hand, her eyes filled with regret. "I only wish you and my granddaughter had met in a different time and place. I hate to think you have lost what you might have shared for a lifetime."

"Unfortunately, wishes don't come true." He had learned that lesson a long time ago. It was a lesson he would never forget.

Seven months, two weeks, and three days. Long enough to forget a scoundrel, Emily thought. If she were ever going to forget him. Still, somewhere around the fourth month she had started to doubt her ability to banish Simon from her thoughts. And now, she knew it was impossible.

A breeze warm with the breath of spring whispered through the open windows of the blue drawing room in her grandmother's London town house, fluttering the blue velvet drapes. Emily stared into the street, watching the carriages rattle past Grosvenor Square on their way to Hyde Park, hoping to catch a glimpse of a face from her dreams.

Rides through the park at five each evening were obligatory, as necessary to a Season as the parties, suppers, routs, balls, and musicales that had kept them busy since arriving in London three weeks ago. Elegant carriages, fashionable men and women on horseback, all paraded along the paths at a sedate pace. Hyde Park was a place to see and be seen, and there was one man Emily wished desperately to see.

Simon.

The thought of him sent a shaft of longing ripping through her. The months away from him had not dimmed his memory. Time had not eased the ache in her heart. Nothing had filled the emptiness within her, that hollow place only he had ever filled. The longing for him had not lessened as she had hoped. Each passing day had only served to chip away at her anger, until none of it remained. Only longing. Only need. Only fear.

The last few moments she had spent with him kept haunting her. She had been so angry, so hurt. And she had hurt him. Deeply. He had offered his love. She had given him anger. He had hoped for understanding. She had found none to give.

Until later.

Until time conspired against her.

Until she realized he was the one man she would always love.

Could they find a way back to each other? She had journeyed to London with her grandmother and Anna, hoping to find some way to mend bridges. Each time she left her grandmother's town house, she looked for Simon. She searched the guests at every dinner, every party, every ball. Yet, in three weeks she had not caught a glimpse of him. She was beginning to wonder if the Mysterious Marquess would come for the Season.

"Emily, dear, are you ready to leave?"

Emily turned and found her grandmother standing just inside the room. Harriet was dressed in a stylish bottle-green carriage gown, ready to join the parade in Hyde Park. "Yes. I'm ready."

Harriet frowned, studying Emily with the keen perception of a woman who could see past her granddaughter's smile to the despair deep within her. She closed the door. "Emily, I can't go on, watching you, knowing you search every day for a glimpse of Simon."

Emily glanced away from her grandmother's piercing eyes. She stared at the black basaltware urn perched on a mahogany pedestal table. Three cherubs stood on a cloud painted on the urn, preparing their bows to strike the heart of a mortal with love's arrow. "I didn't realize I was so obvious."

"I know you well."

"Yes. You know me well enough to predict just how much I would come to regret the day I sent Simon away."

"You still love him."

Emily closed her eyes, fighting the tears that hovered every day. Tears could not wash away the pain of losing him. "More than I thought possible."

Harriet crossed the room, her slippers silent against the Brussels carpet of blue and ivory wool. She touched

Emily's arm, her hand warm and comforting below the scalloped lace of her short sleeve. "I didn't want to tell you this, but now I believe it's for the best."

Emily glanced up into the deep pool of pity in her grandmother's eyes. "What is it? Did you hear something about him? Has he . . . is there another woman?"

"I went to see him."

"You went to see him? In London?"

Harriet shook her head. "He was the friend I was visiting last week. I went to see him at his home in Yorkshire."

"Good heavens." Emily stepped back, pressing her hand to her throat. "Why did you go to him?"

"I thought I might try to bring the two of you together."

"What did you tell him?"

"I told him you still loved him. I told him you regretted sending him away."

The words sank into Emily's heart like finely pointed thorns. "Grandmother, you didn't. The man will think me a pitiful wretch."

"He loves you."

Emily's breath stilled in her lungs. "He told you that?"

"Yes. He said he had tried to forget you, but he couldn't."

The hope surging within her remained captive of the concern in her grandmother's eyes. "There is more, isn't there? Otherwise he would have come to me."

Harriet nodded. "He doesn't seem to think he can live up to the ideal you have created of Sheridan Blake. I believe he spent his life trying to prove himself worthy of his father. He doesn't intend to spend the rest of his life trying to prove himself worthy of your love. As far as he is concerned, it's over between you."

"I don't blame him." *It was over.* All the hope she had sheltered deep in her heart shuddered and died within her. She turned away, stumbling to a Grecian couch near the hearth, all the strength draining from her limbs. She collapsed against the dark blue velvet, leaning heavily on the carved gilded arm.

"Emily, my dear girl." Harriet sat on the couch beside her and rested a comforting arm around Emily's shoulder. "I'm so terribly sorry."

"It's only what I deserve. I turned him away when he needed my love, when he needed my support. Dear heaven, his father had tried to kill him, and I stood there shouting about his lack of honor. I thought only of my own pride, my own feelings. I couldn't see past my fear."

"It will be all right, my girl. In time, the pain will fade."

"He said I wanted a fantasy, a paragon. But it isn't true. I want him. Only him. A living, breathing man who will make mistakes and make amends." Emily turned and sank into her grandmother's warm embrace, resting her cheek against Harriet's shoulder. "What am I going to do? I don't want to live without him."

"Poppycock. You are my granddaughter. That means you have the strength within you to handle all of the blows that life may throw at you, my girl."

Emily managed a smile as she looked up into her grandmother's reassuring features. "I don't feel very strong at the moment."

"You will. Just as you will give that young man a little more time to ramble around his lonely castle, before you storm his defenses."

"Bold words, Grandmama."

Harriet nodded. "I have faith in you, Emily. I know you will eventually find a way to change that young man's mind and convince him to follow his heart."

"I only wish I shared your confidence in me."

"I know you better than you know yourself." Harriet came to her feet and took Emily's hands. "Now come along. A breath of air will do you a world of good. Anna's ball is tonight, and I warn you, I shall expect you to shine."

Emily got to her feet at her grandmother's gentle tug. She forced her lips into a smile, and wondered how on earth she could manage to shine when all the light had vanished from her world.

Chapter Thirty-two

Emily stood near one of the open French doors in her grandmother's ballroom, grateful for the cool breeze that drifted in from the rose garden and eased the heat in the crowded room. Beneath the glitter of four sparkling crystal chandeliers, the cream of London society floated in a mingled sea of pastel gowns and dark evening clothes. People lined the edge of the dance floor, congregating in small groups near the sofas filled with chaperones and their young charges. Steady streams of people flowed in and out of the adjoining rooms, taking supper in the dining room, playing cards in the drawing room.

Emily stood on the fringe of all the activity. She felt isolated, alone even in a crowd of over four hundred people. She watched sets of couples move through the intricate steps of a country dance, trying her best to appear interested in the spectacle. Yet it was difficult to keep a smile on her lips when her mind kept slipping back in time, to the night she had first glimpsed Simon St. James. It seemed a lifetime since that night in her father's home. A lifetime since a handsome scoundrel had taken her in his arms and stolen her heart with a single kiss.

Emily frowned as she noticed Anna hurrying through the crowd, rushing toward her. Anna's cheeks were flushed, her eyes wide, as though disaster had suddenly descended upon her.

Anna gripped her sister's arm as though she needed support. "Emmie, I'm so glad you're here."

"Anna, what is it? Are you all right?"

Anna swallowed hard. "He came."

Emily's heart slammed into the wall of her chest at her sister's words. "Who came?"

"Lord Greville." Anna glanced over her shoulder. "He's over there, talking with Grandmama."

Emily looked in the direction Anna had indicated, stifling the disappointment crowding her chest. Lord Stephen Hudson, Earl of Greville, stood near the entrance to the adjoining drawing room with Lady Harriet. The tall, fair-haired peer had captured Anna's attention the first night they had met him at the Chadwicks' musicale two weeks ago. The handsome young man had soon joined the growing ranks of Anna's suitors. Although there were many who sought Anna's affection, Emily knew that Lord Greville was the only one Anna ever saw in her dreams.

"Isn't he the most handsome man you have ever seen?" Anna whispered, casting a glance over her shoulder.

A man with black hair and eyes the color of midnight came to mind, but Emily kept her own counsel regarding the man of her own dreams. "He certainly is handsome."

"Do I look all right?" Anna touched the golden curls tumbling to one pale shoulder from an artful arrangement of braids high on her crown.

"You look beautiful."

Anna drew in her breath. "Do you think he will ask me to dance?"

Emily watched as Greville wended his way through the throng of people, his eyes fixed on Anna. "I think that is a very real possibility. He is coming this way."

"Oh my."

A few moments later, Greville claimed Anna for the next dance. Emily watched her sister and Lord Greville take their places for a cotillion. He smiled at Anna as though she were the only woman in the room. Anna returned that smile. Emily's heart ached as she saw a warmth enter their faces, the glow of growing admiration. She was happy for Anna. Truly happy. But it reminded her so much of all she had so carelessly thrown away.

Emily slipped out of the ballroom, escaping through the French doors, seeking shelter from the gaiety in the shadows on the terrace. She avoided the couples standing within the glow of the ballroom, taking refuge at the far end of the terrace. Moonlight streamed across the garden, painting the branches of yew silver. She drew in a deep breath, cleansing the mingled fragrances of sweetwaters and perfume from her senses.

It was a night straight from a dream. A night when a bold warrior would claim his lady. She rested her hands on the stone balustrade and thought of her own bold warrior. He had purchased a castle. Did he think of her when he looked at the ancient stones? Did she haunt his dreams the way he haunted hers?

She released her breath in a frustrated sigh. Enough of this terrible waiting. She had never been one to indulge in self-pity and she didn't intend to start now. Simon still loved her. He had admitted as much to her grandmother. It was enough. Tomorrow she intended to journey to the wilds of northern Yorkshire and claim her scoundrel.

Somehow she would find a way to convince him they were meant for each other. If she had to hold him prisoner in his own castle and make love to him until he moaned his surrender, she would win his trust. She refused to allow him to escape their destiny.

"You can't escape me, Simon St. James," she whispered. "I love you too much to let you get away from me."

Although she heard nothing but the lively music of the cotillion, she sensed someone moving behind her. A warmth brushed her back. A strong hand touched her shoulder, long fingers curving against her neck.

Simon.

Her heart froze, then surged, pounding against her ribs. She turned, holding her breath, praying her longing for Simon had not caused her to mistake another man's touch for the man she wanted so desperately to see.

For a moment she could only stare up into his eyes, those midnight dark eyes that looked at her with all the longing she felt swirling inside her. "You came," she said, her voice strangled by the joy surging inside of her.

Simon smiled. "For my lady."

A strangled sob escaped her lips as she threw her arms around his neck. He held her, his strong arms closing around her as though he intended to hold her for all time. She nestled her face against his neck, breathing in the exotic spice of his skin, trembling with the joy of being in his arms. He kissed her temple, her cheek, and she turned her face toward him, like a flower seeking the sun.

She moaned deep in her throat at the touch of his lips upon hers. This was a kiss from her dreams. A kiss of a bold warrior claiming his lady. A kiss she had feared never again to taste. He was here in her arms. Alive and warm and real. And she intended to hold him until the day they both drew their last breath.

She pressed closer to him, absorbing the strong, radiant heat of him through the emerald silk of her gown. She snuggled against him, pressing her aching breasts against the hard thrust of his chest, shifting in his embrace, trying to get closer. Yet she couldn't get close enough.

He lifted his head, his breath falling warm and fast against her face. "You would tempt a saint, my lady. It's all I can do not to drag you into the gardens to have my wicked way with you."

She kissed his chin. "You wouldn't have to drag me, my Lord Scoundrel."

He released his breath in a long, ragged sigh, glancing toward the house, where music and laughter drifted through the open doors. "Don't tempt me."

She cupped his face in her hands and stared up into the midnight depths of his eyes, tears misting her vision. "Do you have any idea how much I've missed you?"

He smiled, moonlight kissing the dimple in his right cheek. "I know I've done a fair amount of missing you."

"I was so angry that last day with you. I said so many horrible things I didn't mean. I was hurt and I—"

"Hush, love." He pressed his fingertip against her lips, cutting off the rush of her apology. "I understand. I gave you cause for your anger."

She rested her hand over his, kissed the tip of his finger, nuzzled her cheek into the palm of his hand, smiling as he sighed his pleasure. "You were only doing what you thought was best."

"I never wanted to hurt you."

"I know. Later, when all the anger was gone, I kept thinking of how you must have felt that day. Your father had betrayed you. And I turned away from you. I felt so terrible. I came to London, thinking we might meet again. I wanted a second chance. But you weren't here."

"I was too busy licking my wounds." He cradled her head, long fingers tunneling into her hair as he slid the pad of his thumb over her cheek, wiping away her tears.

"I was going to leave for Yorkshire tomorrow. I was going to storm your castle." She smiled up at him. "You should know, I had plans to seduce you in your own lair, make love to you until you surrendered to me. I wasn't going to allow you to escape me."

He arched one black brow, as though considering her confession. "I see no reason to alter all of your plans, my love."

Emily laughed as she looped her arms around his neck.

"I hope you are well and truly rested, my bold warrior, because I intend to love you all through this night and the next day. And the next. And the next. And the—"

Simon groaned. "I hope I'm man enough for you, my beautiful tigress."

Emily lifted on her toes and placed a quick kiss upon his lips. "You are all the man I will ever require."

Simon tilted his head toward the house. "Listen."

The orchestra was playing a waltz, the sweet melody of the violins shivering along her skin. It was her favorite waltz. A waltz a daring scoundrel had captured in a music box. A waltz that had haunted her every night since Simon had left. "That's odd. Grandmama only sanctioned one waltz for the evening and it's already over."

"It's just beginning." He took her hand, slipped his arm around her, drawing her into the embrace of the waltz. "You see, I asked your dear grandmother if she might sanction one more waltz. This waltz. For us."

Emily trembled in his arms, awed by the gift he was giving her, a dream made reality. "You remembered."

"Everything."

Music slid around them, delicate threads of notes binding them, one to the other. He held her close, much closer than propriety would allow, but here the moon alone watched them. And Emily knew moonlight approved of lovers.

He drew her farther into the shadows at the end of the terrace, slowing their movements until they were swaying against each other, her breasts softly brushing his hard chest, his thighs hard against her. Emily sighed at the contact, her skin tingling with the promise in his touch. She slid her hand along his shoulder, touched her fingers to his neck, feeling the pulse beating beneath the warmth of his skin.

He pressed his lips to her brow, releasing his breath in a warm sigh against her skin. "I tried to forget you."

"I tried to forget you." She rested her brow against his chin. "But we can't escape destiny, can we? And I am your destiny, Simon St. James. Just as you are mine.''

He held her close, his arms closing around her as though he were afraid someone would drag her away from him. ''I'm not perfect, Em. I've made mistakes. I'll make more. But I love you.''

She leaned back in the powerful circle of his arms, smiling up into his exquisite face. ''How could I ever live with a paragon, if one existed? Perfection would be terribly boring, don't you think?''

He grinned. ''I think you will never be boring my love.''

Emily crinkled her nose. ''I suppose that's your way of saying I'm far from perfect myself.''

''You are perfect.'' He kissed the tip of her nose. ''For me.''

''Simon, I love you. Only you. Please say you want me by your side for the rest of our lives.''

''I have a special license in my pocket. It allows the Marquess of Blackthorne to marry the woman of his dreams.'' His eyes filled with mischief. ''Will you run away with me, Miss Maitland?''

She slid her arms around his shoulders, raised herself on her toes to meet him as he lowered his lips toward hers. ''To the end of the world, my own beloved scoundrel.''

Epilogue

Bristol, England, 1822

The sound of children's laughter rippled on the warm summer breeze. Simon rested his hand on Lady Ravenwood's stone and stared down into the bailey. There was a time when he could not have stood in this place without fear filling him. But now the old memories had no power over him. Now he had love to chase away the fear.

Far below, his daughter and two of his sons sat in a semicircle on a white quilt, gazing up at their great-grandmother. Lady Harriet sat on a stone that had tumbled from the ancient wall, reading stories of bold knights and beautiful ladies. His oldest child, Remington, stood beside Harriet, holding a white lace parasol over her head, a dark-haired knight protecting his queen.

After he had agreed to become a partner in Maitland Enterprises ten years ago, Simon and Emily had built a home near Ravenwood, close enough to spend an occasional evening secluded away from the rest of the world, sheltered by ancient stones. Although they still used Dragonwyck as a hunting lodge, Simon had to admit he preferred it here, surrounded by Emily's family.

Emily slipped her arm around Simon's waist and leaned against him. "Grandmama says Samantha has inherited my stubborn streak as well as my red hair."

Simon moaned. "Then I suppose we should be grateful the boys have all managed to inherit my looks as well as my excellent nature."

She poked him in the ribs. "I suspect they will all grow up to be charming rogues."

He slipped his arms around her, holding her close, breathing in the fragrance of lavender clinging to her hair. "May they each find their destiny."

Emily looked up at him, her lips tipping into a warm smile. "Do you want to make a wish, my beloved scoundrel?"

He looked down into her beautiful face, seeing the love for him shimmer in her eyes, knowing he had everything a man could want from this life. "You have made all of my wishes come true, my beautiful lady."

Author's Note

I hope you enjoyed the time you spent with Emily and Simon. I had a wonderful time writing their story. Since the day I started reading romances, I've loved the Regency period. It was a time of manners, elegance, and fascinating scoundrels.

I enjoy putting twists into my stories, those involving plot as well as character. For my next book, *Lord Savage*, I wondered what would happen if a young man were raised in a culture completely contrary to the one in which his family belonged.

Ash MacGregor doesn't remember his childhood before the time he came to live with the Cheyenne at the age of five. When an English duke claims Ash is his long-lost grandson, the young bounty hunter has difficulty believing the truth. The rugged Westerner has even more difficulty trying to adjust to the role of English gentleman, especially with a teacher as distracting as Lady Elizabeth Barrington. Added to his troubles is someone who would like to see the new heir of the Duke of Marlow dead.

Lord Savage contrasts Victorian England with the old West. It throws together a savage bounty hunter and a proper English Lady in a story filled with adventure, romance, and mystery.

I love to hear from readers. Please enclose a self-addressed, stamped envelope with your letter.

Debra Dier
P.O. Box 584
Glen Carbon, Illinois 62034-0584

THE TARNISHED LADY

SANDRA HILL

Sandra Hill's romances are "delicious, witty, and funny!"
—*Romantic Times*

Banished from polite society for bearing a child out of wedlock, Lady Eadyth of Hawks' Lair spends her days hidden under a voluminous veil, tending her bees. But when her son's detested father threatens to reveal the boy's true paternity and seize her beloved lands, Lady Eadyth seeks a husband who will claim the child as his own.

Notorious for loving—and leaving—the most beautiful damsels in the land, Eirik of Ravenshire is England's most virile bachelor. Yet when a mysterious beekeeper offers him a vow of chaste matrimony in exchange for revenge against his most hated enemy, Eirik can't refuse. But the lucky knight's plans go awry when he succumbs to the sweet sting of the tarnished lady's love.

_3834-X $5.50 US/$7.50 CAN

Dorchester Publishing Co., Inc.
65 Commerce Road
Stamford, CT 06902

Please add $1.75 for shipping and handling for the first book and $.50 for each book thereafter. NY, NYC, PA and CT residents, please add appropriate sales tax. No cash, stamps, or C.O.D.s. All orders shipped within 6 weeks via postal service book rate. Canadian orders require $2.00 extra postage and must be paid in U.S. dollars through a U.S. banking facility.

Name____
Address____
City ______________________________ State______ Zip______
I have enclosed $______ in payment for the checked book(s).
Payment must accompany all orders. ☐ Please send a free catalog.